POSTMARKED FOR DEATH

A Novel

by
JONATHAN LOWE

A Write Way Publishing Book

Write Way Publishing
3806 S. Fraser
Aurora, Colorado 80014

First Edition; 1996

ISBN: 1-885173-13-X

1 2 3 4 5 6 7 8 9 10

Buddy, can you spare a dime?
–'30s saying

Peace and love, brother.
–'60s slogan

I wanna get high. Hurry up and die.
–'90s anonymous graffiti

Prologue

He pushed through the rear swinging doors into the carrier station. People he'd seen every day for years were there, but they were as busy as usual; he walked unnoticed past them. When he got to the big fan set up near the stairwell, he paused and stared into it. Taking off his sunglasses for a moment, he gazed into the polished and spinning surface of the fan's convex center hub.

It was like a circus mirror.

His face appeared fat, and drenched with sweat. His bloodshot eyes stared back at him like a clown's whose makeup had run. He turned to look back at the others, wondering if they saw too, but no one cared for sideshows.

The stairwell's doorknob beckoned. Gleaming. Seeing a tiny but headless reflection of his body mirrored in it, he reached out his hand in fascination. Then he gripped it. Suddenly, resolutely. Like a handshake. Finally, he opened the door and stepped inside.

Once on the staircase, he began to climb methodically, one step at a time. Having come to return his postal carrier pack as he'd been told, he now opened the pack and withdrew the .45 automatic inside. When he arrived at the top of the stairs, he opened the door into the office hallway, and could hear the secretaries chatting together. Laughing.

It was cooler up here. Much cooler.

He ran his hand across his matted hair, feeling for a moment the cold air streaming down from the nearest vent. Then he started down the hallway, walking past the offices, firing as he went. When he got to the corner office, he found station manager Ollie Westover behind his mahogany desk, on the phone. A cup of black coffee was spilled across several papers.

Ollie looked up and said, "No–don't do it ... Thompson, right?"

"Right," Thompson said. And fired.

Afterward, he went to the window, and gazed down at the street fronting the postal station. As he waited, he felt the air conditioning coming from the vent above Ollie's slowly cooling body. Then, in the distance, he heard the expected sirens approach. At last, several police cars and an unmarked white Cavalier arrived, screeching into the front lot, narrowly missing several patrons.

He smiled, sadly, as he put the .45 to his own head.

"*Vaya con Dios*," he whispered.

1

The newspaper reported that recently-terminated city carrier Randall Thompson had entered the rear of Phoenix's Arcadia substation, walked unnoticed past half a dozen sorting cases, two pay phones in use, and a swing room where four female employees, facing his direction, sat watching Oprah on television. He then ascended the staircase to the third floor offices, strode past several offices–shooting–and finally entered station manager Ollie Westover's office.

In all there were thirteen people who hadn't noticed that he no longer had a postal ID card hanging from his shirt pocket. Thirteen who hadn't observed that the shirt he wore was not a postal shirt, but a dirty T-shirt, which hung out of his faded jeans. Of course, the fourteenth and final person noticed. Number fourteen also noticed that Randall carried a cocked automatic at his side. But by then it was too late. Of the fourteen people in the building on that day, nine survived.

Ollie never had a chance. The entrance of the .45MM hollow point was just above the right ear at a downward trajectory. The exit left a ragged hole in the left temple.

Unfortunately, he hadn't planned a good escape route. They never did with crimes of passion, Calvin mused. But then, what difference did it make? A disgruntled employee might blast his way out of the building, might even make it home to barricade himself in his room and wait to see it on the news, but a paper trail would follow him; there were files on him all over the place, like postal exam tests and Probationary 90-Day Performance Reviews, signed off by his supervisor. The mug shot for his postal ID was in personnel records at the Phoenix MSC, and probably in Washington, too. They didn't know him–didn't know how his mind worked, or what made him tick. Didn't know or care. But if anyone saw him and then survived, he would be hunted by the postal inspectors, forever. Even if he hitchhiked down to Nogales and crossed the border into old Mexico, they'd get him in the end.

Maybe Thompson knew that, unless his brain had fried in the desert heat, since they didn't have air conditioning in those jeeps and delivery vehicles, just a little fan that blew hot air in your face whenever your boss wasn't doing it. So, instead of blasting his way out of the substation and killing whoever wasn't hidden behind postal equipment, he'd played it like a regular cliché. When the squad cars arrived, he'd put the gun to his own head, just like so many others before him. Just before he'd pulled the trigger, he'd appeared to say something to himself.

"*Oh, what the hell,* maybe?"

Calvin folded the afternoon's *Tucson Citizen*, and sighed. Then he pushed the paper back across his kitchen table, and picked up his own postal ID:

United States Postal Service
Tucson Arizona 85726
CALVIN BEACH
Social Security No. 295-62-1246
Data Kee 1A #849337

His face in the photo was humorless, the expression of a man who'd just been to a funeral. And he had–his father's on that go 'round. His thick, black hair had been shorter then, too. Much more of his face was visible. He was squinting in the photo; Calvin remembered that it had been taken before he started wearing sunglasses inside ... before he'd started growing more and more sensitive to light, a side effect of the diabetes that had also left him impotent.

He was surprised to notice that in the photo he wore a Madras shirt. A shirt he no longer owned because he wore mostly fatigues now. His usual clothes were Army surplus, and fit his short, stocky frame better than most of the K-Mart or men's store clothes he'd tried. Of course, he still had the white shirt he'd worn to his mother's funeral the day after he'd graduated from Rincon High, but he hadn't worn it since. It probably wouldn't fit him now anyway. He didn't look fat. He was just wider these days. Like a 4X4 with balloon tires. He needed to stop eating so much meat. Fireplug, they called him at work, mostly behind his back.

Calvin went to his closet, and slid open the door. The shirt in back was still white, but not quite as white as it was twenty years ago. Not as white as he remembered it, out in the sunlight. He would have worn one like it to his father's funeral, he realized, except that burial hadn't been much of an affair. No one had shown up–not even Crockey what's-his-name, his dad's fellow postal contract driver during those couple of years when his old man wasn't driving coast-to-coast for Rodeway. They didn't care. None of them. No more than they'd cared about Randall Thompson, whatever his problems were.

He closed the closet door and sat on the bed, looking up at the horned bull skull over his dresser. *Which is worse, Dad?* he thought. *Disease, accident, or suicide?* Alcohol had hastened the end of Ralph Beach's forgotten life eight years ago; a bus on a wide turn had ended his mother's twelve years before that. A bus that had casually squeezed her Valiant into a telephone pole at forty-five MPH, leaving him and his dad with no one but each other.

He went back to the breakfast table, and picked up the letter he'd written the night before. He read it again, one last time.

Hi Dad,

Last week I went to the postal doctor about my eyes. He told me to see an ophthalmologist about my sensitivity. I'm fine otherwise. Good thing I still don't need insulin. My allergies aren't as bad because the pollen count is finally down, too. Spring is almost over and the wind has died down, so I won't have to put up with all those plants the Snowbirds bring back from Michigan or wherever the hell they come from in the fall. Only bad thing now is the heat. Got them to fix my air conditioning the other day, and it works fine, except for the wheezing sound. It was supposed to be 100 degrees today. Yesterday it was 94. Not quite a record for mid-May, but damn close. It's gonna be a long hot summer, and hot as hell, Dad. Humidity's only at 10%, though. It's a dry heat, they say. But who are they, right? At least I got no problems sleeping.

My new motorcycle is running great. It's a BMW, Dad. Did I tell you? Do you know? A GS model, the biggest dual sport bike there is. Goes anywhere—even out into the desert hills, where I can explore all those old ghost towns around here, maybe find that silver vein near some mine great-grandfather wrote about before the Apaches got him. Cost nine grand, Dad, and I paid cash. Can you believe it? I know you want me to buy a house, and I will someday, I promise. Right now, though, I just don't need a lot of space, see. This duplex apartment is fine. I like it that it's only one floor, got nobody above me walking around laughing and screwing around like last time. It's quiet too, not near Broadway or Speedway Blvd. like before, either. Plus, I got a back unit, with a thick wall between me and that retired guy next door who plays golf a lot at Randolph and collects Social Security disability besides. I've learned my lesson about apartments, and people.

Anyway, at work there was a stand-up meeting about another postal shooting, this one in Phoenix. Said this fired carrier killed five people and wounded three, then shot himself. Said they wouldn't know more until the details came out. Then they talked about stress reduction. The usual BS. They gave us a safety talk about suspicious behavior, and firearm safety. Can you believe it? They said any guns on postal property meant termination. Even a BB gun. Like we didn't know that already. They said this guy in Phoenix was a loner nobody really knew. Said they didn't know why he did it. So it was a mystery to them. Can you beat that?

Why didn't he use a letter bomb, I wonder? It would be so much cleaner. He would have been home free that way. But he didn't think. Dummy didn't use his head. I guess he had to be there, to see it happen. I guess that's it. He didn't have much of an imagination, though, did he?

Later,
Calvin

Calvin folded the letter, put it in an envelope, and sealed it. Then he went to the end table in the corner of his living room, and kneeled in front of it. He lit a candle, breathed a prayer, and placed the letter in the copper tray there.

For a moment he stared at the picture behind the tray. It, too, was twenty years old, and faded. In the photo, his mother stood in the kitchen of their apartment on East Irvington. The smile she wore was one of endurance, of hope. It had been Thanksgiving Day, and on that bleak and overcast Thursday afternoon, she'd held up a home-made pumpkin pie and tried to smile that fragile smile for her only son and her mostly missing husband, who was always on the road.

Calvin picked up the letter and wrote IN CARE OF MARY BEACH on the envelope. Then he laid it back in the tray, and lit his match. As the letter burned, he smiled and stared at the candle until it was the only light in the room.

Soon it was time to go to work.

***

Five minutes before midnight he inserted his ID in the sensor at the main post office on Cherrybelle. The gate rolled slowly open, and when it was wide enough he gunned the throttle of his R100-GS, easing out the clutch. He parked in the space closest to the employee entrance, and then turned off the gas pet-cock, put his helmet in the right saddlebag, and combed his hair.

His boss, Gary Lennox, was on the warpath, he learned. Matuska was on Gary's case about overtime, and Fran had called in sick. Whenever Gary walked around with his clipboard and calculator it was a bad sign. Don't even think about talking to him. Gary was a numbers man, up for promotion, and they were looking at him real hard. Once in a while Gary would even glance up at the bridge overhead, where the inspectors sometimes watched from behind those one-way glass panels spaced every fifteen feet. He pretended to use the glass as a mirror to straighten his tie, but Calvin knew it was really to see if the bridge was swaying. That indicated someone might be up there watching. The bridge made a very slight swaying motion whenever someone was walking inside it. It didn't happen often, but Gary was a paranoid SOB.

As he worked, Calvin imagined what Gary was thinking. Was it Matuska, the plant manager, up there? Or maybe Harold Graves, the postmaster? They wanted you to believe that Big Brother was always watching.

Everyone on the floor had learned to stay out of Gary's way on nights like this: Don't even make eye contact. Just do your job, listen to Top 40 tunes or talk radio on your Sony Walkman, and let the hours creep inexorably to dawn.

You had a ten minute break coming every two hours, with half an hour for lunch in the swing room. The rest of the time was spent watching the letter feeding-arm mechanically place letter after letter in front of you for keying. It was boring as hell, and they resented having to use you at all, but if you knew your schemes by heart, you wouldn't even have to think about it. Just hit the right two keys and that letter would be off to the correct bin for further processing. Fifty letters a minute. No problemo.

Of course, they were planning on cutting back the number of Letter Sorting Machine clerks drastically as more Remote Encoding Centers came on line, and technology allowed all the machines the ability to read handwritten letters. But that was still a couple years down the road, and then you could always put in a bid card to train for another USPS craft when they did away with the old line Burrough's LSMs completely. There was always the Bar Code Sorter, the Flats Sorter, and the Optical Character Reader, and all of them were Level 5 jobs at least, paying $15.00 an hour and up before taxes, with time and a half for overtime and double time for any hours over ten per day. Same fringes, too, as the carriers who had to fight the traffic, the dogs, and the heat.

True, you couldn't help noticing all the talking and goofing-off going on over in manual distribution. But once you had six years seniority your postal career was secure, at least until the information super-highway flattened it. Nothing less than an act of Congress could get you fired–the union would see to that, at least while they still could. The only sure way you could screw it up would be to slip a government check or some transparent letter with cash in it in your pocket. Or any other piece of mail. It was that sanctity of the mail thing they told you about in orientation. Translation: if they caught you, your ass was grass.

When Gary went out of sight behind some cages, over to where his computer was, Calvin leaned back to Dave Sominski at the terminal behind him. "Hey, you been to that new place–Fleshdance?" he asked.

"No. Where is it?"

"It's on Craycroft just off twenty-second street."

"Convenient."

He continued keying, then cocked his head back and to the side of the Plexiglas barrier, letting his letters go to the zero bin, unkeyed. "Read about it last week. Got a blond there named Wendy Whoppers."

Dave grinned. "Oh yeah?"

"Yeah, and this week it's Tonya Towers."

"Forty-seven-D Tonya?"

Calvin nodded. "Figured you'd be interested. How about tomorrow night, nine-ish?"

"It's a date! But how come ya never asked me be–"

"What?"

Dave looked back down at his terminal. His face had lost color. Calvin turned just as Gary Lennox came striding up, clipboard held stiffly at his side.

"Our unkeyed percentage is starting to slip," Gary announced, then louder to Dave, "I wonder why?"

"Sorry," Calvin said.

"Sorry?" Gary pushed his glasses back into place with a forefinger. "Sorry? Yeah, I guess you are, aren't you? Learn that from David?"

"It won't happen again."

"You bet it won't, 'cause if it does, you'll get your first warning letter filed. And David, he gets his third. Don't you, David?" Gary pointed his finger at Dave, held it, then dropped his hand and turned away, shaking his head in disgust. When the Flats Sorter manager came over to him with another clipboard, Gary appeared to explain his distress by pointing back at them while continuing to shake his head. The FS manager said something, gesturing with animation, and then both he and Gary laughed. A private joke, probably at their expense.

***

In the restroom at break time, Calvin looked up at the stall door. It had been recently painted, but beneath the layer of paint he could still see the message, carved in with a knife, that someone had left as a testament to boredom or union satire:

GARY EATS HERE

Calvin took out his own pen knife. As he retraced the outline, he thought about all the gossipy manual distribution clerks, the joking bosses, and the other ones he'd read about in the afternoon paper ... the ranks on the outside who often complained about the Postal Service. Some of them were on the government dole, and didn't have to work at all.

He smiled as he flushed the toilet.

2

Victor Kazy waited in the hallway with Phoenix Postmaster Douglas Barnard for the heavy mahogany office door to open. The door was always locked for security reasons, Barnard explained, whether or not anyone was inside. But ten seconds after knocking he rattled the doorknob anyway, just to be sure. Barnard was, after all, a Level 26 official, representing and overseeing the entire operation of a major postal network, which included dozens of stations, thousands of vehicles, and an army of employees, whose payroll stretched into many millions of dollars. With hundreds of customer service managers ranging from Logistics to Labor Relations under him, he alone did not feel intimidated by the engraved seal on the door which read: POSTAL INSPECTOR.

"You in there, Phil?" the Postmaster boomed, knocking even louder.

There was movement inside. A phone was placed back into its cradle, then the door was unlocked and opened.

A woman stood before them. She wore a gray power suit, minus the jacket. Her dark hair was short and neatly styled, rendering a pleasant frame for her attractive Hispanic features. A .38 Smith & Wesson jutted from the brown leather holster at her side.

"Well, hello," she said. "Phil is out, I'm afraid. In the field, as they say."

Barnard nodded, smiled, and then slipped a hand behind her arm. "Maria, this is Victor Kazy. I suspect you've talked before? Victor, this is Maria Castillo, the youngest–and might I say prettiest–field trainer the western region has ever seen. Not to mention the best."

They shook hands. Victor was surprised by the strength of her grip, which seemed to complement the startling intensity of her dark brown eyes.

"Yes," he said. "We've talked ... on the phone, that is."

He'd imagined she'd be a dowdy school marm like some of his colleagues at Greenville High, where he'd taught English Lit, up until four months before. A strong yet feminine woman, she was a pleasant surprise.

"You've settled in?" she asked.

"I'm staying at the Holiday Inn for now," he replied. "Two and a half days from South Carolina pulling a U-Haul by trailer hitch. Stuff's on mothballs at Boxcar Self Storage on McDowell Road." He fingered the key in his pocket, "Number thirty-four, same age as me," he added inconsequentially.

Castillo and Barnard exchanged glances. The inspector moved to her desk, tapped an open file. "You mind if we call you Vic?"

"No, not at all. I didn't realize there'd be such a tragedy here so soon," he said to the Postmaster, who had already moved back to the doorway and was glancing up the hallway. "Are the reporters still after you around here?"

Barnard grunted. "There's a few stragglers. Not as bad as last Friday, though. Wife thought I was a celebrity, said any day now Judge Wapner would call, wanna do lunch." He looked up the hallway again, then motioned to Maria. "You got Vic's badge?"

Maria Castillo opened the desk's drawer, withdrew an ID card and a square leather holder the size of a small billfold. She walked around the desk, and approached the Postmaster. Barnard held out his hand and took the ID and the holder, which he opened to reveal the silver postal inspector's badge beneath. He read the inscription there to himself, then closed it and handed both ID and badge to Victor. They shook hands for the second time.

"Welcome to the Phoenix district," Barnard said. "I'm not your boss, but you can always count on my advice and cooperation."

"Thank you, sir. I look forward to working with you."

The Postmaster left the room; Inspector Castillo closed and locked the door.

"Would you like some coffee, Vic?" Maria asked him. "I've been working some late hours lately; coffee is the only thing that seems to keep me going."

He declined, and tried not to notice her figure from behind. Her skirt was proper and professional, but it failed to hide her perfect hourglass shape. Or to keep his imagination in check. Did she work out? he wondered. Had she thought about teaching aerobics as Karen, his almost ex-wife, had?

"How late is late?" he asked her.

She turned from the Bunn coffee maker with a steaming cup, and smiled thinly. "Lately it's been, well, late. With the reorganization a few years ago, they haven't been hiring many new inspectors. We had twenty inspectors here last year, now we're down to twelve. Tucson had three, now they've got one. When Postmaster General Maxwell gets through, I think we'll have ten and Tucson none. But that's why they call him Max the Ax."

He ventured a smile. "So how do you explain me?"

Maria blew into her cup. "Special circumstances. After they pulled four more of our inspectors three months ago, we had a rash of incidents, and lots of overtime. Mail fraud. A clerk theft of treasury-issued gold coins. A carrier dumping bulk mail. You name it. This bizarre shooting was the last straw, so your final approval came late last week, the day after. Barnard demanded our four inspectors back. They gave us you."

And I'm green, thought Vic, *and a former high school English teacher.*

"Yeah," she added, as if reading his mind, "you got that right."

He glanced at the other end of the office where another desk stood in front of a large bulletin board and book shelf. "So where are the other inspectors?" he asked, hoping to change the subject.

"They're out at the stations. Glendale has four. Scottsdale three.

South Phoenix one. Tempe two. It's just me and Phil here. Phil DeLong. He's out doing background checks on new hires from the clerk-carrier exam they had downtown last month."

"I thought that wasn't done anymore. Not for clerks or carriers, anyway."

"Like I said, special circumstances. But it's no big deal. There were only seven openings, although over two thousand showed up for the test. Maxwell is still in favor of letting attrition and retirement decrease the work force, with automation closing the gap. And Max's ax is mostly chopping from the top down–you don't want to cut at the roots when you prune; they're what keeps the fruit growing–from the branches that survive."

"Otherwise you'd have the union screaming, I imagine," Vic added.

"Exactly." She sighed. "Me, I've been mostly following up leads regarding postal employee complaints against management ... in a vain attempt to identify possible problems on the floor or on the routes, of course. While Phil's out looking at handgun purchase records and asking questions of people's neighbors, I'm trying to get a few bad apples fired for lying on their applications. I'm also trying to get a few others into a counseling program through the EAP."

Vic nodded. "What's the EAP?"

Maria blinked twice at that, and set down her cup in astonishment. "The Employee Assistance Program. You mean they didn't tell you about that at the Academy?"

He tried not to fidget. "I'm sure they did, but there was a lot to learn in eleven weeks. Some of it was a blur. I mean literally. The defensive driving thing, for instance. How to weave in and out of traffic at high speed without ending up wrapped around a telephone pole."

Maria grinned, in memory. "How did you score on the firing range?"

"Top eight percent." He smiled.

She closed his file on her desk. "So how did you like our murder capital?" she asked him.

"Washington? Not much. But I was only in the city once, to tour Postal headquarters. Spent most of my time at the Academy in Potomac. Did you know it used to be a convent?"

She nodded. "Ironic, isn't it?"

Suddenly the phone rang. She picked it up, and her fragile smile soon faded.

"What is it?" Vic asked when she hung up.

"It's your first arrest," she announced evenly. "Let's go."

***

The Arcadia branch had long earned its reputation for trouble, Maria explained in the car. A carrier fight in the parking lot that a third carrier broke up with dog mace two years ago; the suicide of a Level 3 custodian in the supply room eight months ago; a shooting, which drew national media attention by leaving five dead only one week ago ... and now this. Yet, after examining the records and interviewing the employees two days ago, she and Phil had found no conclusive reasons for the problems at Arcadia. There were the usual grievances, of course, typical of the ongoing tug of war between the union and management. But no one could point a finger at a particular manager and claim favoritism, abuse, or harassment. Ollie Westover had been a likable, well-respected station manager there, with an open door policy and a candid approach to complaints. Thompson, the shooter, who had used Ollie's "open door" to blow his own, and Ollie's, brains out, had never been seen arguing with Ollie, or anyone else.

In the end, Maria had concluded that Arcadia had a jinx on it: some voodoo hex an irate postal customer had put on the station, perhaps because it had lost a Social Security check. She seemed to be only half-joking.

When they pulled into the front parking lot, Vic noticed nothing amiss. Several customers came and went with parcels, checking their boxes and dropping coins in the stamp machines; others walked slowly to their cars, reading letters. Only in the station lobby did there appear to be unusual activity: they could see, through the shaded plate glass, a clerk trying to direct customers away from the window station and into the vestibule where the boxes were. A small queue had formed a small semicircle on the left side; the circle included a dog. As they approached the automatic door on the right, Maria nodded to a panhandler at the other door. The man wore a torn and dirty Grateful Dead T-shirt, and was stopping people from leaving by holding his hand open, palm up.

"Take care of him," Maria said, and went inside.

Vic approached the panhandler, who started to raise his hand again, then dropped it when he saw he was about to be confronted by someone wearing a shirt and tie. Just as the man lowered his eyes and turned away Vic said, "Excuse me, sir, I'm afraid you'll have to–"

"Yeah, yeah," the Deadhead said resignedly, waving goodbye.

"This is government property and–"

"I heard ya, man. I'm outta here, okay? Ya happy?"

Inside, Vic found Maria making a real arrest. The suspect, a window clerk, was about to be handcuffed, with the new station manager looking nervously on. When Maria saw Vic, she nodded to the people still in the lobby, and this time Vic got to flash his badge.

"Okay, folks, let's move on, shall we?" he said.

Confronted with a badge now, and not just a wimpish window clerk, they grumbled and started to shuffle out.

"Not him," the station manager said, pointing at the old man wearing dark glasses and holding a seeing eye dog at his side.

"Him?" said Vic.

"Him, yes. Andy will help you lock the door."

The station manager motioned to the other window clerk, who ducked under the partition to return with a ring of keys. The old man with the dog waited, his face blank, as the German Shepherd panted happily in the air conditioned room.

"You'll want to talk to him," the station manager reiterated, seeing Vic's uncertainty. "I'm afraid I've called the police, too. Was that wrong?"

Maria shook her head. When the last customer was out, the other window clerk shut and locked the inner door.

"Okay," Maria said, still holding the handcuffs. "You say you saw him place sheets of stamps under his shirt?"

"Not me," the station manager replied. "Him." Again he pointed at the blind man, who smiled, displaying a lower row of gold teeth.

"How?" Maria asked.

The station manager adjusted his tie. "Well, as Andy puts it, he's been in here since opening, waiting for the general delivery mail to come in."

"And?"

"And when a slack time came about an hour ago Andy went on break, with Tom here covering."

Vic looked at Tom, the clerk Maria was about to put handcuffs on. A tall, slender kid in his mid-twenties, Tom hung his head down, staring in fear at the floor.

"Well, when Andy came back from break the old man there approaches him and whispers that Tom went to Andy's station and pulled out about a hundred sheets of stamps from Andy's stock. Then slipped it under his shirt. Tom's break was next, you see."

"But how–"

"The stamps are out in Tom's car, under the right front seat. When Tom went on break Andy checked his stock, see, then called me. I looked out the window from the second floor toward the parking lot in back and saw Tom putting something there, for sure. His back was to me, but–"

"But how? I mean–" Maria gestured in futility, and finally pointed at the old man with the seeing eye dog. "How did a blind man's dog tell him about Tom?"

The old man cleared his throat. "Excuse me," he said.

"Yes sir?"

The old man shuffled forward to the counter. The dog remained behind, still panting and smiling. "I think I can explain."

"Please do."

He removed his dark glasses. The eyes beneath were not clouded at all, but as clear and blue as the Phoenix sky. "Truth is," he whispered. "*I'm* not blind."

"What?"

"My dog there, he's the blind one. Blind as a bat."

***

When a policeman rapped on the door with his nightstick, they all turned in unison. Everyone, that is, but the dog with the clouded eyes. The patrolman stared with such amazement at the scene that Vic laughed. He tried to stop laughing, but that only made it worse.

Andy unlocked the door.

"What's going on here?" the officer wanted to know, seeing the kid now in handcuffs, and the German Shepherd.

Maria held up her badge, Vic following suit. "We have jurisdiction here, officer," she said, obviously trying to hold in her own amusement. "Sorry about the confusion. When we're done with our report we'll give you a call."

"Okay," he said. "I see you've got it under control. This time."

In the car on the way back to the office three hours later, and with the thief finally turned over to the police for booking, Maria allowed herself the luxury of giving in to a good laugh at the bizarre incident. It wasn't a long laugh, but it was distinctive, and Vic relaxed and enjoyed it. They were going to get along just fine, he realized.

"I'm sorry; I really shouldn't ..."

"No, no, it's okay."

"I mean we're professionals, and it's a serious matter for that kid, and–"

"I understand. Really." He grinned.

She glanced at him, then looked back at the road. "You know who you remind me of? I been trying to think, and it just hit me."

"Who?" he said.

"Agent Mulder on *The X-Files*. Have you ever watched that show?"

"Afraid not."

"Well, you should. Sometimes I think we work on the same kind of cases."

3

The stage at Fleshdance reminded Calvin of a fashion show runway like the ones on TV, except here it wasn't what you were wearing that counted, but what you took off. At Fleshdance they took off everything but a G-string, and of course that wasn't much more than a shoe string. Still, it was high fashion for the beer-guzzlers gawking from the two dozen tables spread around the smoky room.

"Hey Dave, over here!" Calvin called against the loud beat from the driving Bose speakers in the corners of the ceiling. Sominski didn't hear him, but finally saw him and came strutting over. Like a sallow Sean Penn look-alike, Dave was wearing a bright Hawaiian shirt tucked into black Levis, and black leather boots.

"Hey Fireplug, what's shakin'–besides the girls?" He laughed and sat down opposite Calvin at the cocktail table.

"You look like Rick Matuska on his day off," Calvin told him. "You going to work dressed like that?"

"Why not? Place needs a lift. Specially the women. They all wear pants; not a skirt in sight. No leg, man. No leg."

"What about the managers? What about Carole what's-her-name in Personnel?"

Dave made a face like he'd just sipped a Geritol/Pepsi spritzer. "Flat as a pancake, man, you know that. Nice leg, but no shape. An' her face looks like it came outta a potato sack. Has Tonya been on yet?"

"She's up next."

A waitress in fishnet stockings and a teddy came over for their order. "What'll ya have?"

"Whiskey sour fer me," Dave said, as he checked out her backside.

"Mich Lite," Calvin said. When she left, he watched Dave light up a Winston. "When did you start smoking?"

Dave waved his match into smoke. "Every time I come to one a these joints. Might as well. Hell, yer breathin' it anyway, right? If it was any thicker ya couldn't see the meat up there."

Calvin smiled. "The meat. Yeah, I guess that's what it is. Look, but don't bite." When the waitress returned with their drinks on a little green tray he said, "I'm hungry."

She looked at him for the first time, into his eyes. She was a pretty girl, although too short to make it on stage, and her brown eyes were lifeless. She's seen and heard everything there was to see and hear, and maybe she'd done things she regretted too, Calvin thought.

"We have burgers. Four-fifty."

"Guess I'll have to make do without," he told her. "I'm not much of a meat eater lately." He forced himself to smile, and to cover the lie laid a two-dollar tip on her tray. She smiled back, but it was a have-a-nice-day kind of smile. The kind reserved for patrons at the Taco Bell drive-thru window during rush hour.

The girl on stage was a tall blond suggestively turning around a silver pole and doing deep knee bends for the bleary-eyed customers ringing the runway on stools. Her garter belt was a green flower of one-dollar bills. She kept her top on, but no one was complaining because there wasn't much up there to see anyway. It was her ass they were gawking at. A shape to kill for, or to be killed by.

At the end of her set of songs she left the stage to scattered clapping. A moment later she appeared in the audience, going to the ones who had tipped her, thanking them, and asking if they'd like a table dance. An Hispanic guy wearing a lime green tank top popped for the five bucks, and during the next song he got to see the same gyrations the girl had performed on stage repeated within inches of his nose. No one else paid attention, though, because a new girl had just come out onto the runway–a top-heavy bombshell with long blond hair, dressed all in red. By the end of the first song she'd lost her red high-heeled shoes, red stockings, and her flimsy red gauze wrap. By the end of the second song she was dancing without her red-laced corset and panties; by the middle of the third song, she'd lost her bra, amid a cacophony of hoots, whistles, and cheers.

The Japanese guy who caught the tossed bra put it on his head, then tied the straps around his chin. He looked like Little Bo Peep.

Two lines soon formed on either side of the stage. Men with dollars paying homage to Tonya Towers: a woman who possessed breasts bigger than their mothers'.

"Ya comin'?" Dave asked him, fishing in his wallet for a single.

"Naw, you go ahead."

He watched them as she watched them, looking down at them from above, her hands on her hips. A coquettish smile played on her lips as they folded and glided their bills under her garter belt, some of them even daring to touch her thigh. It was as if the operation–the ritual–was a delicate and artful engineering feat requiring a finesse the alcohol in their veins worked against. They wanted to please her, this goddess of sex. Each of them, hoping their offering might be accepted as special to her, glanced up into her eyes before they turned away, trying not to notice the others in line, waiting.

When she left the stage with her skirt of green, Dave returned, beaming.

"You're sick," Calvin told him.

Dave winked at that.

"No, really. You're sick. Weak. She's just laughing at you. This is all a business, and underneath it she hates men. She uses men because that's what she's good at."

"I'll say." Dave laughed. "What's with the Jimmy Swaggart routine? Yer here, ain't ya? Enjoy it. Jimmy did." He ordered another whiskey sour, and scanned the room for Tonya Towers. "I want me a lap dance from Tonya," he said, "even if it costs fifty bucks."

Calvin shook his head. "Ain't gonna happen, buddy. The goddess has left the building. At least until we're keying letters on the graveyard shift."

Dave looked hurt, and lashed back. "You put an ad in the *Tucson Weekly* a couple years back, didn't ya? So what'd ya say, eh? Feel secure in my arms ... Feel the love in my heart ... Feel the hardness in my pants? That close enough? Gail dumped ya quick, though, didn't she? Soon as she met that real estate guy. What's his name, now, uh ..."

"Shut up."

Dave laughed. "How'd it feel when she left ya with only a hand sandwich, anyway?"

"I said–"

"Okay, okay. I'm just sayin' you ain't no different from anybody else in here."

Guess again, Calvin thought.

When the waitress returned with Dave's second whiskey, she asked Calvin again if he wanted another. When he shook his head she gave him that deadbeat look. Like she'd seen his type before–the cheap guys who pony up the entrance fee, leave one tip, then nurse a stale beer for two or three hours. The management no doubt frowned on such types, and smiled on the practice of hounding them until they left the table for paying customers.

After Dave got a table dance from a busty redhead and then ordered a third whiskey, Calvin said, "They've got you by the balls." To the waitress he added, "I'm driving."

"We've got soda," she informed him. "Two dollars."

And tip makes three, he thought. "No thanks. I'm diabetic."

"Diet soda?"

"Sorry."

"Whass with you, man?" Dave asked when she left, his words already starting to slur. "Why'd ya invite me here? Jus' relaaaaax."

Calvin sat back and thought again about the girls he worked with–the sullen cows in denim, who gossiped and griped in the swing room in their little cliques. He thought about the secretaries who worked in the upstairs offices too, high above the LSMs and the workroom floor. Carole and Diane and Rachel so-and-so, who had never deigned to look at him as he passed in the hallway because their lily white hands never touched the mail, and because they worked for the big shot Level 17s while he was a lowly Level 6.

Then there was Gail. She was probably living in the foothills now, in one of those designer split-levels overlooking the city lights. Maybe hubby was teaching her golf, among other things, at the Ventana Canyon resort up there. Or the Westin La Poloma. The good schools were up there too, and so now she could start making babies–if she hadn't already started.

"Ya know what gets me?" he asked Dave. "It's why women crave security. It's in the genes how they zero in on the ones they can manipulate. Gotta have those babies, see. Gotta have their brood, and to hell with everyone else. To hell with us taxpayers who don't have kids, and have to help pay for theirs. Know what I mean?"

Dave continued to watch the stage, oblivious.

"We're just cattle," Calvin told him, "on the way to the slaughterhouse. Rings in our noses. We snort and stamp the earth, but we're not in charge, are we? They got the real power. Use us as they see fit."

"Huh? Ya say somethin'?"

Calvin shook his head impatiently. "Mother of all problems is there's too many mothers, Dave. And we gotta pay for all the little brats in their brood. Not just the ones on welfare. Not just the illegals who slip over the border at night so their babies can be American citizens. You seen your paycheck lately? Seen what gets taken out? Some of that goes for maternity care. To bring their brats into the world with more rights than you got."

Dave ordered another whiskey. Calvin declined yet again.

He leaned closer. "They got it down to a science, buddy. But you know what? It's all starting to backfire on them, now. *Too many people.* Too many baby factories churning out future rapists and carjackers. The idiots recycle cans, thinking that helps. But they didn't expect so many illegal immigrants to get on the dole like this. Didn't think all these retired geezers wouldn't be in a hurry to die, or that our underground water reserves would start drying up. They still don't think it ... They don't see the connection. Too busy primping and posing, planning how to raise and defend their own broods, 'cause that's the meaning of life to them: babies. But I'm telling you, it's like anything else. The more there is of something, the less it's worth."

Dave looked at him. "Ya see that?" he said, pointing at the stage. "Ya see that? Oooooooo, mamma!"

They had the Japanese guy with the bra on his head up there, and two girls danced around him as he laughed drunkenly and snapped his fingers to the beat.

Dave cheered, finished his drink, then glanced at his watch. "One more!" he called to the waitress in his slurred voice. The brunette in the fishnet stockings glanced at Calvin, but this time she didn't ask.

***

At ten minutes after eleven Calvin helped Dave out to his car. "Better come with me," he insisted. "We'll get coffee at Dunkin' Donuts, and walk it off in the park before work."

"Hell, I'm fine," Dave said. "See?" He closed his eyes and touched the bridge of his nose.

"Yeah, right."

When he opened his eyes again, Dave looked over Calvin's shoulder. His eyes widened. "Hey," he whispered hotly. "Hey, look over there. It's–"

Calvin turned. It was Tonya Towers, getting out of a black limo. She wore a big western shirt, blue jeans and sneakers, and was escorted by a club bouncer.

"Dave, no. Wait!"

But Dave was already halfway there, stumbling, imploring, "Tonyaaaa!"

The bouncer turned and smiled as he came up, then lifted one arm. Tonya pulled her hair back and gave Dave a look of disgust.

"Hi there, ba-by," Dave crooned. "I'm one a yer biggest–"

The bouncer's open hand caught Dave in the chest by surprise, and pushed him back, hard. Dave lost balance and fell, hitting his head on the concrete. He tried to get up, but only managed to sit and shake his head as he caught his breath.

"You didn't have to do that," Calvin said, coming to Dave's defense.

"Shut up." The bouncer put his arm around Tonya to lead her inside.

Calvin stepped into their path, blocking their way. He looked at Tonya. "You should apologize, you know."

"For what?" croaked Tonya Towers, sex goddess, hoarsely.

Calvin glanced back at Dave, who sat holding his head. When he looked back the bouncer had moved between him and the girl. He was sizing Calvin up–the dark glasses, Army fatigues, the Sumo wrestler look.

"That's right," Calvin said. "I'm not drunk or a wimp. In fact, I was in 'Nam during the pullout. So whaddaya say, buddy?"

The bouncer smiled, said nothing.

"What's your name?" Tonya suddenly asked.

"Richard," Calvin lied. "But you can call me Dick."

"Dickhead." The bouncer laughed. "I like it."

"He's sorry, Richard," Tonya said. "I am too. Okay?"

Calvin moved aside as they passed, glancing back, but not smiling anymore. *Sure you are*, he thought. *You're sorry, all right.*

***

They left Dave's red Mustang in the parking lot at Fleshdance, and Calvin drove him home in his '83 Ford Econoline van. Sominski's house was neither new nor in the foothills, but it did have trees and grass–two luxuries in the desert, as most of Tucson's homeowners opted for rock lawns and cactus gardens.

Dave switched on all the lights and staggered into the bathroom, where he held a hot washrag against the back of his head.

"I'll make coffee," Calvin said.

"Naw, no time," Dave replied.

"You really should call in sick."

"I'm fine."

"Sure you are. Just look at you. Gary'll think you been in a bar fight."

"Gary's a faggot."

"What's that got to do with it? At least change your shirt."

"Screw it, I'm okay. All right? I'm goin' in. Already used 'nough damn sick leave. Been warned twice."

"Okay, have it your way."

"Screw 'em ... and screw you, too."

Dave slammed the bathroom door. Calvin laughed openly for a moment, but then had to wait for Dave to come out. It was a long wait.

***

They barely beat the time clock. You were allowed to go up to five clicks past, if there was a line, before being counted late. You couldn't do it often, or they'd put a letter of warning in your file. Six clicks past and you had to fill out a change-of-schedule slip and get it signed by a union steward, then hand it to your boss. And pray.

A split second after Calvin slid his ID card into the magnetic reader, the LED indicator went to 12:06. Dave, ahead of him, walked unsteadily toward the letter sorting machines, a look of disorientation on his face. Luckily, Gary Lennox was nowhere to be seen. They sat at their terminals and started to key.

At 12:11 Calvin heard a voice behind him, and glanced back. A man in a blue sport coat flashed a badge in Dave's face. "You'll need to come with me," he said.

Dave cut off his machine and stared up in shock. "Why? W-Wha–"

"You'll need to come to my office," the man told him. "Upstairs."

He waited for Dave to stand and come out of his station, then he motioned for Dave to walk ahead of him. As Dave walked toward the distant staircase, the inspector watched him closely, and did not speak.

They were passed by plant manager Rick Matuska, Gary Lennox, and an Hispanic woman, coming the other way. Matuska held up one hand and whistled. Everyone cut off their machines as Calvin watched Dave and the inspector disappear into the stairwell.

"Got a little announcement for you," Matuska said, beaming. He cleared his throat. "Gary here has been doing a super job. Productivity is up eight percent in the last quarter. Unkeyed mail is down by three percent. He's been a real asset to us this past year, and the postmaster wanted me to congratulate him on the fine job he's been doing, and to let you know that he's being promoted to head of Training. As of next week your new boss will be someone who started on the LSM in Albuquerque six years ago, and worked as manager of mail processing there for a year and a half, after they dismantled an LSM in favor of delivery point sequencing on the new DBCS. She's proud of her Hispanic and Native American heritage, and I know we're going to be proud of her work here as well–Ms. Mariel Grijalva."

The woman between them took a step forward, and smiled on cue. It was the same fake smile as the waitress at Fleshdance, or the hookers on the streets of old Saigon. "Hi," she said, her cheekbones stretching her face as tight as a corpse. "I'm looking forward to working with you all."

Calvin looked up at the inspector's bridge overhead. The bridge was swaying now, very slightly. He tried to mimic the smile that so many had mastered, into the reflective one-way glass above him. But he realized that that smile would come only if you thought the right thoughts: if you saw yourself as part of a big happy family. It was difficult, but if you really concentrated on the present moment by blocking out the past and the future, if you really tried to see the world as "they" saw it, the smile would come.

Calvin blinked. His eyes relaxed. His lips stretched wide.

There it is, Dad. There it is.

At last, he had it, too.

4

"I don't know what you want me to say, Vic," Karen was saying. "I know you think it sounds irrational, but I think we're becoming two different people. And no, I don't think you should try commuting to Casa Grande from there; it puts too much of a strain on a relationship. Maybe we just need more time to come to terms with who we are and what we want."

Victor gripped the telephone tighter, rubbing his forehead with his open palm. "Sounds like you've been reading some dumb pop psychology book, Karen. This is our lives we're talking about here. Shouldn't we at least give it a chance?"

"But we are, Vic. We are. Can't you see that? If our relationship can survive the time test, and we still want to see each other after our heads have cleared ... then maybe. Just not now. Not yet."

He stared out the window at the late traffic along McDowell Road, past the Holiday Inn marquee that said WAY TO GO, SUNS! "'Time is the farthest distance between two points,' Karen," he said. "Even farther than Casa Grande."

"You don't need to quote Tennessee Williams to me. My mind is made up. Mother thinks it's for the best, too."

"Edie never really liked me, did she? She wanted you to marry Bruce what's-his-name ... *Collier*. That ape who lifted tractor trailers with his teeth for a living."

Karen tried to stifle a just perceptible laugh. "He did not! Bruce was a diesel mechanic."

"Same thing. Anyway, you'd think she would have preferred me over him. At least I was a teacher like her, and my knuckles didn't scrape the ground."

"Mother liked you okay, Vic. Don't be paranoid."

"Liked? There's a Freudian slip."

"Well, you're not a teacher anymore, are you? What did you do today, for instance?"

"For instance? For instance, we arrested a window clerk for stealing stamps."

"We?"

"My field trainer and I."

"So was it fulfilling? And did you manage to teach this clerk the error of his ways?"

Vic took a deep breath and exhaled. "Well, he won't be doing it anymore, I can tell you that much. At least not at the Post Office. I don't know, maybe he'll graduate to robbing banks and pushing little old ladies down stairs. What do you want me to say, Karen? I couldn't take teaching anymore. At thirty-four I was already burned out, and scared, too."

"Why?"

"Why? Because those kids don't want to learn the classics. They got street stories about drive-by shootings and gang bangs to relate to these days. It's a regular *Paradise Lost* for them. Except Milton is a junkie and rap star, strumming the same dissonant chord on his guitar. Waiting for the HIV virus to validate the dirge they're all singing."

"I'm sorry you feel that way, Vic. I really am."

"Yeah, so am I." He sighed. "Maybe you're right. Maybe it is time to think about a change."

Silence, then: "We'll talk later on, okay?"

"Just don't marry Bruce Collier yet, and I'll try not to get shot by some disgruntled postal wacko. Deal?"

"Yeah. Thanks for calling, anyway. Did I tell you I'll be out of town for a few days? On a job interview. So–"

"Out of town? Where?"

"Sun City. It's a retirement community just north of Tucson."

"A teaching job?"

"Yes, as a matter of ... Look, I need to go now, Vic."

"Okay, then. Good luck."

"Thanks. Bye."

He listened to the dial tone for a full minute before he hung up the phone. Then he crumpled the letter he'd begun to her. The one which began: "I want to tell you things I could never say ..." He missed the trash can, then slowly pulled the cord that closed the curtains. Finally, he lay back on the bed, kicked off his shoes, and cut the light.

Thanks for calling, anyway, Karen had said. Something about the way she'd spoken those four words told him he might just as well have tried for Seattle or Miami or Honolulu. In fact, he could have studied to become a chimney sweep or circus acrobat for all it mattered. What's done was done, and new lives had begun. As for his marriage, it looked to be over. If it wasn't dead already, it was dying.

***

"How was your night?" Marty Rifkin, manager of plant operations, asked him the next morning in the elevator. "Looking for an apartment yet?"

Victor shook his head, wondering if the fatigue was really that evident on his face. "It's only been two nights so far," he replied, feeling his chin for traces of stubble.

The plant manager, a burly mid-life choleric, nodded as the elevator door opened

The operations floor of the Phoenix MSC was an immense staging ground larger than a football field. The massive concrete posts which held the roof up were numbered so that people unfamiliar with the plant could find any location without becoming lost. The high ceiling of the windowless room was riddled and crisscrossed with piping, conduits, and ventilation ducts. The bright blue walls were mostly hidden by a monotone profusion of postal equipment–the cases, dollies, cages, racks of gray bags, carts, and hampers. Heard over all was the continuous noise of mail processing machinery. Clarion blasts and flashing yellow lights warned of yet another machine's startup.

As they walked amid the pulsing heart of the work floor, Rifkin raised his voice against the din. "I like to say we're in the travel industry," he explained. "Every time someone puts a letter in the mailbox anywhere in the northern half of the state, including Yuma, it comes to this room first. Then we cancel it, bar code it, separate it, and send it on to wherever–Chicago, Atlanta, or Timbuktu. Trucks take thousands of bags to the airport every day, so I guess we work for the airline industry too, eh? Watch out behind you, there."

Victor turned at the beep. A battery-operated car pulling a line of cages shot past, missing him by inches.

"The postmaster wanted me to give you a little tour this morning," Marty continued, as if nothing had happened, "even though you've probably seen other operations like this back east."

"Mostly slides projected on a screen, I'm afraid. In the dark. With coffee."

"Yeah?" They approached a huge machine with belts, turning drums, and a chute where mail shot through into bins. "Barnard wasn't sure exactly what exposure you've had. Of course the postmaster hasn't really been my boss since the reorganization shakeup back in 'ninety-three. Plant operations come under Denver's direction now, and that's where I report. Max the Ax rolled a lot a heads, ya know."

"I heard."

"That right? Well, heads are still rolling. It's a regular bowling alley, and the union's forbidden to strike."

"I'd imagine they're happy about it, as long as it's the right heads."

The plant manager smiled. "But just let some temporary employee come in here and get an hour of overtime and you'll see who gets mad. Are you familiar with this machine?"

Victor looked at the behemoth in front of them. "The Facer-Canceler, yes. It's where letter mail gets dumped first. Goes through the chute there, after it gets turned in the right direction so the stamps can be voided."

"Right. The old machine was a Mark Two, had what was called an Alhambra Retrofit to make it able to identify and separate machinable and bar coded mail. This is the new replacement to the Mark Two. The next generation, so to speak. The FC Two Hundred."

Victor bent over and picked up a letter from the floor beside the feeder belt. It had a heel mark on it, and was partially torn. He handed it to Rifkin. "I guess even the next generation isn't perfect, huh?"

"You can't make omelets without cracking some eggs." Marty laughed and took the letter over to a clerk working a small case against the wall. The clerk was taping together jigsaws of shredded envelopes and putting them in small plastic bags. When he returned he said, "At least her job is secure."

Victor smiled and pointed at the larger case beyond. "What about her?"

"Oh, yeah. Her too, for sure. She's the nixie clerk. Gets mail which can't be delivered for whatever reason, and can't be returned either, because there's not enough of a return address. She looks up what she can in her reference books."

"And what if there's no return address at all?"

"Then it goes to the Dead Letter office in San Francisco, where it's opened. Except now they want to call it a Mail Recovery Center, or MRC. So many damn abbreviations you could go nuts. As for the letters themselves, we just call 'em what they are–dead."

They walked past the FC200 toward one of several long narrow machines with dozens of separation bins along a shielded and speeding belt.

"The OCR?" Vic asked.

"Right again. Unisys and Pitney Bowes have done their magic. Now we have a Multi-line Optical Character Reader, which can read up to five lines of info. See the light at the feeder end, there? Each letter that doesn't already have a bar code is scanned by that Star Wars laser right in there, see? Then the address is sent to a computer, which has the whole damn national directory on it. Well, then the computer looks up the address on the directory, verifies it, and returns a nine digit zip to be sprayed on the letter in a bar, half-bar format. This all happens in the blink of an eye, or less. Imagine a bar code that can narrow down a letter to any particular apartment complex or street in the country. It's sprayed on every letter through this machine at the rate of forty thousand an hour."

Victor shook his head. "Amazing. I didn't realize."

"Now here, see, the letters are sent to one of forty-four stackers, according to zip code. For the breakdown by carrier route, we need to go to over there."

Beyond the OCRs was a larger but similar row of machines. These had stacker bins on both sides. "The BCS," Vic announced as they came alongside one of them. "The Bar Code Sorter, am I right?"

"Yup. New and improved. Separates the mail right down to the mailman, who used to have it rough, casing his mail back at his own station, before carrying it out on his route. We do a second pass with the mail that makes it even easier for him, too. Now let's go over there, and I'll show you how magazines are handled. Unless you already know."

Victor pointed at three long sorting machines which had two keyboard terminals on either end. They were manned by clerks, who placed flyers and magazines one by one into a hole, which paused long enough for them to key in several digits of the zip code. The flats were then carried by belt and dropped automatically through silver chutes into removable white tubs along the sides. A fifth clerk replaced the buckets as they filled.

"The Flats Sorters," Vic said. "I've seen pictures. The clerks that empty the tubs are called sweepers."

"I guess you know about the LSMs too, then," Rifkin said. "But is our layout the same as the one they showed you?"

"Not quite," he replied. "Better take me around and introduce me to the managers. I won't be able to tell who's who from up there on the bridge."

Marty complied by introducing him to the LSM supervisor and the Express Mail manager, then the Bulk Mail processing supervisor. The Parcel and Bundle Sorter came next–a machine which could sort small packages to one hundred sort destinations. The machine was supplemented, Marty explained, by a phalanx of distribution clerks, who tossed bundled letters and parcels into large white bags hung on racks, with the finesse of master horseshoe pitchers.

After passing through a casing area for the clerks who sorted letters which were too bulky or flimsy for the LSM, a Facilities Engineer explained the concept of shrink-wrap technology. Vic soon learned how the fiberboard sleeves and strappings on trays had been eliminated, and how plastic pallets had replaced the old Litco ones. Just in case there was a Trivial Pursuit question in his future, he was also given a summary of how the whole automated staging retrieval system operated. Then a Procurement Specialist told him about the Integrated Logistics Support System at the MSC. A computer programmer described the bugs in the system software of the BCS, and what she was doing about it. She also mentioned RECs, known as Remote Encoding Centers, where clerks sat in cubicles and keyed images of unreadable mail on a screen so the distant mechanized machines could add bar codes. Of course, she used acronyms in talking, too, like DPS for Delivery Point Sequencing, and AMS for Address Management System, just like any government bureaucrat.

Then another training manager described how their ongoing job performance and career enhancement programs supplemented the EPA's own. He met the Manager of Customer Services, whose Computer Forwarding System (CFS) fell under the direction of the postmaster. That manager tried to explain the Customer Satisfaction Index (CSI), and the External First Class Measurement System (EXFC), until the Manager of Fleet Operations interrupted to offer him a lame joke about carriers of the future being robots on whose legs a dog would someday break its teeth.

Later, he was told, he could meet the head of Labor Relations, the Commercial Accounts manager, the Quality Control analyst, the Safety Specialist, and the Manager of Communications. They would all want a piece of him. All of them would want to meet this newly hired gun sent from Washington out to the Wild West to walk the line behind the one-way glass, to spy and to spot check, to investigate and litigate. They all wanted to shake his hand because he was the law above them all, reporting only to his own mysterious branch, and because he held no EAS level responsibilities except to his badge.

Plant Manager Marty Rifkin did not introduce him to a single mail handler, clerk, carrier, or custodian. Nor did he once mention plant security, or the likelihood of what had happened at Arcadia station happening again.

***

Maria Castillo was waiting for him at the corner window table of the Olive Garden restaurant on Camelback Road at 12:30 PM, as planned. She was wearing a navy blue suit this time, and sat sipping an iced tea with a faraway look on her face. When she saw him, Maria smiled. Vic motioned to the waitress, ordered a Pepsi, and then sat down.

"You all right?" he asked her.

"Oh yes," Maria replied, "I'm fine. How was your morning? Did the plant manager take you on the buck-fifty tour?"

Vic frowned and looked down at his right hand resting on the table. Then he lifted the hand and turned it as if it were a sculpture. "A lot of people wanted to shake this," he said. "You'd think it belonged to a celebrity."

"You don't sound pleased."

"I don't know–I get the feeling they're happy to see me, not because I might help make things safer for them, but because I'm a new member of the club."

Maria cocked her head. "What do you mean, exactly?"

"I don't know. It just seems odd that nobody I've met so far has mentioned the killings here last week, except you and Postmaster Barnard."

The waitress came for their order, bringing Victor's soda. After Maria got her tea refilled, she offered her theory. "It's probably just human nature," she said. "You've got to understand what a madhouse it was during the forty-eight hours after the shooting. Reporters, microphones. People are talked out, and they want things to get back to normal. The only folks who can't afford to let their guard down is us. We're paid to think about security and criminal behavior; it's our job, not theirs. They've got deadlines and projections to meet, with over a hundred fifty billion pieces of mail to deliver every year, no matter how bad public perception gets. Think about that."

Vic thought about it as Maria continued.

"Plus, if Mister John Q. Public thinks they're a bunch of lazy bastards, so does Senator John Q. Public. So while the radio talk show hosts make jokes about them, they get new gimmicks like the Performance Cluster concept handed down to them from on high. To say nothing of the union pressure against automation, or hiring part-time temporaries at a lower wage. There's so many variables to deal with here it's mind-boggling. So, can you see, with management's head on the chopping block, why they'd each want to appear important in the overall scheme of things? It's self-preservation at work. Do or die."

"A hundred fifty billion pieces of mail. You sound like Carl Sagan."

"Well, thank you, Data."

"And maybe you're right. It's just that I get a sense they think the shooting at Arcadia was a fluke. What if there's another nut out there ready to spin off the deep end?"

"You mean, what if we don't find him in time to stop him, because they don't have time to think about it themselves?"

Vic nodded. "And what if the rift between management and labor has been such that we don't have access to many true employee profiles, and so the real personalities of the employees we should be examining will be completely invisible to us."

"In other words, we won't find our potential problem employees by looking at EAP enrollment registers because some of the dangerous ones keep to themselves and don't respect all the bureaucracy to begin with. Ergo, they don't enroll or get sent to improvement classes. That it?"

"Exactly."

Maria smiled. "There's hope for you, Vic. You might make a decent inspector after all."

Victor took a sip of Pepsi, and risked a wink. "Was there ever any doubt?"

Field Inspector Maria Castillo slowly nodded.

5

When a cow suddenly appeared in the dirt road ahead of him, Calvin leaned to the left and braked hard. The front tire seized for a split second, so he released it and braked again. After a wicked fish-tail, he stopped at the end of a thirty foot swath, and righted himself. The startled cow made for some thickets of creosote, bent the limb of an ocotillo in passing, and then disappeared down a slope beyond an outcropping of prickly pear.

Calvin stared at the place where the cow had vanished, and breathed a curse under his breath. Then he opened the throttle of the GS again, and this time kept his speed down to twenty, although the desert sun had turned these back roads into a washboard in places, and made it uncomfortable to ride at less than thirty-five. At twenty, the tires of his motorcycle took in every wave and bump in the road, transmitting the vibration to his arms, his feet, and his ass. But this was open range, where it was possible that a bull might decide to cross the road at any time. And then where would he be? Stuck beneath a heap of metal with an angry six-hundred-pound animal stamping around his head. Luckily, most of the cattle were lying in the shade of the surrounding mesquite and Palo Verde trees to escape the hundred-plus degree heat. And the ghost town of Helvetia couldn't be much farther.

At a double fork in the road he stopped and consulted the topo map in his tank bag again. Straight ahead two miles, he estimated. He checked his watch: 2:14 PM. The electronic display below the time read THURSDAY, MAY 26.

His day off.

He took another swig of water from the canteen in his saddlebag, and rode on.

***

After its fifty-year history, Helvetia had died around the 1920s, but remnants of the town lingered on, though not much was left: a few standing walls of adobe brick slowly eroding in the dry heat. A hundred yards behind the Stonehenge-like skeleton walls were the charred remains of a mill, with evidence of its operation: a pool of dead black slag.

Calvin looked north, into the distant haze. There was Tucson, the "Old Pueblo" as it was called. Eight hundred thousand people lived there, trying to accumulate green pieces of paper, which were no longer fully-backed by silver or gold, in a smog-capped valley surrounded on its other three sides by the massive Catalinas, the jagged Tucsons, and the rolling Rincons. Taco franchises, factories, shopping malls, street gangs.

It was a modern kind of Wild West coming, expanding across the desert like a cancer, laying out concrete developments and golf courses to the very edge of the frontier. One hundred and fifteen degrees in June, but it didn't matter. Water brought in by canal from the Colorado river aided this final assault, and the Central Arizona Project gave the expansion its umbilical, just as government handouts gave welfare mothers, and undocumented arrivals, false promise to procreate in exponential numbers. Troops for the war against the haves.

Calvin scanned the horizon, wondering how long it would be before the city reached here. How long before postal substations and processing distribution centers were needed to service all the junk mail, bills, and postcards expressing the singular irony WISH YOU WERE HERE.

He looked behind. Only crumbling adobe walls remained as a token reminder that there were once three hundred people here, living in an assortment of buildings, tents, and shanties. Only a few scattered planks amid the mesquite indicated that this place was once home to humans whose skulls were now cavities buried somewhere in the hot sands. The Old Frijole Mine, the 150-ton smelter, and all the investments made by the Helvetia Copper Company of New Jersey, where were they now?

He took out a photocopy of the letter from his great grandfather, Willard Beach.

> *...and on the promontory there's this big rock, like an anvil, and below that three smaller boulders. Under the center of the smaller three there's the ledge where I found some rich ore. Dug a hole there, and guess what? There's more down there. Lots of silver, I can smell it! Maybe a vein. Maybe a mountain of it, all under this here hill, and within sight of a mine shaft below that turned up nothing! Soon as I stake it, I'm filing my claim in town, and then I'll come for you in Tucson quicker than a rattler can strike. So don't you worry none, now. We be rich soon, no more scraping to get by!*

He contemplated the date on the fragmented letter he'd saved from total deterioration: 1885. Then he climbed a slope to a point overlooking the entire site, and saw no distinctive boulders of the size referred to, no place where such boulders could be hiding. Below and surrounding him the desert was punctuated only with low rounded hills, abandoned mine shafts, and sparse vegetation. The one rift in the terrain, where a creek had once run through, bore no singularity except for the skeleton of the mill. And the only large boulder was the peak of Old Baldy in the Santa Rita Mountains to the south, which was not a boulder, but the massive crown of a nine-thousand-foot tooth.

So Helvetia was not the right ghost town, as he expected. The easiest to get to, but not a likely prospect. Still, he had to mark it off the list. One down, and how many to go? He figured on a dozen at least: Contention City, Gleason, Courtland, Harshaw, Mowry, Cerro Colorado; Total Wreck; they were all out there, waiting.

After a solemn walk through the debris he found the town's tiny cemetery, and checked for names amid the weeds and cactus. Then he scanned the mountains with binoculars, and finally mounted his iron steed. He was about to restart the bike when he saw a man in a white hat on horseback approaching.

"Howdy there," the man said, pushing back the brim of his hat to admire Calvin's bike. "Nice motorcycle."

"Thanks," Calvin said.

"Hope you're not gonna go off the trails with that."

"Not me." Calvin took out his map. "Can you tell me where to find this other place?"

"What other place?" The rancher climbed down to examine his map, then looked at him in obvious bewilderment. "Why you lookin' for that?"

"Because that's where a man named John Dillon discovered a silver-lead mine in eighteen seventy-nine. When they asked him what he'd name the place he said it looked like a total wreck. Then in eighteen eighty-one the Empire Mining and Development Company bought the place, and constructed a mill. The town grew up around it."

"What town?" the rancher asked.

"I just showed you. Total Wreck. Fifty houses, four saloons, three hotels, a butcher shop, general store, and lumberyard."

"Well, there's none a that there now! Just like Greaterville. Mostly jackrabbits and Gila monsters, a few ranches, cattle. Oh, and an abandoned Titan missile base from the Cold War."

"Really," Calvin replied. "So I suppose no Apaches are gonna be coming down from the cliffs to surprise some Mexicans cutting wood, like they did in eighteen eighty-three."

The rancher chuckled. "If you're looking for Geronimo, he's gone, too. Only outlaws out there now are drug runners from Mexico."

"Few and far between, I take it."

"If you're lucky.

Calvin shoved his map into his pack, cranked up, and climbed the bad road in one long second gear moan. It would be a bumpy forty minute ride to Total Wreck, but he already felt a strange anticipation about what might be awaiting him there.

***

Sominski kept one hand on the lintel, casually barring Calvin's entrance. Squinting at him as if at an intruder.

"You got a girl in there?" Calvin asked, and glanced at his watch. "If so I can come back in five minutes."

Dave dropped his arm to rub the stubble on his chin. "What is it you want, anyway?"

"Just wondering what happened last night. You letting me in or what?"

Dave stepped aside to open the curtains. The Arizona sunset lit the room like a flood lamp on a stage. The scene was Oscar Madison's living room the morning after *The Odd Couple* was canceled. Set decoration was by Jack Daniels and Frito Lay. An open Dominos pizza box on the floor beside the couch bore two dried crusts in a mock happy face. Only Sominski did not smile.

"Bastard put me on probation," Dave explained. "Gotta go to some half-ass substance abuse sessions set up by the EAP, too. Can ya fuckin' believe it? If there wasn't a backlog of mail to be processed they'd actually be suspendin' me instead of just cuttin' out my overtime."

"A bummer. Coulda been worse, though."

"Worse? Hell, why'd you tell me about that Tonya bitch in the first place? All ya did was complain." Dave sank into his sofa, angrily brushing away several crumbs. "Yer one weird dude, ya know that?"

Calvin laughed. "*Moi?*"

"Well, hell, here ya are, forty years old, got no family or friends. Not even a girlfriend."

"Look who's talking."

"Well, at least I'm tryin'. You gave up, didn't ya? Don't even like girls no more. And what beats all, it don't bother ya any. How do ya do that, exactly?"

"What?"

"Go on like this without carin' whether ya end up an old man livin' in a trailer somewhere on the south side with nothin' an' nobody."

Calvin shrugged. "I got money. Bought a new motorcycle, didn't I?"

Dave shook his head in frustration. "No, I mean what kinda life is it? Damn–don't it bother ya? How do ya stay sober thinkin' about it? Here we are, a couple of lifeless fools workin' the graveyard shift, think we escaped marriage and babies, but what we got, eh? *Nada*. Zip. Couple a robots servin' our fuckin' purpose 'til they're done with us. Then we can spend our wad at the liquor store, clean the place out, an' kick back an' watch *Twilight Zone* reruns. Waitin' for the end."

Calvin smiled. "Think that's the score, huh? Look at you ... you're the one gave up, not me."

"How ya figure? What you doin' with yer fuckin' life besides jackin' off?"

"For one thing," Calvin replied, "I'm not falling for it."

"For what?"

"*It*. As defined by *them*." His smile widened. "Maybe you wanna be one of them, but I don't. Not anymore."

Dave rubbed his forehead. "What the hell does that mean?"

A pair of A-10 jets roared by overhead, back to base. Calvin walked to the window and stared out at cars passing on the hot asphalt. When the sound faded and the house stopped vibrating, he finally said, "Means I'm in a war here, and they're the enemy."

"Who? Who's whose enemy?"

"All of them. The world loves the lovers, gives 'em all the breaks. It's true, just like you say. But me? I don't fit in, and women know it and hate me. Everywhere I go it's like I'm abnormal, subhuman. It's the way they look at me, alone. Like if I don't get a wife and start making babies like everybody else, then to hell with me. I'm a freak. A loser."

"Well," Dave responded, "maybe you are."

Calvin turned and curled his lips. "That's what they want me to believe. Want *me* brainwashed, too. To think like them. Like sex is all that's left. Sex and babies and a dream house with a white picket fence. Onward and upward to the end, until there's no more room to breathe."

"Ya sound paranoid, now."

"Do I? You walk over to the flats sorter sometime. *Parenting, Baby's World, Family Circle*–to say nothing of *Penthouse, Playboy, Climax*, and *Screw*. Tub after tub of 'em. And the poorer you are, the more babies you have. The more likely you'll be a deadbeat parent."

"So?"

"So open your eyes. You've seen those government checks coming through for years. Thousands of 'em, right there in front of you, one by one. Now they're testing plastic cards here, so they can go to any ATM machine and get instant cash. Money *from* you and me, buddy. Every dime of it. And it's never enough. I read this morning they're talking about raiding our pension funds, taxing our four-oh-one-K, plans, too. Increase your property tax and sales tax to pay for more schools and prisons." Calvin paused, seeing Dave's bewilderment. "You don't see the connection? It's ... I mean ... their entire *purpose* in life is making babies. The Pope is their God, telling everybody not to use birth control. Won't be long their babies will have bloated bellies too, just like in the third world, or in the Book of Revelation. All you gotta do is just stop working, get your free health care, welfare, and sue anybody who looks at you wrong. Why work? I'm telling you it's a war, and you don't see it."

Dave laughed. "Sorry, but if yer gonna bring the Bible into this it's jus' too–"

"What? You don't believe the Bible, either? You've never read about the war of Armageddon, where everyone has let everything good slide, so they can curse God and screw like rabbits? Never heard about the cashless society and the number six six six? It'll be six six six, and sex sex sex."

"Come on, man, don't ..."

"Don't what? You know where I went this afternoon? Visited a ghost town named Total Wreck. Place had a history you can't even imagine. No shopping malls, no television. People talked to their neighbors then; they didn't build walls and fences with razor wire ... or line up their kids to be fingerprinted. They didn't expect other people to pay for their kids either, but when it was necessary people did it out of charity, not because someone was lazy or claimed discrimination. They called the town Total Wreck, right? Well, the name didn't fit the town like it fits Tucson today. Tucson is gonna be Phoenix is gonna be Los Angeles. Or Sodom and Gomorra. This is the true wreck, and the people here are a total loss."

Dave squirmed in his seat. "For one thing, how would you know what it was like then? An' what the fuck does that have to do with–"

"You really don't get it, do you? Can't you see it? Even automation can't keep up with it."

"With what, fer godssake? With overpopulation? Socialism? What?"

Calvin walked past him into the kitchen. "With all of the above," he said, "and war." He smiled to himself and opened the freezer compartment. He took a pair of ice cubes out of the bin, and popped one in his mouth. Then he walked back out to the front door, where he turned and looked down at Dave Sominski, the dumb Pollock, sitting there sweating in his underwear. "I know all about it," he added, "because I've been there before."

"Where?"

"Total Wreck. I've seen it. Recognized it. Might even be the town I lived in once. One thing I know: the Indians didn't get me. I fell. See? I fell into a mine shaft on the run from them. The mine shaft right near a vein of silver I found then, and an anvil-shaped rock I found today. Except now there's an old missile base there. The silver is long gone."

"What the hell are you talkin' about this time?"

Calvin sighed. "You believe in reincarnation?"

"Hell, no."

"I didn't think so. You know, Jesus once said 'I and the Father are one.' It makes sense to me now. Has to do with time. That's right. And no one really understands that concept, either. You substitute great-grandfather for father, and maybe I can say the same thing."

Dave blinked. "You sayin' yer God, now?"

"Not at all. I'm just a postal clerk. A loser just like you. Except I know it, and accept their label. Means nothing to me. At least, not like it does to you. What I'm saying is what if maybe, just maybe, I was my own great-grandfather, back when the country was a country and not a screwed-up collection of gutless victims? At the very least old Willard, he's left me a different kind of legacy."

Dave laughed and covered his face with one hand.

"Go ahead, laugh. But I'm the one dealing with it, see? I mean the cold war." Dave watched him as he held out his arm in the doorway. The ice cube in his hand had melted and now dripped between his fingers. He let it all drip out, and then turned up his palm like he'd just done a magic trick. "Have a nice night at work with the new boss," he said, "'cause I'm going to plan my next sortie into the desert. Hey–maybe I'll even draw a line in the sand."

"Yeah, Fireplug, you do that, ya hear?" Dave laughed again, then raised his voice. "'Course yer a real nice guy underneath it all, ya know? Real nice."

Back at his Beemer, Calvin put on his helmet, then waved at Dave, standing there inside the screen door, still laughing and mocking him.

Dave didn't wave back.

6

"A pretty dreary drive," Vic commented thirty miles out of Phoenix on I-10 South.

Maria turned down the radio, and nodded at the bleak terrain beyond the windscreen of her Lexus. "Yeah, and we may be taking this trip more often than you think."

"Why is that?"

"They're pulling all but one inspector out of Tucson, and since Tucson is under our jurisdiction, guess who'll have to fill the gap?"

Vic frowned. "Can't we fly or something?"

"Why do you think they're cutting the other two inspectors?"

"Silly me. Well then, how often do we go?"

Maria smiled at him. "You're taking this pretty well. Better than I did, or Barnard ... Well, it's not so bad there, really. Tucson has less traffic, at least so far. The mountains are sure nicer. And it's a bit higher than Phoenix, so it's not quite so hot. I figure one trip a month for each of us, staying two days at a time. I'm guessing, of course. It depends on what we need to investigate. Today we're doing a surprise audit of Cherrybelle station's bulk mail unit because there's been reports of an advertiser defrauding the Postal Service of revenue, by falsely claiming non-profit status. But it won't be the same thing next month. That's what I like about this job–you never know."

"I thought our special priority was employee background investigations, plant security, that kind of thing."

"Somebody's got to write those contract audit reports. If they pull the inspectors who do it, then it's up to us."

Vic shook his head. "It still makes no sense. Why'd they hire me if they were gonna let two other inspectors go? Just last year the Service saved fourteen million in revenue deficiencies, forty-seven million in workers' comp fraud, about a hundred sixteen million by inspector recommendations to strengthen operations, and thirty-nine million in property was seized. And I haven't even mentioned all the mail order marketing schemes which were stopped before some little old ladies sent off their nest eggs. Or the child porno convictions and illegal drug arrests. What gives, anyway?"

Maria switched on the cruise control. This time she gave an acquiescent smile. "I'm shocked. You've done your homework. But it's like I said: you never know what may happen. You've got to remember, this is civil service. Government. It's like them trying to handle health care. Don't try to make sense of it. Sometimes they throw the baby out with the bath water as standard procedure." She paused, then suddenly asked: "You're married aren't you, Victor?"

"Uh-huh. Recently separated, actually. Karen didn't much like my career move, especially the law enforcement part of it. Her father was a cop, got killed breaking up a domestic dispute. Guy used a kitchen knife. Karen was only ten. She grew up in Casa Grande, with her mother, who was a teacher, too. Still is. Anyway, Karen's staying with her for a while. I requested Phoenix mostly because of that."

Maria pointed at a sign ahead which read, CASA GRANDE 22 MILES. "How is she?"

"She's ... not there," he said. "She's on an interview in Sun City. Gonna be an aerobics instructor or something, for the retirees. Teach Spanish, too."

Maria nodded thoughtfully, said nothing.

"Actually, it's been pretty rough for us lately, since I joined the Service. Don't know if we'll make it. How about you?"

"Me?" Maria looked into the rear view mirror. "What about me?"

"You're not wearing a ring. Are you seeing anyone?"

"I've been seeing a man named Carl, a lawyer. He's even proposed."

"And?"

"And ... I'm not sure if he's my type."

"Do you love him?"

Maria looked over at him, studying him. "You come right out with it, don't you?"

Vic let a smile spread slowly across his face. "I speak my mind, if that's what you mean."

***

They stopped in Casa Grande at the Cactus Flower Cafe for a late breakfast at 10:00 AM. Vic ordered a western omelet, and Maria an egg and ham burrito with homemade salsa. As she called ahead to Tucson, using a pay phone in the corner of the nearly empty restaurant, he looked out the window at the flat, quiet town, already simmering in the early summer heat. A sign across the road read RUINS AHEAD TWO MILES, and he remembered that Casa Grande meant "big house," for the enigmatic four-story adobe structure left behind by the Hohokam Indians in 1450. Tourists visited the site in droves, bringing their thirsts to the Cactus Flower for quenching. But the season was over now, and their numbers had dwindled as the thermometer rose into the triple digits.

He thought about calling Edie, his mother-in-law, to let her know he was passing through, but decided against it. They'd never spoken much in the past, and there was even less to talk about now that their association appeared to be over. He wondered what it might have been like had he moved to Casa Grande with Karen, and taught school there instead of dragging Karen with him back to his home in South Carolina. Would they all be friends now, sitting on Mother Burrow's front porch, sipping iced tea and discussing babies or outcome-based education curriculum? What would they do for fun, out here in the middle of nowhere? Pitch horseshoes? Chase butterflies? No, Karen wouldn't approve of that. Besides, there weren't many butterflies to chase in this arid climate.

"John is out," Maria said, when she returned.

"John?" Vic asked.

"Maybe we should call him Lone Wolf McQuade. He's out investigating the theft of a food stamp shipment from the Rincon station there."

Vic took a sip of coffee, and considered what Maria was wearing for their trip. Slacks this time, and a blue cotton blouse with a pattern of tiny red peppers along the shoulders and sleeves. "You look more relaxed than usual," he said. "Not as intimidating."

Maria sipped at her orange juice and considered the statement. She settled back and looked out toward the street. "I'm trying to relax," she admitted. "Thinking of selling my Lexus and getting a jeep."

"Really? The Postal Service would frown on that, wouldn't they? I mean if they have to pay your gas bill?"

"I'd get the same if it was a tank," she replied. "Actually, I could drive a postal vehicle, but they're all plain Jane white. Lately, at least when I'm on the road, I don't want to think that I'm at the office."

Vic nodded. "Why a jeep?"

"I don't know. I saw some ASU girls riding in one last week; it looked like a lot of fun."

***

The Tucson Processing and Distribution Center was not as large as the Phoenix MSC, but since it was once an MSC itself–pre-reorganization–the identical layout was there, if at a slightly smaller scale. The bulk mail unit was at the rear of the plant, giving business customers access to the facility without having to interrupt private customer use at the window and box section units in front. After notifying Postmaster Graves of their audit commencement, Maria opened her briefcase and began to tackle the books, following the guidelines established by the inspection service in Potomac, Maryland. She refreshed Vic on the procedure step-by-step, although at several points she had to repeat herself as Vic quoted passages he remembered from *The Waste Land*, by T.S. Eliot.

"Sorry," he explained, with a shrug. "I was never very good at math. It's how I impressed my math professor at Clemson, but I guess it won't work with you, huh?"

After they completed enough of an examination to pass as a spot audit, it was mid-afternoon. Checking documentation on a questionable non-profit client, and verifying the client's status via several long distance phone calls, brought them to five o'clock.

"Short day," Vic said, checking his watch. "Went by like a flash. Guess it's the company."

Maria lifted her index finger in front of his eyes, and waved it. "Not so fast," she said, grinning. "Our day has just begun. After we grab a sandwich in the swing room, it'll be time to go over the personnel files John hasn't had time to look at."

"John?"

"You know–Lone Wolf McQuade. I mean McDade. That's his real name."

"No kidding? Not that it matters; I'll probably never meet him, anyway."

"Why do you say that?"

Vic spread his hands. "I've never even met Phil, your partner in Phoenix. The closest I've come to that is a warm cup of coffee and half a jelly donut on his desk. Forensics could match the teeth marks on it to him, I suppose. But they couldn't tell me much about him."

"Well, Phil is busy, what can I say? He's covering for me while I'm setting you up with your training wheels. Anyway, half a jelly donut is pretty damn close. You should be happy. Phil wouldn't leave that behind unless he was in a hurry, so you must have just missed him."

They entered Personnel, and just as it was closing Vic told her, "I'm missing Phil more every day."

"And night," Maria added. "Because tonight we get to man the bridge, and do a little spying."

"We? In your case don't you mean woman the bridge?"

"I'm not a radical feminist," she said. "But just bear in mind that if I had to, I could knock you for a loop."

You already have, Vic thought. *And I'm not complaining.*

***

The bridge which traversed the plant above the workroom floor consisted of two shielded corridors two hundred feet long, crossing at midpoint to cover all the major work areas where clerks and mail handlers operated below. Rectangular 12" X 18" one-way glass ports were fit into both sides of the walls, at roughly twenty foot intervals. The walls sloped inward toward the narrow metal footpath, a grid which was lit by tiny bulbs much like the aisles in a theater. It was a dim and spooky place, reminiscent of the corridor of a sf/horror movie set. Vic half-expected to see Sigourney Weaver appear at the distant intersection with a flame-thrower, looking for aliens.

"It's safe up here, right?" he asked. "It doesn't feel too stable."

"It's held up by metal rods in the side walls," Maria explained, pushing him forward with one hand between his shoulder blades. "The rods come from connectors in the ceiling and attach to the metal walkway below. They also support the framework. Watch your head."

Vic ducked as they walked along the metal span, expecting obstructions along the dark ceiling. "Jeepers, Lois," he said. "If I was as tall as Superman, I might damage something."

Maria laughed. "I just hope you're not afraid of the dark."

They came to the first one-way glass, which was angled downward toward what looked like a honeycomb of manual distribution cases. Only two of the cases were manned, by what looked like high school girls in blue jeans and T-shirts.

"Who are they?" Vic asked.

Maria glanced down at the luminous dials of her watch, then looked through the pane. "It's not quite time for the shift. They're probably temporaries, called Casuals. They get short-term assignments of thirteen weeks to cover some of the Regulars who go on leave during prime time vacation, which begins in March. Sometimes they get reassigned to box mail or to sort Express packages, but most of them are laid-off after prime season, or after Christmas. They get few of the benefits the regulars do, and the wage isn't even half as much." Maria clicked on a pen light and scribbled something on a pad. "Girl on the right down there is reading a postcard. You'll find they do that a lot."

"So would they be more likely to steal, too?"

"A thief is a thief or he isn't."

Vic chuckled. "He?"

"Mostly he. Or she. But you're right, a casual is probably more likely to steal than a regular career employee, but a regular who's also a thief is more dangerous than a casual."

"Oh? And why is that?"

"Because a career employee would know what to steal, and when."

"Not to mention how," Vic added.

"Exactly. The risk of being caught is remote because we're so understaffed, but if they are caught the punishment is severe. And they never know if we're up here watching them or not. They could lose their job, and end up working at Circle K selling fountain drinks to gang members at the minimum wage. No more four weeks paid vacation, paid sick leave, practically free health insurance, four-oh-one-K matching retirement. Bye-bye new car, steak dinners, and job security, too."

Vic nodded. "And hello night classes, hold ups and have a nice day?"

"Uh-huh. That's why whenever the postal exam is given thousands show up for the test, although only a few make the waiting list. Because once you're in, you're in for life. No more competing for dollars in the real world. You're in a monopoly, and get dollars thrown at you just for showing up. At least that's the way it used to be for some."

"You mean until automation and restructuring started up, and they stopped hiring so many new employees."

"Not just that. I mean until others started competing against the Postal Service to deliver magazines and bulk mail. The gravy train is coming to an end for them. Every day we're tightening the belt a little more, and looking more and more like a private, competing enterprise. It won't be long before what regulars are left will start worrying about job security, if they haven't already."

Vic peered down at the empty distribution cases, with racks of mail waiting between them. "Does any of this explain why that guy Thompson went berserk at the Arcadia station?"

"Who knows? It could have to do with anxiety and resentment. Maybe when he lost his job he went nuts thinking about what he was going to do next. Someone with nothing who ends up with nothing isn't shocked. But give someone with just a high school education a job at forty grand a year, and then snatch it away ... well, it depends on what his personality is as to what he'll do. And his age. Some may go work at McDonalds and be fine. Some may go back to school. But once in a while there might be one who'll pick up a gun and come in blazing."

"You mean like the Son of Sam? He was a mail handler in the New York post office, you know."

"Or Tom McIlvane. Five dead and then himself at the Royal Oak, Michigan, post office in 'ninety-one."

"Isn't he the one who put a gun to the head of a girl hiding under a table and said 'Don't worry, you're not one of the ones'?" Vic asked.

Maria looked at him oddly and then tapped the glass panel with her index finger. "The most we can do is offer employee counseling, and follow up on problems. Of course, if they have as many problems as the guy in Edmond, Oklahoma, back in 'eighty-six, then we've got problems."

"Fourteen dead. I see what you mean. But isn't our job mainly to check security, and watch 'em like hawks?"

"That, too. Maxwell has been trying to warn employees about the competition coming–electronic mail, alternate delivery–trying to get them away from this idea of easy job security. Maybe it's working, but it causes tensions, too. Especially in middle management. A lot of heads have rolled there already. I'm surprised there aren't more bizarre incidents in that arena, and why it's almost always some lowly clerk who goes off the deep end."

Vic considered it. "Education?"

"Could be. A healthier self-image, perhaps. The main reason may be there's so many more clerks and carriers than managers, and so statistically there's more disturbed people in the larger group. Veterans get first jump on the waiting list roster too, and first shot at the tests."

"So?"

"So we get quite a few ex-Vietnam types with long-standing problems. By and large most clerks are responsible, honest, and hardworking, though, like any place else. We've all got our problems, but we've got a lot to be proud of, too."

Vic sighed. "After all the negative press and all the bad news, that's good to hear. I was beginning to wonder if I'd ... well ..."

"Made the right decision? We'll find out soon enough, won't we?"

***

At 8:00 PM the main shift came on, filing past the time clock as they pushed their ID cards through the magnetic sensor, which electronically logged their hours, in military time. Crews assembled at the BCS, the OCR, and the LSM. Mail handlers shuttled cages of Priority packages down the narrow pathways between the machinery, beeping horns on their battery-operated cars at every turn. As Vic watched the show from his box seat, the Tucson P&DC came to life, processing the mail, which had been placed in thousands of boxes and delivered by hundreds of vehicles from the entire southern half of the state during the day.

Maria showed him how to operate the swinging camera mounts, which were installed above the recess of each viewing pane. The camera fit into a ball joint on each flexible metal arm, and could be popped in and out quickly and easily as an inspector made his or her way up the corridor. "Same mount for the video camera," Maria explained. "Except you won't be carrying that one around much. Mostly you mount it and leave it to run."

"You mean if you need to observe someone for a while, and you can't stay and watch."

Maria nodded. "It's not just to watch for theft. If people are consistently goofing off, management wants to know about it. That's a judgment call, of course. We watch the tape in fast forward mode later, if we have time."

"What about the camera you carry with you from window to window? What kind of film does it use?"

"High speed black and white, thirty-six exposure rolls. They showed you how to use a camera at the Academy, didn't they?"

Vic smiled in the close, dark quarters. "Even if they didn't, do I really look that stupid?"

Maria didn't reply as Vic set up the video camera over the LSM section, got it running without mishap, then joined her above the noise of the Facer/Canceler. He peered over her shoulder down at two men below, who were separating thick letters and cassette mailers from the machinable letter mail. The men were both in their fifties, seasoned veterans with T-shirts reading UNION? YES! Their hairy hands glided over the mail moving on a belt into the feeder, feeling for anything which might stick in the throat of the hungry FC200.

"So if that guy, say, suddenly shoves one of those envelopes in his pocket," Vic said, "how in hell am I gonna photograph it in time?"

"Maybe you won't," Maria replied, "but you can photograph him anyway, and keep photographing him."

"Like a reporter on *A Current Affair*, except I haul him up to the office, then try to get him to confess."

"Exactly. Nine times out of ten he'll hand over what he has right then, and sign your report."

"What does number ten do–pull out a forty-five?"

"Not funny. That's why I bring a witness with me, and why I've got a brown belt in Karate."

By midnight they'd seen enough, and even Maria was complaining of fatigue and eye strain. For the last two hours she'd been sitting on a metal chair at the cross point of the two bridge corridors and reading a selection of personnel files under a 40- watt bulb, as Vic tried all forty-seven camera mounts with the Nikon FE she'd given him. As the graveyard shift came on, she finished up her summary report, and closed the file and her briefcase for the last time.

"One more round to check out the late shift," she said with a sigh, "then we're outta here."

"That's a relief," Vic replied. "Back to Phoenix, or a hotel?"

Maria looked up. "This is a two day stay, I think."

"Late breakfast?"

"Very late."

Moments later, Vic ejected the videocassette from the video camera, and was detaching the camera body from the mount when he saw one of the LSM clerks below in an argument with a supervisor. The clerk stood up from his station, and started yelling.

"Oh damn. Maria? Maria!" Vic shoved the videocassette back into the camera and hit RECORD. Then he angled it down and narrowed the focus. "Maria, over here!"

Maria came at a run. "If you call, you should use your walkie-talkie," she scolded him. "Someone down there might hear you."

"Sorry. Look at this."

"What is it?"

She bent forward to the window. Vic tried to look over her shoulder in the tight space. The supervisor, an Hispanic woman, was pointing at the sandy-haired man, and then away. Motioning him to leave. The clerk was cursing and backing her toward the racks of mail behind her.

Maria detached her walkie-talkie and depressed the button. "This is Castillo," she said into the radio, "we got an incident on LSM Two." She turned the squelch knob. Static greeted her. "Damn, I forgot."

"What?"

"Plant manager's off tonight too. No one in the office."

"McDade?"

"He's put in his sixty hours."

Vic stared down at the confrontation below. "He's picked up a chair, now."

"He's *what*?"

"And he's gonna throw it."

Maria ran for the bridge exit. "Follow me," she ordered,"and keep the camera running!"

7

When he heard the commotion behind him, Calvin turned off his headset and looked back.

"Hell, no, I ain't been drinking!" Dave lied. "Why the shit do ya ask?"

"Clock out right now," Mariel Grijalva commanded, standing at his station. "Right now! *Go.*"

"Fer what? Fer what? Ya got no damn right! Who died an' made you God?"

Frustration lit Mariel's face. She felt everyone watching her now, the new boss in her first test. But Dave Sominski just sat there at his terminal with disrespect and a two day stubble on his face, staring up at her with bleary disgust.

"Go," she said evenly, "or I'll call security."

Dave stood to face her. His shirt was in as much disarray as his hair. "You will, will ya?" He even looked drunk. "What, am I keyin' too many damn nixies, that it?" He stepped toward her. "You gonna call somebody ta throw me out? Eh? Why don't ya do it yourself, bitch! Got no balls for it?"

"That's it," Mariel announced. "You've had it. You're fired. Get out."

"Fired?" Dave laughed. "Hell–you can't fire me, I'm in the union."

Mariel was hyperventilating now. "You just threatened me. It's in the contract. You're fired!"

Sominski shook his head once and briefly closed his eyes, absorbing it. He had been drinking too close to work time again, and he knew that, too. "You can't ..."

"Out." Mariel turned to Donna Cortez, the chubby girl at the last terminal. "Dial sixty-three, tell inspector McDade we need him," she said. "Now."

Donna went for the phone, which hung on the post marked C8. The others stared, stunned. Dave watched her too, dimly; the reality of what was happening was finally dawning on him.

"Ya can't," he repeated.

"Don't bother clocking out," Mariel said as the final LSM terminal shut down.

"You ... you ..." Dave stepped toward her as Mariel backed into a rack of mail, trapped. "You ... fuckin' *bitch*!" He whirled drunkenly and picked up his chair. He lifted it, and held it in the air as if he didn't know what to do next. Then he hurled it toward her. The chair crashed into a U-cart beside her, careening off the top, spilling the uppermost tray of letters.

It's all over now, Calvin realized, watching. Threats, and willful destruction of postal property. Maybe even a violation of the sanctity of the mail.

What a fool.

Two inspectors he'd never seen before arrived within seconds; Donna was still on the phone. The female–another Hispanic–handcuffed Dave, while the male held him from behind in an arm lock. Spittle drooled from Dave's mouth as he bent over in pain. Once handcuffed, he was escorted away.

When Mariel finally returned, she had a burly mail handler with her. Nick something. The mail handler righted the U-cart and began picking up the spilled letters.

Donna slipped back into her terminal. "I never even got a call through," she said. "How did those inspectors know ..? "

"Everyone back to work!" Mariel commanded. She even clapped her hands together. "It's all over for now."

Yes, thought Calvin grimly. Now he had no one to talk to at all. But Dave was just a dumb Pollock anyway, he consoled himself. When would he learn?

***

He banged on Sominski's door a full minute before it opened. Dave looked sleepy, even with a half-empty Corona in his left hand. A ragged Van Halen T-shirt hung out of his shorts, and he still hadn't shaved.

"What the hell do you want?"

"Just wanted to see how you're taking it," Calvin replied.

"Takin' what?"

"Being fired."

Dave belched, then laughed. "It won't stick," he said.

"Why not?"

"I'm in the union. Got eight years service, an' a good sick leave record. That's why not."

Calvin smiled thinly at the unwitting optimist behind the screen door. "That what they told you?"

"Not yet, no. I jus' woke up."

"I can see that."

He tried to peer into the dim room, but Dave blocked his view. "Like I said, what the hell ya want, Fireplug? Come over here ta gloat or what?"

"Why would I do that? I thought we were friends."

"That's what I thought, too. But I got to thinkin' ... guess we never were, eh? Probably never had a friend in your friggin' life."

A military transport plane roared overhead. The screen door hummed. Calvin glanced up at the hot morning sun. "I'm here, ain't I?" he said, "when I should be going to bed."

Sominski considered it. "Yeah, yer here, for sure. Ain't ya. But I figure it's curiosity. And I ain't too far out of the way, am I?" He glanced at his watch. "Yer shift ended, what? Ten minutes ago, countin' two hours overtime? That about the size of it?"

Another swig of beer. Another burp.

Calvin grinned. "That's the way you want it, huh?"

"Thass the way it is."

"Right. Well, I guess you don't need my recommendation when the union tries getting you reinstated, then."

Dave shrugged. "Who would listen to you, anyway?"

"For one thing, I've got a better record than you do. And no disciplinary letters on file in Personnel."

"But yer one strange dude. So it would help a lot, wouldn't it?"

"It might. Of course, I don't think you got a prayer, as it is. You blew it by throwing that chair. It's all over now."

"Think so, huh?"

"Know so. Nothing left for you except the Burger Barn. But hey–maybe after a few years, if you can keep your nose clean, you can make night shift manager at two hundred a week, unless you wanna get on relief now, and make us all pay for your stupidity."

"Screw you, Calvin."

"No, you've screwed yourself, you dumb Pollock."

Dave slammed the door. End of conversation. End of friendship.

Calvin looked up as another pair of A-10s droned overhead. He smiled. Guardians of the country's demise? he wondered. The opposing Air Force which has outlived the American Dream only to defend the American Nightmare?

The enemy, yes. With maybe even women in the cockpit now, protecting the teen mothers below. Mothers pushed double baby strollers through the malls. If Sominski didn't see it, then to hell with him. He'd go it alone. Maybe throw his own spanner in the works. Something to really get their attention. Maybe it wouldn't stop the baby machines in their war against the quality of life, or the liberal freeloaders in their war against capitalism, but there had to be a way to slow down delivery of their new government ATM cards and green cards. Maybe nothing would stop all those SSI payments to drug addicts and alcoholics like they talked about on *Dateline NBC*. Not in a country where they gave free fertility drugs to welfare mothers, and called food stamps Food Redemption Certificates. But he could sure slow things down. He could call the Food & Nutrition Service what it *really* was–free lunch on the taxpayers.

Naturally, his own taxes would continue shooting for the moon.

The free-lunchers would continue to invent new ones too, while raiding retirement money and levying fees on things meant to be free. Oh, yes. So whatever he did, it wouldn't be much, he knew. But it would be something, by God.

***

"Keep driving, he's got company," Vic said, then as Maria passed the cottage-style tract house, added: "Who do you think that was?"

Maria stared back in her side mirror at the man in the blue button-down shirt entering the home of David Sominski. "Who knows? Union man, maybe. Want to feed the ducks at the park for a bit?"

She crossed Country Club road and entered the shaded refuge of Reid Park.

"Shouldn't we watch his house?" Vic asked.

"I want to study his file some more," Maria replied. "Besides, there're trees here. We can get out of this nuclear furnace."

"The sun. Right. I guess if you keep the AC on, your car will overheat."

"But Vic–it's a *dry* heat, you know." Maria winked. Then she parked and took a thin manila folder over to a park table near the pond, which proclaimed itself as Reid Park Lake, complete with tackle shop, paddle boats, and a snack bar. "Go get yourself a frozen yogurt or something. And relax. This won't take long."

Vic wandered over to the snack bar and ordered an ice cream sandwich. He stood on the sidewalk near the water, unwrapping the treat, when he was surrounded by several dozen quacking beggars. "Sorry guys, it's my turn. You got the water to cool off in." The ducks soon waddled off, pegging him as a deadbeat.

He pondered the sculpture which grew from a mound of grass beside the lake. It looked like three upside-down barren red trees. Beyond was a baseball stadium, spring training home of the Colorado Rockies. Beyond that were the Catalina mountains, majestic, craggy, and certainly cooler at the top, where the vegetation lived. Looking the opposite direction he saw a fence surrounding a rose garden. The flowers there seemed wilted, dying.

When he rejoined Maria, he got her summary of the Sominski situation. "Not much more in here," she explained, "than we learned from the Personnel manager and Sominski's old boss. It appears Sominski has a temper of long standing."

"That's obvious. What about his alcohol problem?"

"It's not even mentioned in the disciplinary letter he got two years ago. Could be he just started drinking recently, and it aggravated his other problems. He was scheduled to begin an EAP substance abuse program next week after McDade caught him drunk at work a few days ago."

"Why wasn't he suspended?"

"It's prime vacation time, and they needed him. Plus, it was his first offense."

"And yesterday was his last offense?"

Maria nodded. "The union can't help him now. He went over the line, and there's no turning back. If that was a union rep on his porch–and I suspect it was, because his old boss claimed Sominski was a loner–then he's getting the bad news this very moment."

Vic shook his head. "Great, now we go in and mop up what's left of him."

"Them, as they say, is the breaks. It's also our job to collect any other postal ID he might have, with a warning to stay away from the plant. Of course we want to gauge his reactions too, to see whether we have a problem here."

"You mean like Thompson at Arcadia?"

"Or the Son of Sam."

Vic ventured a mortician's smile. "Well, I guess it has all the earmarks. A disgruntled ex-Army regular who's a loner, with a temper to boot. I suppose we'll be checking gun registrations later, looking for Sominski's name."

"You bet."

"Unless he bought an AK forty-seven under the table, in which case–"

"In which case we watch him round the clock, and get used to eating take-out. Burgers. Tacos. French fries."

"Sounds like heaven. We can die young. In the meantime I'm glad you got that brown belt ... although I wish it was black."

"Did I tell you what a great job you're doing so far, Vic?"

"No, you didn't."

"Good."

***

The doorbell was silent. Vic banged on the screen door. After half a minute the inner door opened, and there stood David Sominski, ex-postal employee. He looked like a shell-shocked infantryman just told that his girlfriend had married an old high school rival.

"David," Vic said cautiously, "we'd like to talk to you for a minute."

"Can we come in?" Maria added.

The door widened. Sominski retreated to the couch, and slumped down into it. "Why the hell not," he said at last, and stared at the ceiling.

The room was a mess. Empty beer bottles littered the coffee table. In the past twenty-four hours he must have been watching a lot of television because the set was on a cart pulled near the couch, and several near-empty bowls still possessed telltale chips. Fritos Barbecue Corn Chips from the look of it, Vic guessed. But the TV was off now, and the look of denial on the ex-clerk's face had been replaced by a rare expression of shock, which didn't fit the mood of the room.

"How are you doing, David?" Maria asked.

She got no reply. Sominski just sat there, one hand shielding the right side of his face.

Vic examined the western art on the walls. Though expensive, it was dusty and mismatched–as if placed there haphazardly, without thought. This, he concluded, was a house inhabited by a bachelor with few social contacts and limited self-esteem.

"David?" Maria tried again.

"What the hell do ya want?" Sominski replied, finally.

Vic stepped closer to the painting of Geronimo, which hung slightly askew over a bookcase with no books, but dozens of video cassettes. "Nice picture," he said, then glanced down to read some of the movie titles: *Cliffhanger. Terminator II: Judgment day. The Horny-mooners. You Bet Your Butt.*

"How are your parents?" Maria asked. "And your sister, Julie."

"They're in Michigan," Sominski informed her. "Ain't seen 'em in years." He looked up. "What's gonna happen to me now?"

"You'll be fine," Maria replied, a little too quickly.

"Think so, eh?"

Miami Blues. The Fugitive. Ball Street.

Maria tried to smile. "You're still young, and you're–"

"I'm forty," Sominski corrected her.

"But forty is young, considering. Besides, I think–"

"Besides that," Sominski continued, "I got no skills. Ya know what I did in the Army? I reconned M-sixty machine guns used in tanks and APCs. Between that an' the LSM I really got it knocked. They'll snap me right up, won't they?"

Maria fidgeted. "Have you thought about sales?"

Sominski chuckled. "Sales. What ... tuxedoes? How 'bout another fuckin' chance?"

Maria glanced at Vic. "Rules are rules, I'm afraid."

"Yeah? Well, the rules suck." He put his face in his hands, then looked up again. "What if I got help, quit drinkin', got a doctor to sign off on it?"

"I'm afraid it's too late for that."

"What if I posted a bond?"

"A *bond*?"

"You know, my thrift savings. Four-oh-one-K. Put it on the line if I screw up again."

Maria shook her hand slowly. "It's over, David. You need to move on. Get help, yes. Go to counseling, yes. But think about what you want to do next, and then take it one day at a time." She paused. "About your thrift savings plan, you should contact Personnel in the next few days about rolling it over into an IRA. They can help you with that."

Sominski nodded. "Can they help me spend it? Forty grand'll buy a lotta booze. Hey–maybe I'll throw a big party. You two can come too, flash yer badges whenever ya see somebody havin' too much to drink."

Vic asked to use the restroom. "Mind if I ..?"

Sominski laughed; his mood had transformed completely. "Sure, go ahead. The seat's already up for ya. Too many Bud Lites this mornin', eh?"

Vic found the restroom and shut the door behind him. He looked into the medicine cabinet as Maria asked about postal ID. Nothing out of the ordinary here: aspirin; calamine lotion; a few bandaids; some hydrogen peroxide; a pair of nail clippers; antacid.

He shut the cabinet, and then flushed the toilet, noticing a copy of *Playboy* beside it on the floor. On the way out he peered into the bedroom: clothes in heaps, unmade bed, a musty odor.

Then he saw it: on the wall over the dresser, a gun rack. Empty.

He quickly rejoined Maria in the living room just as she was reminding Sominski of the off-limits policy for ex-postal employees.

"That's okay," Sominski said, getting up. "Guess I don't have any real friends there, anyway. Probably all had it in for me, jus' like Gary did."

"We're sorry you feel that way. Don't you have any other friends you can call?"

Sominski thought about it, then shook his head. "Nope. Not anymore." He saw them out. "But listen, don't worry about me. I'll find me a woman, make some babies, and get on AFDC and food stamps. Her'n me, we'll watch the soaps together. Maybe even get on the Sally Jesse show an' tell our stories. You be watchin' for us now, ya hear?"

On the way back to the car Maria said, "We'll be watching him, all right."

"Yeah?" Vic said. "You know, maybe we should. Could fit the pattern ... he's certainly disgruntled."

"Think he's dangerous, though?"

"Well, there was a gun rack in his bedroom."

"Rifle or shotgun?"

"Don't know. The gun was missing. Makes you wonder, doesn't it?"

"What?"

"Where the gun is."

Maria spoke little on the way back to the Tucson post office, but seemed deep in thought. When they arrived there she opened her briefcase and took out a three-page form, which she handed to Vic. He took it and stared at the title:

SECURITY CHECKLIST, TUCSON P&DC.
PHOENIX PERFORMANCE CLUSTER

"We go back to Phoenix tonight?" he asked. "Or do we stay longer on account of Sominski?"

Maria didn't smile. "I'm afraid it'll be up to Lone Wolf McDade," she said, "for now."

***

Calvin was awakend at 9:00 PM, by a hand on his shoulder.

"Sorry sir, but we're closing now."

Calvin glanced up, nodded, and rubbed his face as he reoriented himself. Then he got up and started gathering his books. One fell. The librarian picked it up, and while waiting to place it on the stack in Calvin's arms, looked at the title.

"*The Anarchist's Cookbook*?"

"Sorry," Calvin said. "I'm writing a term paper. Went back to college, see. Trying to work, too."

"Where do you work–the morgue?"

"Yeah, the graveyard shift." He laughed. "Sorry."

He made it outside, then glanced back. The security guard had followed him to the door, twirling a key chain. Calvin turned the corner in front, and set his books down on a concrete bench next to a pay phone, out of sight. He fished out two quarters and dropped one in the slot. Dialed. "Hi. Can you tell me if Bud Gessel still hangs out there? Forties, tall, ex-Army Special Forces. Brags a lot."

"Ain't seen him lately," the scruffy tobacco voice on the other end said. "Wait a sec an' I'll ask." A long pause, the sound of a jukebox playing Tonya Tucker, then finally: "Yer in luck. Billy says he saw Bud shootin' pool over at the Buxom Bandit on Speedway less than an hour ago."

"Thanks." Calvin hung up, then dropped quarter number two. He connected with the Tucson Post Office in a couple of minutes. "Hello, is Mariel there?"

"Not yet. Comes on at eleven tonight."

"Well, tell her I won't be in tonight. This is Calvin Beach."

"Beach?"

"Yeah. Calvin Beach. Something I ate. Think it's food poisoning. Been hugging the toilet for the last three hours."

"Oh, God."

"Yeah. It's the dry heaves now. Think it was some leftover tuna. I'm pretty weak."

"Sounds like it. Okay, Calvin, I'll let her know."

"Thanks."

It took both saddlebags to fit in all the books he carried. He put the ones on ghost towns in the right saddlebag, and the ones on explosives in the other.

He rubbed his face again, then slipped on his helmet and straddled the Beemer. At startup, the quiet rumble of the twin boxer engine sounded reassuring, powerful. He gunned it, and watched the tach needle dance up and down as he tried to remember what Gessel looked like. It had been two years since he'd heard Gessel talk. If Gessel was still hanging out at a biker bar, maybe times were tough for him, and talk would be cheap. The Beemer would need to be parked out of sight; at the Buxom Bandit you didn't want to park a Honda or BMW with all the Harleys out front; the human debris which inhabited the place called them rice-burners and kraut-burners, and had been known to make a party of one with an ax.

Of course they didn't know who they were dealing with.

Not a nice guy. Oh, no. Not anymore.

An *ice* guy.

8

"You again?" asked Bud Gessel, unscrewing his pearl-handled cue stick. "I thought I told you the other night: I ain't the man you're looking for."

Calvin sank into the nearest red-cushioned booth and took out his wallet. He glanced around the Buxom Bandit to see if any of the few bikers inside were watching. Then he withdrew the bills. Ten of them. All hundreds. He counted them out on the table.

Gessel stared down at the money. Then he laid his pool case on top of it. Almost, it seemed to Calvin, on impulse. "Keep that outta sight," he said quietly. "Might be a narc in here. Hell, the bartender might be a narc."

Calvin smiled. "So you're talking to me today. Don't take me for a loser now. That it?"

Gessel's weather-beaten face showed more wrinkles than an iguana. He sat across from Calvin, clenching and unclenching his left hand as if trying to get the stiffness out. "Let's say ya got enough under there for a listen. You want more, it'll cost ya more."

"So you are the right man."

Gessel leaned back and put his muscular arms up on back of the booth. He looked around casually, then smiled through a row of crooked teeth, "Maybe I'm paranoid, but convince me yer not a cop, an' I might play along."

Calvin told him about Vietnam–a rambling of what he remembered, and some of what he'd tried to suppress. Then he talked about hard times, until his recent interest in mining and prospecting brought him some luck. He said he was tired of panning, which was for sissies. That what he really needed was to blast into a rock face near where he'd discovered gold, to see if there was a vein like he suspected. He explained that it was on remote public land, so he needed to get in and out quickly and easily, and not be caught carrying a load of dynamite. He'd heard that Gessel was an ex-Special Forces operative who once specialized in explosives; that he was a soldier of fortune for a few years after that, until the South Africans jailed and then deported him. What he had in mind wasn't legal, but if Gessel could help him obtain the items he needed, he'd let him have the grand right now, and give him two more just like it on delivery.

"Did I hear ya right?" Gessel asked, leaning forward at last. "You wanna make plastique? Ta blast some rocks?"

Calvin put a finger to his lips, and nodded.

Gessel chuckled. "Sure your wife's not screwin' around, an' you figure to blow her lover six ways from Sunday? You got no ring, but it might be in yer pocket."

"Wanna check?"

Gessel held up one hand. "Don't wanna know. Except maybe yer name."

"It's Alan. Alan ... Cooper."

They shook hands. Gessel lit a cigarette, assessing him.

"It's Alan something, but not Cooper, right?" Gessel shrugged, then opened the pool case, lifted it, and slid the bills inside. In three seconds it was done. "You, ah, think I got access to some police munitions bunker or somethin'?"

Calvin looked away. "Or something."

Gessel smiled, and ran a hand through his thinning hair. "Okay. Plastique for a would-be miner." He paused. "So here it is. I can get ya the ingredients for five G's, or I can make it for you for ten. Take yer pick."

Calvin coughed. "Can you be trusted?"

Gessel thought that one over throughout one long inhalation and an even longer exhalation. "It's yer money," he said, finally.

"Just so we understand. I'll give you three grand if you get me enough materials to make three big charges."

Gessel blew a smoke ring. "How big is big?"

Calvin waved the smoke away. "Enough to shatter a two-ton boulder. Each, of course."

"Of course." Gessel lowered his voice and leaned closer. "And what exactly is yer expertise in making plastique that ya think you can pull this off without losin' yer balls?"

Calvin looked away again, and smiled to himself. He said nothing.

"I thought so. Been doing some readin', have ya? Well, it's trickier than ya think, kid. Let me tell ya, you might be able to make a primitive blasting gelatin with eight percent nitrated sawdust, but it's the ninety-two percent fuming nitric acid and glycerin you gotta worry about. You ever worked with that? You know what it does to soft body parts like arms and legs? Ya don't get a second chance if ya make a mistake. Can't say 'oops, I'll be more careful next time.' I say, if you're doing this yourself, ya better stick to something less volatile. Get you some ammonium oxalate and nitrate, a stabilizer like Glauber's salt, and the kinda saltpeter they use to keep prisoners from gettin' a hard on. Or just fertilizer, fuel oil, and a blasting cap. Don't mess with higher explosives, kid. Got better odds playin' Russian roulette."

Calvin shook his head. "It's gotta be compact. A small charge with a big bang."

Gessel tapped his pool cue case. "You wanna try nitrogen triiodide? Want me to get you somma that? A fly lands on it an' it explodes. Or hey—maybe you want some trinitrotoluene, otherwise known as TNT. Use it in grenades and pipe bombs. Got two million pounds per square inch of power."

"Sounds good. What do I need—sulfuric and nitric acids? Toluene?"

Gessel laughed. "Yeah. You make it in an ice bath, need a good centigrade thermometer, too. And a crucifix."

"What's that for?"

"You keep it around yer neck so yer fuckin' head stays put."

Calvin didn't smile. " You got access to these ..?"

Gessel studied him for a moment, then said, "I can get them if I have to." He continued staring.

"So why you looking at me like that, then?"

"Because I think I'm lookin' at a dead man." This time Gessel looked away. "Listen, you'll need sulfuric and nitric, yeah, and dimethyllaniline too. Keep it in an ice bath, then filter and wash it, boil it in fresh water with baking soda, test it with litmus paper until yer sure it's free of acid. Then ya filter that and let it dry."

"What is it?"

"Tetryl. That's what ya want. I've made it before. The end product is easy to work with, relatively stable. An' a little blows a long way."

Calvin nodded. "You'll get me the stuff I need to make it?"

"Yeah. For five more grand. An' good luck; you'll need it."

"How do you set it off?"

"Tetryl? Number a ways. Spring action shock is one. I've heard of it used in an ordinary fountain pen that way. Guy presses the plunger and bammo–he's lost his hand, maybe his whole arm. Or in a smoking pipe. Guy lights up an', well, there's no public viewing at the funeral. Of course you just wanna blast some rocks, though, don't ya?"

"You don't believe me?"

"Hey, like I said, it's yer money. An' yer life."

Calvin scanned the bar once more, then looked directly into Gessel's lizard face. "Would you believe me if I made it ten grand for the finished product?"

Gessel blinked at him like an old cash register ringing up a sale.

***

Calvin stopped at the Safeway market on the way back to his apartment. The sun was just setting out past the downtown cluster of office buildings. As he crossed the parking lot toward the store, he made out the familiar whitewashed "A" that the University of Arizona students had painted on top of the peak overlooking his bank–the First American Bank.

Once inside the cool grocery store he remembered to check his wallet. Only four dollars left. What could he get for four dollars? He decided on a cheese-filled croissant and some bottled water. The Colorado river water the canals brought to the city (due to overpopulation) tasted faintly like dead catfish.

He was standing in the checkout line behind two women with full carts when he noticed that the black woman directly in front of him was pregnant. As he watched, she casually rummaged through her purse to produce a packet of food stamp coupons. No wedding ring adorned the chubby fingers which now counted the twenty dollar coupons in the booklet. Although her lips moved as she added up her total, Calvin decided to interrupt anyway.

"Excuse me," Calvin said. "Mind if I ask you a question?"

The woman turned, looking confused. "Yeah?"

"Why is it you keep having kids if you can't afford them?"

"What?"

"You heard me."

She stared at him for a moment as his question fully registered. Then: "That the mos ... you ..." She turned to the woman in front of her for support. "You hear what he jus' say?"

"If you don't have an answer," Calvin said, "it's okay. I'll understand."

She was aghast. "Jus' who ya think you be, mister?"

"Me? Oh, I'm just a guy helping support your babies."

"Like hell ya are. I's a taxpayer too."

Calvin grinned, and looked down into her cart. Atop her stack of groceries, next to the package of Pampers, lay a *TV Guide*. "Sure you are," he said. "You just can't handle the whole bill, so you need me."

Her eyes narrowed. "Is that right?" Now the checker was listening, too, as she continued ringing up the items of the woman in front. "Lordie, lordie ... Ya got it all figured out, don' ya?"

"Damn right," Calvin replied.

"Bet ya don' got no kids yerself neither, do ya?"

"I can't afford it; I've got yours to pay for."

Her eyes were slits now. She cocked a finger at him. "Do I know you? When you done anythin' fo' me?"

"Every payday, see, they take a cut out of my salary? Give it to you." Calvin pointed at the food coupons in her hand.

Now her eyes got wide. "Lord God ..."

"Where do you think it comes from–thin air?"

"Lord God Almighty. You a racist."

"You got it all wrong. You're the racist."

"Me? How ya figure that?"

"You brought it up. Must be important to you, huh?"

"You think you smart ... but who is you ta judge me?"

Calvin smiled. "I help buy your groceries, that's who I am. What you got there, anyway–any steak, liquor? You get SSI payments too, for that? AFDC?"

She pointed at his two items, defensively. "Pear-yea? A qua-saunt?"

Calvin held them up. "Bread and water. It's all I can afford, after taxes."

Now a tide of anger washed her eyes. "Let me tell ya somethin', mistah. You been oppressin' us for decades, now it come full circle, be justice time."

"You mean like Reginald Denny got?"

The woman in front of them began writing a check for her groceries. At first Calvin thought she wouldn't react at all. But her look, when she glanced back, was a commingling of shock and amusement.

The pregnant woman finally began loading her own groceries onto the checkout belt. "I was a-gonna let you go ahead a me, too," she said.

"Sure you were. You voted for Clinton, I bet. Soak the rich."

"Amen, Lord! But ya jus wait'll Jesse gets in, then you see."

Calvin laughed. "Jesse."

"Or Louis. Ya won't be laughin then!"

Calvin stared at her in pity. "Why don't you just get the President to make Haiti and Cuba part of America? That way you liberals would have a lock on votes, and you wouldn't need to keep having ten kids each." He glanced at the checkout girl, and winked. "Look at this ... bacon, donuts, soda pop. She actually feeds her kids this crap, too."

The checkout girl looked down without smiling.

"You no tell me what ta eat neither, mistah," the black woman said.

"Why not? I'm paying for your health care, too, ain't I? You eat that junk, get sick, and they raise my premiums, don't they? I got a right to complain."

"You sick."

Calvin nodded. "Sick and tired, you got that right."

The checkout girl reached for the intercom. "Mr. Rogers, can you come to the front, please?" she called.

Calvin grinned. "What? You gonna have me silenced, now? She's had equal time. But then she doesn't want equality, does she? She wants revenge."

The black woman stabbed her finger at him. "You jus shut up an' leave us alone, sicko."

Us?

Calvin saw into her purse. Three ten-dollar bills lay loosely inside. He looked into her dark eyes. "You think there's no end to this gravy train, don't you? You're all on a roll now. Think you're justified cheating the system. Gonna get a slice of the pie at last ... until the pie's gone forever. Meantime, you ain't worried about welfare reform. No, that's a joke. A ruse, right? They'll be pouring more money into it for better benefits, more government jobs. Truth is, though, you got no ambition. *Nada*. Zip. Except maybe to have more kids. So you won't really have to train for anything, will ya? Except Lamaz classes. Tell the truth, now."

"Only truth here is you's a racist an' a bigot."

"*And* a homophobe, *and* a radical right wing kook who needs sensitivity training, that it? Huh? I'm just another WASP bastard who goes around sticking pins in puppies, an' gets his jollies sitting on juries and stickin' it to all the minority criminals–that what you think?"

"You said it, not me."

"But you thought it, with that brainwashed mind. But you didn't consider how us white males can't get promoted anymore. You didn't think about what's gonna happen when everybody's making the same paltry wage, set by Big Daddy. Ain't gonna be any health care, then. Or food, either."

"Mr. Rogers?" the checkout girl called again.

Calvin's grin widened. "*Et tu*, Brutess?"

The checkout girl winced. To the pregnant woman she said, "I need a bagger. Do you remember the price of this, ma'am? It won't scan."

"Can't she bag her own?" Calvin asked.

"She's pregnant, sir."

"She's always pregnant. God bless her, it's not her fault if three or four of her brood end up in prison some day. She's got her hands full raising more." He watched them bag and scan, oblivious to him now. "Boy, she's got a lot of them little suckers, don't she? Been wondering why those payroll deductions been gettin' so high lately. Suspected this, of course, but I had no idea."

"Please, sir."

"Please? You know you've thought it, too. Admit it."

To the black woman she said, "Not even once."

"Not even *once*?" He looked back at the pregnant woman, then laughed and gestured toward her. "Oh, I see. We've gotta be kind, compassionate, and understanding here. Poor helpless thing, she's just struggling to endure all this prejudice and inequality. She *needs* a helping hand. My God, how would she survive without it? Heaven forbid she'd have to actually be responsible for something. Right?"

He dropped his water and croissant amid her pile of groceries, and pushed his way through. The pregnant woman's belly bumped the rack of women's magazines in front of her, and she turned venomously to watch as he flourished a white plastic sack.

"Bas-turd."

He started to bag her groceries, then punched two holes in the sack instead, and slipped it over his head. At the door, he turned and waved, tossing the sack aside.

Once outside again he felt better. Better than he had in a long time. But still, it wasn't enough. It didn't feel nearly as good as he wanted it to feel.

For that, there was always tomorrow.

9

Maria stopped Vic in the third floor hallway of the Phoenix MSC by grabbing his arm.

"What's up?" he said.

"Whoa–wrong way," she replied. "You just passed the conference room."

"There?" He pointed at a closed door marked Room 812.

"That's it. It's the grievance I'd like you to sit in on with me." She glanced at her watch. "They're already waiting."

"But," Vic glanced up the hallway toward the inspector's office. "when do I ever get to meet Phil?"

"Later."

"Later? Later he'll be out buying jelly donuts or something. I'll miss him again."

Maria shrugged. "Maybe so. But it doesn't matter. We attend a station manager's meeting right afterward. Where I get to discuss security, and where you get to answer questions."

"I do?"

"If you get stuck on something, I'll be standing by, don't worry."

"What about Phil?"

"Phil won't be there."

"Lone Wolf?"

"Of course not. McDade's back in Tucson."

"Somewhere." Vic shrugged. "Not that it matters."

Maria stared at him with curious deep-brown eyes. Then she grinned, and punched his arm with her free hand. "You're a strange one, you know that?" She laid her hand on the doorknob of Room 812, and winked. "Not that it matters."

Waiting for them inside the conference room at the polished wooden table were two women in their mid-twenties and a man in his late forties. The women were average-looking, slightly overweight, one blond and one a redhead. They wore clean white union T-shirts and blue jeans. Green IDs indicated their clerk status. The man had a pock-marked face, evidence of severe acne as a teen, and wore a tan shirt with brown tie and brown slacks. His ID was red–a manager.

"So, hello," said Maria, taking a seat at the head of the table. "I'm inspector Castillo, and this is inspector Kazy. Shall we begin, Mister ..?"

"Blanchard," the man with the red ID said, not looking at the others. "I'm the new flats sorter supervisor here. Transferred in from Spokane last week. That's why we've never met." He tried to smile, but it was forced. "Anyway, the thing is, I was always allowed to assign overtime whenever I needed to in the past. So I don't understand why–"

"Excuse me," the blond opposite him said. "What happened was, he brought in two casuals on Monday an' let 'em work on their day off, eight hours. Contract states if you call in the temps on their day off, you gotta work the regulars on the overtime list twelve hours. And the ones not on the list get to work ten."

"That right?" Vic asked.

Maria nodded. "That it, Miss ..?"

"Kay Richards, the union steward. That's not all, no. Sally here says there's favoritism involved. Says Mr. Blanchard let Susan Woods take leave without pay on Saturday afternoon. I mean, instead of using her annual leave, like normal."

"Susan Woods?"

"We were finishing early," Blanchard said defensively. "Nobody knew on Saturday there'd be so many catalogs on Monday." He looked to Vic for sympathy. "Besides, Susan wasn't feeling well, and she'd already used all her annual leave."

Probably a good looker, Vic thought. Probably one of the few clerks who dared to wear tight jeans. "So why didn't she take sick leave, then?" he asked.

"Come on, you know how it is. Everybody frowns on doing that. It wasn't like she needed to visit the hospital or something."

"Truth is," said Kay, "Susan already has a bad sick leave record, so it's not like she wanted to keep her record clean and get the leave bonus at the end of the quarter."

A very good looker, this Susan Woods, Vic decided. And getting better looking all the time. "That right?"

Blanchard spread his hands. "I call it as I see it at the time."

"Yeah, that's true," Kay told him. "That why you didn't work the list overtime on Monday? That why you turned down Sally's leave request for Saturday on the second day you got here?"

Blanchard folded his hands. His smile faded. "How would I know it wouldn't be busy on Saturday? Or that we'd be swamped by Tuesday? They're both flukes."

"And you're a flake," said the redhead, Sally.

"Now, now," Maria warned. She opened her briefcase, found a blank form, and began writing up her report. They all watched her in silence.

Then Sally spoke again. "Susan has a nickname you may want to write down," she told Maria, and then pointed at her form for emphasis. "Know what they call her? I.P."

Maria looked up, pen in hand. "What's that mean?" she asked.

"It means Ice Princess. Means she usually gets what she wants. Except she hasn't found her Mr. Right yet. Donald Trump and Bill Gates are already taken."

Vic suppressed a laugh.

Maria looked at him sternly, but for just an instant the trace of a smile flickered on her own lips. As she continued writing, she asked, "Anyone have anything to add?"

No one spoke.

"Okay, then, it's pretty cut and dried. It is true that the contract states you must use the overtime list if you call in any casuals on their day off, Mr. Blanchard."

"But–"

Maria raised her hand. "I don't know how long you've been a manager, but you should have known this. As for the favoritism allegation, we'll let it ride this time, with the understanding that this won't become a pattern. In the future I suggest strongly that if someone is feeling sick you require them to use sick leave. Especially if they are already abusing their sick leave as it is."

Blanchard turned away and ran a hand through his thinning hair.

"Now, normally your plant manager would listen to any grievances, but since this is his day off, " Maria turned to Sally, who was now smiling faintly, "we won't let him know there was any name calling here. And I suggest–again, strongly–that if someone has a problem with respect for his or her supervisor, he or she should bid out to some other job. Bulk mail or rural carrier, for instance." Finally, she turned to Kay, the union steward. "Is this agreeable?"

The blond girl nodded.

They all rose.

"One moment please, Mr. Blanchard," Maria said. She motioned to Vic, and in a low voice told him, "Wait for me in the office."

***

Vic found no trace of Phil DeLong in the inspector's office. No jelly donut, no smoking cigarette in the ashtray. Not even a photograph of the wife and kids. Nothing. He frowned and sank into Phil's swivel desk chair. When Maria finally entered the room she found him going through Phil's top drawer and coming up with paper clips.

"Having fun?"

"Sorry," he said. He waved his hand. "It's part curiosity and part frustration, I guess. I wonder what people I might have to work with actually look like." He stared at her staring, and almost blushed. "You know ... what they're really like." He sighed. "Forget it. What did you tell that guy Blanchard, anyway? You read him the riot act?"

"Him? Oh, I just asked what he did before he came here. He was a flats sorter clerk. Twelve years at it, mostly doing it by hand until automation came along. Not much management experience."

"Obviously. Is he married?"

"You wanted me to ask him? I don't think so." She checked her watch. "Okay Mr. Curiosity, you've blown another chance to meet Phil, now it's time to go."

Vic sighed again. "Sure you don't have his photo on file anywhere?"

"No, but I can tell you this: Phil is married, and he's not your type." Maria winked. "Not that it matters."

He winked back, twice. "How do you know it doesn't matter?" He winked again, and pinched his ear lobe.

Maria laughed. "You can't fool me," she said. "I saw the way you looked at me when we met."

"You mean like this?" he asked. He stood and came to her, staring right into her dark eyes for one long and rather interesting moment. Then he made a funny face.

"Careful," she warned. "I'm grading your papers."

He followed her down the hall into the elevator, and out to the side parking lot, admiring the way she walked in front of him–self-assured and sexy. Very definitely sexy. He tried to imagine what her boyfriend looked like ... perhaps she had a photograph of him? He couldn't ask, of course. No, it wouldn't be right. Or would it? She'd been friendly with him more than she had to be–maybe even more than she should. Perhaps if he told her it was really over with Karen she would become even friendlier, off duty. True, it was almost never a good idea to begin a relationship with a colleague or boss. The chances of it working were low. Even lower than his chances with someone as sensitive as Karen had been. But they seemed to hit it off, and the vibes were more than pleasant. He certainly wouldn't find anyone more attractive at some singles bar or through some dating service. No one with that subtle smile, that laugh, or that perfect–utterly perfect–view from behind.

Getting into the car, he was fantasizing about the various methods for the murder he intended for her boyfriend, when they heard the shots. Three distinct gunshots. Then two more, coming from the rear of the building.

Maria glanced at him, then pulled her revolver. "Let's go!"

They sprinted along the side of the long, red brick, MSC plant, Maria in the lead. As they came into view of the dock area, Vic pulled out his own pistol. Was this for real? He remembered what Karen had said about her father. His heart began to hammer at the thought, something it hadn't done in training.

Two men on the dock, he noted. Both were looking south toward the supply building; one of them pointed there.

Suddenly another shot. Then four more in rapid succession: whump-whump-whump, whump. From the south–the supply building.

"Get back inside!" Maria ordered as they passed the two dock workers.

The supply structure was a massive gray prefab with a closed corrugated steel door, and two smaller doors with small windows. It was situated in the rear corner of the employee parking lot. Fifty yards to the west was the open entrance gate to the fenced and tree-ringed parking lot. Beyond that was the service station for postal vehicles; a postal mechanic stood in one of the three service bays there, wiping his hands with a rag and looking in their direction.

Maria motioned. They split up, each to one side as they approached the supply building. Vic took the left door ten feet from the closed bay. He peered through the window quickly but cautiously.

It was an empty office, cut off from the warehouse by prefab walls. No one inside.

He opened the door, then lifted his gun and slipped inside.

Not a sound. No sense of movement beyond. Had the shooter killed everyone? And was he now standing over the bodies, contemplating suicide? Vic edged forward to the inner door. Then he took another split-second peek, ducking his head quickly in and out of the open space.

He'd seen a high metal ceiling with skylights. Below, long gray racks filled with postal equipment blocked any eye-level view. Should he wait here, he wondered, in case the shooter came out this way? Where was Maria? What if she was in danger?

He crouched down and took another peek. Then he made for the first row of racks. The boxes behind which he kneeled read USPS CHANGE-OF-ADDRESS KITS. Above him was a shelf of broken postal meters. He strained his neck around the corner.

No one. And still nothing but ominous silence.

He bit his lip and broke for the next row. He could see an open space through the racks beyond the office supplies and chair parts, but he couldn't see what might be there. Stacks of wooden pallets and boxes of labels were in the way.

He inched forward, his revolver gripped in both hands. Then he cleared the next row of racks. The central space was just ahead. Anticipating the worst, he cocked his pistol, which gave out with an audible click.

Had the shooter heard?

He stepped out, still trying to see past the obstruction. Suddenly, from behind him, came footsteps. He whirled, gun raised.

"Maria?"

"Over here," Maria called from the other direction.

He pointed his weapon into the space at the end of the last row. He crouched and waited, his finger firm on the trigger. The footsteps got louder.

"Vic?" Maria called from the other end of the warehouse. "You over there?"

His arms trembled. The .38 felt like it weighed twenty pounds.

"Vic!" Maria called again, from somewhere behind him.

The footsteps came at a run now. Vic tensed. Then, through the metal shelves, he caught sight of a big man, something swinging in his left hand.

"Drop it!" Vic ordered. "Drop it or I'll shoot!"

The man stopped dead in Vic's gun sights, and opened his left hand. The object he carried dropped to the floor and broke.

It was a telephone. A cordless telephone. Vic stared at it as it turned like a compass at the big man's feet, a crack and hole now in the tan plastic of the headset.

He lowered his revolver and looked into the man's face as Maria came running up to join him.

"I'm Eddie Cassaway, a supply clerk," the man said, after swallowing. "Heard some shots out back, so I ran out ... seen some kids shooting at a beer can beside the street back there. Called nine-one-one. That the right thing to do?"

Vic nodded dumbly.

"The kids still out there?" Maria asked.

"Naw, they drove away. Kid shot from the passenger seat of this red Camaro. Don't think they hit the can–it's still there, don't look like it's damaged."

Vic coughed. "You didn't, ah, make the license plate by any chance, did you?"

Cassaway looked at Maria, then back at Vic. Then he bit his lower lip. Maria patted Vic's shoulder in passing.

***

After filing the police report, and after their station manager's meeting, they ate at Mi Nidido, a tiny Mexican place near Maria's condo.

"You were good," Vic told her.

"So were you," Maria conceded. "Back at the supply building, I mean."

"Thanks for not mentioning that to everyone. Dinner's on me."

She smiled. "Trying to bribe me, huh? So I won't write you up for destroying postal property?"

"You wouldn't."

"How do you know what I would do?"

"I don't know how. I just do." He swirled his Margarita. "Somehow."

She nodded slowly and pursed her lips. "You know," she said, "Carl would kill you if he saw you with me like this."

"I thought he was a lawyer, not a postal clerk."

Maria wagged her finger at him.

Vic sipped from his salted glass. "Funny you should say that, though, since I've been thinking about Carl a lot lately."

"You have?"

"Oh yeah. In fact, if that supply clerk had been him I might have pulled the trigger. By accident, of course."

"Of course." She leaned back. "So ... you think this is a date, then?"

"It could be. What do you think?"

"Better yet, what would Max the Ax Maxwell think?"

"Forget him. He's in Washington. Besides, he's not as attractive, so his opinion doesn't count."

"So you think I'm attractive, do you?"

"Did I say that?"

"Yes, you did. Didn't you?"

Vic scratched his jaw. "Only if that means this is a date."

Maria shook her hand. "A real date means going to a movie ... or dancing. Like that. We're just sitting here getting fatter."

"A couple of gluttons, that's us." He winked. "Incidentally, what movies haven't you seen yet? Not that it matters."

10

Hi Dad—

Funny, I can't remember seeing photos of Total Wreck, although it might be possible I did. It would explain why it seemed so familiar to me. Anyway, I'm not 100% certain it's the town great-grandfather referred to, but I have a feeling Total Wreck is the right town. I don't know what I'll do if I find the silver vein. Maybe blast in for a look. There might not be anyone around for miles, if I'm lucky.

We haven't been very lucky in the past, though, have we? Always scrambling for a buck, letting Ma down again. But at least we tried. At least we worked hard, unlike some.

I tried, Dad, I really did. But what can you do? The Army let me down when I became diabetic, and the Postal Service let you down by dropping your driving contract. Of course I haven't touched a bottle like you did, yet. Been afraid to. But if I don't do something soon that may be next, because the country has gone even more to hell since you left. It's not the same anymore.

Even people in Washington pass the buck. They don't want to solve any problems. Not really. If problems were solved we wouldn't need them to try anymore. It's a joke.

I been thinking, see. This may be the end times coming up. What if God put this maternal instinct in women as a blessing at first, but meant it to be a curse later on? Or maybe it's the devil doing this. I don't think it's greed will do us in like liberals think. It's not the greed that's so bad, see. People still need money, and they still want it, but the main thing is, nobody cares anymore. There's no more standards anywhere. They don't teach morals in schools like they used to. Kids are having kids and they think one thing is as good as another. They don't want to make judgments about anything. They got no work ethic either. Hell—no ethics at all. Violence and revenge is all they understand. Right? They wanna have someone else pay the bill, and then to hell with them. Get on the government dole. That's the ticket. Claim discrimination, claim abandonment, claim anything it takes. But something's gotta give or it's the end of everything.

Sterilization, and a stiff immigration policy, and the death penalty. We need all three in spades. Even the environmentalists screw like rabbits, and then they talk about recycling. What hypocrites. They don't talk about the real problems. They don't try to repair the dam. No. They're all downstream telling people how to live. Talking about diversity, instead of freedom. So now we're becoming a third world country, and before long kids'll have bloated bellies and flies all over them. Soon as the pot is empty. Soon as inflation kills everyone's savings.

It's time somebody wakes people up to what's happening! If not we'll become like Guatemala or Somalia where every woman is pregnant and your life ain't worth shit. People gotta know where we're headed, or one day we'll wake up in a socialist hell-hole with all the trees clear cut for more housing projects, just like those hypocrites feared. No one talks about the source of the problem, but I'm gonna make them talk, Dad.

Gonna tell them about the war too. Not 'Nam. That was nothing. The war now is against all us white males, and we're losing. We get blamed for everything, and while we're off working to pay taxes, those whiners get on the dole and screw some more. They get us to pay for their screwing too, see how it works? Free prenatal care, free health care. It's the perfect setup! And the AARP too—they're no different. Rich old geezers out there playing tennis and golf every day, you should see them. Maybe you do. They've already collected three times what they put into Social Security, but they keep cashing those checks anyway. They know it'll go bust before the people putting in money now will ever see it. Oh yeah. They got their excuses too. They can say "don't worry, when your time comes ..." (Ha ha.) They know it won't be there. They know checks go to winos and drug addicts to support their habits. They know Capitol Hill has raided the funds and blown it all on pork barrel projects. So they want every damn dime they can get. Just like everybody else. Every damn dime.

It needs to be D-Day. Like in the Big One, remember? Call it Demolition Day, this time. I'm only one soldier, so I can't stop it alone, but maybe others will enlist later when they see what I'm doing. It could happen. It's possible. I can pick them out in a crowd—the frustrated ones forced to wait in line, behind a food stamp recipient. Once you come to the conclusion that people should pay their own way (like free enterprise capitalism is supposed to work), the rest comes easy. Hey—maybe the courts will excuse them too, for whatever they decide to do. Like those judges excuse the killers and rapists and gang bangers by saying they grew up deprived of love in dysfunctional families, the poor victims of society's awful discriminations. (I know—fat chance, right?)

I just know something's gotta be done, Dad. Maybe I can't stop it, but maybe I can slow it down. At least here. At least for now. I think I've got a plan too. Part of it involves the BCS and the LSM. If I put a charge between them, it should take them both out. Then they can't sort those bar-coded government checks except by hand, one at a time. If I'm lucky maybe the charge will take out LSM T2 as well. I can rig it to go off in the morning when nobody's there except all those checks waiting to be processed that afternoon. Besides burning them it'll cripple the system beyond repair. Not just electronics, but mechanically too. The stuff I'll be using is great, Dad. It's like C4, the military explosive. Be bigger than if a howitzer hit.

I'm gonna send a typed letter to the Arizona Daily Star, too. The letter is ready now. Says the country's got too many takers and not enough givers, so I'm going to give everybody a little wake up call. I typed it on a display typewriter in a department store. Right there, in front of everybody!

Nobody paid any attention to me, but they'll pay attention when their government freebies get delayed. Oh yes! You hold back some money people are used to getting and they go apeshit.

That'll be a kick to see, too, won't it, Dad? I can watch it all on TV too, on the same news report where they tell us every day about new taxes for schools and cops and illegal aliens coming across the border at Nogales so their babies can be born here. And that's just part of my plan. I've got a few other letters to write too, see. And I've already put in a bid to transfer over to CFS so I won't have to work all that overtime that'll be coming for the LSM clerks. So I can go home, kick back, and watch the damn city council deal with all the complaints. Hey, maybe Dan Rather will even read my letter to everybody, too. It's possible, right?

I wish you were here, Dad. I feel alone sometimes. There are still some places out there, like in the hills or the ghost towns, where I can think and write you letters like this. But I feel lost a lot of the time. Like I got no identity anymore. Like they've taken it from me. The free lunchers and New Agers—they're taking away the past, stealing our legacy. They call me Fireplug at work, and laugh, but it's a label like nigger or spic used to be. So they don't have to see me. I guess that means I'm a minority now, huh?

Before, Dad, I wanted to be somebody, if even in a previous life. I guess you'd know the truth about that, wouldn't you? Or maybe this letter is like a prayer going into the void. Maybe it's just a black hole out there. Maybe it's where I came from and where I'm going. You never answered me before, even on my Ouija board.

They say at the other end of a black hole you can emerge into another universe. I don't know. If you're over there maybe you can't hear me, but when I'm there maybe I'll understand. Thing I wonder about sometimes, though, is when they say it's like going into a tunnel of light when you die. See, some scientists say it's just visual receptors in the back of the brain firing as the brain closes down. So to anyone who's dying it just looks like a tunnel. Before it turns all black.

So which is it, Dad? Is it love there where you are, or oblivion?

Wish me luck,
Your son, Calvin

He placed the letter into the silver tray on the table, then reached for the volume control on the television and turned it back up. Dan Rather was talking about some teenagers outside Oklahoma City who'd used an Uzi to kill twenty head of cattle in a drive-by stockyard shooting spree. The veteran news anchor hid a mild amusement as he shook his head. Then he came on with a report of rising inflation, and how the President was going to fight homelessness with another two billion in appropriations. Of course the President would have to get Congress to raise Social Security payroll taxes again, but he would also increase import tariffs on Japanese goods. It was a tough decision to make in an election year. But the children of the future didn't deserve anything less, while the Japanese still had an unfair trade surplus from flooding the market with all those high quality goods. Anyway, didn't we all need to do our part to end poverty and hunger?

He cut Rather off in between-the-line implication and carefully pulled out one of three boxes from beneath the TV stand. Then he took off the lid.

Inside was a large clear plastic cylinder filled with a gray jelly-like substance. It looked like play dough or bread dough. Or even, considering the folds and crevices along its surface, like a five-pound oblong human brain.

He reached for the second shoe box. Packed inside were wires, electrical contacts, three smaller gift boxes, a roll of wrapping paper, plus tape, rubber gloves, a 9-volt alkaline battery, and a compact traveler's alarm clock.

Wake up, wake up, wherever you are.

He took the slip of paper that was stuck between the pages of a phone book, and scanned the three addresses on it. The first address was:

Cheryl Nagen
(aka Tonya Towers)
639 McCauley Rd.
Boston MA 02154

He smiled.

Then he struck a match, and slowly–carefully–lit his father's letter in the tray.

He thought about where his letters might have ended up had he mailed them. The Dead Letter office in San Francisco, probably. Except now they tried to call it an MRC, or Mail Recovery Center. Sounded like a recycling center–the kind he wished they had for lost souls.

As the flames died and the letter crisped and turned to ash, he put on the rubber gloves. In a few hours, he realized, it would be time to go to work.

Wish me luck, Dad, he thought.

Like Gessel said, he would need all he could get.

11

Vic knocked on the postmaster's door, and when it opened Barnard's secretary stood there, a tall middle-aged redhead with bifocals the thickness of the bottoms of shot glasses. "Yes?" she said through thin, pursed lips, focusing on him with a mildly critical curiosity.

"Hi, I'm Victor Kazy, and ..."

"Yes?"

"Yes, well, I'm looking for Inspector Castillo. Or the other guy, Phil what's-his-name."

"DeLong? You should try the inspector's office, sir. It's right up the–"

"Excuse me, I know where it is," Vic interrupted. "It's just that no one's shown up yet, and Maria doesn't answer her pager either, and it's almost noon, already. I was wondering if maybe the postmaster knew something about that."

The secretary stared dumbly. "Why would he? The inspectors here are independent and don't report to–"

"I know that! I'm an inspector here, too!"

She blinked at him, her glasses magnifying her incredulity. "You are?"

Vic rubbed his eyebrows. "Look–I'm sorry. Yes, I'm an inspector."

He produced his badge as proof. As she studied it he added, "So can you tell me if Mr. Barnard is in?"

"Oh, no. He's in Denver. Flew there yesterday afternoon for a meeting with the division supervisors. The plant manager is in the building, though. You want to talk to him, you dial fourteen."

"Yes, I know. Okay, thanks, Ms ..."

"Arbuthnot."

The door closed. Vic trudged back to the office. He slumped into Phil's empty chair. Where the hell was Maria? It wasn't her day off, and it wasn't like her to be over an hour late. Phil, yes. Phil might not show up until the Christmas party, if then. But Maria? Something was definitely wrong.

He thought back on the previous night, on their first "date." Dinner, then a tepid romantic comedy, and then at her door, a hug. That was all. Just a hug.

Well, not just a hug. A great hug. The kind of hug that had made him whistle all the way back to that antiseptic hotel room which served as stand-in for a real home. The kind of hug which felt so right that you knew, in the middle of it, that there was a God, and that He expected something like the return of the Holy Grail before He'd be dispensing such rapturous epiphanies again.

Still, he hadn't kissed her, or gone inside. Their professional relationship should still be intact. Was it even possible she'd expected more?

No, that was insane. Even if she had, which was unthinkable because he couldn't be that lucky, Maria was not the kind of lady to sulk. She was the most non-neurotic woman he'd ever met. Erotic, yes, but not neurotic. She hadn't a screwed-up molecule in her body. If she was late there had to be a damn good reason. So if she wasn't home, why hadn't she called?

Suddenly the phone rang. Vic stared at it, and smiled. Bingo. Here it comes, he thought. A textbook excuse. Not some lame sleepy voice telling him she'd stayed up late at her boyfriend's place, and would be in just as soon as she got dressed. That was impossible.

He picked up the phone after the third ring. "Hello?"

"Is Inspector Castillo there?" a deep voice asked.

Her boyfriend? If so, he didn't sound happy. "No, she's not," Vic replied. "Who is this?"

"Postmaster Graves, Tucson. We need someone here immediately to sign off on this report. You hear? Right now."

"What report, sir? What's going on?"

The postmaster paused to catch his breath. Over the phone line, Vic heard a siren go by in the background. "Inspector McDade is on vacation. His plane left this morning for Miami."

"And?"

"And there's been another incident."

"Incident?" Something in the way Graves said it sounded ... grave. "You mean a shooting incident?"

"No," the postmaster corrected him. "I mean a *bombing* incident." Another pregnant pause. "The police are already here, with a bomb squad, to see if there's more. The building's been evacuated. But it's policy that an inspector be here. So we need someone pronto."

"Really?" Vic glanced around the empty office. He imagined he could be there in two hours, if there were no delays getting to the interstate.

"Is Barnard there?" Graves asked suddenly.

"No, sir. Nobody but the plant manager, Rifkin. Why?"

"Okay, then. I'll call the Phoenix PD. There'll be a helicopter there in ten minutes. You be in the parking lot and they'll pick you up. Got it?"

"I got it. But can you do that?"

The line went dead. Evidently, in a bombing situation, Graves could do anything.

Vic tried to imagine the scene at the Tucson P&DC. All operations suspended, the building evacuated, fire trucks and police cars converging on the Cherrybelle plant ... and not a single inspector around. Not McDade, who was probably somewhere over the Gulf watching an in-flight movie. Not Phil DeLong, who was probably swapping jokes at some unknown greasy spoon in Tempe with all the other inspectors. And not Maria Castillo, who was ... where? With Barnard, eating canapés in Denver? Wind surfing with her cryptic lawyer boyfriend Carl in Acapulco?

As he was about to leave the phone rang again. It was a Dr. Abrams this time from the Bethany Clinic in Glendale. "I'm calling on behalf of a Ms. Maria Castillo," the doctor told him.

"Oh, no," Vic said, expecting the worst. "It's not a ... a car accident, I hope."

"No, it's a rather severe case of food poisoning. We've pumped her stomach and given her a sedative. She was feeling pretty weak, but she's resting now."

Vic shook his head numbly. "Thanks for the call, Doctor. Oh! And be sure to tell her when she wakes to contact me at the Cherrybelle Post Office in Tuscon. This is Victor Kazy. It's very important."

"Vic-tor Kat-zy."

"Kazy. K-A-Z-Y."

"Okay. No problem."

He hung up, took Maria's briefcase from beside her desk, and left the office. The question now was, if the postmaster could get the Phoenix PD to drop everything and shuttle him like a VIP to Tucson in order to save a one-hour delay, just how big had the explosion been–and what other strings were being pulled? The governor's, perhaps? Max the Ax Maxwell's?

He walked out to the rear parking lot, scanning it for the largest open space where a helicopter might land. Amazingly, he didn't have to wait long. A blue and white helicopter with the insignia of the Phoenix Metro Police approached and descended near the supply building. When it landed several dock workers came out to watch. Then a Plexiglas door on the chopper was thrown open, and Vic bent to edge his way under the still-whirling blades. He caught a glimpse of the helmeted pilot's dark visor, then scrambled up with his briefcase, and buckled himself in.

"The latch," the pilot shouted over the engine noise as the chopper's main rotor accelerated again.

Vic turned the handle, felt it snap in place. Then the pilot pulled on his stick. They heaved upward and forward, turning as they did.

"You Katz?" the pilot asked.

"What? No, name's Kazy. Victor Kazy. Okay?"

The pilot glanced at him and nodded as they continued their turn to the south. "You know what this is all about? Sounded pretty damn urgent." He held out his right hand. "My name's Jim Lucky, by the way."

Vic only shook his head. "I don't know much, Jim. There's been a bombing at the main post office in Tucson and they need an inspector there pronto."

The pilot withdrew his hand and shrugged it off. "Anyone killed?"

"Sounded likely, but I didn't ask."

"Why not?"

"It's the postmaster's name, for one thing. Harold Graves. Plus, I haven't been very lucky since I been here, Lucky."

The pilot looked out over the terrain ahead. "Well," he said at last, "maybe your luck is due to change."

"Let's hope so, anyway."

The city thinned below them, turning into subdivisions of red-tiled rooftops. Then, past the retirement communities and industrial parks, came the vast Sonoran desert–a lunar landscape except for patches of mesquite and that occasional symbol of the southwest, the majestic saguaro cactus.

He thought about David Sominski, the LSM clerk who'd been fired for throwing a chair at a "stupidvisor," as he'd put it. Had David been the one? Was Sominski the reason for the helicopter trip at high speed and taxpayer's expense?

As the ribbon of I-10 snaked below them, off to the west, the desert surface heat reflected glints of sunlight off the line of vehicles like the scales of a rattler. Their own route, straighter and delay-free, bore southeast over the Gila River Indian Reservation, the Sacaton Mountains, and the Picacho Mountains east of Casa Grande–which was where mother Burrows was probably sipping lemonade on her porch swing and contemplating the final dissolution of her daughter's marriage. From there they followed I-10 like a shot toward the Tortolitas, over the vicinity where western film star Tom Mix had met an untimely end.

Next, in short order, came signs of suburbia and approaching urban development, including the infamous Biosphere II, a space-age habitat nestled against the north side of the Catalinas. Red-tiled roofs to the west indicated a massive retirement complex–perhaps the very one where Karen had gone to work. And soon they passed Pusch Ridge and then entered the Tucson Valley itself, flying over the largest of the city's shopping malls, two golf and tennis resorts, and a dizzy grid of interconnecting streets.

"You know where you're going?" Vic asked.

The pilot nodded. "Main office on Cherrybelle, right? I know where it is."

Or where it was, Vic thought whimsically.

They came down in the west parking lot of the post office, in a space beside a fire truck and three police cars. Smoke still rose from the rear dock area of the plant, but it was more of a drifting smoke, like tear gas. Not the billowing black of a major fire. The parking lot itself was almost totally devoid of cars. Perhaps the management had sent the day-shifters home, and then gone home themselves. As they set down, Vic noticed spider webs of yellow police tape encircling the building, and more: out front, policemen on foot directed traffic away from the scene. A woman reporter stood across the street next to a TV news van; she spoke into a microphone as her cameraman filmed them landing.

He recognized Postmaster Graves coming across the parking lot from a side entrance. Vic opened the Plexiglas door and stepped down.

"Inspector?" The postmaster shouted with one hand atop his head in a vain attempt to preserve his groomed appearance.

"Victor Kazy, sir." Vic shook Graves' hand as if they hadn't already met. "How bad is it in there?"

"Bad. Follow me."

***

The central floor of the plant was murky and eerily lit by a ring of workman's lights tied to the tops of mail cages. The overhead bulbs had been extinguished by the blast, and the concrete floor was wet and gritty with glass. As they approached ground zero, Vic was reminded of the scene he'd read and later seen in *2001: A Space Odyssey* ... the alien monolith uncovered on the moon, with lights on tripods surrounding it. Only this time the monolith was a complex high-tech mail processing machine which had been blown almost in half and now jutted unnaturally in acute rigor mortis. But not only had the number one BCS been decimated, number two was stripped of electronics as well, as if a high school vandal had happened by. The same with the LSMs. All the intricate plastic separation bins were strewn like shredded insulation on the floor, and the innards of the first LSM were a concave jumble of burst framing, belts, and wires.

"Beyond repair," Graves announced grimly. He pointed at the other LSM, whose metal manufacturer nameplate–Burroughs–now hung on one rivet. "I had an ET look at that one, and–"

"Excuse me. An ET?"

"Electronics technician, of course."

"Sorry."

Graves frowned. "And he said we might have that one up and running in a week or so. If spare parts are available, that is."

Vic nodded. "If we're lucky, you mean."

"Right. As you can see, we now have no means to process mail, except by hand. So, with the damn mail volume this time of year, I predict we'll have a warehouse full of it by the time we can get back on line." The postmaster covered his eyes for a moment with one hand. "Maxwell will not be pleased."

"You mean Max the Ax?" Vic saw Graves glance at him between his fingers. "Sorry." He looked across the bone yard of twisted carts, cages, and distribution cases. "Anyone killed here?"

"Luckily, no. At least not that. Two people are in the hospital, though. One was a custodian, the other a CT. That's a computer technician."

"Ah."

"Both were a good seventy feet from the blast area, with lots of equipment between them and the explosion. It's a miracle there wasn't a crew working or something. We could easily be looking at dozens dead here."

"I believe it."

A plainclothes cop with a badge on his belt approached. Graves introduced him as Detective Vince Manetti. The stocky Italian had a half-moon scar on one cheek, like a smile. But the man himself had no time for smiles.

"I need your signature on my report before Mr. Graves here says anyone can release what's happened to the press," Manetti explained.

"I understand," Vic said, taking a pen. "What's your theory about what's happened?"

"Figure it's plastic explosive of some kind. That's what Joe on the bomb squad says, anyway. Figure it's an inside job, too. Your security here is pretty tight lately, I understand. That true?"

Vic glanced at Graves and nodded once. "There was an incident in Phoenix not long ago."

"So I heard. By the way, thanks for the little tour of Hiroshima, gents. And, there's no need for you to stick around until after the bomb squad's done over there, sir." He nodded toward the far side of the plant. "Mr. Kazy and I will brave the risk from here."

Graves nodded dutifully and walked toward the exit, glancing back jealously, as if he preferred immolation to facing the waiting press.

"Now then," said Manetti, when Graves was gone, "it looks like you got quite a mess here. Lucky for you, you also got a high stone ceiling. Otherwise you'd be looking at major structural damage, and not a little sunlight. Far as the mail goes, it's so much confetti or soggy ashes now, but I guess that's not so unusual, is it?" He winked. "'Course, what I mean to say, nobody's celebrating. Don't get me wrong. Thing is, before everyone starts rolling up their sleeves, I need to know if you got any suspects in mind for this. Or do you intend to play lone wolf on this, too?"

"I'll let you know," Vic told him, then took his card. "I'll call you soon as I have a clue. If I can have dupes of the photos you must have taken here, that is."

"Sounds like a fair trade to me. Just don't take too long gathering your thoughts. We got the press on our backs too, you know. And besides–they may decide to draft you to help clean up this mess. I'm sure you're used to that, though, being with the postal service and all." Manetti finally permitted himself the luxury of a smile.

Vic smiled back. "A lot of people like to complain about our service," he said. "Makes a good stand-up routine. Leno, Letterman. But you gotta wonder ... what would the public do without us?"

"I'm sure," Manetti replied, evenly, "we're about to find out."

12

Calvin opened the evening paper and almost laughed. There on the front page was a grainy picture of the Cherrybelle plant. Taken from outside and in front, the photo showed a line of yellow police tape crossing the customer lot, a motorcycle cop directing traffic to use the drive-through mail box, and a helicopter being refueled in the employee parking lot at the left edge of the frame. The headline was:

BOMBING AT MAIN POST OFFICE INJURES TWO

The report detailed the human injuries first. Roberto Horas, a custodian with eleven years service and three children, had suffered a concussion and broken collar bone when struck by a metal cage. He'd been mopping the floor at the entrance to an employee restroom. Cynthia Franklin, a computer technician who had just returned from her honeymoon in Cancun, suffered a burst eardrum and several cuts from flying debris. Her quote was: "I'd just dropped a floppy disk out of my case, and I bent over for it when it happened. A terrible blast. No heat at first. No, it was like being inside a bellows. A sucking-in, then a tornado force wave of wind. Solid air, you know? Hard as this desk. Threw me across the floor like I was a rag doll. Luckily, I was down low, because I saw stuff fly by overhead. A chair, maybe? I didn't really hear it, it happened so fast, though. Funny about that–it must have been damn loud."

Regarding postal equipment, the damages were estimated at three million dollars. This included two automated processing bar code sorters, and two letter sorting machines. Plastic explosive was the culprit; the motive was unknown. Directing the investigation was postal inspector Victor Kazy, with help from the Tucson PD and the FBI. Postmaster Harold Graves, in an interview, tried to reassure the public that service would not be interrupted, although there would be significant delivery delays until the damaged equipment could be replaced.

Calvin folded the *Tucson Citizen* and considered the battle so far. Neither rain nor bullets nor bombs shall prevent the Postal Service from returning to their rounds. So be it. In every war there were set-backs.

He switched on the TV for the national news. Had the explosion been heard around the world? He changed the channel to 13, the CBS affiliate, to see. Yes.

There was Dan, using KGUN footage and playing it up big with references to postal violence in the past–ever since the Pony Express crossed the Wild West. Then came speculations about whether the bombing indicated an escalation of the service's disturbing trend. They'd tried to reach the Postmaster General in Washington, but he was unavailable for comment. A spokesman for Maxwell said the incident was a tragic fluke which would be investigated for evidence of terrorist organization ties by the FBI, and for employee links by the Postal Inspection Service. Luckily, it was reiterated, no one was killed in the blast, and the service was committed to working hard in order to lessen the potential impact the bombing might have on postal customers in Tucson. Dan Rather concluded the report by saying the postal service had thousands of offices nationwide, all part of the infrastructure, so it was understandable that this American institution might become a target for subversive entities. What was next? he asked.

Indeed, thought Calvin, and pulled out his two boxes.

He removed the lids. Inside were the two small boxes and the letter. All three were addressed and stamped. What remained in the plastic cylinder was small. Less than a pound.

He was listening to Rather talk about a Mexican man who'd floated north on an inner tube, when the phone rang.

"Hello?"

"Is this Calvin Beach?" a woman's voice asked.

"Yes."

Dan Rather was now saying the Mexican man had gone directly to the L.A. Medical Center ...

"This is Carole Sherwood from Personnel."

... where he got a liver transplant ...

"I wanted to let you know there's no need to come in tonight."

... at a cost to the taxpayers of California of one million dollars.

"Due to a bombing. Your transfer into CFS has been approved, but they'll be using that area for manual distribution because of the damage on the work floor. So you'll have to wait until CFS can be moved out to the supply warehouse. No one is working tonight, actually."

"No one?"

"That's why I'm calling everyone. Maybe not tomorrow either ... at least until the fire inspectors approve the sprinkler repair. I'll call you back and let you know then, okay?"

"Okay. Thanks."

He hung up. Rather was now recounting the current cost to California's taxpayers for illegal aliens on welfare, in schools, and in prisons. Almost three billion a year, and rising. Government efforts to stop the flow were inadequate and failing. So the governor was taking heat from both sides.

The phone rang again. He snatched it up.

"Yeah?"

"Why'd ya do it, Calvin?" a voice said.

His heart skipped a beat. "What? ... Who is this?"

"It's Dave, remember me? Yer old buddy Dave?"

"Sominski? What do you want?"

A pause. "Oh, I dunno. How about ten grand?" Another–and longer–pause. "I could use the money, see. Won't say a word. Promise."

Calvin laughed. "What is this?"

"Don't play dumb. We both know ya did it."

"You think I–" He swallowed involuntarily, and gripped the telephone tighter. "You talking about the explosion at the plant?" He tried laughing again, wondering if it sounded false, even over the phone. "You're crazy."

"Listen who's callin' who crazy," Dave said. "You ain't just crazy, yer a regular walnut if ya think you'll pull this one off. Ya got a better chance of crossin' town on ice skates."

A long pause. Calvin said nothing.

"Ya hear me, Calvin?"

Still, he said nothing.

"You better come across with some cash or I'll tell 'em what a crackpot you really are. Ya hear me, Fireplug?"

Faintly, he could hear it now. Over the receiver, the distant ghost of a sound. Like a whirring. Like a tiny motor. A hiss, barely there at all.

Dave Sominski was recording their conversation with a cassette recorder held to his headpiece. A tiny metallic bump confirmed it.

Calvin decided to turn the tables.

"You ... you did it ... didn't you, Dave?" he said, his voice registering shock. "My God, I can't believe it. It was you! You did it because you were fired. What have you done?"

The line went dead.

Calvin replaced the receiver.

Then he picked up the letter he'd addressed to the editor of the *Arizona Daily Star.* He remembered what he'd written. Some of the same words he'd used at Dave's house. If Dave suspected now, what would he do when he saw the same ideas expressed in the paper? His call may have been a joke, but it wouldn't be then.

He picked up the first of the two small packages, and tore off the Tonya Towers address. With a pen he wrote:

DAVID SOMINSKI
2813 WESTERN AVE.
TUC

He stopped.

No.

Using a razor blade, he carefully cut through the left end of the box.

Then he peered inside.

The spring mechanism was primed and ready. But if he could reach in with a pair of pliers and disconnect the 9-volt battery, all would be well.

He peeled away the wrapping blocking his view, careful not to disturb the reinforced cardboard lid of the 4" X 5" box. Now he could see the battery, and the plunger/detonator linked to two tiny electrical contacts. The Tetryl charge was small–no larger than the size of an eyeball. It even looked like an eyeball, lying there in its plastic cocoon with two wires feeding into it like optic nerves. The charge that had destroyed half the post office had been half again the size of a human brain. Now one of the brain's two jelly eyeballs waited in the darkness. When it saw the light, someone's lights would go out. Permanently. Along with whoever else was standing nearby.

Having disconnected the battery and extracted the makeshift bomb, he went to his bookshelf and withdrew a thick hardback titled *The Collected Stories of Ray Bradbury.* He opened the book. The interior had been gutted for preparation of the remaining Tetryl. But he could use another book for that. Maybe his *AMA Medical Guide*, or Stephen King's *Nightmares and Dreamscapes,* he thought ironically.

He placed the bomb into the cavity, and reset the spring to activate when the book's cover was opened. Finally, through a break in the pages made by his needle-nose pliers, he managed to reconnect the battery after four tries.

He sat back and waited for his heart to settle down. Then he carefully slipped a rubber band around the book, and smiled.

***

At eight-thirty he parked at Reid Park and walked down the alley that went behind Eastland Avenue, carrying a plastic grocery bag. A dog behind a wall sensed him and barked. Calvin cursed under his breath, and continued walking. When he came to the fence behind

Sominski's house, he saw that Dave's car was gone. Even the moon was gone, somewhere behind a high bank of clouds. The gate Dave used to deposit his trash into the green dumpster in the alley was unlocked, too.

He was in luck.

He scanned the darkness, then swung open the gate and entered Dave's backyard. He could see that there was a dog next door, chained to a stake, but its head was down, asleep. Quickly, he went to the lawn chair that Dave had set up on his veranda, took the book out of his sack, slipped off the rubber band, and laid it on the plastic table next to the chair. Next, he went to the small utility building against the house, and slid open the rusty door, using part of the plastic bag as a glove.

The dog next door raised its head, but it was looking in the wrong direction. Calvin waited silently until the dog's head lowered again. Then he let the shoe box inside the bag slide out onto the floor of the shed. He opened the lid with the plastic bag, and adjusted the contents. He righted the tape and placed the razor atop a small box of electrical connectors. He positioned the knife, with a trace of Tetryl on it, in the center, and covered it with gauze. Gently, then, he pushed the shoe box with his toe into the inside left corner of the shed so that it would not be visible from the opening of the door, then he replaced the lid. As a final precaution, he swiped at any marks on the floor with the plastic sack, carefully slid the door closed again, and then stuffed the bag into his pocket.

The dog's head remained down as he backed out of the gate. But, when he shut the gate with his forearm, there was an audible click; the dog looked up, and turned this time. It looked right at Calvin, but didn't move. Calvin remained frozen in the darkness, like a fence post. After almost twenty seconds the animal's head finally bobbed and went down again. But when it did a car pulled into Dave's driveway; Calvin glimpsed the car's grille as it came to a stop just out of sight.

It was not Dave's.

A police car?

Calvin walked quickly in the opposite direction, and did not look back until he was out of the alley, across Country Club road, and into the dark safety of the park.

On the way home, he stopped at the Sun Station post office on Speedway Boulevard to mail the other unopened surprise package and letter to the editor. Then he picked up a bucket of chicken at the KFC on Broadway–Extra Crispy–and soon after settled into his couch to watch *America's Most Wanted* on TV. As usual, there were no messages on his machine. The phone rang one time around ten o'clock, but whoever it was didn't allow enough time for him to answer.

13

Detective Vincent Manetti and FBI agent Frank Delany were watching Vic's videotape of Sominski for a second time when a knock came at the door of McDade's office. Vic opened it, and saw Maria standing there. She was wearing blue jeans and a pale blue knit pullover, but it was the white sneakers and her pale face that threw him—even for a Sunday morning.

"You all right?" he asked.

"I'm getting there," Maria replied. "I ate some peanuts on the commuter flight from Phoenix, but the cab from the airport had faulty air conditioning. Must be a hundred and two degrees out there already."

"A hundred and five," Manetti corrected her. "In the shade."

"Ugh ... Vince, this is Maria Castillo, the head inspector for the Phoenix PC."

"Psychologist?" Manetti asked, brightening. He grinned. "You did say head inspector, didn't you?"

A dutiful laugh.

"Maria had food poisoning yesterday," Vic said.

Maria nodded. "I'm not sure if it was dinner or breakfast that did it."

Vic introduced them then, and they all shook hands. Manetti

seemed particularly attentive to Maria, despite her tired, listless eyes. He wasn't looking there anyway, although Vic had personally decided Maria's eyes were usually her sexiest asset. Now he felt embarrassed for her at Manetti's gaze. Even protective. As for Delany, the man was polite, but impervious. A dark and lanky Robocop with little evident emotion, he was probably always on duty for the omnipresent Bureau.

"So is this our only lead?" Maria asked suddenly, and pointed at the TV monitor.

They all turned to see now ex-employee Sominski picking up a chair to hurl at his supervisor.

"Appears that way," Vic interjected, stepping between Maria and the lecherous detective. "The employees that were hurt in the bombing are recovering, although one may have permanent hearing loss in one ear. We've made copies of Sominski's photo to show to employees, and we plan to set up the conference room for interviews to see if we can learn anything else from them ... just as soon as they get back to work tomorrow."

"The lab report is back, too," Manetti added. "Guesstimate three to four pounds plastique. High-grade stuff. Very professional. Set off by a timer."

"So it wasn't from the mail stream?"

Manetti leaned forward so he could see the pretty lady inspector. "Not unless you people lose lots of packages under postal furniture. Best they can figure, the bomb was placed under a small wooden cabinet directly between your two most expensive pieces of equipment."

"It was a maintenance-built software cabinet," Vic explained, "that had computer backup disks of operating software for the BCS. The cabinet was kept locked, but there was a phone on top, and a space underneath to store phone books. The computer technician who was hurt had been in the cabinet earlier that morning, but doesn't remember seeing anything unusual."

"So the bomb could have been hidden inside somehow, then. Like maybe inside a hollowed-out phone book."

They all looked at Maria in amazement.

Agent Delany nodded thoughtfully. "That's it, I think," he said.

"Not so fast," Manetti cautioned. "The Tucson yellow page directory is thick, but I don't think it's that thick."

Delany crossed the room to McDade's cluttered desk in three long strides. He opened a bottom drawer and came out with the directory. He hefted it, then turned to the back page. "Fourteen hundred and sixty pages," he announced. "I think you're wrong."

"Thin pages," Detective Manetti countered, not to be outdone. "And you got at least three pounds of plastique, not to mention a detonator and battery."

The tall G-man shook his head slowly. "I've seen it done. In a space smaller than this." He dropped the book for emphasis onto McDade's desk; it landed with a heavy thump. "The bomber could have come in with a phone book, made an exchange, placed a call to the weather channel, and then dropped this other phone book on another desk on his way out. He could have come in with a tour group, or he could be this guy Sominski. Either way, it would be the safest course. On the off chance someone was watching, he might not even be questioned."

"Agreed," Vic said. "So what about motive. Is it revenge?"

"Revenge of some kind," asserted Maria. "So, instead of watching a tape, how come one of you isn't at least questioning Sominski, and getting a search warrant for his house?"

Vic turned to her, lowered his voice. "Vince and I went over there last night. He wasn't home, and hasn't been home since. In the meantime, the house is being watched, and the search warrant should come soon."

"How soon is soon?"

Manetti checked his watch. "Less than an hour. There's an APB out on the weasel, too. Wanted for questioning. May be a long shot, but hey–it's our only lead. Guy's a loser, right? No friends, no family in the area. His car's not at the airport. Maybe he drove to Michigan to renew acquaintances. If he shows up there in a couple days the police there'll question him. And if he doesn't, and there's evidence in his house, the APB'll go national, and maybe we can pick him up on the interstate."

Maria went to the monitor. She tapped the screen where Sominski was now being handcuffed. "I'm still not totally sure it's him," she said. "I'm not sure why; I just can't see him doing it."

"You can't see?" Vince asked. "You mean like women's intuition? Some kinda clairvoyance?" He winked at her.

Maria cut off the monitor. "I can't see him making a bomb. Where would he get the materials, for one thing. Plastique of that quality isn't easy to make, either. Plus, someone's been watching him ever since his incident that night, and he knows it. Not closely watching, of course, but he doesn't know that."

"He's not around anymore, though, is he?" Manetti asked.

"No, but he hasn't cleaned out his thrift savings account yet, either. That's forty grand."

"So how do you know he hasn't killed himself by now in a fit of remorse?"

"Unlikely," said Delany. "Bombers aren't usually into suicide, unless it's a religious thing."

Vic shook his head, remembering the X-rated video tapes he'd seen in Sominski's book stand. "I didn't see any evidence of that," he said. "There was a rifle rack in his bedroom, though. So he may be a hunter. Of course, the gun itself was missing."

"How come you didn't tell me this before?" complained Manetti. "I thought we were cooperating on this investigation."

"I am," Vic said, defensively. "We are."

"Uh-huh. Okay, then. This loner, he's ex-military, but maybe he's got old contacts. Some friend of a friend who can smuggle the stuff off a base or bunker. It's unlikely, that's true, but it's happened before somewhere, hasn't it?" Manetti turned to Delany. "Am I right?"

Delany nodded noncommittally. "It's a remote possibility."

Vince chuckled. "Remote? It's happened, friend. You want me to show you the hole in the floor again? Wanna try to find that cabinet or those computer disks in all the debris?"

The FBI man smiled thinly. "I'm already ahead of you. As soon as I heard the material might be C-four, I contacted the commander at Davis-Monthan and requested a C-four munitions check through their supplier at Hughes Missile Systems. He should be paging me in ..." Delany checked his own watch. "Very soon."

The phone rang. Manetti looked at Delany, who looked at Vic. Vic turned to Maria, who sighed and picked it up after the third ring.

"Hello, this is Inspector Castillo." Maria's face suddenly went even paler as she explained their situation as calmly as she could. Then she listened for almost a full minute. "Yes sir," she said, finally, and "Will do." Then she hung up.

"Who was that?" Vic asked.

"That," Maria announced, "was the Postmaster General, Max the Ax Maxwell himself. He just got back to Minneapolis after cutting short a fishing trip, and heard about the bombing. He wants us to keep him up to date on this every four hours. He said all the major media want answers, and he wants to be able to give them some, soon." She turned to Vic. "By the way, how's the media here handling this so far?"

"I can answer that," Manetti offered. "They've had their cameras in your Mr. Graves' face ever since noon yesterday. Vic here, and me, been listening to Graves complain about it for almost as long. Only now that Mr. Delany is with us, Graves doesn't bother us as much. I think he's afraid of the Feds. Think maybe he's got income on the side he's not reporting to the IRS. What do you think?"

"I think you may be right," Maria conceded, with a chuckle.

Manetti glanced at Vic. A look of success flashed in the Italian's eyes.

"You know," Vic said, "there's something we haven't considered. Tomorrow is the first of June. That means mail should be heavy. Heavier than usual, I mean. With a lot of people moving."

"Yeah?" Manetti lost his momentary sense of humor.

"I see where he's going," said Maria. "All the remaining snow birds are heading north, along with the college students. It means extra work for the carriers and the clerks in forwarding. Plus, there's a lot of catalogs, bulk mailers, and Publishers Clearing House kind of contests coming up. Mail volume will be high this coming week, and our bomber couldn't have picked a better time to blow away half the plant's automated processing machines."

"Couldn't anyone know this, though?" Delany asked. "Would it take a postal employee to figure out the timing? It seems pretty obvious to me."

"That's true," Maria replied. "But it does add a check mark to the employee side of the ledger, especially considering the placement of the bomb. The bomber knew exactly when to set it off, it seems to me. At a time when there were few people around."

"You mean like himself?"

Maria smiled. "Or herself. And another thing. They didn't tell me this on the phone, but what exactly was destroyed in the blast besides equipment?"

Manetti blinked at her. "What–you mean like mail?"

"Exactly."

Vic produced the inventory list which Graves had given them. He handed it to her. "There were fifteen cages of mail in all," he said. "Seven were only slightly charred. Should be recoverable, eventually. The others are mostly ashes from an electrical fire. The sprinklers overhead got blasted away, see, though they did manage to work in other areas of the plant, soaking a ton of other mail."

Maria shook her head. "I mean the mail near the target–do we know what it was?"

Vic shrugged. "First class letter mail, mostly. The usual: love letters from the IRS; rent checks; utility bills; bank statements. A shipment of government checks."

"Government checks?" asked Delany, suddenly alert.

"You know–savings bonds, Social Security, welfare, that kind of thing."

"But I thought that was going to be done electronically now, through ATM machines."

Vic glanced at Maria. "Ours is the first test shipment of those plastic ATM cards in the whole country. Tucson is coming onto the system early, as a kind of trial pilot program. But there's still some of those old checks involved here, too."

Maria nodded. "Yes ... and both would come in batch shipments, and the BCS separates them into routes." She looked up. "Make another check mark in the ledger. I may be wrong about Sominski; he's the only one we know with a motive. He would know about the ATM cards too, and how the postal service would catch hell for their loss. It could be weeks before the government can reissue checks to everybody, and some of those poor people live from check to check." She brushed her hair aside. "I remember one time when a man didn't get his pension check, and I had to help find it in the mail stream when it got sent to forwarding by mistake. Guy was furious. Cursing like a sailor high on speed. Can you imagine how it'll be in the coming week when hundreds, maybe thousands, of people can't buy groceries?"

"I can see it now," said Manetti, with a cynical grin.

"Even if their cards or checks weren't in that batch, it'll be the same situation. They'll still have to wait weeks while the machinery is being repaired. Won't matter to them that every clerk on the payroll is working twelve-hour days doing it by hand, either. They've got to eat. Got to pay the rent and buy medicine. And so they'll be forced to complain, even if they never complained about anything before in their lives."

"I *can* see it," Manetti repeated himself, now staring at the ceiling. "Long line wrapped around the building, and when you get inside? You gotta take a number." He chuckled. "Then when ya finally make it to the front, the window clerk's gone on break!"

Maria glowered at him. "Maybe we should draft you to help out," she said. "I'm sure if I called Mr. Maxwell he could pull some strings and–"

She stopped as the telephone rang again.

Vic answered it, then handed it to Manetti. "It's for you."

Manetti listened, said "We'll be right there," and then hung up. He stared at everyone, each in turn. Then he announced lightly: "Case closed. Our suspect has returned, and the warrant's on the way."

***

They drove to Sominski's house in two cars. Manetti's unmarked Crown Victoria passed them at the first red light to lead the way. It was a supercharged pursuit vehicle, and Vic didn't even try to keep up in their white postal Caprice. Besides, he'd decided not play the macho Italian's subtle game of dominance. Let him think he was in charge. Let him imagine himself the gallant knight, wary of Maria's safety. He would anyway. As for Delany, the G-man had stayed behind to pursue other possibilities. It was not an ego thing with him, Vic hoped. There was no open competition, anyway; Delany worked in an entirely different arena that had to do with conspiracy and terrorism.

In addition to the surveillance car, another police car was already there, lights flashing. Sominski's red Mustang was in the driveway; Sominski himself stood just inside the front screen door. Waiting.

They all approached the house together–including the cop who handed Manetti a twice-folded form.

Sominski squinted out at his uninvited guests with a look of resigned disdain. "What is it?" he asked. "Come ta crash my party, or you jus' wanna arrest me again, so ya won't get outta practice?"

Manetti stepped up close to the screen door, looking past the shirtless, barefooted man, into the living room. Then he lifted the papers up to Sominski's unshaven face behind the slightly warped mesh. "We've come with a search warrant," he said. "Are you alone here?"

"I'm always alone here," Sominski replied. "Whaddaya think–I got some hot-ta-trot blond babe in the back room? Think they like unemployed alcoholics, do ya? Get turned on by old vets with no education? That what ya think?"

Manetti laid his hand on the doorknob. "Step aside. Over in that corner." He pointed. "Over there."

"What's it all about, anyway?"

Manetti opened the door, handing him the search warrant. Sominski backed away as they all entered, including the uniformed policeman, and the other surveillance detective. The half-dressed man lost his half-smile while reading the warrant.

"Where were you last night?" Manetti asked, as the other detective and officer went into the bedrooms.

"Wait a minute," Sominski said. "You don't really think I–"

"I asked you a question." Manetti stepped closer, cornering him. "Where'd you go to stash the evidence?"

"Hey. *Hey* ... What's yer problem? You people don't talk to each other? I was in jail last night. That's right. Made me stay 'til jus' an' hour ago."

Vic exchanged glances with Maria. "In jail for what?" Vic asked.

"DUI. Whaddaya think? They picked me up comin' outta the club parkin' lot at ten o'clock. Friggin' strip-searched me. Hosed me down in the damn tank. Put me next ta this asshole kept whistlin' an' clickin' his teeth all night."

"That right," Manetti nodded. "You got the arrest receipt, I imagine."

"Damn straight. Gonna frame it. It's my first friggin' arrest."

"Second," Vic corrected him.

Manetti frowned. "And the name of the club is ..."

"Fleshdance. You should go there. Might do ya some good."

"Cute."

"Yeah? You people are really cute if ya think I'm the one blew up the plant. Personally, I can think a four or five more likely suspects. One of 'em might a done it jus' fer kicks."

They waited, listening to the rummaging sounds. Done in the bedrooms, the other officers finally moved into the kitchen and began pulling the drawers and looking through the cabinets.

"These other people," Maria said, "can you give us their names?"

"Why should I? What you ever done fer me but get me fired?"

"This is serious, David," said Vic. "You got any information, you should let us know. Might get you off the hook."

"I got nothin' ta hide. An' I'm sick a jerks like you tellin' me what I should do."

He sat on the stool nearest the corner, and crossed his arms. When the clanging and rattling stopped in the kitchen, it began in the dining room and bathroom.

"Be sure to check the baseboards and walls for signs of disturbance!" Manetti called, still staring at Sominski. A faint smile traced his lips. "You hear me, Roger?"

"Yes sir," came the reply. "We've been doing that."

The rattling and tapping continued.

"The living room is next, kid," Manetti explained. "Then comes the attic and the yard. Then we go talk to your neighbors, ask 'em if they've seen anything suspicious over here. Ask 'em what kind of person you are, and did they see you with anybody. Then we go through the whole house again, and through your car. You got anything you want to say about this?"

"Apparently I don't. Do I?"

"No, you don't."

"Then get off my fuckin' back."

The other detective stuck his head around the corner. "All done. Vents too. We do in here next?"

"No ... not yet." Manetti wriggled his fingers in Sominski's face. "Car keys."

"Yer really somethin', ya know that?"

"Yeah," Manetti replied, and glanced around at Sominski's cluttered furnishings. "So are you." He took the keys and threw them to his assistant. "You got a real nice place here. Real nice." He picked up an empty Tecate bottle by the top and turned it, as if looking for fingerprints. Then he bent to read the video titles in the bookcase. "Not much of a reader though, are you?" He withdrew one of the tapes and showed it to Vic. "Have you seen this one?"

Vic shook his head at the glossy image of a woman in a white teddy holding a long white staff in her hand. "Really, it's–"

"What? Not relevant? I think it is. Look at this. Besides *Snow White And The Seven Hunks* we got *Under Siege Two*, and *Above The Law*. Sex and violence. American staples, for sure, but what you want to bet Tinkerbell here went over the edge when he got him a lady boss. Always had trouble relating to women. Just couldn't handle it. So he freaks, loses his cushy job, then plots revenge. Simple as ABC, one-two-three baby, you and me, girl ..."

Maria turned away. Vic looked at Sominski, who sat with his head in hands.

"Come on, Davy boy," Manetti prodded. "You can tell us."

"Tell ya what? Where to pick up some plastique?" He laughed. "Haven't got a clue. And neither do you."

"One of your buddies helped you out, maybe," Manetti suggested.

"What buddies?"

"Or ... maybe you paid somebody. Organized crime, a militia nut case, a gang member."

"Yer fishing, an' it smells fishy. Even ta me."

"That right? Well, you tell me how you did it, then. Go through it, step by step, nice an' slow, smart boy. See, I'm just a dumb fuck. I don't understand how a genius like you can–" Manetti looked up as the patrol officer came in. "What is it?"

"Sorry, sir. We're about done, except for in here."

"Did you do the attic already?"

Sominski laughed. "Ain't no attic. It's a flat roof. No basement either. House is on a slab."

"You're on a slab." Manetti turned back, "Do the yard, then. Look for signs of disturbance, holes, that kind of thing."

"Yes sir. Detective Bates is checking the shed out back now."

When he was gone, Manetti dropped the car keys in Sominski's lap. "Now where was I? Oh, yes. You were gonna tell me what idiots you think we are."

Sominski gave Manetti a sick smile. "You said it, not me."

"This is getting nowhere," Maria concluded. "Let's wrap this up." She turned to Sominski. "You haven't been back to the plant since you were fired?" she asked.

"Hell no."

"Not even to mail something out front?"

"What did I just say? No. I wanna mail somethin', I put it in my mailbox an' put the little flag up. Then the mailman, he comes along an' he takes it out. Got it so far? Then he, like, puts the flag back down. And he drives to the post office an' empties his white sack into this big, big bin. Then that bin gets dumped onto a belt so these other mailmen can take out the thick stuff before it goes into the Canceler chute. Then, see, it–"

"You little faggot," Manetti breathed.

The rear door in the kitchen opened. Detective Bates appeared, standing next to the refrigerator. He looked between them. "I think we got something," he said.

"What?" Manetti said, almost in surprise. "What do you mean?"

"In the shed," Bates replied. "There's a box."

Manetti slowly smiled. He took Sominski by the arm. Sominski stood, a look of confusion on his face. His eyes darted from side to side. Manetti got behind him and pushed him toward the kitchen. "Out back, kiddo," the Italian said, with a laugh. "You got a date with destiny."

As they moved into the kitchen Manetti took out his handcuffs. Bates went outside and held open the door for them.

A sudden explosion rocked the house. Shattered window glass burst into Vic's face in a blinding flash.

Vic yelled as Maria fell on him. From the floor, he blinked up at the gaping hole above the sink where the window had been. He couldn't hear anything but the howling in his head. He put his hand to his face, and when he withdrew it, it was covered with blood. He sat up and turned Maria around to face him. She seemed dazed. A thin sliver of glass was stuck in her eye.

"Maria!" he cried. But he couldn't hear his own words.

He turned to Manetti for help, but the detective was kneeling in the living room, holding his own mouth as blood dripped between his fingers onto the carpet.

Ex-postal employee David Sominski was gone.

14

Calvin woke from a chaotic dream of fighting incoming Viet Cong. From a sandbag bunker outside Bok Thoh, to the reality of the wheezing sound of his air conditioner. He blinked at the ceiling as the transformation firmed. Then he became aware of a light coming from the end of the hallway. From the bathroom. Had he left the light on? He couldn't see, so he turned his head to look at his alarm clock, instead. Somehow, in his sleep, the clock had turned away. He reached for it, but found that his left hand had been handcuffed to the bed post.

Then he heard a sound from the bathroom.

Water running.

He jerked up in bed, pulling at his restraint. No use. The bed post was tubular metal. The handcuff only scraped along the bar's antique finish.

Now the water stopped. The air conditioner cycled down. A cold stone silence. Calvin took in a breath and waited. His heart was a quick, shallow pounding in his temples and upper throat. He felt, rather than heard, the bathroom door widen. The light played on his bedroom wall nearest the door, getting brighter. Then it went out. Slow footsteps on the hall carpet in the darkness ...

Suddenly he remembered his pistol.

He flung himself across the bed, his free arm lunging under the space beneath. His right hand slid across the shag in a jerky semicircle, flailing back and forth. Back and forth. Frantically.

The bedroom light came on. He stopped, his heart hammering so fast it was painful. He pulled himself up, slowly, and turned to face a cocked .45 automatic aimed at his head.

"Looking for this?" David Sominski said, with a twisted grin.

"D-D-Dave?" he said, squinting up at the stark figure behind a barrel that had a black hole in the end of it the size of eternity.

Sominski continued grinning, as if the grin was stitched on his face. He wore the brown polo shirt that Calvin had purchased at JC Penny for $14.98 the previous Saturday. His hair was awry, his chin bruised. His forearm had three Bandaids on it, with a pink stain of blood showing along the edges.

"Dave ... what the hell is going on?"

Sominski laughed dryly. "As if ya didn't know."

"Tell me."

Sominski backed to the dresser and sat beside it on the foot stool, never once losing his aim. "Why'd ya do it, Fireplug, huh? How'd ya get so low so quick? You one a them sociopaths ya hear about–got no emotions, like a serial killer? Who was gonna be next, anyway? The Postmaster General? The President?" He paused, his wide and wild eyes never once blinking. "'Course I'm the perfect patsy for ya, ain't I? At least I was. You was gonna blow me away, make 'em think I had a little accident while I was puttin' together another bomb or somethin'. Only it didn't work, did it? And now here we are. Jus' you an' me. Buddy."

Calvin stared, said nothing.

"No denials, huh? No confessions or denials?" Dave shook his head. "No. That's not how we gonna play it. What it is, yer gonna write up a statement on paper and sign it. Then yer gonna call the inspectors an' tell 'em ya wished you'd got counseling. Otherwise, I'm blowin' yer fuckin' head off right here an' now."

Calvin glanced up at his handcuffed hand, stalling for time. "Where'd you get these?"

"Never you mind where. You jus' come to a decision. What'll it be?"

Calvin looked back at him. *Was his hand trembling slightly? Was it rage or fear–or both*? "You musta got in a fight, didn't you? You musta come out on top somehow, got these handcuffs as a souvenir. Was it inspector Kazy? These cuffs his? And is he dead now?"

"I'm not a cold-blooded bastard like you," Sominski said. "But it won't pain me none ta rid the world a one."

"So they're alive. And now they're looking for you. And there was nowhere for you to go, so you came here. That about sum it up?"

"Shut up and decide!" Sominski glanced at the clock; he could see it from his angle. "It's ten-fifteen. You got five minutes. At ten-twenty, if you ain't agreed, I pull this trigger. Got it?"

"I'm supposed to be at work at midnight."

"You ain't gonna make it."

Calvin fidgeted. "Oh. That's right. We don't start until tomorrow. Then it's overtime up the wah-zoo."

"Goodbye, Calvin."

"Hold it!" *Five minutes? Was it enough time*? "You ... left me no choice, you know. Threatening me on the phone like that. What was I supposed to do–let you turn me in?""

"Oh, right. Like I really knew you was the damn bomber ... that it wasn't a Priority mail package or somethin' that blew. Yer weird, Fireplug, but I didn't know you was insane. Until now."

Calvin lifted his free hand in a casual gesture. "Like I said, I couldn't take the chance." He coughed. "Nothing personal."

Sominski laughed. "Yeah. An' in four minutes it'll be nothin personal when I carve a bloody hole between yer lyin' eyes."

Calvin shrugged. "What would that get you?"

"How 'bout a big slice a satisfaction."

"Or revenge? So you are like me, after all."

"Not hardly."

"Oh really? You kill me, what's the difference? I mean ... I'll tell you the difference. Okay? You'd be a killer, which is something I ain't."

"How ya figure that?"

"You don't understand, do you? I'm a *soldier,* not a killer. And this is a *war*. Sometimes innocent people die in war. It's sad, but it's not for nothing if it turns out okay in the end. After the war, I mean."

"Yer sick. You need therapy if ya think what you done helps anybody. You shoulda called the EAP when ya had the chance." He gestured with the gun. "By the way ... what was it, exactly, exploded out in my shed?"

"Book bomb. Next to your lounge chair."

Sominski nodded thoughtfully. "I don't read enough. So where'd ya get the plastique?"

"Does it matter?"

Sominski sighed. "Not really. Ya got two victims in yer friggin' war already. Cops. An' in three minutes you can join 'em in hell."

Calvin shifted on the bed. "It doesn't have to be that way."

"Don't it?"

"Not if you join the war. Not if you're an ally, and we're on the same side. The right side."

"So you wanna recruit me now, start a little fag outfit? Think that'll save yer fuckin' life, do ya? Yer a joke a minute, Fireplug. Yer hilarious."

The air conditioner cut on again, none too soon. Calvin wiped the cold sweat from his face. "You must have thought about it."

"'Bout what? Hatin' women an' babies? Thinkin' it's some kinda conspiracy? Hatin' Mexicans an' blacks, thinkin' they're the ones causin' all the problems? What is it you're fightin' anyway, Calvin? What kinda racist war you talkin' about?"

Calvin sneered. "I'm talking about a new civil war. A war that should be happening against the ones bringing America to its knees. I'm talking about the socialists and do-gooders, like those in the Post Office, who think they know better than you do how to run your life, Dave."

Sominski's eyes narrowed for a moment. He blinked twice. But he said nothing.

"You know, they want to talk about you being fair, and about justice ... while they stick their dirty hands in your pockets and grab you by the nuts. They wanna talk about diversity and the great melting pot that never mixed right. As if that's what America's all about. But I'm telling you, Dave, that ain't it. Not even close. You know what made this country great? Huh? You got any idea what it is we had, and now we're losing? It's called freedom, Dave. That's what made this country. Not diversity or fairness or poverty programs. Freedom! That's all. That's everything. And it's going down the tubes, buddy. Going quick! You wanna have your damn social justice and civil rights, and you wanna cling to that hypersensitive PC crap, you go right ahead. But you leave me out of it! 'Cause the government doesn't own me. I own myself, you understand? I own me! Which means those bastards in Washington and at City Hall ain't supposed to tell me what I gotta pay to be fair, and what I gotta eat, and where I can shit. And they ain't supposed to take care of me, either. Because I'm responsible for me. And me alone. It used to be called freedom. It used to be called opportunity. It's why the founding fathers came here in the first place. And it's why somebody's gotta make a statement about all the leeches who wanna suck all our freedoms dry by ending any chance you got to succeed."

Sominski looked away, still silent.

"You know they won't rest until everybody's equal, don't you? But it's a myth, isn't it? Everybody's not equal, and they can't be made equal. You can drain every dime the rich and the middle class have and give it to the poor, and in five years it'd be back the way it was. Why? Is it because of discrimination? Unfairness? Racism? No. It's because some people got ambition, Dave. Some people got a work ethic. And other people just don't give a shit. They'll have their babies, and get other people to foot the bill. Because they can. While they whine about anybody who's got more than them. While they talk about getting even, and getting their fair share ... which all comes down to the same thing. Free lunch."

The .45 slowly lowered. Sominski now stared at the floor.

"There's more and more of 'em now, ya know. Got nothing to do with race. But if you want to talk about that part of the class war, you must know the Mexicans hate you for being a middle class, white, male gringo. Because that's what they're taught. That you're the cause of all the problems in America. *You*, Dave. Your greed and racism is what keeps them where they are. Except I'm not just talking about that, am I? I'm talking about the bigger war, not just one battle. I mean all the people trying to get on the dole, not just those coming over the fence in places like Nogales. Ninety-one billion a year on Food Stamps, AFDC, supplemental income, and housing aid. Another seventy-eight billion a year on Medicaid. And a whopping three hundred twenty billion a year on Social Security–a lot to people who don't need it, and already collected three times what they put it in. You know how many zeros it all is? Add it up, and you're left with a big goose egg for your own retirement. All because on one side you got uneducated, unwed mothers on the dole for years, having two, three, and four babies. And on the other side of the vise you got retired geezers driving Lincoln Town Cars, playing golf, and collecting money they deduct from your paycheck. You already know who's stuck in the middle, getting squeezed, don't you? And how before long the system'll go bust. Then we get a police state, Dave. You're gonna love that. Be like the Army, except everybody's poor, and you got no choice but to reenlist. It ends up with everybody working in factories like the post office, but at whatever minimum wage they think you deserve. Forget about choices. You got none. Your freedoms are gone once that happens. That what you want? You want to let them win? Because they're soldiers too, ya know. Think they got us outnumbered, but they wouldn't if some people would wake up. So to hell with the leeches, I say ... to bloody hell. There's gotta be consequences for your actions, or it's the end of freedom. And I say 'give me liberty or give me death.'"

Sominski continued staring at the floor. The .45 slumped in his limp hand, and looked for a moment like it might drop.

Calvin rattled his handcuffs. "My five minutes are up," he concluded. "So either shoot me or give me back my freedom so we can figure out what to do from here."

Sominski's eyes moved slowly from side to side. "Shut up an' let me think," he said, dully.

"Take all the time you want," Calvin told him, and almost smiled in relief.

After another full minute, Dave finally looked up. A tired disappointment now shadowed his face. "I think the best thing," he said, "is I jus' leave you here. I phone the police, lay out the story, an' let 'em search yer place better than I could after I broke in through yer back window. I'll warn 'em about yer book collection, too. Then I wait somewhere ta see what happens. Like at the zoo, where I spent the afternoon."

"I hate to break it to you, buddy," Calvin told him, "but the zoo's closed by now."

"In the mornin', I mean."

"Oh."

Sominski stood and stuck the .45 in his belt. "I gotta hand it to ya, Fireplug," he said. "I didn't think there was anything you could say ta change my mind 'bout pluggin ya. You wouldn't a signed a confession either, I bet, would ya?"

Calvin shook his head. "Not on your life."

"You mean yours." Dave moved into the hallway. "You probably ain't sleepy, but I am. I been keepin' normal hours lately. 'Course unlike you, I'm a light sleeper, so try ta keep quiet in here, okay? Otherwise I'll change my mind again."

He cut the light, and shut the door. The hall light went on under the door, then went off again. Sominski would sleep on the couch. He wouldn't be reading any Stephen King.

After half an hour, Calvin sat up, slowly. He turned the clock to face him. Somehow, in eight hours, he had to get free. If he only had a knife, he might saw through the bed post in that time. Or through his hand, after applying a tourniquet. The tempered steel of the handcuffs was out of the question. Of course, he didn't have a knife, so the idea was futile.

Or was it?

By the light of the clock's numerals and the dim moonlight on the closed window drapes, he took stock of everything in the room. He tried to remember what was in his dresser drawers. Socks, underwear ...

Polo shirts.

Sominski had been in his dresser. Yes, and probably removed

anything metal or sharp in the room, along with the bedroom phone. He might try to pull the bed over there, break off a metal drawer handle. But what good would that do? And what if the dumb Pollock heard him?

He examined the bed post, where it was welded to the frame. The weld was strong. And although the post itself was hollow, it was too thick to bend and weaken. Besides, it had a middle brace, so he couldn't pull it from the center anyway.

The wall socket. Wires, electricity. The clock. Or the lamp! Maybe the center rod of the lamp could offer some kind of leverage.

No, he decided. The rod would be too pliable. It was useless.

He lay back and tried to think. How would Houdini do it? Or Gessel, the Special Forces vet? Was there no way? If he didn't come up with something, he'd have a lifetime in prison to think about what he might have done. Or what he might have said to make the idiot take off the handcuffs. The only thing he'd managed to do was prevent Sominski from pulling the trigger. But, considering a lifetime in jail with all those leeches and losers, a shot through the forehead might be a preferable alternative. Of course, he could get lethal injection in Arizona, but there was always the CLU in the way of that. Liberal bleeding heart protesters who would try to save his life to the very end, and then force the taxpayers to pay thirty grand a year to incarcerate him.

He thought about the two cops Dave had mentioned. That must have been the reason. His "sometimes-innocent-people-die-in-war" hadn't washed. The idea of a class war had made sense, but actual casualties had been too much. The idiot didn't realize how serious it was. So he took the bait, but not the hook.

Now what? Try again in the morning?

The answer came to him in a flash.

He moved to the side of the bed, put one foot on the floor and stood up, carefully. Then he lifted the mattress and peered down, closely, bending as far as he could.

Yes!

That was it, then. So simple. Maybe he wouldn't need eight hours; maybe one hour would do it. He'd have to wait, though. It was risky, and he'd be giving up the chance that Sominski would have a change of heart and let him go.

He lay back on the bed and went over the idea, looking for flaws. There were many, and they all had to do with Sominski hearing. Which is why he needed an hour, and not ten minutes. Of course, he'd read somewhere that REM sleep usually occurred in cycles, and the deep sleep characterized by rapid eye movements couldn't be predicted.

It was almost eleven o'clock now.

In three hours, at 2:00 AM, he'd make his move.

Hoping Sominski was counting sheep somewhere in Scotland.

***

The digital alarm clock clicked over at last: 2:00 AM.

Calvin moved slowly to the side of the bed. He removed the sheets with his free hand, rolling them into a ball. He tossed the pillow and the sheets aside. Then he slid the mattress off, an inch at a time, while listening for noises from the other room. Always listening.

The box springs were next. It was difficult to clear it from the bed frame with one hand, without making a sound, but he managed in about eight minutes to get it out and upright. Then he leaned it gently against the wall.

Finally, he kneeled inside the frame and felt the rigidity of the connection he'd checked. The nuts were tighter than he'd expected. For an instant he panicked–his fingers didn't make a good substitute for pliers. But with a strain that bruised and cut his forefinger and thumb, he managed to loosen them. After that, a simple jerk on each side lifted the bars away.

He used the pillow to shield the sound.

The frame was free.

He lifted the head piece carefully, estimating it weighed about fifty pounds. This molded metal ribbing was bulky too, and long. It would be difficult to maneuver it out the door and along the hall. Then there was the sharp curve he'd need to take in order to get into the living room. At any point, if he slipped or bumped something, Sominski might wake up. And Dave had claimed to be a light sleeper.

He sucked the blood on his finger, then put his hand on the doorknob, and turned slowly. He kept the little finger of his right hand between the handcuff and the frame's bar.

The door whispered open.

Calvin listened for the sound of breathing, hoping for a slow and regular inhalation and exhalation. There was nothing. The hall was dead. The house was dead. Every creak would be loud, every scrape like fingernails down a blackboard.

He waited for the air conditioner to come on again, and then lifted the head frame and took his first step forward. Then a second. The frame cleared the door by less than an inch, even with his stomach sucked in. Luckily there were no pictures on the walls of the hallway. It was relatively smooth, although he feared to touch it, much less slide along it. He moved agonizingly slowly, wary of every minute sound, wary even of the kitchen clock, which couldn't keep up with his heart. Suddenly, halfway down the hall, the air conditioner cut off and he stopped.

What was that?

He heard it, now. Faintly. Sominski's breathing. Very shallow. Not slow, but not fast either.

Was he awake? Was he waiting?

No, he couldn't be. But it wouldn't take much to wake him up. A sneeze would do it. A bump. The phone ringing. A dog barking. Or even a wasted driver taking the turn onto Treat Avenue a little too fast.

And what are you dreaming about, Dave? he thought. Are you at Fleshdance with your head between Tonya's towers? Are you at some base PX, buying hot dogs, while I'm over in 'Nam dodging bullets? Or are you in a mine shaft near Total Wreck, loading ore cars into the elevator ..?

After an eternity, the air conditioner came on again. He lifted the head frame and stepped closer to the turn. A slight creak in the floor–not from the wood, but from the carpet. He waited: nothing. Just the fan and compressor. The wheezing sound he'd grown used to, and knew that Dave had not.

When he finally got to the turn, he realized that the frame would be seen first. If there was movement now, he would have to blunder in somehow and try to rush Dave before he could get to the gun–pin him with the frame before he could fire.

Unless the gun rested in his lap.

Unless Dave's forefinger was already on the trigger.

Or unless he got stuck in the turn.

He placed the front of the head frame perilously close to the wall beside the bathroom door; it was in view of the couch, now. He strained as far forward as he could, but still he couldn't see anything except the distant moonlight streaming through the slats in the front mini-blinds. Craning his neck farther, he glimpsed Dave's foot. Pointing up. Which meant Dave was on his back, not on his stomach as Calvin had hoped.

As he watched, the foot moved. A jerky movement to one side, like a tic. As if something had happened in his dream. Something bad.

Calvin slid the head frame forward. It was the only way, now. Sliding and then touching and then finally scraping the back wall. Quicker and quicker.

Screeee ...

He was going to make it. It would be tight, but it would fit. After all, how had it gotten inside in the first place? He almost laughed as he pulled free.

Dave opened his eyes. But it was too late now.

Pulling free, Calvin lifted the frame and turned it. Before Dave could reach for the .45 on the coffee table, Calvin came down on top of him and then fell on top of the frame. Dave screamed as his forearm snapped, caught between the couch and the table. Calvin punched him again and again through the metal bars of the frame until Dave's front teeth were gone and his bottom teeth had splayed into a sepulchral grin.

Dave was breathing heavily at last. A sucking sound. A gurgling sound.

He felt into Dave's pockets for the cuff key, found it, and then released his left hand from the restraints. As he rubbed his wrist Dave said nothing, just stared up at him with his new grin–a grin that would require stitches. The eyes, though, were definitely readable. Fear was the key.

Calvin leaned back, took the .45, and then got up.

Dave lay there, the frame still on top of him, not moving.

Waiting for the end.

"Well, well," Calvin said at last. "You are a light sleeper, aren't you? You shoulda listened to me, buddy. Now I'm gonna have to take you out to the desert, to this place I found. You're really gonna get a kick out of it, too. It's an old missile silo, been abandoned and gutted for years. But it's nice and cool down there below, although it'll be pretty dark for you. Not to worry, though, I'll bring you bread and water every now and then. Until you decide you want to confess."

He reached with one hand to pull the frame off Sominski, keeping the .45 aimed at Sominski's face with the other. "Sorry about this, Davy boy, but you know it's nothing personal."

He swung the butt of the gun down hard onto Dave's head.

Amazingly, it took three times to do the trick.

15

When Maria came out of the treatment room, Vic rose from his seat and stared at the bandage which covered her right eye.

"Is it going to be all right?" he asked.

She tried to smile. "They think so. You don't look so good yourself, with that gauze on your cheek. Will your cut leave a scar?"

Vic shook his head, touched by her concern, considering. "Well, maybe. Twelve stitches. Let's get out of here; we look like a couple of war victims."

"Yeah, you shouldn't have punched me like that, darling, and I wouldn't have had to scratch you with my long nails."

They left the Tucson Medical Center. Vic drove her to the nearest Taco Bell for a breakfast burrito. "I assume you haven't eaten anything," he said.

"No. I just hope they've got some strong coffee. I didn't get much sleep." He started to park, then entered the drive-thru, instead. "Good idea," she said. "No point in being ogled."

While waiting, he handed her the newspaper from the back seat.

"Did we make the news?" she asked. He nodded, but didn't smile. "So how is our wonderful Mr. Manetti doing, anyway?"

"Physically or mentally?"

"That bad, huh?"

"Worse. He made the mistake of heading the search and arrest, so he gets the blame for what happened, too."

"Better him than us."

"Yeah. But I'm sure there'll be enough to go around."

As he took their order, Vic stared down the checkout girl. "Its okay, now," he confessed. "We've made up."

The checkout girl smiled. "Have a nice day," she said.

Maria opened the paper and lifted it in defense, and focused her good eye on the headline:

BOTCHED BOMBER ARREST
KILLS TWO POLICEMEN

"There's more," Vic said. "The editor-in-chief got a letter from our fugitive, Mr. Sominski, just in time for the early edition. They printed it, too."

Maria scanned the page. "Where?"

He took the paper back, and turned the page. "Here–let me read it to you. It says, 'Dear Editor ...'"

"I can read, teacher," Maria said. "You just drive."

Maria read silently.

Too many people are abusing the system, so I have taken action to slow things down in the hope that others will also take whatever steps they can. STOP THE FRAUD. FIGHT THE SOCIALIST POWER GRABBERS AT THE BALLOT BOX BEFORE IT S TOO LATE!

Otherwise we will continue to lose more freedoms as we have been, one by one.

I am not a "nut case." I am not a "radical right wing kook" as you will want people to believe. I am a FREEDOM FIGHTER, and you should join me. If you do not join me, and if you do not print this letter, I will continue to give you occasional wake-up calls until you do. For it is time to end the prejudice against the workers and the producers which made this country great. It is time to stop the racism and hatred against white males who just want to live in peace without being blamed for things they have no responsibility for.

It is time to deport the illegals and to stop financing the leeches who would only buy more drugs and have more babies. I am not to blame for all the rotten parents who would end us all in crime and famine and poverty. Everyone should be responsible for themselves, and if they are not, then I say to hell with them! GIVE ME LIBERTY OR GIVE ME DEATH!

—A TRUE American (with no quotations!)

"I'm thinking maybe you were right before, about Sominski. Somehow I can't see him writing this letter. The grammar, the sentences. Something about it. It doesn't fit his style."

"He is a little rough around the edges in person, isn't he? But he might have carefully composed the letter. Taken his time with it. Wasn't a typewriter found in his apartment?"

"It was typewritten," Vic added, when she'd finished. "The envelope was printed in block letters."

"Can we get the originals?"

"I don't know. I don't know if we're in charge anymore, either. I called Maxwell this morning, and he said he's sending two special inspectors from Washington. It's not clear whether they're supposed to help us or replace us."

Maria seemed startled. "He didn't say?"

"Not really. He kept asking about our injuries, and I told him I was fine."

"But not me."

"I didn't know what to say. He suggested pulling two inspectors out of Phoenix, and then he said he'd be sending two more."

"To head things up?"

"I don't think he used that phrase. So I assume we're not off the case unless we need to be. Is Maxwell our boss, anyway? Can he do this?"

Maria shrugged. "Technically, no. In actuality, yes. At least he's in charge in a case like this, with the press on his back. We'll have to wait and see."

"Can we afford to wait, though, with Sominski on the loose?"

Maria felt her eye patch. "I didn't mean that. Are you kidding? We need to put security on red alert. No one in or out of the plant without an ID badge and a search. I mean everything, too. Lunch boxes, thermos bottles, purses ..."

"Phone books?"

"Especially phone books. We'll get the plant manager–Matuska–to see to it. And the station managers at the stations. Anyone complains to the union and we haul out the agreement every one of them signed when they first got their postal jobs. Searches can be made on postal property, anytime, anywhere. We'll bring in dogs if we have to. We've done it many times before, looking for drugs."

Vic nodded. "Matuska is already alerted. I talked to him first thing this morning."

"You did?" Maria focused her good eye on him. "I guess you think your probationary training is over, huh?"

"Hope springs eternal, as they say."

Maria looked back through the windshield as they approached the cordoned-off P&DC. "It's going to be a rough week for the Postal Service, and we'll have to keep our three eyes open. Your two and my Cyclops." She winked at him, beautiful and confident even now.

"I'm glad it's not just my two eyes," he admitted. "I don't know if I could handle it without you."

"It's nice of you to say so, anyway."

"It's the truth." He took her hand and squeezed it. He felt her squeeze his fingers back, and smiled. Then a patrolman appeared at the employee gate, and he had to show his inspector's badge to get in, so their hand-holding went on hold.

Agent Delany was waiting for them in their office.

"How did you get in here?" Maria asked the G-man. "This door is always locked."

Delany smiled briefly. "I didn't know when you'd be showing up. Here's the deal. I've taken the letter and envelope the perpetrator wrote to the local FBI lab, and–"

"You got it from the paper? The originals?"

Delany smiled again. "And they should render a report by this afternoon. The base commander reports that no C-four ordnance is missing, although there is a discrepancy in one of the chemicals Hughes Missile Systems have stockpiled ... which might be used to make the explosive. I've rechecked police bomb squad practice stockpiles too, and they check out. Oh, and the KGUN and KVOA news teams called for an interview, which I declined for you." Delaney paused. "And your wife called too, Mr. Kazy."

"My wife?" Vic asked, exchanging glances with Maria.

"Wants to know if you're all right. I said yes, you were. But she insisted you call her anyway."

"Thanks, Frank. Thanks a lot."

The FBI man's smile broadened. "Now, if you'll excuse me, I'd like to start arranging personnel files so I can start interviewing employees. I've taken the liberty of setting up room eight-twelve, where I'd like the opportunity to ask each employee a few questions as they report for duty."

"What are you looking for–a conspiracy?"

"Perhaps. Perhaps not. One never knows. One can only watch and listen."

"You're right, of course," Maria told him. "It has to be done. I was going to recommend Detective Manetti do it, with Victor sitting in. But it's a very time consuming thing, and I imagine the Tucson PD are expending most of their time trying to find our Mr. Sominski. I could help, I suppose, but how would it look–me with this eye patch? I look like Patch the Pirate. From Disneyland."

Delany left the room, the unusual smile still on his face

Vic took a seat at McDade's desk."So you want me to help him? Sounds like it'll take days, if we're talking about everybody."

Maria nodded, and began pacing. "While you're doing that, I need to visit the stations and check security."

"Can you drive, though?"

"I can manage. I'll call Phoenix for help, too."

"I already have," Vic said. "Barnard is sending Brown and Weaver from Glendale."

"Where is Phil?"

"You're asking *me*?"

Maria chuckled, then checked her watch. "You've got a few hours before a floor crew comes on. Maybe you better go see your wife."

"Whaddaya mean, *see* her?"

"She's in Sun City, right? On the way back you can stop at Casas Adobes station for me."

"Really, I mean I ... we're not seeing each other."

"She called, didn't she? If I were her, I'd want to see you."

But you're not her, he thought, *thank God*.

"Besides," Maria added, "I need you out of here so I can call Carl in Phoenix."

"Oh." His heart sank. "He didn't call *you*, though, did he?"

Maria stopped pacing, and stood at the window looking down. "Carl is very busy. There's also a chance he hasn't heard; we don't know what was in the news in Phoenix about this." Maria turned. "I know what you think, and maybe you're right. I should call my mother in San Diego, anyway. Tell her about our bomber."

He stood to his feet, and checked his watch. "I'll be back in two hours–tell Delany. I'll stop by Casas Adobes branch on the way. You want me to bring you back some lunch?"

"I better not risk it," Maria replied. "Nothing personal, but it's those mom and pop places I fear, and I don't need to revisit the hospital right now."

They avoided each other's gaze this time.

***

Sun City was a world to itself. A gated community laid out in the middle of the desert northwest of the city. Driving in, Vic was observed by the gatehouse attendant, who marked down his license number for the records, just in case.

The houses were all new, and all made of identical materials, which included tons of stucco and red tile. Only the floor plans and number of bedrooms lent distinction to their pink exteriors. Landscaping wasn't exactly desert kitsch, but it too was uniform and low maintenance. Gravel lawns with barrel cactus, saguaro, desert spoon, Palo Verde. Air conditioning was standard. There were few swamp coolers because the residents who lived here didn't need to pinch pennies on their power bills. If they got senior citizens discounts at stores in town, it wasn't because they needed to. Sun City homes started as low as a hundred grand, the sign said, but the community also boasted its own private shopping center, bank, and restaurants. Not to mention the golf and tennis club, the clinic, the bowling alley, and the spa and health club, where Karen worked.

He found a space marked VISITORS at the clubhouse, not MEMBERS ONLY like the others. The receptionist behind the desk wasn't a cream-cheeked teenager; she was a deeply tanned collection of sinews and wrinkles, and while she might inspire members to emulate her shape, she wouldn't be flaunting her age. She was sixty at least, Vic guessed. Maybe seventy.

"Can you tell me where Karen Kazy is?" he asked her.

The receptionist frowned. "I don't believe I know her, sir. Where does she work?"

"Here. I mean as an aerobics instructor, among other things. Water aerobics."

"Karen Burrows, you mean?" She bit her lip. "Oh, I'm sorry. You must be her ... I mean ..."

"It's okay," Vic said. "Is she around?"

The receptionist pointed. "Out by the pool, I believe. Her workout class should be over by now."

"Thank you."

So Karen had already relinquished her name. That meant it was really over. He wondered if she'd even thought about it, or if it had been a natural progression from moving back in with her mother and separating from her hazard-loving husband. Out of sight, out of mind. Had she forgotten her married name already? Or had she never thought of herself as a Kazy to begin with?

He found Karen laughing with a virile-looking man in his late fifties. Plenty of dark chest hair, otherwise the man was bald. Vic watched them surreptitiously from inside the glass doors that led out to the pool area. Karen and the possible former Mr. Universe sat at the edge of the Jacuzzi in the blazing sun. Both of their bathing suits were wet, and others were toweling off, so her class had probably just ended. He waited for Karen to get up, to stop talking and laughing, but it only continued. And when she looked away, Mr. Muscles took the opportunity to stare at her bust, except she didn't look away often: she admired his physique, too. A widower, perhaps? Plenty of secure, income-based mutual funds? No doubt he was telling her all about it.

Vic slid open the French doors and stepped out of the shadows into the heat. Karen looked up as he approached, and put a hand up to her forehead to block the sun.

"Victor," she said, in surprise. "What are you doing here?"

Mr. Bald Universe looked away as if irritated at his presence.

"Well," Vic replied matter-of-factly, "when my wife calls I usually come running, don't I?"

Karen didn't smile. "Victor, this is Matt. He's ... one of my students."

The big man lifted a hairy fist, dutifully. "Matt Devons," he said.

Vic shook the hand when it opened. The grip was absent. It was like shaking a dead fish. "Pleased," Vic said. *Thrilled*, he thought.

"Victor is a postal inspector," Karen said, with just a trace of sarcasm. "He's got a bandage on his cheek because he nearly got blown up yesterday, and it made the paper."

"Yeah, it happens all the time," Vic said, and flashed a cheap grin. "Can I, ah, talk to you for a minute, Karen?"

Karen stood. "Excuse us, Matt," she said. "I'll be right back."

She passed him on the way inside. Vic turned in time to see Devons checking out the way her pear-shaped butt moved as she walked. Not only wasn't Karen's relative youth bothering old Matt any, but he stared for a full two seconds after Vic caught him. Then, finally, he looked away.

"A little old for you, isn't he?" Vic asked her in the safety of the clubhouse. "I half-expected to lose you to some young brainless stud driving a red Corvette, but I didn't expect you'd fall for some member of the geriatric set."

Karen gave a short chuckle the same way she always did when they argued. "Matt is my student. Drives a Park Avenue. He's also a nice man."

"Nice and quick, you mean. And with a sharp eye, I might add."

"Like you don't have one of those."

"He wants to be your teacher too, I bet."

"I don't discriminate because of age."

"No, but you discriminated against using my name. I asked for Karen Kazy and they didn't know who I was talking about."

Karen sighed. "Look, Vic. Maybe it's just as well. Maybe it's time to end it and move on."

"You mean like get on with our lives? I hate that phrase. Sounds like life is some program. Like you can plan it to work out just the way you always read about in those women's magazines."

"We didn't plan any of this to happen, Vic. It just did. Now it's different. It's just not the same as it was. That's all I'm saying."

He looked into her eyes. She held his gaze for a moment, then looked back out the window–back at the few people braving the heat to sit beside the huge and sparkling pool. "Are you really happy here?" he asked.

She nodded, once.

"Then I guess there's nothing else to say, is there?"

"I guess not."

"We can get an uncontested divorce in Phoenix. Should be easy with no kids and no property to speak of."

"Yeah. Easy."

"Thanks for asking about my injury. It's nothing, really. It'll heal."

"Given time," she added.

"Yes, given time," he said as he turned to leave.

"Good luck with your new job, Vic," Karen told him.

On the way out of the building he walked past the staring receptionist, who almost started to speak. Two smiling retirees approached the door then, and he held it open for them. "Thank you," the old man said, beaming.

He accidentally dropped his keys beside his car while fishing them out of his pocket. He stood there and just stared down at them. The apartment key for their Pelham Court apartment in Greenville was there. The duplicate he'd asked for, and forgotten to turn in. He picked the keys up, slowly, and looked back at the clubhouse sign–SUN CLUB.

How strange, that it had come to this. He felt an almost paralyzing awe, as if the next question should be: *And who are we now?* Except that it wouldn't be asked, at least not by Karen. Because she was already getting on with her life, and getting on meant accepting all the little deaths that life had to offer. Just like this one. Maybe even the final death–the Big One–would be accepted too, when it happened.

He asked directions to the Casas Adobes station at the gate house. Then he drove there, made his inspection, and warned the station manager to check all employees upon entering. He tried not to think about the possibility of death, but that was impossible now, considering the previous twenty-four hours. Impossible as well because it was now his job to think about it. To risk it. Just as it was Karen's job not to.

Out of sight, out of mind?

He wondered where Sominski was–and if the bomber struck again, who might die.

16

A pounding sound coming from the trunk began just south of I-10 and continued for another ten minutes along 83 to the turnoff of the Old Sonoita Highway. When the road turned to dirt, the pounding stopped and a moaning took its place. Calvin ignored that, too. They were already well outside of Tucson into what the ranchers called "big sky country," and the barren Empire Mountains already loomed from the desert ahead. In another twenty minutes they'd be at the site of that so aptly named ghost town, Total Wreck.

When a jeep passed, going the other direction, Calvin rolled up his window against the blowing dust, and turned on Dave's air conditioner. He knew the cool air wouldn't reach the tight trunk compartment where Dave was probably suffocating by now, but that, he reckoned, was the fortunes of war. At least he didn't have to worry about some highway patrolman pulling them over. Not only didn't he resemble Dave, but he'd managed to switch plates with another Mustang he'd found in an apartment parking lot while Dave was handcuffed to the drain pipe beneath his kitchen sink. The plan now was simple. Stash Dave away for a while in a nice safe place. Ditch Dave's car where it wouldn't be found, even by helicopter. Then hitchhike back to town from Highway 83–a ribbon of asphalt only a mile or so across the desert, due west of where he was headed.

No problemo.

At the third turnoff the moaning got louder as the road got rougher. But the sound was soon eclipsed by the staccato *carummph* of the Mustang's tires bumping the wheel wells, and the scraping sound of the carriage bottoming out, as he took the rutted and rocky trail that led across the wastes. A startled coyote darted in front, its head low, making for a tendril patch of cholla cactus. A Cooper's hawk drifted down from overhead, attracted by the rattling sound the muffler made as it dragged the ground. After another ten minutes the muffler and exhaust pipe, fittings and all, fell off.

"Hey, hey," Calvin said, with a laugh. "They don't make 'em like they used to."

Near the old town site he found what he was looking for: a large Palo Verde tree in a dry, sandy stream bed. He turned the steering wheel toward it, and then floorboarded it. The Mustang left the trail, shot through a thicket of mesquite, blundered over a boulder the size of a desk, and turned on its side to crash into the sand eight feet below.

"Heeeeeee–hawwww!" Calvin yelled as the right front tire exploded on impact.

The engine raced, and began to smoke. Steam boiled from the radiator. He turned the key to OFF, and quickly released his seat belt. Then he climbed out.

"How ya doing in there, Davy?" he asked, after the sizzling sound died.

There was no reply. Silence had returned to the desert.

He opened the trunk, pulling at the bent lid.

Dave was bleeding again. His bandages had come loose, and his eyes fluttered spasmodically above the gag. Sweat drenched his clothes.

"You dumb Pollock," Calvin chided him. "Don't you know better than to drive from behind the back seat? And handcuffed like that, no less. My God, man." He pulled Dave out, dumping him on the sand. "Look. There was water and supplies back here with you, too. Is there no limit to your stupidity?"

He took off Dave's gag, and then opened the lid of a five-gallon Army surplus water canister. He tilted the canister to pour water on

Dave's head, then into his open mouth. He continued pouring until the shattered mouth closed.

"Sorry we couldn't visit the dentist there, old buddy. No time for it. You can always get dentures later, once you sign your confession. A mechanical arm too, if it comes to that. In the meantime, let's get you outta this heat. I know a nice cool place that's just the ticket."

He tried pulling Dave to his feet by the cuffs, but Dave only blacked out and slumped to the hot sand. He tried it again after pouring more water in his face to wake him up, but Dave's knees seemed made of jello.

"Good Lord. Am I gonna have to drag you all the way? Okay, then. Climb on my back. I'll come back for the water later."

He pulled Dave up again with the other arm, and leaned over. Dave fell across his back, only half-conscious.

"Damn, you're light as a feather! How do you manage to drink so much and stay so thin, anyway?" As an afterthought, he bent to pick up the water canister, too. "Hell, why not? May get thirsty myself before I make it back."

Getting out of the stream bed was difficult with the load, but he managed to bull his way up the rocky slope. Dave wheezed with his every step, breathing shallowly by comparison. Exhausted, Calvin set down the water on the trail, then kept walking.

"Whew! Guess you ain't so light after all, buddy. Never underestimate the desert, they say, but I'll be back shortly. After I rest. Ain't too far from here, now."

The ghost town of Total Wreck waited for them a mile to the south of the trail, at the intersection of two low hills. There was a skeleton of buildings left, but what else was there seemed a total wreck: heaps of blackened boards; shards of adobe brick; an excavated depression in one of the hillsides where the mill had once operated; scattered and rusted rivets. A mine shaft too, which had since been plugged with the carcass of what looked like, by its narrow rear windows, a 1940 Ford. Somewhere to the left lay the cemetery Calvin had found. Only one of the graves was marked by anything more than a pile of stones or a long-rotted cross. He remembered what the stone had read:

EMIL BOSTROM
1841–1884

He smiled in the blazing heat, and trudged on, thinking: *I might have lived here, Dad. Or I might have been your grandfather. It's possible, anyway, isn't it? Now, if only I could go back to then–to the way it was. Find my fortune on the frontier, in the wild west. When men were free, and the law was maintained by a gun and a rope. Because men were equal then, Dad. Free to do and be anything they wanted. Anything they could. They'd laugh at us now, Curly Bill, Johnnie Ringo. Even Wyatt. They wouldn't understand how we can live like this, or how it's come to this.*

At the edge of town, or so he guessed, he stopped and turned for a final moment.

God's cursed me, Dad, placing me here instead of there and then. If only I could go back. If only it was really true that I was him. Even if I didn't find the silver vein, and the Indians got me. Or if I fell into a mine shaft. At least I would have felt alive. At least I would have had my chance. Now all that's left is the lottery, and they have you wait in line at some convenience store for a ghost of a chance. Then, if lightning strikes, you got to pay half to Uncle Sam because they want you to be fair about it. But I'm sick of playing fair, Dad. Aren't you?

Dave suddenly wheezed and sucked air. Calvin walked on, more determined now. The frustration was real–the only real thing left, besides the anger.

Don't get mad, Son, a voice inside him said, *get even.*

He came to the fence at last. The barbed wire was high, but there was a broken post and a few loose strands sufficient to bend away and squeeze through, just like last time. He laid Dave across the top strand and rolled him over. Dave fell heavily, with a thick blubbering moan, ripping his shirt. Then Calvin looked up at the sign before squeezing through:

POSTED: KEEP OUT
MILITARY FACILITY
TRESPASSERS WILL BE PROSECUTED

"Yeah, right," he said. "The nearest coyote will turn me in."

He picked Dave up again and approached the base, or rather the shell of it. Faded tire tracks surrounded a level, twenty-foot square of concrete in the middle of the clearing ahead. In the center of the square was a square hole. In the distance, along the perimeter of the clearing, were three round slabs of concrete ten feet across, covering the missile silos themselves.

He laid Dave beside the hole atop the control room bunker. Dave groaned and then blinked up at him.

"Coming 'round at last, buddy? Arm hurt? You need a cast for it, you know, but I guess that wrap I made will have to do for now. Think you can make it down the ladder, there?"

Dave turned his head. His swollen lips moved, but no words came out. Calvin peered over the edge, down at the three-foot-thick steel door thirty feet below. It was still open.

"We're in luck, buddy. No one's disturbed the door. Not since they finished gutting the place. You're gonna love it down there, I'm telling you. Nice and cool, see, because you got ten feet of high-impact sand about you, outside eight-foot-thick steel-reinforced concrete walls. A jacket of steel inside that, too. No need to worry about earthquakes or the like, either. Rooms are suspended on giant springs. Someone drops an H-bomb right on your head you might be in trouble, but short of that, no. They built this place at a cost of millions to fight the cold war, buddy. It's obsolete today, of course. Been abandoned since the mid-'seventies, along with six or seven other bases just like it. They made a museum out of one of 'em, you know, over in Green Valley. This one here is ours. For our own little war, you might say. You ready?"

Dave's lips curled again, and this time he managed to form a word. Calvin crouched down beside him to hear the word repeated.

"Crazy? You think I'm a lunatic, buddy? If you want to believe that, go right ahead. But it won't get you anywhere. At least not out of here." He hoisted Dave to the edge of the pit, took off his handcuffs, and then pulled his foot to the first rung of the ladder. "Yeah, it's rough out here in the real world, once you lose your postal job. Guess you're just finding that out, huh?"

He pushed Dave from behind. Dave tried to grab his leg, but he kicked the hand aside. Once on the ladder, Dave's knees wobbled; he pinwheeled for balance.

"Careful there, buddy."

Just in time, Dave gripped a metal rung near the opening. It had a pulley attached to it, which swung back and forth. He regained his composure, then slowly started down, one rung at a time, hugging the ladder as he went. His strain and terror were unmistakable. Calvin smiled.

"Let me know if there's any rattlers down there, okay? I thought I heard a noise sounded like a bunch of 'em."

At the bottom at last, Dave slumped to the floor. And Calvin began to pull the heavy ladder up.

"N-n-nooo ..." Sominski moaned.

"What's that, buddy? Don't want me to leave you here? Don't worry. I'm just gonna go get the supplies you'll need." As an afterthought he lowered the ladder again, instead. "On second thought, I don't think you got the strength to climb out of here, do you? Besides, where would you go without water, right? So you just wait right there, and you think about how you're gonna word the confession letter, so it sounds real convincing in case you ever think about implicating me from Mexico in any of this sick, twisted revenge of yours. Hold on, now, while I go get some stationery."

Back at the Mustang, he collected the canvas sack containing the chain, the rope, the flashlight, the pen and stationery, along with the groceries. He wiped his fingerprints off the steering wheel and trunk with a rag, just in case. Then he collected the water canister, and on the way back through town nodded at the ladies, said, "Howdy, Marshall," and shooed an imaginary dog out of the way.

Dave was waiting at the bottom of the "mine shaft" that Calvin imagined, laid out on his back and holding his broken arm. Dave stared up at him as he slid the rope through the pulley.

"You woulda let me ... fall an' die ... wouldn't ya?" Dave finally said, thickly.

"Well, well. Our crazed bomber speaks." Calvin grinned. "Voice sounds different, though. I wonder why?"

"Because yer a bastard."

"*Moi?* Last time I checked it's you they're hunting. Probably in Utah, California, and New Mexico, too, by now."

He lowered the water canister to the concrete floor below. Then he tied the canvas sack containing the other items to the other end of the rope, and lowered it, too. It went almost half way down on the fifty-foot inch-thick nylon.

Finally, he started down the ladder himself.

"What ya gonna do?" Dave asked him. "Keep blowin' up post offices? That the plan?"

"Maybe, maybe not. Maybe I won't have to. Maybe other people will begin doing it for me. Start by blowing up that ATM entitlement card manufacturer and a few Affirmative Action offices. Finish by voting the remaining bastards out of office. The ones who block every budget cut."

"Don't count on it, Fireplug."

Calvin reached the bottom, and pulled down the canvas bag to retrieve the flashlight. "Oh, I haven't quite given up on you yet, old buddy," he said. "You might just need a little lesson about the birds and the killer bees. After that, who knows–you might be begging to join my special force, and making special deliveries on your own." He gestured toward the opening beyond. "Now, you want to hobble in there on your own power, or am I gonna have to carry you across the threshold, darling?"

Sominski continued to lay there, motionless, staring up at the sky as if at a fading light at the end of a tunnel.

"What–you don't think you'll get out of here alive? Think this'll be your tomb?" He reached for Dave's broken forearm. "Up we go."

Sominski jerked away. "Don't touch me, ya faggot."

"Oh! So you think I'm gay, now. Or maybe you thought it all along."

Dave grunted, his eyes narrowing below the purple bruises on his forehead. "Ain't it true?"

"No, Davy, you poor boy. I'm afraid, for you, it's not. What it is,

I'm impotent. Can't get it up. Not for years now. Can't jack off like you do, either. And most of all, I can't make babies. So I'm a useless son of a bitch, ain't I? You want to crack some jokes about that now?"

"I don't believe you."

Calvin adjusted his glasses. "No? You ever had diabetes? You ever had one of your gonads removed?"

"Yer lying. Why wouldn't ya have told me before?"

"You said we were never really friends, didn't you? Look around you, now. Maybe what you said was true."

Calvin grabbed Sominski's fractured arm, and pulled. Sominski screamed, and struggled to his feet. The screaming went on through the dark opening, past the steel door, and into the musty-smelling interior of the Titan crew quarters. When Calvin finally released the arm to turn on the flashlight, Dave started making his old blubbering sounds again–the air sucking through the holes between his shattered teeth. It gave Calvin time to retrieve the canvas sack.

"Look at this," he said on returning, and shined the beam around the room. "They took out the bunk beds, but they left the latrines. No water anymore, of course, so you won't be able to flush. But hell, you'll get used to the smell after a while."

"What ... do you want ..?"

"I told you what."

Dave's eyes widened just above the flashlight beam. "Then ... ya gonna jus' *leave* me here?"

17

"I'll be back," Calvin told him.

"When?"

"When you agree to write that letter. See, I already got a way to pre-cancel the envelope. I work at the post office, remember? You will have mailed it yesterday morning, before the little fiasco at your house." He shined the light directly into Dave's eyes. "By the way, are you left- or right-handed?"

"Right ... I mean left."

"Right. Good. So your handwriting shouldn't suffer."

"I won't do it ... won't let you get away with this."

"You have no choice. Otherwise, I break your neck."

"How would that look?"

"Bad, for you." Calvin laughed. "There's another tunnel over there leads to a staircase and down to the control room. When they took out the fixtures and control panels they left some big holes in the floor. Some of 'em drop a good twenty feet. Down there where the generator used to be, that's where they'd find your skeleton. With its broken neck. As for me, who's gonna suspect me of anything? I've always kept my nose clean, paid my taxes, been a fine upstanding citizen."

"'Til now."

"Even now. Not even a traffic ticket on my record. I served in

'Nam too, got me a Purple Heart trying to save my buddy Kyle. Then later Kyle got liver cancer. Tried to link it to Agent Orange, but the VA didn't want to hear about it at the time. Died on morphine."

"Ya never told me ..."

"I'm telling you now. You didn't seem to care, before. You were too busy chasing women like everybody else. It's all you ever wanted to talk about."

Sominski sucked in another breath like he was taking a drag on a final cigarette. "What about you an' Gail?"

Calvin chuckled. "Bitch wanted to get married and have babies, like they all do. As they say, what's love got to do with it? Nothing. They all read romance novels and watch soap operas like the welfare mommas do, settling for some wimp in the end ... unless some knight in shining shark skin comes along. But it's all an illusion, isn't it? Love's not just blind, it doesn't exist. Not anymore. It's all about sex now. Sex is the biggest drug there is, buddy. And love's just another needle to stick it to you."

"Thass ... you ..."

"You oughta try impotence sometime. Your eyes will open. You'll see it, like a revelation. People OD'ing everywhere. Sex and babies. Sex and violence. It's a setup from hell. Men like you screwing teen girls at every opportunity, and all the unwed mothers screwing the taxpayers so they have to support their little shit-meisters from cradle to grave."

"They don't–"

"Don't they? You got no kids, Dave, but you're a homeowner–paying, anyway. What if National Health Care comes back, and National Day Care? Pay up, Davy. Then watch the punks grow up to join gangs that require them to break into your house. Watch 'em end up in jail or in politics ... as liberal Democrats. I'm telling you, World War Three could be going on, and all the bitches would still be talking about having more of the brats and having you pay for them. Only way to stop it is to drop a bomb on their heads, which is one of the things I'm thinking about convincing them is gonna happen. An H-bomb, from right here."

Dave sneered. "Right ..."

"Think I'm kidding? What if the government forgot to take out one of these missiles? What if the ones who know the truth can't convince the news anchor who gets a letter from me, with details of another explosion? They could come out here, but they'd never get that door open, if it's locked from inside. And I could make it look like there's been a lot of activity here."

"Yer one sick SOB, ain't ya?"

"They're animals just like you, Dave. All women. Size you up on how good a provider you are. For the nest. For the brood." He snapped his fingers. "Leave you just like that, once you ain't up to their agenda. Just like that."

He snapped his fingers again. Sominski laughed out loud. The laugh echoed in the metal room. Air sucked in over his teeth, and he laughed again.

"Shut up," Calvin told him.

But Dave wouldn't stop. The laughter got louder, more real. So Calvin hit the Pollock in the face. Sominski went to his knees, bleeding from his mouth again before the laughter finally stopped. "Get a fuckin' life, Calvin," he said. "Thass what ya really need ... a fuckin' life." He squinted up into the flashlight beam with a twisted and bloody grin. "Yer pathetic. They all thought so. Every damn clerk on the fuckin' LSM. And now yer gonna make 'em pay, ain't ya?"

Calvin smiled in the dark. "Making other people pay ... isn't that what it's all about?" His smile widened, but Sominski couldn't see. "They don't know it yet, but they're ducks in a shooting gallery."

"But you ... yer not William Tell, Fireplug. Yer the fuckin' bad apple with the worm inside it."

"Whatever works for you, buddy. Whatever works."

Calvin opened the canvas sack at his feet, and took out the chain. Sominski lost all trace of his grin.

"Yer not serious ..?"

"Hey, I can't have you wandering around when I'm gone, looking for something to use as a weapon. Besides, you might fall through that hole in the floor down there in the dark. Prematurely, I mean." He held up the chain, and rattled the shiny links in the flashlight's beam. "You gonna write that letter now, or do I put you on a short leash?"

Dave sucked air. "You'll kill me once I write it. Won't ya?"

"If I was gonna do that, I already would have. No. See, you're here so I could try to convince you to join the war as my General."

"Don't ya mean Field Marshall, *Herr Fuhrer*?"

"Academic now. You're a lost cause. Wanna be a victim like everybody else. Actually, I'm trying hard now to save your worthless life. Once you write the letter you can go free. Go down to Guadalajara or somewhere. Eat tacos and find some Mexican chick to make babies with. I'll even spot you a grand to get there and set up your little love nest."

"Whudabout my forty grand in savings?"

"Take it, too."

"What if I ain't got it outta the damn four-oh-one-K plan yet?"

"Then kiss it goodbye. Chalk it up to stupidity."

"Right."

"You see any other options here?"

"How 'bout ya turn yourself in, claim insanity, and get EAP counseling?"

Calvin laughed, and put the light under his chin to make a scary face. "You ready to compose that letter yet?"

Sominski wheezed, and tried to blow the blood in his nose onto his shirt. "Yeah," he announced, flatly. "I been thinkin' maybe it should read 'Dear Calvin, I blew up the PO, an' now I can't live with myself. Goodbye cruel world. David.' How's that sound?"

"You don't trust me much, do you?"

"Not as far as I can carry ya, Fireplug. Thing 'bout it is, why would ya hold that letter? Be like holdin' back evidence."

"Okay, ya got me. I was going to turn it in tonight."

"An' risk bein connected ta me? They'd be investigatin' you; maybe implicatin' ya, if they find somethin."

"There's nothing to find. Like I said, I'm clean. Unlike you."

"But what if somebody saw ya do somethin', or they recognized ya on TV?"

"I won't go on TV."

"How could ya prevent it? By bombing them? An' jus' where'd ya get the stuff to make the bombs in the first place?"

"I could tell you, but then I'd have to kill you. Wouldn't I?"

Dave nodded, thoughtfully. "What kinda guarantees I got you ain't plannin' to do that anyway?"

Calvin giggled. "Guarantees? You want guarantees, now? Sound just like a liberal. Think everything in life should be risk-free. Like you can create some kinda Socialist Utopia if only you can get those greedy rich bastards to pay everybody's insurance premiums." He rattled the chain again. "Make up your mind. Now. What'll it be?"

He shined the flashlight in Sominski's bruised face, waiting for an answer.

"Convince me, Calvin," Dave said, at last. "Lemme write the letter down at the border, in exchange fer the thousand bucks."

"No deal. It's here and it's now. I ain't gonna be seen with you."

Dave's eyes searched for him, rolling back and forth. "Ya won't have to. I could go over at Lochiel, jus' south a here. No border guards, no ID needed."

"Forget it. I'm on foot from here, anyway. It's thirty miles to the border, and it's the wrong direction."

Dave clamped shut his eyes briefly. He opened them to slits. "Then I guess I'll jus' have ta think about it, won't I? Come up with a better idea. 'Cause you ain't gonna believe me joinin' yer fag Army, are ya?"

"Not anymore." Calvin took out the handcuffs and slapped one end on Sominski's right wrist. "Yeah, you think it over real good," he said, and dragged him toward the wall. He threw the chain around a toilet, and then slid the other end of the handcuffs through both links to lock it down.

"Hey, wait a fuckin' minute," Dave complained. "Ya got more length ta this chain than that!"

Calvin shined the flashlight on the arrangement, then into Sominski's eyes. "You got room to sit on the crapper, don't you? What do you expect for not being fair with me–a reward?"

"Fuck you, Calvin!"

"Sorry, I can't do that anymore. But you can keep doing it to yourself, letting women and liberals dictate your life."

He cut off the flashlight, and walked toward the dim light down the tunnel at the threshold.

"Wait! What about the damn water? The food?"

Calvin ignored him. Once outside, he picked up the water canister, untied the knot, and then opened the cap. It was warm out here. It would be hotter than hell topside.

"Calvin!" the voice echoed from inside.

He lifted the canister to his lips, and drank until he could drink no more.

Half-full now. Maybe less. Maybe only two gallons. Sominski would need to conserve.

He took the canister back in and set it beside the man chained to the toilet. He shined the beam on the canvas sack over near the middle of the musty room. Far out of reach.

"Food's over there," he announced. "Help yourself. It's a buffet. No table service here, I'm afraid. But look on the bright side–there're no tips, either."

He shined the light back. Sominski was speechless. In shock.

He moved toward the door again, and cut the flashlight for the last time. "Oh, I forgot," he called back. "I guess there's no bright side in this for you. At least not until there's an attitude adjustment."

He pushed on the thick steel door from behind. Surprising, how easily it moved once the initial snap of frozen metal gave way. At the last moment, before the door clanged shut, he heard a scream. But the sound was cut off by three feet of heavy metal. The only sound now was the cry of a hawk somewhere above.

He pulled the rope free of its pulley, and slipped it through the door's handle, which he tied on either side to the twisted reinforcement rods protruding from the concrete. He ran the rope back through several times and made triple knots. Then he climbed the ladder, pulled it up and ran the sections together so it would be easier to hide. He used it to get over the fence, then carried it for at least a hundred yards until he found a suitable ravine.

Done. Now, with Dave out of the way, it was time to make it back for work. The postal service frowned on its employees being late.

***

The hike to 83 took longer than he'd anticipated, but he enjoyed the walk anyway. The desert was the best place to be, he'd long decided, because the tourists mostly stuck to the clichés of woods and lakes and beaches, their RVs rolling in formation from one honeycombed campsite to the next. Winnabagos had difficulty maneuvering down bumpy desert roads, thankfully. Without their microwave ovens, refrigerators, and satellite dishes, the RV zombies would feel insecure, disadvantaged. Of course, their spoiled children would whine anyway because there were no video arcades and pizza joints, just Game Boy cartridges to play with and roasted hot dogs to cook over the tiny metal box where they allowed you to build a safe little fire.

He was considering the idea that everyone was a tourist now, just going through the motions of living, when a pickup truck stopped in response to his thumb. The driver wore a cowboy hat, was a big muscular dude in boots, and had two kids with him. The kids even climbed into the back so he got to ride in the air conditioned cab.

"Threw a rod in my Chevy," Calvin explained. "Can you drop me at a garage somewhere in Tucson?"

"Sure thing. You want some water? There's a canteen under the seat."

"No thanks; I'll be fine."

They said little on the ride north toward I-10. Then suddenly the rancher asked, "You hear about the bomb went off at Tucson City Hall today?"

Calvin shook his head. "No, what ..?"

"Letter bomb. Killed the mayor."

"No shit."

"That's what I said."

"Anyone else hurt?"

"Just his secretary."

Calvin sighed. "What in the world are we coming to?"

18

"Where's Delany?" Vic asked Maria, who was standing by the window looking down at the news van below. "I checked room eight-twelve. Checked the head, too."

Maria turned. She seemed distraught. "There's been another explosion," she explained. "The mayor is dead."

"The mayor?"

"No accompanying letter with the package, unless it was incinerated in the blast. His secretary was going to open it, but it was time for her coffee break. The mayor passed her going in, declined a second cup. Went to his desk. Her back was to him when the thing went off. Knocked her out of her shoes. Hairline neck fracture and broken nose, among other things. Mayor's on a slab. *Two* slabs, actually."

"My God."

"Sominski must have mailed it yesterday or the day before."

"So you think he still has access to explosives?"

Maria appeared uncomfortable with the thought. "Seems likely. We won't know for sure until the police find him. So far they haven't spotted his car anywhere, even with the help of traffic helicopters. Delany did get called away on another lead, though. He heard from Hughes Missile Systems, out near the airport. Apparently they do have a shortage in their inventory of one of the chemicals which could be used to make plastique."

"But how would a postal clerk ..?"

"Who knows? Only thing for us to do now is to put Brown and Weaver on security. In the meantime, we stay insulated from those reporters and complaints, so we can do the interviews ourselves. You ready?"

Vic nodded. "You don't want something to eat before we start? Looks to be a long day."

Maria started collecting the Personnel files. "I'm afraid I've lost my appetite."

Vic helped her. "Did you reach your mother?"

"Yeah, I did. She's worried about me. I tried to reassure her, but it wasn't easy."

"I'll bet. What about Carl?"

"Not a word. Did you talk to your wife?"

"Ex-wife. It's just a formality, now. She's found Mr. Right, I think. A retired executive who looks like an older version of Bruce, this trucker she once had the hots for before we got married."

"I'm sorry."

"Don't be. Karen was never right for me, anyway." *Not like you are.* "Shouldn't you, ah, at least try to reach your friend?"

"Friend?" She looked at him, and for a moment he felt like biting his tongue. Then she brushed away a wave of dark hair hiding the patch on her left eye. "Carl and I are ... we're about finished too, and not just because of this. I guess I don't fit into his circles, and maybe I should stop pretending it'll work out. Who would want a one-eyed postal inspector, after all?"

I would, for one, Vic thought.

"Anyway, he's probably making it with his legal assistant or someone. He's surrounded by beautiful women at that office of his."

"Whoever he's surrounded by," Vic heard himself say, "the view is still nicer in here."

Maria smiled at the compliment, and touched her patch. "Even with this?"

"Even if you lost the eye, which you won't." *Why did he say that?* "You probably wouldn't want to date me again, though. Wake up with food poisoning. Or the hiccups at least." *Dumb.*

Maria laughed anyway.

Amazing, he thought. Karen would have looked confused or just stared.

They went to room 812 with the Personnel materials. Luckily, there were no windows in the room, so they wouldn't have to watch the line forming out of the front lobby below. The police and news media would be out of sight too, although not quite out of mind.

Maria poured water from a pitcher into two glasses. She slid one across the polished conference table to Vic's side. Then she looked up at the wall clock, picked up the phone, and asked Carole in Personnel to alert the first employee on the list. They waited as cool air blew down on them from the air conditioning ducts overhead.

The door opened momentarily, after a knock. An older man wearing a blue union shirt stepped into the room at Vic's motioning. He'd lost most of his hair, and what remained was white. He had a big belly, but looked otherwise fit, with the tattoo of an anchor half-hidden by the thick hair of his right forearm. His other arm was bound by elastic at the elbow. He smiled at the sight of Maria, but was taken aback when she turned and he finally glimpsed her eye patch. He slowly took a seat at her invitation.

"You're Mr. Chambers, is that right?" Maria asked the man, who now stared at them as if at Frankenstein and bride.

"Rudy," Chambers insisted, at last. "I'm dock manager. What's this all about? The explosion?"

"We were wondering," Maria said, nodding, "if you knew anything about that."

"What–ya mean if I saw anyone suspicious carrying a phone book?"

"Who told you it was a phone book?"

Chambers glanced between them, then chuckled. "I heard it on the news this morning. Channel Four."

Vic slid a photo across the table to him. The old man picked it up and studied it. "Ever seen him before?" Vic asked.

"Sure I have. He's worked on the LSM for years. Saw him on the news, too. Didn't know him, a course. What's his name?"

"David Sominski," Maria replied.

"A Pollock?"

"We don't use that term here."

"Why not? Ain't he the bomber? Ain't he a killer?"

"That might be true, but it has nothing to do with his ethnic background."

Chambers hid his smile unsuccessfully. "Sorry."

"We were wondering," Vic stressed, "if you remember seeing him any time after he was fired early last week."

Chambers shook his head slowly. "No, not me. 'Course I do a lotta paper work, mostly. I'm usually not one a the ones loading the trucks." He felt his left arm. "Got two years to retirement. Put in thirty, total. After the Navy."

Good for you, Vic thought. And me–*I got thirty to go. If anyone's that lucky.*

"Could Sominski have walked past you without your noticing him?"

"Possible. He was a fixture around here, wasn't he? You guys never checked ID badges much, either. What makes you think he came in through the dock, anyway?"

"It's possible, isn't it?"

"Oh sure. There's the bulk mail unit back there, and you got customers out back all the time. But there's a sign forbidding entrance to the plant itself. Be easier for this Polish guy to come in through the employee entrance, as usual."

"Without a badge for the gate?"

"I was gonna say, if someone let him in. You know, you hold the gate for someone behind you. Someone you recognize even if ya don't know their name."

"You ever done that, Rudy?" Maria asked.

"Me? Well, yeah. But I guess I won't anymore, will I? Not after Matuska laid down the law. Not after Arnie Huff ruptured a disk that time and got fired for coming back and taking a swing at Carter."

Maria rose. "Thanks for coming in," she said. "I trust you'll keep your eyes open for us?"

"Looks like you need help in that department. Sure, I will. By the way, you in on the lottery pool? Twenty million this week."

He moved to the door, and actually waved goodbye.

Maria picked up the phone and asked Carole to send in the next employee. "If they don't laugh at us," she told Vic as they waited, "it may mean there's a conspiracy, and they're in on the plot."

"I'll be on the lookout," Vic said.

Maria blinked at him, rapidly, a dozen times.

***

The interviewing continued all day and into the night, with breaks for dinner–consisting of Dominos pizza delivered through the Express mail unit to the inspector's office–and two interruptions from a stymied Delany and a beleaguered Graves. The news was not good on any front. No cause for the Hughes discrepancy could be found. The press still wanted answers no one had. And the flight on which Maxwell's special inspector was to arrive was canceled, requiring a rerouting through Indianapolis, Denver, and Phoenix. Inspectors Brown and Weaver arrived to assist in security at the stations, but they wouldn't be much help in investigations. By midnight, when the late shift came on for their twelve-hour tour, Sominski had still not been captured in the police dragnet, and the growing number of cages containing unworked mail had already begun filling the dock area.

Vic was dead tired. The air conditioning had dried his nose and given him a headache. Maria had a legal pad filled with notes, but she tapped her pen on it with a look of futility. After putting in twelve hours themselves, though, they were beginning to see the light at the end of the tunnel. Or so he thought.

"If nothing else," Vic said grimly, "we've managed to make all the employees paranoid. That should come in handy whenever somebody drops a tray or backfires a car in the parking lot."

Maria shook her head. "It's not over yet," she told him. "We still have a dozen more LSM clerks to go. The important ones, because they knew Sominski. Although we've already talked to a few acquaintances."

"We have?"

"I have."

"Who's next?"

She gave him a tired smile, and checked the files. "One Calvin Beach. Eight years' service. A decorated Vietnam vet. Has a good record. A Type Two diabetic with retinopathy, but only one sick leave absence in the last three quarters. He's been seen talking with Sominski, and they've occasionally gone to lunch together at the Mexican restaurant on the corner, according to Gary Lennox, his former boss. But they only get a half hour to eat."

"You mean like us–today, anyway? Why haven't you talked to this guy yet?"

"Well, we've been busy, you know."

Vic felt the bandage on his cheek. "Tell me about it. I feel like a war vet myself."

"Or someone on disabil–"

They were interrupted by a loud knock. But when the door didn't open, Vic had to call "Come in!"

The LSM clerk who entered was a stout man wearing dark sunglasses. He grinned widely.

"Calvin Beach?" Maria asked.

The clerk nodded, removing his dark glasses. "What's the scoop?" He stared at Maria's eye patch. "What's happened to you?"

"A little accident. Have a seat, will you? Just a few questions."

"Questions?" Beach glanced at Vic. "You mean about David?"

"That's right," Vic told him. "We won't keep you long from your job."

"No problemo. This is my last night, anyway."

Maria tapped her notes. "Yes; you're starting in CFS soon, aren't you?"

"I think I might like the day shift for a change," Beach confessed.

Vic motioned to him. The clerk sat without hesitation as Maria turned a page. "You have a nickname, don't you?" she asked.

Beach nodded. "They call me Fireplug. Yeah."

"Fireplug?" Vic chuckled. "With a name like that you couldn't be a carrier, could you? The dogs would be after you." They both smiled dutifully, although neither of them laughed. Vic considered about apologizing, but skipped it as trivial.

"You were in the Army too," Maria noted. "Along with Sominski, I mean."

"Yes," Beach admitted, "I was in the Army, that's true. But not with David. I was in Vietnam. Based in Bok Thoh the year before the pullout. Got me a medal for it. I don't think David ever left the States, did he?"

Vic glanced at Maria, who nodded. "How well did you know Mr. Sominski?"

"Oh, you know how it is. You find somebody who understands the lingo, you shoot the bull in the break room. That's about the limit of it. We didn't share any deep secrets, if that's what you mean."

"So you have no idea why he might have done what he did?"

"Just what I read in the paper." He paused. "David was a loner. Didn't have much in common with the women in the unit. Neither do I, come to think of it."

Maria scribbled a note to herself. "What do you mean–because they're married, with families?"

"That, and because their interests are different. Sure. Why would someone like David–or me, for that matter–be interested in pie recipes and soap operas?"

"Yet this was all a surprise to you?" Vic asked.

"I'll say. He went off the deep end, didn't he? So something must have set him off. 'Course, I knew he had a temper." Beach glanced between them. "Who knows why anybody does anything?"

"Where would he get explosives?" Maria asked. "Plastique, specifically."

"You're asking me? I wouldn't know where you can get firecrackers on the Fourth of July."

Maria made another notation. "He ever talk about bombs or explosives?"

"No."

"Revenge?"

"Against what?"

"You tell us."

"Hey, the main topic with him was women. Ask anybody. Except the women, of course."

Maria sipped from her coffee cup. "He have a girlfriend?"

"Not that he mentioned. Like I said, I wasn't in a position to know about that. We killed ten minutes here and there. Small talk. Jokes. Gripes about the boss granting leave to some and not to others. The usual." He looked at Vic. "Anything else?"

"Yes," Vic said. "Do you know where he'd go?"

"No idea. He mentioned his mother once, I think. Wisconsin or Michigan ... or was it Minnesota?"

"Michigan." Vic corrected. "What about other friends, like from the Army, for instance?"

Beach thought it over. "No, can't recall. Like I said, he was a loner."

"Like you."

"Well, not like me, obviously."

"You got any girlfriends, hobbies?"

"Not right now, no. My hobby is my bike. Got me an off road thousand c.c.G.S."

"What's that?"

"It's a BMW. I use it to explore some old mining towns. That's my hobby. Lot's of history out there, you know."

"That's what I hear. By the way, where were you wounded?"

"Does it matter?"

"Not really, " Vic conceded. "Okay then. If you remember anything about Sominski that might help ..."

"If I do, I'll let you know for sure. But like I say, he was just another Level Six like the rest of us. Did his job and went home, and then started up again the next day. Same clothes, same Walkman, same small talk on breaks."

Maria turned over Beach's file onto the stack, said, "You hear from Mr. Sominski again, you let us know immediately, okay?"

"You kidding? I'll dial nine one one. Call the FBI, too."

Maria tapped her pencil idly, then wrote something on a card. "No need to do that. Agent Delany may not be available. You just call me. Maria Castillo. Or inspector Kazy." She handed the card to Vic for him. "Anytime, understand?"

"Will do." Beach got to his feet. "But David was never my friend, really. It doesn't work like that in the unit. He even told me that, not long ago. Said he never had a real friend in his whole life."

"Interesting," Vic said. "Okay, then."

"Oh–one more thing," Maria added, as Beach vacated his chair.

"Yeah?"

"In your opinion, do you think David was capable of doing this alone?"

Beach had walked to the door, and now turned. His eyes squinted at the fluorescent lights overhead as if the answer was up there. Finally, he looked down. A slight smile played on his lips. "I don't know," he said. "I was just thinking. I saw something scratched into the stall door in the men's restroom a week or so ago. Said 'Gary eats here.' And there was the letter D under it. Like an initial, or the beginning of another word. Like maybe the clerk had started carving another sentence, but got interrupted."

"Oh really?"

Beach nodded. "I was just thinking about the D being David. I never thought about all the words it coulda been. Lots of bad D's in the dictionary. Death. Destroy. Demolish. Or how about debauchery, demean, dungeon. Demonize ... dementia ... delusion? Or for David ... Democrat? Maybe your agent D-lany can figure it out."

Vic coughed. "Yes, well ... Thanks for your help."

"Any time." Beach opened the door, and slipped on his dark sunglasses. "Oh," he explained with a gesture. "I got diabetes, myself. Sensitive to light, you know."

Vic nodded. The door closed. He looked at Maria. "What was that all about?"

"Strange," Maria conceded.

"Does strange merit a background check?"

She shrugged. "A gun check, maybe." She finished off her coffee, and massaged her throat. "Let's finish up; this caffeine isn't working anymore."

***

The Park Hotel on Grant road was unexpectedly filled with last gasp tourists and not a few media types. Vic was about to pull out of the parking lot and check the nearest Holiday Inn when Maria shook her head.

"We do have reservations here. Let's not start looking now. I'm beat."

The clock over the clerk behind the reception desk in the lobby read 1:15. "Two single rooms for Castillo and Kazy," Vic said.

"Sorry," the clerk replied, oddly cheerful. "We only have a double left."

"But we have reservations."

The clerk shook his head. "We don't hold them valid past ten o'clock, sir. Just a double left. Sorry." He smiled, politely.

Vic started to turn away, but Maria grabbed his hand and squeezed.

"We'll take it," she said.

Soon, as he followed her into the elevator, Vic felt his stomach tighten with a sense of giddy fear.

19

The night was long. Twelve hours of working the mail by hand. Worse, the bitch Grijalva required that they separate out all government checks and ATM cards first. Of course, he'd managed to separate his own share of these "entitlements" into the wrong zones of his labeling case, after satisfying himself that no one would be checking his work. Meanwhile, the others were busy enough themselves culling through their endless trays of letter mail in search of what remained of the blasted shipments, and with Grijalva herself watching the ETs attempt to repair some of the relays on LSM II.

The plant floor was cleared of the bulk mail, which was not a priority. That area soon served as a staging ground for newly incoming first class letter mail, coded by colored flag as to day of delay. Nixie mail and the burned fragments of letters were moved into the breakroom and the various offices, much to the chagrin of the administrators who'd never touched live mail before. On his way to the restroom, Calvin glimpsed a pile of ashes on Gary's desk, and then throughout his time at the urinal he chuckled to himself at the look of frustration he'd seen on Lennox's face.

By the end of the tour and its four hours of overtime, Calvin was exhausted. On his last night as an LSM crew member, he'd diverted over six hundred checks intended by Uncle Sam for all the poor and helpless little nieces and nephews. Twenty or so of the first shipment of ATM cards were accidentally dropped into the waste bin, or hidden inside empty bulk envelopes. Several dozen more were accidentally dropped and kicked underneath the postal equipment. Most, of course, were overlooked, and the supposedly checked trays set aside for further delay. As a reward for his efforts, he would be paid an average of twenty-five dollars an hour on overtime. Plus, he was granted a day off, so he could sleep before reporting to his new assignment, which would be on tour one, the first Wednesday shift.

It was just after noon when he parked the BMW at his apartment, and he thought about what the inspectors had asked him. They suspected nothing, of course. They were just fishing, and with a big net at that. Looking for minnows perhaps, since they couldn't find the shark. As for Sominski, he probably wouldn't write a confession, nor could he be forced to write a suicide note. A short scribbled note on the floor with a stick might have to do. Then it would be a scene from *Hang 'Em High*. Or, considering the broken arm, the movie might have to be *Cliffhanger.*

Sleep came quickly. Dreams, however, were chaotic. At one point he was in jail, in a tiny cell with a small barred window. Out there, in the street, horses were tied to a hitching post. A man leaned back on a stool, a gun at his hip. A wooden platform with a cross piece supported a noose. The dream was in black and white, like in old photographs. It seemed to go on forever.

When he woke it was almost 8:00 PM. He ate two cherry Pop Tarts and a glass of orange juice. The evening paper reported eleven hundred more Cubans and Haitians picked up by the Coast Guard to be processed for asylum; the seizure of a hundred and twelve kilos of cocaine found hidden inside hollowed-out watermelons shipped up from Sonora; and the failure of more budgeting legislation to make it through the scandal-ridden Senate.

But what took up most of the front page was an account of the hardships to be suffered by welfare and Social Security recipients forced to wait for their benefit checks due to Postal Service inefficiency and the terrorism against it. Predictions were of starving babies robbed of sustaining formula, and of heartless capitalist landlords evicting without mercy. Already, the Food Bank was being called on to help, as well as the Salvation Army and local charities. Homeless shelters were being alerted to the growing dilemma, with extra staff donated by local churches. Phone numbers were given, too, for anyone to call and offer assistance to the poor victims of this horrendous violence, caught as they were in this temporary glitch in the money-flow from Washington. Reporters ended their stories on page four by quoting Hispanic mothers on the south side, claiming they had always lived from paycheck to paycheck, and that the entitlement money had never allowed them to buy extravagances like Big Macs or Pampers. Who was going to bring the bomber to justice for this? And when he was, would he get off because he was white?

The one article hot on Sominski's trail began with a headline on the bottom of page one titled **BOMBER STILL AT LARGE** and continued on page seven with Dave's photo and a brief bio, including an offer of reward. Ten thousand dollars was the going rate today, and you didn't have to give your name and number to collect. Inspectors Kazy and Castillo were mentioned, as investigating Sominski's possible contacts. Agent Delany and Detective Manetti were looking into the acquisition of explosives made by Sominski, as well as any other leads. And a special inspector from Washington had just arrived to take over security at the city's postal stations, with the help of other inspectors from Phoenix.

Calvin thought for a moment about Gessel. If the ex-Special Forces man could add two and two he'd certainly put it together by now. Still, it was unlikely that he'd go for another ten grand, even anonymously. Not only had Calvin gotten it clear that Gessel was discreet, but there was the matter of Gessel's own illegal acquisition of dangerous chemicals. Complicating the problem for Gessel was how to identify the buyer of his plastique without involving himself by looking through postal personnel records. No—even if he wanted the ten grand, there would be no way to collect and be sure the real bomber wouldn't look him up one dark night with a silenced 9MM automatic to the back of the head. Gessel would remain quiet. He'd just keep reading the paper out of intense curiosity.

Of more relevant concern was his letter to the editor, and why they had stopped running it. He worried about whether the FBI man could trace the explosive to Gessel later. If Gessel was caught, then he'd worry. For now there was too much emphasis on the so-called victims of his action, and not enough on the reason why he'd done it. Sominski, it was said, was a "right wing extremist." Just another wacko. They weren't getting the message, as usual, even with the mayor dead, and a hole in the post office floor, and a line of welfare recipients out the door.

But he did have one more little bomb to drop. Hopefully, it would be a significant call for freedom, since it was his last one. And he would need to issue further warnings to publish before the bomb went off, and after it went off, too. With promises of more. Of course, in Revelation, God sent plagues and diseases, and the sinners didn't repent or change their ways.

Something else was needed, in addition perhaps, to get their attention. The Irish Republican Army hadn't achieved much success with bombs, after all. He needed something big. Something to generate more national attention.

Like a kidnapping.

Yes, there it was. That might be the ticket. If only he could kidnap someone, like from the City Council. Or from Affirmative Action. Or a liberal judge. That would be a blast, too. Throw him in with Sominski, let him fight over scraps of beef jerky soaked in urine. Take recordings of the judge telling the taxpayers how much it will really cost them to incarcerate another five or ten thousand illegal aliens, or else neither of them would get any H^2O. In the end they'd both be victims, regretfully, but didn't all of America consist of victims now? That was what reports on *World News Tonight* suggested, anyway. No one was responsible, except the good old boys: the angry white males.

As he checked his blood sugar level with a small kit, Calvin suddenly remembered something from his interview. He took out the card in his pocket. MARIA CASTILLO, POSTAL INSPECTOR it read. He remembered what she'd said too: *Call me anytime.*

Yes, he could give her a call. She would make a nice abductee and partner for Dave, for sure. It could be dangerous, though. She would be wary, and probably not alone. Women like that were never alone. After the self-preservation instinct came the sexual instinct in a close second, and both instincts factored in here. Still, it was exciting to think about, anyway. Even if he couldn't do it because it was too risky, it was a pleasant daydream to occupy his time while he composed another warning "letter to the editor" for Sominski to sign. And if Dave refused to sign the letter, then he could go ahead and push him into that hell hole, head first. Or maybe he would anyway. Doing even that would take guts enough. Like in combat, in 'Nam when he'd hit one gook in the teeth with the butt of his M-16 and dropped a dozen more in a muddy rice field with an M-60 at one in the morning. But luckily he remembered the quip his buddy Kyle had told him the next morning. *A gook's a gook, and they all oughta be shot.* Dave wasn't a gook, of course, just a dumb Pollock.

The girl, though ... that would be even better. The thought of getting revenge, if only symbolically, against all the lazy do-gooders who wanted to tell people what was fair, and how to live. A kidnapping of one of their kind would be great, as a sacrifice to the great god of Mediocrity. What did it matter, anyway? Most liberals and New Agers didn't believe in God. They believed man was an animal, with even less rights then certain spotted owls. So it would just be an animal sacrifice. Wouldn't it?

He thought about it. Sominski and the spic lady, together. If only he could watch them. Listen to their prayers. Be their God. The dumb Pollock and the pretty, dumb, liberal bitch inspector who probably voted for Clinton, and mostly sat in her office doodling and drinking coffee like all the useless union types whose ranks he'd never joined. Maybe he could wire them to blow together with the last bomb! A lover's embrace ... or perhaps the cornered, misunderstood bomber and his bleeding-heart tree-hugging nemesis on the government payroll ...

He closed his eyes, imagining it.

Momentarily, something moved in his pants. He slipped his hand down into his jeans to check.

It couldn't be, but it was: His penis had partially filled with blood.

Not fully erect, but not flaccid either. Somehow, he was getting there. Perhaps if he could actually witness the bombing–what then? Ejaculation? It had been years. He'd forgotten what that was like.

As quickly as it had come on, though, it vanished. He went limp again in seconds, as if the Thought Police were exacting justice. Nothing there anymore. But he hadn't imagined it–it was the real thing, this time. The thing that had overpopulated the world. The mother of all problems.

He decided to visit Fleshdance as an experiment. To see if that was the link that had done it ... the purported link in the brain between sex and violence.

***

The club was full that night. Loud and smoky. He ordered a Heineken and sat in the back, near the side rail where the girls entered onto the stage. When a tall, busty brunette came over to ask him if he wanted a table dance, he unfolded a five dollar bill and laid it beside his drink. Then he smiled.

"You hiding from somebody?" the girl asked, and pointed at his dark glasses.

"Prescription glasses," he told her. "The better to see you with, my dear."

"Oh." She grinned and leaned forward, pushing her breasts together, making them bulge, presenting them like fruit. Then, as the song began, she writhed to the music, turning to arch her back and push her shapely butt almost in his face.

"This is what it's all about," he said. "Isn't it?"

"What?"

"Everything," But she couldn't hear him over the loud stereo. And at the end of the song, he only patted the flat space between his legs. "Nothing."

She lost her sense of humor, and took the money. Then she moved on to the next paying customer.

Three more table dances and five beers later, and still no effect.

He again took out the card the inspectors had given him. Below the office number was another number written in pencil. It was faint, but he could make it out. Perhaps a home phone? He bought a pack of Marlboros from the back bar and asked to use the phone. He took the phone book, dropped a dollar tip, and then looked up Castillo. There were a number of Castillos but no Maria or M. Castillo, as women sometimes listed themselves to hide their sex from the heavy breathers.

He dialed the number. A sonorous male voice said, "Hello? This is the Park Hotel. How may I help you?"

He hung up. *I'll be damned.*

***

At his van, he checked the rear. Green carpet on the floor, ceiling, and sides for insulation. Not just for the AC, but for sound, too. Gas can, empty. Tire iron, spare tire. A rope. No windows, except in back.

How would he do it?

Silly. It was just a fantasy, anyway. Not even an experiment, yet. Insane too, as Sominski claimed he was anyway. He would be a lunatic to try it. He could be shot, or identified, at the very least. The woman was a professional, after all. Being female, she was wary and suspicious of all men by nature, like any girl in Fleshdance, who teased the money right out of your wallet but would sic a bouncer on you the instant you touched her thigh.

Still tipsy, he withdrew his .45 from its hiding place inside the torn passenger side cushion where he sometimes kept it. He checked the clip, then shoved it back and fumbled for his keys. He should have eaten something, he decided. Maybe the beers wouldn't have affected him. But he was only going over there for a peek. Nothing would happen just thinking about it, if afterward he only visited Dave on the GS and then took a nap before work. Nothing, except maybe something in his jeans.

20

"Did I tell you about my parents?" Maria asked.

"You said the other night that you were an only child," Vic replied. "Just like me. Spoiled."

"Yeah, rotten." Maria grinned as she dried her hair. "They're sweet folks, though. You would like them."

"I really would, huh?"

"Mom makes great enchiladas."

"I'll bet you do, too. I prefer beef ribs, myself. And speaking of food, I'm starving. How about you?"

She came to him unexpectedly again, and put her arms around him to squeeze him tightly. He squeezed even tighter. At that, she squeezed tighter still–a hugging contest they both won.

"Famished," she whispered in his ear, at last.

He smelled her sweet dark hair, fresh from the shower. Then he cupped her head in his hands and kissed her eye patch, gently. Her lips trembled slightly as they met his at last, but then the kiss firmed and lingered just as Vic remembered it during a long day of distraction.

They hugged again, tighter even than their first night together.

"I like your other side too," he confessed. "The side that slips through now and then. Especially now."

"And I'm loving your hugs," she told him. "The tighter the better."

"You mean like this?"

"Yeah," she confessed, giving a little sigh. "Just like that."

"Didn't Carl ever hug you?"

"Who?"

When they finally parted, he moved toward the door. "I'll be back," he promised, "with lots of goodies. We'll pig out, okay? Watch the late show. Just don't you chicken out on me, now."

She smiled teasingly. "What's it going to be? Pork or chicken?"

"Beef. If I can find my shirt." He began looking beside the bed.

"Don't forget these," she reminded him, and jangled the keys from atop the TV. She picked up the plastic ice bucket on the dresser. "I'll get ice for the drinks."

"What kind do you want?" he asked.

She went outside without answering. The door closed. He stared at the door for a moment and then found his shirt, but it was slightly damp from sweat. He would need a clean one from his suitcase. Rummaging through his suitcase, he found a red pullover, but before he put it on, curiosity got the best of him. He went to the door, and opened it. He found Maria filling the ice bucket at the ice machine just outside their room.

"What kind of drink do you want?" he repeated.

"Anything wet," she replied, and smiled.

She gave him the ice bucket, and he took it inside. They hugged quickly yet again. Finally he pulled on his shirt, and took the keys.

"Drive carefully," she told him, "with all that food."

He opened the door, and backed slowly out, unable to take his eyes off her.

"Goodbye already," she urged with a laugh.

"Bye," he said, half-heartedly.

"Hurry back. No, I mean don't hurry."

"Oh. Okay, I won't, then."

"Promise?"

"Cross my heart."

He smiled and then turned away to walk quickly toward the stairwell. Only after she was out of sight did he think of Max the Ax. What would the Postmaster General say of their new collaboration?

Not that it mattered; Maxwell wasn't as pretty, so his opinion didn't count.

***

The Park Hotel was off one of the city's busiest roads. Calvin drove carefully into the lot, and pulled around to the back, where a side street connected. He backed into a space nearest the street, and killed the engine and lights. He could see the entire back side of the hotel's four floors now, with its entrances from both lots. Had she arrived yet? He lit up another Marlboro while waiting, and looked out the window at the man in the moon.

Tell me, Dad, is there a final justice? Is this fate, or is it all just chance?

He tried to imagine the inspector lady down in the hole with Dave, but oddly he thought about what it would be like to have his own family instead: Dinner at a family buffet restaurant with the twins crying and junior playing under the table. A G-rated movie requiring two buckets of politically correct Canola Oil popcorn at four bucks a pop. Toys R Us, dental fillings, report cards, church services. Maybe a bridge or poker game now and then with friends. The television set always on. Whining in the background from the kids or the dog, or both at once–like a wasp trapped in a bottle. Nagging reminders of duties shirked or put off, like cutting the grass or painting the kitchen. Rituals too, such as the Thanksgiving turkey dinner or decorating the Christmas tree. Mother's Day flowers and Father's Day ties. College education funds. PTA meetings with group discussions on gangs and teen pregnancy and low SAT scores. Endless shopping trips for groceries and clothes and furniture. Just like the neighbors, and the neighbors next to them, a*d infinitum*.

Even their fights over money would be just like the people on the next street, and the next. While thousands, even hundreds of thousands, of people across the city did the same things, had the same arguments, ate the same food ... on and on. While mounting each other out of habit or boredom or fear, an average of two and a half times a week.

Am I the weird one, Dad? Is it me?

He finished his cigarette, and flicked it out the window.

He looked at his watch: 11:17 PM.

The buzz was starting to leave him. Maybe he shouldn't try to tempt the fates, even if they didn't exist. They'd screwed him enough up to now, as it was. Not as much as the poor overtaxed slobs who were married to fat wives that wanted more kids, of course. Not as much as the swarthy regulars at Fleshdance, who were prisoners of their sex drives, thank God. Not like David Dumbass Sominski. But ...

I'm not a robot like them, am I Dad?

He turned the ignition. The van shuddered to life. It was time to go home, finish that letter, and think about what to do with the last bomb. He couldn't risk bringing it into the post office, but it would make a nice housewarming gift for the local president of NOW or the NAACP or the ACLU or the NEA. Postmarked for death.

On the way out of the parking lot he glanced back at the hotel and saw a woman on the third floor at the ice machine.

A woman with an eye patch.

It was her. Maria Castillo, postal inspector. From Phoenix, he'd read. Yes. No doubt about it–it had to be fate! Because the chance of seeing her alone and at this last possible moment was astronomically tiny. Better odds could be had betting on a sled dog pulling a plow around Churchill Downs.

Fate or luck?

He turned the wheel and circled around for a closer look, stopping the van directly below her and leaning forward to peer up at her almost bare ass as she leaned into the silver ice bin to scoop the cubes into her bucket.

He felt his penis fill with blood as he watched. His heart became a sudden metronome battering his temples. *Just do it*, he remembered the slogan on TV.

He scrambled for his .45, shoving it into his belt, and then covering it with his shirt. He opened the door, intending to leave the engine running.

A door opened, up there beside her. A shirtless man stepped out. It was the other inspector–the one named Vic.

Victor.

Calvin shut his car door again, and quietly pulled the van away, back to his former spot. The male inspector didn't have a bandage on his cheek anymore, and now took the ice bucket inside. The woman followed. Just before their door closed they both seemed to be smiling like idiots.

Calvin stared at the empty balcony and felt numb. His penis drained and went as limp as a discarded banana peel lying in the noon Tucson sun.

So close, and now they were in there, safe, the two of them getting ready to hump at taxpayer's expense, on the USPS per diem, sans any ethics at all.

He began to imagine what they could do with the ice when the door opened again. The one called Kazy had a shirt on now–a red pullover. He talked to the woman inside, and then started down the balcony toward the staircase and elevator. He chose the staircase. His walk seemed brisk, happy. He got into a white Cavalier and drove off around the hotel to exit the front entrance. His tires skidded on the concrete entry. He was in a hurry to get back. An errand. Late night fast food, maybe. Chicken McNuggets or chili dogs.

Which meant the pretty lady inspector was up there alone, with at least a ten minute gap in her illusion of security.

Just do it, Son.

But how? By knocking on the door? By calling her room and asking her to come down to the lobby? She could take ten minutes just to dress, and she'd have a gun ready in either case. Any quick moves and a bullet would bore a hole deep into his *medulla oblongata*. Or she'd kick what remained between his legs, and then deliver a karate blow to his solar plexus.

But not if she was off guard, of course.

Calvin edged the van back under the railing, toward the elevator. He got out. His heart began to race again, although the banana peel there between his legs only got staler.

He took the elevator up, praying that no one would exit one of the curtained rooms along the third floor balcony. When it opened, he pushed the HOLD button. The door remained open.

He walked nonchalantly to the room, which was two doors to the right of the ice machine. Room 312.

He sucked in a breath, and knocked.

Knock, knock ... knock-knock, knock. Like a friend, or a lover.

He stood to the side, against the wall, in case she used the peephole.

She didn't. The door opened without a word.

"That was–"

Quickly, he bulled his way inside, and roughly pushed her down. In another second he had his .45 out and aimed at her face. "Not a sound," he said.

She rose from the floor and then slunk to the bed. Her shoulders sagged.

Now who's the victor, he thought.

"You're ... Beach, the LSM clerk," she said weakly.

He reached behind him with his other hand, and with the side of his index finger turned up the TV. David Letterman was going through a top ten list–why the President's cat didn't like to be called Pussy. "Good memory," he told her. "Now let's go. Sominski called, and he wants to meet you."

She looked at the floor, and then up again, up and down, her head bobbing in disbelief. "Were you part of this from the start?"

He didn't reply, but when she looked down again he feinted to her blind side and then brought the pistol down on top of her head. Hard. She collapsed forward in a heap.

Done.

Hiding the gun under his shirt, he quickly gathered her up into his arms, then edged her sideways out the door.

The balcony was still vacant. The sound of air conditioners hummed. He made for the elevator warily with her limp and unconscious body.

Stand aside, people! My wife's collapsed, and we have to save the baby!

He released the HOLD button with a middle knuckle, and hit GROUND. The door slid shut. The elevator descended, then opened again after an interminably long wait at ground level.

A car went by. Not the white Cavalier, but a blue Buick. He paused until it passed, then blundered out of the elevator, toward the still-running van. He noticed that her legs were cool to the touch as he reached past them to open the back door latch. He heard another door shutting somewhere above, but didn't look. He merely laid her inside, his heart in his throat now, and then pushed her, rolling her torso forward.

He shut the door carefully, and glanced up. No one there.

Hugging the far side of the van, he circled around to get in.

Fearing someone might glimpse him out of a window, he pulled slowly away, toward the rear exit, headlights off. Not until he made the turn away from Grant, toward the residential neighborhood beyond, did he finally put the lights on. In his side mirror he thought he glimpsed two other cars enter the hotel's parking lot. One of them was white. The third floor room door was open back there, just as he left it–a rectangle of light. But Inspector "Victor" Kazy would find the room empty, except for David Letterman. So maybe he would watch some stupid pet tricks before he dialed 911. Certainly he would check the lobby first, and interrogate the desk clerk. Or perhaps he'd assume she'd tired of him and left. Maybe he'd even wank off in the bathroom in frustration.

Calvin almost laughed. If no one had seen him, his insane gamble had actually paid off. On the chance someone had seen the van or read its license plate number, though, he'd best ditch it. Then what? Call it in stolen? Stolen by Sominski?

It was stupid to risk such an act. A lunatic thing to do, just like Sominski throwing that chair at the boss. But he'd pulled it off, hadn't he? Like a Special Forces operation. Somehow, with accumulated luck or fate on his side. Or maybe it was God, or–

Thank you, Dad.

***

He pulled over to the side of the dark street when he heard a moan coming from the rear. He climbed in back and tied the pretty lady inspector's ankles and wrists together behind her in a very politically incorrect position. Halfway through the procedure she became groggily aware of what was happening, and began making louder moaning sounds.

"That's it, baby," Calvin urged her in falsetto voice. "Don't stop."

He completed the packaging by creating a gag from the rag he used to check the van's oil.

"Don't worry," he consoled her. "It's not fattening."

Next stop was his apartment, to pick up the flashlight, another chain and padlock, the remaining book bomb, and two plastic one-gallon milk jugs, which he filled with water. When he returned to the van, Inspector Castillo was wide awake, taut, and shifted to the other side nearer the rear door. The bruise on her head was a clotted tangle of hair in the flashlight beam.

"Now, now," he whispered, raising his finger. "You mustn't fight your destiny. Otherwise we'll have to stop your biological clock a little early, won't we?"

She laid her head back on the stained green carpet. Then he slammed and locked the rear doors.

Calvin stopped at a Blockbuster on the way south on Campbell toward I-10. He parked at the far side of the lot, went in and rented a movie for later. Back in the van, he explained his selection.

"You ever seen *Blown Away*?" he asked. "Stars Jeff Bridges and Tommy Lee Jones. Sorry there won't be a VCR for you and Dave to watch. Guess I'll have to see it alone, before I catch a nap and go to work. Had to do it on the way down, see, because by the time I get back here they'll be closed." He glanced back at the hog-tied princess in the back. Her one eye was wide and fixed on him. He smiled and winked. "You're enjoying this, aren't you? Well, I'll have to see if I can make you enjoy it even more. You just hold on tight–it won't be too much longer. Promise."

For her entertainment, he turned on the radio. Elvis was singing "Return to Sender," and as he drove and sang along, they headed deeper south toward an address unknown.

21

His watch read 1:35 AM by the time the dirt road off the Old Nogales Highway turned into a trail. Then the way got even rougher—the ruts too deep for the van, and the rocks too large.

Calvin pulled to the side at a point where he could turn around, and killed the engine. Then he got out and opened the rear door. He pulled the girl back toward him and used a knife to release her legs, leaving her hands tied. The relief on her face was evident, but it didn't last. Not when he pulled her to the edge, sideways, and pulled down her briefs to press himself against her bare butt.

He lingered for a moment against her tensed thighs, waiting to see what would happen. He bucked against her once, twice, in the desert silence.

Nothing.

He laughed, as if at a joke. Then he pulled her upright, to the ground. And pulled her shorts up for her.

"Had you going there, didn't I?" he said. "If they instituted an erection tax like I think they should, they wouldn't even bother auditing me. Now. Looks like we got us a bit of a hike ahead. Lucky for you it's night, and cool. You'll have to walk ahead of me, but don't worry, I'll tell you where to go. Besides, the moon's just about full now."

He took the water jugs and the plastic bag with the chain, the bomb, and the other items inside it.

"Watch out for rattlers, now," he warned, "with those bare feet. And don't get any idea to run. Not only don't you know where you are, but I got the flashlight, and the knife. Only thing you got are good jugs." He held up the water jugs to his chest, and chuckled again. "Not as good as mine, though."

It took twenty minutes of hiking in rugged terrain before she seemed to be losing strength. So he took out his knife again. She looked back and her good eye widened in fear.

"Hold on now, just gonna take off your muzzle so you can drink some water. No one can hear you out here, anyway."

He cut the gag from the back, and pulled it out. She sucked in several breaths as he took the cap off one of the water jugs. Then he lifted it to her lips. She drank three big gulps.

"Why?" she asked at last, her voice choked.

"Why you ... or why me?"

She nodded.

"Why not?" he asked. "It's still a free country, isn't it? Not for much longer, a course. You might say I'm a man long past my time. And you? Well, you're just another victim, aren't you? A prisoner of war for now."

"What ... are you saying?"

He motioned for her to start walking again. "I'm saying ... what does it matter, anymore? We're all running on empty. I'm saying you wouldn't understand."

She seemed confused for just a passing moment. "Tell me."

Calvin laughed. "Why–so you can try to talk me out of something? So you can go back to your dickhead inspector Kazy and fool around some more?"

"I wasn't–"

"No? I remember seeing a ring on his finger, too. Not sure if it was at the interview ... maybe when you two arrested poor screwed-up Davy boy. Where's your own ring, by the way? You take it off before you seduced him?"

"I'm not married. Neither is he. I mean ... he's separated. And what business is it of yours?"

"Oh, I make it my business to notice things. You do that when you're single and alone like me, see. You notice everything when ya don't have kids yelling and dogs barking and some hag asking you to do the dishes ... fat hag, now that she's had her quota of brats. You step back and watch people from a distance, from the silence where the truth is. You read and you think, and you remember, too."

"What do you remember?"

He thought about it, walking behind her. "I remember the bitches in 'Nam that'd sell themselves for a carton of cigarettes. Give the GIs the clap, or knife 'em through the back. My buddy Kyle, he got screwed too, by a nasty mama named Agent Orange. 'Course the punks who didn't wanna go over there, like your prickster Victor, they just dropped acid, threw beer parties, and screwed teenagers, while pretending moral superiority. Laughed at us when we returned too ... except that didn't bother me as much as what came later. What's happening now."

"And what is that?"

"Never mind. Just keep walking, and shut up."

They came to the place where Sominski's Mustang had left the trail. They continued on, Calvin shining the flashlight's beam through the pretty inspector's scratched legs. Once they neared a tarantula walking slowly across the path, atop a central boulder. He shined the beam on it and it hunched back in defense, legs wriggling in a slow motion spider dance. But the girl wouldn't look, and bypassed it to keep walking. At any moment she might have run, he realized, but then there were a billion more such spiders out there in the dark. And scorpions and Western Diamondbacks and coyotes and poisonous Gila monsters. It wouldn't be much fun sleeping on the ground with creepy things crawling on your body, and you with your hands tied behind your back. In the daytime, in the blazing heat of one hundred fifteen degrees, the creatures slept. But at night they all emerged. On the hunt. On the prowl.

"Victor is too young to have dodged the draft," the woman said, as they approached Total Wreck. "I thought you should know that."

"And I know it," Calvin admitted, noting the careful cadence of her voice. "But he would have if he could have, wouldn't he?"

"What makes you think so?"

"You liberals are all alike, that's why. Weak, pathetic. You're still flower children, talking about peace and love, and forgetting that mankind has been at war since Cain killed Abel. Forgetting that it's part of nature. Like dying. Like eating meat. Like fucking. But fucking is all you do now. You do it to us all too, don't you? While blabbing on and on about how evil we are for smoking or running a lawn mower or driving a car or drinking a beer or having money in the bank. You're planning for some bogus Utopia to break out once you redistribute the wealth and make everybody equal and happy and having a nice fucking day. But I tell ya, it ain't gonna happen, sweet cheeks. No way. Kiss it off. *Adios muchachos!* 'Cause the world's not like that. Never has been, an' never will be. So you go ahead and do away with the military, an' you see what happens next. Do away with the wealthy, an' see what kinda starvation you get in the streets when the shopping centers close down. Take away religion and responsibility and making people pay for their actions, an' you get people like me running things. Except I ain't a criminal, though, am I? A criminal's somebody who's out for their own good at other people's expense—like quite a few senators I could name. No, I'm a soldier now, an' there's no laws I got left to consider, except what's good for the country. Because the country's in a civil war, see, an' people just don't know it yet. A class war. An invasion of its borders. Meantime, Arizona is the second fastest growing state, but with the worst teenage pregnancy rate in the country. Maybe the world. And you're letting it all happen, aren't you? Well, not me, baby. Not me."

Total Wreck, as they approached it, was eerie silver in the moonlight. Like the set of *Twilight Zone*. Like the old version with Rod Serling, in black and white.

Are you there, Dad? Are you watching?

"Did you know Rod Serling died of lung cancer?" he asked the woman.

"What?"

"Yeah. My dad had it too, when he killed himself. But that's not the only reason: he was screwed by the Postal Service. This–what I'm doing?–it's not because of that. Call it an extra. The job has been pretty good to me, personally speaking. I got my reasons, and Dad's had his."

"What ... do you mean?"

"Keep walking. Through town, make a left in another hundred yards by the ridge, and you'll see a fence. I'll have to tie you up there, so I can get the ladder."

"Ladder?"

He took a swig from the water jug. "Oh, you're gonna love it."

"And Sominski is waiting?"

"Oh yeah."

"Tied up too, I imagine."

Calvin smiled. "Hey, you're good. How'd you guess?"

She didn't answer, but seemed to be getting tense now. She tried to hide it, but he could tell. It was in the way she walked, like she was gathering strength to spring away for the run of her life. Finally, closer to the fence, she said, "What made you think I was a liberal?"

"Hey," he laughed, not to be diverted, "it's a liberal town. Environmentalists and knee-jerk tax lovers."

"Because I'm a registered Republican," she insisted. "And I always have been."

"Right. And I bet you like to watch Rush, too."

"As a matter of fact, I appreciated what he said tonight on TV about the liberals going after the other half. You know, with taxes already effectively taking half your income."

"Yeah?"

"Yeah. I mean Federal income tax, Social Security tax, state tax, sales tax, property tax, and more. Rush said they're talking about new taxes too, and a higher capital gains tax, and a national sa–"

"Save it," Calvin said, and reached to suddenly grab her arm from behind. "You were watching Letterman, not Rush. I was there, I saw it. Remember, honey buns?"

"No, really, I ..."

He gripped her tighter, until the tenseness left. "You're not so tough, are you? Besides, Rush is wrong. You think I record his program and get his newsletter, you're wrong there, too. You may be a Republican, but you're deluded like the rest of em. And personally speaking, I'm more of a libertarian. I listen to local talk shows. I hear how they're screwing up this town, and I worry for the whole country."

He tied her to the first fence post they came to, taking extra care on securing the knots. Then he went for the ladder, and returned with it to find that she'd almost cut through the rope, using the barbed wire. She wasn't exactly delighted to see him.

"Well, well. Seems I underestimated you, huh?" He dropped the ladder against the fence, and cut through the remaining stands, making sure not to let go of her wrist this time. "Okay then, up and over you go, and be careful about it." When she made it to the top, and was about to jump awkwardly, he added, "Keep in mind this is a small compound. The fence goes all the way around it. There are holes, so running now won't get you far in the dark."

She started to turn around for a possible kick in the face, but he scrambled up behind her. Then she jumped and fell, looking down at her ankle in pain.

"Careful," he warned, and then landed beside her after dropping over the jugs. He held up the plastic bag he carried and grinned. "Get up now or I'll strap you to this."

"What is it?"

"Plastique."

"How'd you get it?"

"Good question."

Her eyes shrank from the flashlight's beam. "What is this place?"

"A missile base. At least it was. Call it my combat HQ now. For you, it's the brig, or boot camp."

"There're no buildings."

"Underground. Nothing to see from a helicopter."

She struggled to her feet, with his help. "I've hurt my ankle."

"Sorry about that. Fortunes of war."

She limped forward. "David Sominski is here?"

"And waiting breathlessly." Startled, she froze. Calvin chuckled. "Just kidding."

He telescoped the ladder out and ran it down the hole forever as she watched, dumbfounded. Finally, it clanged at the bottom.

"You can't see it," he explained, "but there's an iron door down there leads into the base itself. Davy boy is inside, and that's where you'll be staying."

"Until what?"

"Until I decide what to do with you both, darling. Remember, you're a Level One here, and I'm Postmaster General. Friggin' Max the Ax in the flesh–that's me."

She peered down, edging slowly toward him. "He's been down there since–"

"Since the night of the little mishap at his place." Seeing that she was looking for an opportunity to catch him off guard and push him over the edge, he hopped back and grinned at her. "Don't worry, though; Dave had nothing to do with it. That booby trap was meant for him, for suspecting me."

He came toward her now, but she backed away, fear in her eyes. "You're going to kill us, aren't you, Calvin?"

He smiled in pity. "Why do you say that?"

"Because you have to, in the end. Because no one knows you're the bomber. You kidnapped me to blow the two of us up together. Make it look like a struggle, or a murder-suicide–while you walk."

He pursed his lips, as if considering it for the first time. "You know, you may have an idea there. Of course, I intend to have some fun with this first. Send your lover boy some clues as to your whereabouts. Get Dan Rather and Peter Jennings, and all those other liberal broadcasters here on the story. Hell, it might be months before I actually detonate you and Dave. In the meantime you'll have food and water, and a nice cool place to contemplate joining my war."

As he came for her, she sized him up one last time, straining at her bonds. "You don't have to do this."

"Don't I?"

"I'm not a liberal. I can help you get your message out. Get you help too, if you want."

"That's good to hear. Dave hasn't been too cooperative so far. About the help for me, though, I don't need that. Try helping Tucson. Try helping the ones who don't claim to be victims, and just want to be left alone."

"You mean like me?" she asked.

He took her arm, and led her roughly to the ladder. She descended first, slowly, one rung at a time, with her legs only, hands still tied behind her. Then he followed, with the water jugs tied together and slung over his shoulder. He held the bomb gingerly. He shined the flashlight beam down with his one free hand. The beam was weaker, but it was sufficient. He could get more batteries later. Or a penlight. If he had to, he could use matches.

The steel door was undisturbed. It took a couple of minutes to untie it before he could pull it open. There was no sound inside the crew quarters, though. It was oddly silent. He pushed the girl across the threshold into the darkness beyond. Then he followed her in.

"Hey, Davy!" he called. "You here, kiddo? Got a present for you. Something you've always dreamed about."

He shined the flashlight over at the far end of the room, where the toilets were. He stared in disbelief at what he saw.

One of the toilets had been broken into pieces.

The toilet where Sominski had been chained.

"Well, I'll be a–"

The blow came out of nowhere–a sudden whipping rattle against his shoulder. Calvin pitched sideways, yelping in pain. He dropped the water bottles and whirled in time toward the blow's direction to see Sominski's form moving into the dim rectangle of light. Dave trailed a loop of chain behind him as he stumbled out. He must have been waiting near the door.

I'll be damned.

"Yo–Dave!" he said as he came up behind Sominski at the ladder and grabbed onto his leg. "Where ya going, buddy?"

He jerked Dave down, kicking.

The Pollock's head hit the concrete in the fall, just like it had in the parking lot at Fleshdance.

But then the girl struck, too–with a kick aimed at the small of his back. Luckily, that missed its mark, just as the chain had missed his head. Calvin bulled her back into the door, putting his face against the side of her head as he gripped her by the hair.

He spoke in a close, hot, gutteral voice: "Go ahead and knee me in the groin now, baby, if you think that'll work. Come on. There's not much left to knee, though, and it'll only make it worse for you." He kissed her on the cheek. "Love ya, sweetheart! Love both of ya! What a fine team you are! Lotta good you'd be in combat, though. Davy boy watching X-rated movies and fondling himself, and you pushing papers and doing your nails. I'll make soldiers of you yet, though. Or roman candles. Take your pick."

He picked her up around the torso and carried her back inside. She didn't resist. Then he returned for Sominski, and carried him inside, too.

Using the handcuffs, he chained them both to one of the giant springs, which was suspended to the floor from the sloping, circular wall. He put the remaining food and the water jugs beside them. Sominski came around, finally. When he did, Calvin shined the flashlight in his pale face, and saw the pupils of his eyes go to dots before he closed them and turned away.

"Not a bad try there really, old buddy. You must have banged at that toilet chip by chip for hours to get it to crack like that. Then you ate, got your strength back, and planned this little surprise for me. Too bad you couldn't see too well after so long in the dark. Kinda stinks in here now too, don't it? Not just a musty odor. Don't you just love the smell of urine in the morning?"

"Yer sick, Calvin."

"Oh, I'm sorry, Dave. I forgot to introduce the lady. This is inspector Castillo, and she'll be your hostess for the night. You two can do whatever comes natural here too, I want you to know that. It's none of my business anyway, right? You have to take a crap, you can do that together too, except without a toilet now. Oh well, them's the breaks. By the way, what you been using for toilet paper, buddy? You look a mess."

"Get outta here."

"You want me to leave?"

Sominski started to cry. "Get the fuck outta here, Calvin! Ya damn ... ya damn bastard."

"Oh, poor Davy. Bruises and wounds getting infected, and here I am babbling about feces. I'm sorry. Really, I am. I'll bring a first aid kit when I come next time, I promise. You been getting a lotta knocks on your head lately, haven't you? Though you can't hit me in the head to save your life. As for you, honey ..." He reached down and ripped off the girl's eye patch. Her right eye, milky, clotted, opened and blinked into the light. "As for you, you got to pay for your actions. That's what's wrong with this country. Didn't I explain that to you?"

He walked back to the entrance door, and turned for a moment to hear Sominski weeping.

"Don't do this," the girl said. "What if there *is* a God?"

"Then don't curse him," Calvin replied. "Curse the devil, 'cause he's the one'll be sticking a pitchfork in your ass."

He angled the book bomb against the wall near the door, and took off the rubber band. If it was accidentally knocked or opened now, July Fourth would come early. But then he decided against leaving it, and slipped the rubber band back on. He might need it sooner than he expected, after all.

"Too-da-loo, now," he called.

He closed the heavy door on them, and used his extra chain and padlock this time to secure it. Then he climbed the ladder, stowed it, and hiked back through Total Wreck toward the van. Still, he caught himself looking into the shadows along the way. A chill swept him.

God is *on my side, isn't he, Dad?*

***

Once past the ghost town, the flashlight's battery died as if on cue. Luckily, the sky was cloudless. So he used the moon's reflected sunlight. When he finally made it to the van, he checked his watch. The luminous display read 4:22 AM. In a few hours he would be starting his new job in Forwarding. He needed a nap to adjust. There wouldn't be time to ditch the van somewhere outside town and hike back. He'd simply have to take his chances, hoping no one had seen.

Just before he started the engine, a coyote howled somewhere off to the west. Like a premonition.

22

For lunch, Vic ordered a Corona and two shredded beef tacos from the tiny Mexican place nearest the P&DC. As he ate one of the tacos, he ordered a second beer. He knew he'd need it, and knew as well that no one would care today. Not even if he was wearing a carrier's uniform.

The political cartoon in the *Arizona Daily Star* showed a postal jeep equipped with machine gun, bullet proof glass, and a mine-sweeper attachment on front. But Vic didn't laugh this time; it wasn't funny, anymore. Maria had vanished, had possibly been kidnapped, and no one knew anything. He hadn't slept–hadn't even bothered to shave–and no one cared about that, either. Certainly not Vince Manetti, who'd questioned him at the hotel that morning. Manetti had a stubble of his own, and his thick eyebrows were probably still raised at the suspicion of him and Maria sharing the same room. Was this the *modus operandi* of the United States Postal Inspection Service? If so, he'd implied, maybe he needed to change badges. Score some of those fringe benefits.

Now it was Wednesday, and even the window clerks dreaded coming into work. Earplugs were needed in the lobby, although they weren't supplied. Yet. As for the plant floor, it was barely navigable to the electric cars the mail handlers used. Cages and pie carts of delayed mail now filled every corridor in the building, including the one outside Graves' office. By Saturday, it was predicted, they'd have to start storing mail in the parking lot, covered with tarpaulins. Already the LSMs and the two bar code sorters were being dismantled and carried away, piece by piece. The decision for that had come from Maxwell himself on a conference phone with the Western Division manager and with Graves and Matuska. Two new LSM and BCS machines would be installed at a cost of nearly three million dollars. It made sense, because the time frame that way was six days instead of the eleven minimum needed to repair the damaged processors. But that was only if all the ETs and CTs worked around the clock.

Meanwhile, Sominski was out there somewhere, still at large, planning his next move. He'd already killed two police officers accidentally, and the mayor on purpose. Who was next? Would Graves be laid in an early grave? Would one of the City Council be targeted? One who'd recently voted to award a legal immigrant one point two million of county taxpayer dollars for false arrest? Surely they must all be suspicious of packages by now, Vic mused. Especially with local news shows flashing photos of the bomber every half hour on channels four, nine, and thirteen.

Yet it was the possibility of Maria with this nut that bothered him the most. He shuddered at remembering the X-rated movies Sominski owned. If the Pollock was smart, of course, he should have left the city at least, or gone to Mexico. But since when were killers rational? Had Thompson been logical to blow away Ollie Westover and then himself, at Arcadia? What about David Koresh or the ATF at Waco? Or Oklahoma City? Or the man who'd opened fire in a crowded McDonalds, or in a crowded Luby's in Killeen, Texas? Such killings had become hyped so much by the media that even the movie *Naked Gun, The Final Insult* had half a dozen postal carriers with submachine guns blasting away at innocent civilians like gangsters.

Art imitated life, no doubt about it. But where was the sanity in any of it?

On the way back to the office, Vic thought about Maria with not a little guilt. He went over in his mind their last words together.

Nothing extraordinary. She'd confessed hunger after they'd made sweet, but passionate, love. He'd gone for beef burritos with extra hot salsa, and ten minutes later he'd returned to find the door open, the TV blaring, and Maria missing. Fingerprints taken in the morning had failed to uncover clues. Next door guests reported hearing nothing. Of course, Vic had omitted the part about their making love. Manetti was curious, but it was none of his business.

***

He found Delany waiting for him in the office. He ignored the method used for the intrusion, and asked what the FBI man wanted. Delany produced two sheets of paper in reply. "A fax to the editor of the *Tucson Citizen*," he explained. "One of Manetti's men just brought by a copy."

Vic took the fax. "What are *you* doing here?" he asked.

"My trace of possible sources for the plastique has come to a brick wall. A prison wall, to be specific. The one lead I had left turns out to be a con doing time in Florence. Our local office is still going over my report, looking for holes, but until something else turns up we're out of luck."

Vic tapped the sheet. "And this is from Sominski?"

"That's what it says. He got the description of the inside of his house right, anyway. Although he didn't need to do that, I'm afraid. You'd better read it."

"Where was it faxed from?" Vic said, stalling.

"One of those rental fax places. Self-service, this one. Owner was shown a photo, but it didn't ring any bells."

"When was it sent?"

"At eight thirty-five this morning."

Vic nodded. "Why address the *Citizen* and not the morning newspaper?"

"Maybe it's the one he reads. Remember, he was on the night shift."

Vic read the fax at last. He didn't want to. After the paragraph which established the writer's identity was the bad news. The news he'd hoped and prayed wasn't there.

> This is to inform you that I ve taken a hostage until you meet my demands. The hostage is a postal inspector named Castillo, and it s a she. If you do not comply with my demands, I will sacrifice her and find another hostage. If you do not take me seriously I will detonate my biggest bomb yet, where it will do the most good. As you see, I am not just another disgruntled ex-postal worker. I am a citizen and a freedom fighter, and we are all at war.
>
> My demands are simple. First, you will stop publishing my photo on the news and in the paper. Next, you will stop doing stories on the "victims." They are to be referred to as "casualties." Finally, you will publish the following statement in the paper tomorrow.

Vic paused, swallowing hard, and looked up to meet Delany's gray eyes. Neither spoke. He continued reading.

> America as we know it will come to an end unless drastic measures are taken soon. Freedoms are being eroded, and there is little time to stop it. Solutions are these:
>
> A flat 10% tax imposed on all goods and services to eliminate all other taxes, while preventing the Tax Code to be used to promote Socialism.
>
> A moratorium on all immigration from the Caribbean and Mexico, until all countries from which the immigrants come curb their popula-

tion growth.

An end to foreign aid, because we re not just broke, we re in debt.

Swift death penalties to all drug dealers and "entitlement" defrauders, with speedy trials and justice system amnesty from all frivolous lawsuits.

Caning, as in Singapore, for all major and minor offenses. In public.

More attention paid to crime victims, instead of bogus victims and other criminals.

Disposal of TVs in prisons, and the installation of manual mail processing equipment so that inmates can distribute bulk mail, and thereby eliminate plans for more government subsidies to the Postal Service.

Military boot camp, with road construction work, for carjackers and other young punks who now think minimum wage jobs are for losers.

Mandating only one child per couple, as in China, with the proviso that more than one child is possible only to those who can prove success with the first. Rebates of tax funds to single people who have no children, but are forced to pay taxes for the so-called "education" of those who do.

A censure of the Pope for helping cause all the 3rd World s bloated babies, passing his hand over the masses in blessing, and then blaming us for not sending more food and medicine.

Term limits for the career criminals and wolves-in-sheep s-clothing on Capitol Hill.

Tort reform to end never-ending lawsuits for things like breast implants and Gulf War Syndrome, as well as fines for ambulance chasers.

A balanced budget amendment to make people pay up front for what they receive.

Finally, a total end to the welfare system, plus needs-testing for Social Security and Disability (to stop "crippled" defrauders from playing golf, tennis and racketball).

We have chosen quantity and poverty and laziness over quality and prosperity and work. It is time to start demanding responsibility for one s actions. Everything which is done must point toward stopping people from thinking that the world owes them something, or that the U.S. government is a bottomless pit of money. We are digging our own graves. So-called "entitlement" giveaway programs are bankrupting us, as well. Let everyone pay their own way without regard to race or religion, and let the government stay out of the way of those who work hard and have more ambition than their neighbor. This is the American way.

You have forced this first battle of the Second Civil War with your treasonous actions. You know who you are. Many more will die unless you act responsibly now to consider the laws outlined here. These things must go through, and not be blocked. They must be implemented, not vetoed. I will release my hostage as soon as progress is seen, and if it is not seen by the Fourth of July, then I say let the fireworks begin again, and GIVE US LIBERTY OR GIVE US ALL DEATH!

—David S. Sominski

"What's the 'S' for?" Vic asked, as he dropped the fax onto McDade's desk.

"Stupid," Delany replied, dully. "Talk about a Contract with America. Who's he kidding? His wouldn't even make it through the house."

"Progress. What does that mean?"

"Only the devil himself knows."

"Or a man with a brain the size of a postage stamp." Vic took a seat, and ran a hand through his hair. He thought about Maria again—her eye bandaged, probably tied up and gagged somewhere ... maybe even being raped. He imagined Sominski leaning over her, leering. Touching her. He must have used the gun they hadn't yet found to get her in this position. He couldn't imagine Sominski overpowering her so quickly and spiriting her off without it.

"And what would he say to her? Something bothers me," Vic said, thinking out loud. "The same thing that bothered me before."

"What?"

"Maybe nothing. Just the writing. It's too intelligent. I can't see Sominski writing this. It's not his style. Of course I'm going by the way he talks. Maybe he took his time with this, to get it right; he's certainly had some time."

"Damn lucky time, if you ask me."

"And then there's the matter of how Sominski got the bomb into the post office to begin with. No one recalls seeing him, you know."

There was a knock on the door; Delany opened it. It was Graves' secretary. She looked solemn as she edged in and handed Vic another sheet of paper.

"A fax," she said. "For you."

"When did you get it?" Delany asked.

"Just now."

Vic read the crisp, freshly dried paper:

Roses are red,
Violets are blue,
In the garden 'neath a bench
You'll find your first clue.

"Thank you," he said absently to the secretary, who left the room with a look of disappointment. Then he shook his own head in bewilderment. "My God."

Delany took the fax from his hand, read it, and smiled. "Can I have this?" the G-man asked. "It may be a lead."

"What do you mean?" Vic replied in frustration. "A nursery rhyme ... as some kinda half-ass runaround? What garden could it be, anyway?"

"A public garden, obviously, since neither you nor–"

"Wait a minute! The park. What's that place near Sominski's house?"

"Reid Park?"

"Right. There's a rose garden there, I remember. But he'd be insane to go so close to the crime scene, wouldn't he?"

Delany shook his head. "It's a cliché, but–"

"Don't say it, then. I'll agree with you: it's the only lead we've got. You coming?"

***

He followed Delany's Crown Victoria in the Cavalier along 22nd Street, and then left onto Country Club and into the park. They circled and parked in front of the rose garden–a round, fenced area a hundred yards in diameter. In the center, at the end of a footpath, were three benches facing each other around a cleared span of packed sand. No strollers or attendants were to be seen. They got out and started up the path.

"How hot you think it is?" Delany asked, offhand.

"Not quite as hot as where Sominski's going, I trust," Vic replied.

They kneeled beside the first bench. Delany put his hand up to stop Vic from coming closer, then peered underneath the bench, and finally felt the soil around it carefully.

"You think one of these is booby-trapped?" Vic asked, from a distance.

"You never know. He might have taken the chance he'd be seen by one of the maintenance people, or he could have scaled the fence at night to do what he needed to do."

"Kill me, you mean. But why?"

Delany shrugged. "Because you were with Inspector Castillo. Because you interviewed him at his home. Because your name was in the paper."

"So was yours."

"True." Delany smiled, albeit half-heartedly, and continued carefully examining the undisturbed soil. Bench number two came next, with identical results. Finally, Delany approached the last bench–the one facing the lake some four hundred feet away, where the ducks were huddled now on a tiny island of oak trees for shade.

Vic turned. The roses surrounding them had long receded into hard brown nubs in the cruel summer heat. Their blooming life had been brief, even with the sprinkler system active. Now he saw that the name plate on the bush nearest him read NEW BEGINNINGS. That was what he needed, he thought wistfully. Something Karen had already found, and certainly in a more settled form than he himself had, so far.

Delany kneeled beside the third bench. Then he pointed at a spot near the bench's left rear leg. Vic approached and saw the place where he pointed. The ground had been excavated and refilled there, in a space no larger than a human hand. Delany bent his head, presumably searching for wires or tripping devices.

"It's probably just a note," Vic told him, wiping his own forehead.

The FBI man didn't reply, but took out a pocket knife and began to carefully scoop dirt away from the edges of the disturbed area.

"He probably enjoys playing these little games," Vic added. "It's how he gets his jollies."

Delany kept digging, methodically. Soon the edge of a piece of paper appeared. Was it a trigger? Taking no chances, Delany dug deeper, sticking the blade slowly into the soil. Finally satisfied with his probe, he cautiously pulled the note free of the hot sand. He looked up at last, almost triumphantly.

"Better than nothing," Delany announced.

When he got up and unfolded the paper by the edges, Vic read what was there over his shoulder. It was handwritten on crisp bond paper this time.

Hi Victor, remember me? My old man used to come here and sit right on this bench. Thinking about death, just like you are now. You think I'm just a dumb Pollock, don't you? Well, I got news for you, bud. I'm not drinking anymore. Thanks for sobering me up, because I'M THE VICTOR NOW. You're the enemy, all of you, and it's time you started losing the war. So I've changed my mind about leaving you any clues. Sorry.

Now here's what I want you to do. Get the 40 grand from my 401K and put it in a brown envelope and leave it beneath the rock at the base of the sign marking Soldier Trail in the Catalina Mountains. Old bills, unmarked, non-sequential. Don't try and observe the site. I could see you from miles away with binoculars, anyway. I see anyone suspicious and the bitch dies. Then you'll know that you're the one who killed her. (By the way, those handcuffs have sure come in handy.)

About my money, I earned it, unlike some of your Food Stamp defrauders who stole four billion last year. (That's FOUR THOUSAND MILLION, KIDDIES.)

Have all this done, including what I said in my fax, by July 4 at midnight.

—Dave

PS: By the way, you DO know what July 4 is? It's Independence Day. A celebration of freedom. Something all you weepy preachy socialists wouldn't understand as you complain about the noise and air pollution, and then force us fed-up taxpayers to give block parties to homeless people.

Vic sat down on the bench and looked up. "What is it with this guy?"

Delany placed the letter inside a small evidence bag taken from his pocket. "He's a terrorist, and he needs to be treated as such. What motivates him should be none of our concern. We need to eliminate him, not meet his demands."

"But what about Maria? What about what he said in the fax about another bomb?"

"We can appear to go along. Maybe get the evening paper to print a story suggesting some progress on what he's seeking. It's the paper he reads, apparently."

"And television news?"

"They can stop showing his photo. People have seen it enough at this point anyway, I think."

"Easily said. But can editors and station managers be manipulated like that?"

"They can be convinced to cooperate, if they see awards for cooperation in their future."

"Can we get the money he wants?"

Delany wiped sweat from his eyebrows. "A radio device could alert us, triggered when he moves the rock. A police helicopter with a searchlight could be waiting on Mount Lemmon, after a police unit was dispatched to cut him off."

"He'd go at night, then."

"Obviously."

"But he wouldn't stay with the trail."

"Probably not. That's why the helicopter."

"So the money would be bogus ... shreds of paper, maybe?"

"It could be real. Then we might have the surprise advantage a while longer. I doubt that he'd go when we predict he might, on the night of the fourth. He would probably wait a few days for safety's sake."

Vic shook his head. "Maria doesn't have that much time. He said he'd kill her."

Delany looked away, grimly. "He might anyway. She could already be dead, for all we know."

Vic stared out beyond the rose garden at the brick barbecues stationed on the wilted summer grass. Sominski could be out there, watching them from behind any of a hundred shade trees. They were fenced in here, as if in the center ring of a circus. And disgruntled ex-postal clerk David Sominski was now a circus clown. A sad clown with a madly grinning face.

Delany's beeper went off. Vic followed him back to his car, where he retrieved a mobile phone and dialed it in. "I'd better go," the agent said at last.

"What's up?"

"Another lead relating to the plastique. I'll call Manetti about this letter, and we'll have a conference about what to do." He checked his watch. "I'll get back to you by three-thirty. Don't talk to the press about this."

"Don't worry," Vic said.

He watched Delany circle and exit out of the park. Then he got into the Cavalier, started it up, and turned on the air conditioning. He tilted the vent to blow cool air into his face as he sat looking up the path into the rose garden. He wondered where Maria was–and if she was cool there.

Then he thought about Sominski again, too. *My old man used to come here*. He couldn't remember reading anything in the records about Sominski's father. Only his mother, who'd heard nothing of her son in years. Could it be a clue, after all? He decided to check into it. The indefinable apprehension begun with Sominski's letters continued to bother him, just as another slice of pepperoni pizza might on a peptic ulcer.

Now if only someone like Maria were around to help. Or even one of the other inspectors assigned to security. Maybe if he called Washington, they'd assign him one. But probably not. Maxwell–and therefore Graves and Matuska–were mostly interested in getting plant operations back to normal, and in letting the police ferret out the bomber, while protecting the premises of the various postal centers. That he'd been assigned to investigation of the terrorist act at all was possibly political. It looked good. At least up until Maria had been kidnapped. Now it was one big black mark across the Service's reputation, and probably a black mark on his own record once the report was read that he'd been sharing the same room with her. He tried to shut the thought of that out of his mind as irrelevant for the moment.

We have chosen quantity and poverty and laziness over quality and prosperity and work.

He imagined the residents of Tucson or Phoenix reading the statement. The homeowners at the edge of the desert who complained about new developments blocking their view of the mountains. They would certainly disagree about the poverty and the work aspects. After all, the newer residents that they complained about would be complaining themselves about others farther out, before long. But what else were they going to do? It was ludicrous to imagine actually stopping the expansion. It was the way of the world, to to raise families and retire, everyone hoping their children's or grandchildren's lot would be better somehow.

Somewhere, he realized again, Maria was waiting–bound and gagged–for her rescue or for her death. Somewhere Karen was being massaged by a retired trucking executive too, and forgetting all about her past.

Both seemed to be his fault.

***

In the office he found another intruder. From the back, this one was even taller, and with more angular bone structure than Delany. The man flipped a ring of keys in his hand, and wore a checked blue blazer, dark pants, and dully-shined leather shoes. He was chewing gum as he turned around, and then something about his face seemed suddenly familiar–the blue eyes, wide thin lips, jutting chin. The box on the desk in front of him clinched it.

Not gum, after all. It was an open box of jellied donuts.

"Phil!" Vic exclaimed, and ran forward to pump the man's crumbed hand. "You don't know how glad I am to see you!"

"Have we met?" the tall, gangling man asked, dumbfounded.

23

When Calvin got back from lunch two clicks late, seven trays of CFS letter mail awaited him at the copy machine. Although Paula Rodriguez–a fat Hispanic girl in her mid-twenties–had promised to train him on the mechanized terminals used to label and sort letters to their forwarding addresses, she explained that it would have to wait until the backlog could be processed. In the meantime he should continue photocopying the letters which requested forwarding and address corrections.

It was a simple task, repetitive and boring. Slap three yellow-labeled letters down on a template, hit COPY, and take them off. Then slap three more down. An idiot could do it ... or a Pollock. The Kodak Ektaprint 150 copied the old and new addresses onto card stock paper, automatically cut it into thirds, and ejected it into an output tray ready to be run on the LSM as RETURN TO SENDER. The template added the Postal Service symbol, along with the notice POSTAGE DUE.

Calvin smiled. It wasn't so bad. Inside a week he'd be doing a number of jobs here, including labeling magazines by hand for forwarding, via the Flats Sorter. Pulling full, and then re-hanging empty, #3 green sacks on racks. Tearing magazine covers to return with their new addresses to publishers. And keying old addresses at the computer-operated terminals so labels could be printed with the new addresses. Best of all, CFS had its own special room off the main work floor, and the air conditioning worked better here ... plus there were no peepholes for inspectors. He could reroute as many checks and ATM cards as he wanted, and no one could see. On the off chance that he was caught, well, he was new in here, wasn't he? In point of fact, it was already afternoon, and they hadn't even bothered to introduce him to everyone yet.

Not that he wanted that. Looking around at the other clerks, what he saw was mostly cellulite, and tired will-the-day-never-end expressions. Being mostly women, he could imagine what they were often whispering about when they should have been working, too.

Babies.

Even the CFS manager had long been referred to as a woosie by everyone on the main floor. Gilbert Allen was his name; he was thin and pale and rumored to be gay. A regular walking cliché, he might have made poster boy for a *Mad Magazine* rendering of a postal clerk, right next to the nerd with the taped glasses. The wimp didn't have the guts to tell anyone to stop talking and get back to work, either. Not that he even could, because CFS clerks were Level 4's, and the union contract forbade any mention of speed or output at that level. So Gilbert buried his face in the computer screen at his desk and mostly talked on the phone instead.

What a crew, Calvin thought. *And what a country we got now, Dad.*

Of course he was one of them, now. For a while anyway, until his seniority built up enough to get a rural route carrier job. With any luck, he'd outdo them all, too. Beside him, their inefficiencies would pale. He would prove to be the most inefficient clerk since the Postal Reorganization Act of 1970, and no one would know. On the expense scale, he planned to rate straight Tens in cost to Maxwell's bottom line of red ink. The added zeros might even force the Board of Governors to consider raising postage rates. Maybe, given enough time, his war would contribute to privatization of the Service, wrenching it from the hands of government bureaucracy and waste and favoritism. Then the right heads would roll at last. Competition would triumph. And the union's deadwood would be hacked off better than Max the Ax could ever have dreamed.

Already he was eyeing the IBM System 88 mainframe computer in the corner. What if it short-circuited? What kind of delay would that cause?

***

After work he drove the Beemer to Eegees for one of those Galactic Grape drinks a geek named Ernie had recommended. He ordered a ham and cheese grinder, too. It wasn't bad, but it didn't end his growing jet-lag-like disorientation. As he sat looking out the window at all the deluded taxpayers driving by, he caught himself thinking about what Dave and the bitch inspector might be discussing there in the perpetual darkness. Probably rehearsing what they would say when he came back.

If he came back.

Not tonight anyway, he decided. Maybe not tomorrow, either. He needed to get better on track with the shift change. It would feel odd to sleep at night again like normal people did. But it could be done, even after three years of sharing a vampire's world. It was amazing what the mind could do once it was allowed to gain control of the body.

You can't do this, Calvin.

Maybe she was right. Maybe it was a mistake recruiting her to the A team. Stone sober, he'd realized she had the situation summed up when she'd said that he had to kill them both. Except maybe he didn't–at least not with his own hands. Maybe he'd forget about them for a few weeks. Forget about risking getting Sominski's money in the Catalinas, too. Promise more bombs, but do nothing. Let it all ride. Then take all the evidence away from the missile site, and drop the dead bodies in that big hole beneath them–where it might be years before their skeletons would be found. After all, he'd made his statement. He'd done his duty. Now it was other people's turn.

He got an evening paper from the machine rack out front, and skimmed through a report of post office boxes in Nogales being used by Mexican nationals to obtain government checks. His fax wasn't printed yet, but at least they'd stopped using Sominski's postal photo. That was a good sign. Maybe they would cooperate after all. Maybe they were scared shitless not to.

***

He sat on a bench outside the restaurant and listened to the radio station playing through the exterior speakers. Love songs sung by hormone-crazed punks promising the moon and stars and then singing about moving back and forth, going deeper, getting sweaty, finding sweet release. Every song, he realized, had the same message, whether rap or not: Do It As Often As You Could. Obsessing on it. Sweet-talking girls into their own fantasies of love and family so you could go back and forth some more. And the only thing eternal about the love they described was their eternal and transparent hunger for more flesh–for a new jigsaw collection of shapes and sex organs. Mix and match, that was the game, all right. Oh yeah. Fit as many pieces together as possible, even if they didn't fit. Even if the picture wasn't any clearer. Because, of course, they couldn't step back and look at the whole jigsaw. Not like he could. They couldn't see that the picture they were trying to make was the picture of a smiling face.

Have a nice day, Calvin thought, *you fucking slaves.*

In a way, it felt good to be free of it. To be free of the thing so many had sacrificed their futures for, or even their lives. He felt a strange privilege in not being on the mailing lists of all the sleaze merchants his mother had once warned about–and which came through the post office in sickening regularity–advertising interracial videos, dildos, blowup dolls, anal lube, and edible undies. He alone was rid of it, forever.

Or was he? He remembered his partial erection. Had it been the excitement of the moment? A fluke?

He finished off his frozen drink, and tossed it in the outdoor bin. Then he went out to the Beemer and cranked it up, thinking about the van. It was too late to ditch it–the timing was wrong to report its theft. He would leave it parked in back instead, and take his chances. If they didn't make the plate he'd be okay. If someone had seen it, he would have heard by now. It was time to forget about it. Forget about everything. Wait and see what happened next with the media. In the meantime he would sleep it off.

You can't do this, Calvin.

You can't do this ...

You can't ...

Oh, but he could.

***

He parked beneath his bedroom window as usual, and was in process of covering the bike with a nylon tarp taken from his saddlebag, when he was reminded that he couldn't chain the Beemer to the gas meter anymore. The chain was being used elsewhere. He almost smiled at that.

What stopped him was seeing the back door.

Which was partially open.

He ran to it, noticing now that the frame was cracked. Someone had forced his way inside.

Detective Manetti, perhaps?

He retrieved a tire iron from the van and returned to edge his way inside, cautiously. The first thing he detected was the missing Sony Trinitron. Then the missing Fisher stereo system. Someone had gone through his classical and jazz CDs too, looking for what–rock? Rap? Norwegian folk medleys? The CD jewel boxes lay scattered, possibly with fingerprints on them. Not that it mattered: He didn't have apartment insurance, and so a police report wouldn't do any good. Even with prints the odds were long on recovering anything. The stuff was probably in a third party's hands by now, anyway.

He checked the book case and located the Stephen King novel: still intact.

In the kitchen he noticed the imprint on the counter where his juicer had been. The refrigerator door was ajar, and he opened it now to discover a half-empty jug of apple juice. He took it out and drained it in the sink.

Couldn't find any beer, could you, fellas? Sorry about that. It's hard work, and I know you get thirsty.

In the bedroom, all the drawers had been pulled out. Suddenly remembering the gun, he kneeled beside the bed, and felt under it. Amazingly, the .45 was still there. He hefted it and cocked it lovingly.

Pretty dumb, boys. Not professionals, are we? Punks, maybe?

He noticed that the spare change he kept in a jar on his dresser was empty. The clock radio was gone, too. They'd used a pillowcase for a bag: his pillow was uncovered.

Missing from the bathroom: his digital weight scale, and his practically-new Remington microscreen electric razor.

The indignity of it. He was getting mad now.

He checked the closet, and yes–his toolbox was not there anymore, either. All the Craftsman wrenches and sockets and screwdrivers were history, their lifetime warranties expired early. Ditto his Powercraft half-inch reversible drill and twenty-piece drill bit set.

He closed the closet door carefully, then rammed his fist through the sheet rock in the hallway. He stared at the hole he'd made, and realized he'd have to repair that too, along with replacing the cracked rear door frame and the door itself.

***

He decided to take a ride to the bank to calm down. After all, he told himself, he still had a few thousand waiting for access via the automatic teller. Uncle Sam hadn't taken everything as deductions from his direct deposits. The State hadn't made everyone equal yet, although they were working at it.

He took the gun with him just in case someone else wanted to make a withdrawal while he was gone.

The cooler air of evening felt good in his hair. But on the way down Broadway he caught every traffic light, and was forced to wait and witness laughing couples on their way to theaters or restaurants. So he began to gun the BMW, peeling away at each successive green signal. His rage grew as a woman in a station wagon with four kids passed him without even having to slow down. It was the same woman from three lights before, driving steadily and cheerfully along. Oblivious to him. One of her kids even pointed at him as he roared past, taching out at 8000 RPM. Laughing and pointing. The little snot might have been pointing at one of the Power Rangers come to life out of his Gameboy or Nintendo.

Beside the closed bank was a boarded-up convenience store with graffiti all over it. Four Hispanic youths were passing around a joint in back. One drank from a Styrofoam cup. They saw him pull up to park next to the teller machine, but paid little attention, and continued in their animated conversation. Then, as he cut off the bike's engine, one of them turned to watch him. The kid pointed at him as he withdrew his cash. Now two others looked.

Calvin waved.

They didn't wave back. He got his money, retrieved his card, and waved again, finally holding up the three hundred he'd just withdrawn. He grinned maniacally.

At least now he had their undivided attention.

He glanced at the graffiti on the wall nearby. The only legible thing amid the scrawlings read: *I love Ramona–and hate everyone else.* He stuffed the money into his shirt pocket, making a display of it. Next, he gave them the finger, and strolled back to the bike.

All four, as if on cue, were walking toward him. Walking fast. The one in front was the biggest. They all looked to be around seventeen, wearing oversize dark blue pullover shirts and jeans two sizes too large. Two wore baseball caps turned backward, and all four had stern expressions on their swarthy faces.

Calvin waited until one of them reached for something in his hip pocket before pulling out the .45 and kneeling behind his iron horse for cover. He aimed over the seat, using it for support. They froze. The one in back dropped his cup. But the other three clung stubbornly to their attitudes.

"What's up, boys?" Calvin said, and then flashed his postal ID. "Detective Manetti's the name. Gang squad." He grinned. "You fellas the Who-twos or the Tootsies?"

They looked at each other, said nothing.

"What's that you dropped–ice tea?" Calvin asked the one who'd dropped the cup. "Littering is a serious offense in Singapore, you know. Get you fifty lashes. Rip the skin right off your back. But maybe you didn't know that 'cause you can't read."

Still nothing.

"You punks don't listen to good music either, do you? Never

heard of Rachmaninoff or Gershwin, I'll bet. All you're good for is jumping people in the dark, and screwing your tramp girlfriends. Right?"

The big one said something in Spanish. They began backing away.

"Hey, don't leave! Talk to me. In English, if you can. This is America, you know. Or at least it used to be."

But they turned away, still glancing venomously back. When they made the corner of the bank, the big one returned his upraised middle finger gesture, giving it an additional upward thrust for emphasis. Then they disappeared.

Calvin started the Beemer. *Most people would let it go now, wouldn't they, Dad?*

He hesitated, looking up at the crescent moon from which he imagined his father watched. Then he cut off the bike again, got off, and followed.

All four, he saw, were getting into a maroon Buick Regal parked in front of the abandoned store. The car had tinted glass, a low body, and extra wide tires. Luckily, the bank's landscaping was mostly stone. Smooth, round stone.

Palm-sized and ideal for throwing.

The first rock he hurled hit their roof, skipping off, but leaving a dent. The second was dead on target–the back window shattered before the car could get away, burning rubber and skidding sideways as it roared for the side street.

An arm came out the window from the Buick's back seat. Calvin ducked as a pistol fired and a hole was punched in the bank's thick green plate glass behind him. Quickly, he kneeled and returned fire with the .45, aiming with both hands. A plume of blood jumped from the head of the kid in the front passenger seat. He fired again, but the car went out of his sight and sped away.

A hit, Dad! Did you see? A head hit!

"You lose," he breathed. "How do you like frontier justice?"

Back at the GS, he cranked up and throttled off in pursuit. It had been ages of routine and boredom since he'd shot a Commie gook in 'Nam, and shooting a street punk did feel better than any imagined sexual release. But he couldn't find them now. They must have turned off onto another back road, making right hand turns back toward Broadway, where there was traffic. Where people would see. After that they would go back to their own turf on the south side. South Tucson. Home base for their own operations, preying on each other in meaningless posturings and feudings and killings.

They had no purpose, of course. To hell with them. They weren't worthy to be recruited for the real war. They were too much on the other side. They were the enemy.

***

He rode without direction for awhile, passing the bars and nightclubs along University Boulevard. He noticed two cop cars parked at the Dunkin' Donut shop on the corner of Tyndall. Not far away, a coven of hookers plied their wares for the frat boys on the corner of Euclid ... the college kids who screwed and ate pizza while learning how to accept the coming bad years.

Listless, he turned south, circled around, and was cut off by a freight train on South Park. Then, as he sat watching the Southern Pacific coal cars and the CTXL tanker cars bringing Texas crude oil to California, he sang a song for his father, up there in the moon. By the end of it, though, he changed the words slightly.

"Oh, say does that star spangled ban-ner yet waaaaave...o're the lannnnd that cannot reeeeeeead ... and the hooooome ... of the ... slaaaaaave ..."

At last, the final freight car passed.

He paused, watching the train dwindle toward the desert darkness beyond the Tucson mountains to the west. Then he let out the clutch slowly, his anger gone as a weary disgust took its place.

24

Vic arrived early on Friday morning to find that the line of customers waiting for access to the harried window clerks stretched almost to the road. Some of the faces seemed familiar now, and most of the indigent or elderly seemed either angry or resigned. Three bearded men had set up camp with sleeping bags under the Mexican palm trees in the little rock garden to the side. A pup tent had been erected by a fourth. Dozens more sat against the wall or along the plate glass of the lobby inside, waiting numbly in their shabby clothes for nine o'clock to arrive. All had ignored the sign which indicated that they would be telephoned as soon as their checks were processed. Most of them could probably not be reached by phone anyway, Vic realized. Maybe they were General Delivery customers without an address either, and without cash they had nowhere else to go. The shelters were already full, he'd read, and that explained why they'd ignored the second sign, too, the one which read NO LOITERING.

"What do you think," the guard at the parking lot gate said, as Vic flashed his badge out the car's window. "Should I clear the bums outta the lobby so people can get in and check their boxes?"

The big blond kid was eager, hoping for an override of standing orders probably given him by Matuska. With an inspector's permission he could risk doing what he really wanted—ordering people around. Vic had seen the type before in his class at Greenville High: the obsequious bully who tried to cover his prejudices by becoming teacher's pet.

"Isn't Inspector DeLong here yet?" he asked, shunting the question.

"No sir. At least, I haven't seen him."

"That's why a police officer is not guarding this gate?"

"He is ... I mean, he's inside on break now. They asked me to cover for him. I'm checking all IDs coming and going, like I was told."

"Which means you know who to look for, right?"

"Anyone without a photo ID?" The kid asked. "David Sominski, sir?"

Vic frowned. "Any idea what Mr. Sominski looks like?"

"I've seen him on TV."

"Uh-huh. But what if he has a gun? Like an AK-forty-seven or an Uzi?"

The kid was taken aback. "Then I guess I'm ... dead?"

"Exactly."

Vic drove past him into the lot, and parked. Upstairs, he'd barely made it into the office when Graves came in, one hand to his forehead, pacing. The postmaster looked like he hadn't slept in a week, which was probably true. "My God," he said feebly, "my goose is cooked. The pin has popped out. Get out the ax already."

"What's up?" Vic asked him. "Is a *Sixty Minutes* crew on the way?"

"How did you know?"

"You're kidding."

"Am I? Max is coming, too. He's en route now on a private jet. He's been taking heat from the media, and he wants to put this thing behind him. Trace the fire back to the source. Stamp it out with his own foot."

Vic nodded. "It's a pretty big foot."

Graves continued pacing. "A foot that could come down on my neck ... just before the blade."

"I don't think he blames you, sir. It's a good PR move, to be here.

He probably wants to make a statement to the press from here. Show he's on top of it. Reassure people about Postal security and the commitment to on-time delivery. Not to mention expressing his concern for the victims."

"Don't you mean the casualties?" Graves laughed glibly. "I shoulda let you make some of my speeches."

Maybe I should, Vic thought. "When's Maxwell due?"

Graves checked his watch as if it were the countdown timer of another bomb. "We got one hour."

"Then I suggest you order breakfast for the people out front. Donuts and coffee, anyway. It would look good when the cameras return."

Graves shook his index finger at the air. "Good idea. Damn good."

Carole from Personnel came in, after knocking on the door frame. She handed Vic his paycheck. "For you," she said, and smiled.

"Thank you," Vic said, with plastic charm. He slipped the check quickly into his pocket without peeking.

Graves followed her out. "Consider yourself compensated," the postmaster said as he closed the door.

***

At nine o'clock, as he was reviewing his files for a third time, Vic heard running in the hallway outside. He went out to investigate.

"What's going on?" he asked the girl at the window in the office across the hall.

The commercial accounts manager did not turn around. She tapped the window instead. "He's here," she said simply. No elaboration was needed.

Vic walked to the window and stood beside her. "You mind?" he asked.

She shook her head as if a fly had landed on it.

Below them now, parked near the road, was the familiar KGUN remote truck, its dish antenna being positioned for a live feed. Other film crews, including KMSB and a Phoenix station, had camera tripods swiveled to film the airport limo as it entered the protected gate to the east. The sleek white Caddy parked under the close surveillance of the two uniformed police now posted, but there was a pause before the car door finally opened. When it did, a brown-haired man in his late forties stepped out.

"Who's that," Vic said, "the bodyguard?"

"No," the account manager replied. "It looks like Steve Croft. From *Sixty Minutes*."

Vic shook his head. "But I was just ..."

"What?"

"Nothing. I just ... can't believe it."

The other door, on the far side, opened next. A tall, stout man, with gray streaks in his hair, got out. It was the Postmaster General, Max the Ax Maxwell himself. No doubt about it. He looked like an executioner looking for a big, thick post.

"He's quite handsome, actually," the girl commented, more to the window than to Vic. "If you like older men."

"I'm afraid I don't," Vic informed her.

The two were met by Graves now, and would go inside first. They walked toward the side, then out of sight.

The girl left the window, but Vic stayed. The line directly below was shorter now, he saw. The tent was gone, as were the sleeping bags. Two giant silver coffee urns had been set up on a table. Another table held at least twenty boxes of donuts. The man behind the first table was the plant manager, Matuska. The one who manned the table with the donuts was none other than Phil DeLong.

"I'll be damned."

"What is it?" the girl asked, as she checked her hair in a small mirror.

"Nothing. Thanks."

Vic left her to her work and took the stairs down two at a time, hoping guiltily not to run into Maxwell on the way up. Luckily, he guessed right about them taking the elevator.

When he approached Phil DeLong, the gangling man was munching merrily away on the leftovers. "I should have known," Vic said.

Phil gave a bulging smile. "What? No 'hi, Phil, how ya doin' buddy?'"

"How do you eat so many of those things and not turn into a blowfish?"

"I'm blessed with what's known as reverse metabolism. Don't much like glazed, though. Stupid to pinch pennies at this point, am I right?" He washed down another bite with some coffee. "The show's about to start. Got your ticket?"

Vic scanned the growing crowd of reporters, half-expecting to see big Al, the NBC weatherman, cracking jokes about the dry heat. "As long as there're no fireworks. Who told the press to be here?"

Phil turned to Matuska, who wore an out-of-character white shirt, but with a colorful Hawaiian tie. "You call them in, Rick, hoping for a screen test?" Phil asked.

The plant manager grunted. "Not me. Maybe the old man phoned ahead."

Vic nodded. "Where's the *Sixty Minutes* cameraman?"

"The *what?*" Matuska was aghast.

Phil pointed at a short bald guy adjusting the filter on a steadicam. "Over there, I think. He's the one they let out on the road, anyway."

"I hope they don't ask me to speak," Matuska muttered as he adjusted his tie.

"Hey, don't worry," Phil reassured him, mopping up crumbs. "Be happy. We're just the catering service."

Vic pulled Phil aside. "Where you been? I wanted to go over those other files with you, like I said. We need to find out why Delany didn't call back about that lead he had, too."

"Relax! Had to make some calls, tie up some loose ends on that stamp washing operation in Mesa. Hell, its only nine o'clock anyway. You really think Sominski's not–"

"Hold it down, will you? I don't know. Maybe he's got himself an accomplice."

"He was a loner, you said."

"Yeah, but that doesn't mean ..." Vic broke off, seeing Graves coming through and now beckoning him. "I'll be back."

"Okay," Phil said, and grinned. "I'll save you a seat."

***

Maxwell was waiting for them in Graves' office upstairs, alone. On the way up, Graves warned him about the man's temper. In public Maxwell was a diplomat with a silver tongue and knack for escaping being cornered. In private he was a shark, fully capable of devouring fools. After a successful career as CEO of Reprotek Engineering and Automation, he'd been tapped by the Board of Governors as *the* innovator needed to lead the Postal Service into the 21st Century. The man himself was no robot, though. He was a motivator, an ass-kicker, and a lie detector to boot. Heads had rolled in every department he'd investigated, and in some he'd only heard about. But the USPS was just too big, and so his frustration inevitably led to anger.

"And you're ..."

"Inspector Victor Kazy, sir. Nice to meet you."

The handshake was more like a vise or trap than an indication of affection. Maxwell obviously used it to put people in their place at power luncheons and power conferences. Standing so close now, he reminded Vic of his dead father, re-animated by force of will, complete with an extra graying of the hair follicles at a point marking his time of death–or maybe his entry into union contract negotiations.

"I want to know where I stand," Maxwell said evenly, "before I go down there and face the press. I've got a crow sitting on my neck right now, and I've been trying to tell him nevermore. But there're some vultures out there too ... like the ones from *Hard Copy*. So let's have it."

Vic looked at Graves for support, but the postmaster moved closer to Maxwell. Postmaster and Postmaster General stood side by side now, both likely hoping somehow that they were looking at their scapegoat.

"Well, sir, there's the letter from Sominski to the *Tucson Citizen*."

"I've read it."

"And the previous letter, and the note left in the park."

"Faxed to me by the FBI. What else?"

Vic figeted. "Then you know we've decided to plant the retirement fund money on Monday night as demanded, and have it monitored?"

"Tell me something I don't know. What about this guy Gessel?"

"Who?"

Maxwell glanced at Graves, who shrugged. Vic swallowed hard. "You mean the FBI's got information they're not sharing with you? Gessel. Some renegade ex-Special Forces operative who may have connections to missing chemicals at the base. The one they're trying to track right now."

Vic shook his head. "I wouldn't know about that, sir. I haven't talked to Agent Delany since yesterday afternoon, and he said nothing about it then."

"Really? And just what exactly have you been doing lately about our kidnapped inspector?"

Vic swallowed again, involuntarily, trying to cover it unsuccessfully with a hand to his chin. "I've been going over the letters from the bomber, sir. And my notes about him. Developing a suspicion."

Maxwell turned to Graves. "What suspicion?"

Again, Graves shrugged. He was getting good at it.

Maxwell scowled impatiently. "Come on, son. Out with it! The President personally expressed his concern to me about this situation, and I need all the ammunition I can get."

They both looked at him, waiting for the bone. Or the boner. He threw them a big one. "A suspicion," he divulged, "that David Sominski is not our bomber."

25

When they came out, through the lobby, the cameras started rolling. Phil DeLong looked satiated at last. Matuska looked envious. Vic moved to one side, outside of Graves, and watched the audience of mostly reporters as they were flanked by security inspectors Carl Brown and Jack Weaver in dark blue sport coats. He noted two uniformed cops near the road too, watching the scene through dark sunglasses, and then he began looking for Steve Croft of *60 Minutes*. Where was he?

There. Next to the one Phil had pointed out as the cameraman. Croft's arms were crossed, and, unlike the others, he seemed to be serene, certain of the questions to be asked. Perhaps even of the answers.

Maxwell stood at a small lectern which had been set up in front of the automatic doors. He did not have to run a hand over his hair to check it. He was perfectly groomed, stately in his light gray suit. On display for viewing, Vic thought darkly, like a handsome corpse.

"Before I answer your questions," he began, "I'd like to express my condolences to the mayor's family, and to the families of the injured clerks. Also my prayers on behalf of the parents of one of our finest inspectors, Ms. Maria Castillo, whose abduction you learned about earlier. This is a tragic day for all of us. We do our jobs and live our lives, never expecting something like this to happen. When it does, some of us ask why. Others point the finger of blame. No matter what our reaction is, though, we're left with a terminated employee who was a loner, and who somehow managed to hide his deeply disturbed feelings from those around him. He's someone whose mental problems eluded detection from day one of his entry into the Service, hidden among thousands of normal people who entered with him. This might have happened anywhere ... in a fast food restaurant, a manufacturing plant, a shopping mall. But it didn't. It happened in a United States Postal Service facility. One of over twenty-eight thousand post offices. One of more than a hundred processing and distribution centers. That makes it a Federal crime. It also means we are very concerned about apprehending the person or persons responsible, and in saving lives in the process. If anyone has any information regarding these crimes, they should contact the Tucson Postal Inspector's office. In the meantime, as I told the President this morning, we plan to be busy following up on leads and ferreting out the whereabouts of the ones responsible."

The pause was not long.

"Excuse me–what do you mean the 'ones' responsible? I thought there was only one felon."

Maxwell nodded solemnly at the KGUN reporter. "We are ruling nothing out. The bomber may have had an accomplice on the outside. Someone supplying him with explosives."

The same reporter: "Military explosives, as Mr. Graves suggested?"

"We're looking into that. Mr. Sominski is a vet, and although he had no direct contact with explosives at the time, he may have formed friendships, which he maintained. The FBI has not discovered how it might have been done, but there are missing chemicals. So security has since been tightened." The Postmaster General began pointing at individually lifted hands amid the confused babbling. "Yes?"

"Is there a connection between this and what happened in Phoenix?"

"Absolutely not," Maxwell told the cynical reporter, sternly. "Yes?"

"Do you believe that Ms. Castillo is in the city, and that she's still alive?"

"We have no way of knowing for sure. We have to assume she's well, and that what the bomber told us is true. We can only hope, and continue our investigations."

"What about his demands?" the KOLD reporter asked. "Will they be met?"

"I can't comment on that." Maxwell glanced at Graves: Had the news anchor seen the demands before they were printed in the evening paper? "There will be an announcement on that tomorrow morning."

As a KMSB reporter asked her question, Vic watched Steve Croft. The *60 Minutes* investigator stood, arms still crossed, watching with a barely perceptible smile and narrowed eyes.

"What could the Postal Service have done to prevent this?" was the question.

Maxwell held onto the lectern for support, and looked down. When he looked up again, his tone bore a hint of the frustration, which he'd so far held in check. "We are not sure there is anything we could have done. As you know, every time there is an incident involving Postal Service employees, the press is there to point out our problems, and to remind people of our supposedly violent past. I would like to remind you here and now that our past has been one of continued public service, marked by steady increases in efficiency and productivity. Incidents such as these are rare and bizarre aberrations, not commonplace occurrences. We have almost seven hundred thousand career employees, after all. The vast majority of these people are just like you. They have families to support, bills to pay. They volunteer for community service. They attend church. They take their kids to Little League games. There is no difference between them and the general population in terms of race, creed, or gender. The only difference which may affect some, is the repetitive nature of what they do. I have to tell you, some may not be suited for the job. For these and for others we have counseling services available. Our Employee Assistance Program helps thousands of employees in all eighty-five postal districts, with over three hundred clinical counselors provided by the Public Health Service, through an interagency agreement."

"And did Mr. Sominski use the program?"

A few chuckles. Maxwell was not rattled. "In many cases, the employee seeks advice for himself or herself. But in Mr. Sominski's case a drinking problem was observed, and he was scheduled for EAP counseling and put on probation. So, when an incident of violence occurred, in which you should know no one was physically hurt, Mr. Sominski was fired. We cannot have employees threatening anyone under any circumstances. Such actions are not tolerated, any more than the presence of weapons on postal property. Be clear on this point. Safety has been, and is, a major focus for us. Our customers and employees should not fear conducting postal business, and I believe it is, shall we say, inappropriate to give the impression that it's dangerous to *now* do what so many have done safely in the past. Namely, mailing letters or delivering them."

"What guarantees are there this won't happen again? Or do you think the bomber has moved on to other targets?"

Maxwell paused five long seconds. "There are no guarantees, first of all. I must be honest with you about that. I can tell you that Mr. Sominski would never make it onto postal property again without being apprehended. So I seriously doubt that he would try it. Regarding mailed packages, we are screening them carefully. As to his other targets, I can only speculate. And so I will leave that up to our inspectors, the detectives on this case, and the FBI."

"Have you been in contact with Ms. Castillo's relatives?"

"I have. As I said, we are all praying for Mr. Sominski to come to his senses so as to avoid another tragedy."

"What do you think about his political statements?"

"I have no comment on them."

"Even if they are phrased as demands?"

The last question came from a new voice. Several cameras turned. It was Steve Croft, the *60 Minutes* reporter, who'd spoken. Croft's cameraman, Vic noticed, had moved to the side in order to more easily film both Croft's questions and the Postmaster General's responses.

Maxwell straightened and tried to keep his composure, but for a moment surprise lit his face. Vic couldn't guess his thoughts, though. It depended on whether Croft had also seen the as yet unpublished fax supposedly from Sominski.

When he spoke it became clearer.

"I really cannot comment more than I already have at this point," Maxwell said at last, avoiding Croft's gaze.

So he *had* seen, Vic decided. They'd gone over this ground before, maybe in the plane. Croft had tried to draw him out, to see what the man was like under pressure, and Maxwell had been unwilling–or unable–to respond. Was the president's friendship on the line? Or did the union trouble him? They'd probably already had this discussion, only Croft wasn't giving up.

Vic turned to get Phil's reaction, but Phil was missing. Only Matuska stood there, oblivious to everyone but Maxwell.

"Tell us this, then," Croft tried, his arms still crossed. "Do you see the Postal Service ever privatizing, or will it continue to endure deficits as a government entity? In other words, is this bomber's attack motivated by seeing the Service as just another bureaucracy–part of Big Brother's agenda, if you will–or was he just trying to blow up a test shipment of entitlement ATM cards as a political statement?"

Maxwell did not seem flustered, but his knuckles whitened as he gripped the lectern. "I will not speak for the criminal mind. I can only tell you that, no–we have no political agenda, and neither are we seeking privatization. Our job is to supply the best possible service to our customers at the lowest cost, and we intend to be the most effective and productive service in the federal government and the markets that we serve, well into the next century. Look at our guiding principles: people; customers; excellence; integrity; community responsibility. We have teamwork here. In floods and hurricanes and tornadoes. And yes, even through this. We will make it. Why? Because our people are committed, dedicated. Like Becky Randall, who works as a keyer on the parcel sorting machine in the induction unit of the Bulk Mail Center in New Jersey. Just yesterday I learned that she was walking her dog down the street when she saw smoke in a neighboring house, and a baby crying upstairs. What did she do? She risked her own life to save that child, and to help the mother, who was in a wheelchair. These are also the kind of people that we have working for us. You seem to forget that. It's true that we face challenges now in terms of alternative delivery. Competition from second and fourth class private mailers. But that's where the competition comes in. And we intend to meet it head on, streamlining our operations with automation, and utilizing our strong technological base. Today we have expertise in high-speed electronic recognition, infrastructure maintenance, and message interchange, which will help us develop an electronic commerce system–an 'on ramp' to the information superhighway, if you will. The Vice President has even asked us to develop an interactive information kiosk to provide a platform to be used by other federal agencies to serve their customers. And we're well on the way to accomplishing this. We're going high-tech very quickly, you see, with Remote Encoding Centers and new management tools. But we won't neglect the people in our performance clusters, either. There will be fewer employees in the future, but equal opportunity for all and a continuous improvement in all aspects of human relations. Bank on it."

"Does sensitivity training figure into the improvement?" Again, Croft.

"Yes it does, where needed. No differently than in any other agency."

"It sounds to me like your performance cluster concept–and I take it we're in the Arizona Performance Cluster right now–reads a bit like PC. Even has the same initials, doesn't it?"

"We embrace Total Quality Management. That's TQM. Quality first is our motto, and we've chartered teams in all our Performance Clusters to address obstacles and issues that need to be improved."

"Sounds like Big Brother to me."

A few more chuckles. Maxwell ventured a smile. "Just because we have 'United States' in front of our name? Isn't it time a government agency proved to be competitive and effective?"

"It would be a first since Hoover, I'll admit. So with all this high tech, I assume you're going to have the processing problem here cleared up by next week."

"We're working on it, yes."

"And in the meantime your inspectors are not looking for missing money orders or Express Mail corporate account defrauders anymore ... they're all after Sominski, right?"

"Security is our main concern." Maxwell glanced at Vic. "But we do have someone investigating leads relating to the bomber, of course."

"Streamlining means more firing, though ... and possibly more disgruntled employees?"

"We plan to achieve our goals by attrition, mainly. Mr. Sominski is, we hope, a unique case."

"I hope so, too." Croft smiled. "Although some in the tabloid press may not." Laughter. On a roll, Croft took out a piece of paper and held it up. "Got a cartoon here I'd like to share with you. Shows a postal uniform salesman, with a clerk asking him if he's got any uniforms made out of Kevlar. Is this as much the future of the Postal Service as doing away with the union and going to eight bucks an hour instead of eighteen?"

Maxwell laughed dutifully with the others. "We have no such plans," he confessed. "At least I haven't seen them."

***

As the meeting began to break up, with promises of further news in the near future, someone nudged Vic from behind. Vic turned to see Phil DeLong staring at him with wide eyes. "We've got a problem," Phil whispered.

"What is it?"

"I think you better come see. I've called the bomb squad."

Graves whirled, overhearing. "What? The bomb squad?"

Graves' voice had been a little too loud, as well. Maxwell turned, his face going white at seeing the three men's expressions.

"What's wrong?" asked the KOLD reporter in front.

Maxwell looked out over the audience and the still-focused video cameras. "Everyone please back away from the building," he announced, suddenly lifting his hands. "We've had a bomb scare inside, and, just to be on the safe side ..."

His words trailed off. Already the reporters were in a panic to pull back. They left Maxwell alone to stare at the wall of glass fronting the Post Office. A glass wall which might at any moment explode into shards, like the one which entered Maria's eye. Inspectors Brown and Weaver had to take Maxwell's arms and pull him away. He seemed to watch, as if in a trance, as Vic and Phil entered through the automatic doors.

"Get those people out of there," the Postmaster General said, as an afterthought.

***

The building was cleared using the fire alarm system. It took longer than it should have. Vic followed Phil toward the nixie station, through the narrow corridor between endless cages of unworked mail, and noticed that the machines had been left running without human supervision. He was reminded of the promise of automation, to do with two people what once took fifty. He imagined all the displaced postal workers who might one day be out there, a few of them building bombs.

The nixie station was abandoned, too. Its clerk had fled. On the desk, beneath a shelf of reference books and directories used to find addresses, lay an envelope with a bulge in it.

"That's it?" Vic asked dubiously. "That's all there is?"

Phil shrugged and nodded. The envelope was a standard business size, with a scribbled address on it, almost illegible. Its two stamps had been hand-canceled.

"I tried not to make a fuss," Phil contended, defensively. "But the bomb squad should be here to check it out, anyway. Standard procedure."

Vic nodded. "I know. Why did the nixie clerk suspect it was a bomb?"

Phil looked like he'd just eaten a lemon-filled donut. "Turn it over," he said.

"What?"

"Go ahead. It's been handled enough already. I don't think it's primed to go off until it's opened, anyway."

Against his better judgment, Vic picked up the letter by its edge and carefully lifted it.

"Easy," Phil warned. Vic glared at him. "Just kidding."

He turned the letter over and laid it back. The operation took half a minute. On the back side now, written in small but legible block letters, he could see a word.

KABOOM.

"You're kidding me, right?" Vic grabbed Phil's bony forearm. "You didn't really alert the press and the Postmaster General because of this. Tell me there's a big box somewhere, and it's ticking. Please!"

Phil spread his hands. "No, that's it. I'm telling you. I didn't intend to alert anybody, even though I'm supposed to clear the building at once, regardless. I wanted to see what you thought about it first."

"Well, I think it's a crank. That's what I think."

"You mean because of the word there? Kaboom?"

"Not only that. You can't read the addresses. They're like squiggles. Whoever mailed this didn't care about the target."

"You mean like Sominski?"

"Possibly. Except I don't think our bomber has anything against the nixie clerk. He's out for bigger fish."

"A teaser then, maybe. A letter bomb that ends up at the Dead Letter office. Sominski, the standup comedian."

Vic shook his head. "Sominski's got no sense of humor, either. This is from somebody else. Like the other notes were."

"But who?"

"Maybe somebody who knew Sominski. You heard about this Gessel character that the FBI's after?"

"Who's he?"

"I don't know, but I'm gonna find out soon as I see Delany. Find out why he never answered my calls, too. In the meantime I'm working on my own theory."

"You mean your inside theory?" Phil asked laconically. "You really think the answer's in those files upstairs?"

"Could be. I'm thinking: What if the bomber's still here, still working at the Post Office?"

"What if? That's nuts. That would mean Sominski–"

"Was never our man. Yeah. It could be. Think about it. What if the explosion at Sominski's house was meant to kill him ... because he knew too much, say. What if he's in hiding–or dead–somewhere, while the real bomber has taken on his identity? It would be the perfect cover. You could get away with murder."

"You told your theory to Maxwell?" Vic nodded. "What did he say?"

"He's dubious, but said he wants a list of suspects, anyway."

"Really. And you got it narrowed down?"

"To three. Yeah. Acquaintances, actually. Not friends. One is more likely than the other two because he's a Vietnam vet. Been seen with Sominski at lunch. Wears dark glasses, Army fatigues. Has insulin-independent diabetes. The more I think about the interview we had, the more I can see this guy writing those letters, too."

"What's his record like?"

"That's the thing: it's spotless. He was even given a merit citation for excellent productivity two years ago. His Army record's the same. He's got no criminal history, either–not even a traffic ticket."

"Sounds like you're reaching on that one. He'd have to be one sick puppy."

"Maybe. But he is a loner like Sominski. No parents, no visible friends. Maria had me run a gun check on him because she had a reaction to his behavior at the interview, and I came up with a .45 automatic."

"Registered legally, of course, like thousands of other people."

"Of course. But if we turn up Sominski's skeleton in the desert with a .45 slug in his skull, we'll know where to look, won't we? In the meantime, I'm gonna watch him like a hawk, especially around the Fourth of July."

Vic picked up the letter again and turned it over. He wasn't as careful this time, and Phil backed away instinctively.

"What the hell are you doing?"

"Checking out the handwriting ... what there is of it." He held the letter over the desk's light, suspending it with finger and thumb.

"There's no battery or detonator mechanism here. Just the end of a wire going into a rubbery substance."

"Plastique. Put it down!"

"Meanwhile we got a bunch of employees out back twiddling their thumbs, and a dozen reporters out front with the Postmaster General trying to calm everybody down ..."

Vic ripped open the end of the envelope.

Phil's eyes widened–"Holy shit!"–and he dove for cover behind the desk.

Almost casually, then, Vic blew into the envelope and then peered inside.

"Just as I thought," he announced at last. "Silly putty."

26

Calvin picked up the newspaper, and read the letter he'd faxed to them, again. Below it, he saw another editorial denouncing his actions. On the opposite page were three more editorials by liberal writers, using his words and actions as clear proof of the "true radical right agenda" which must be stopped at all costs in November.

On the next page was an article about Tucson schools on the south side being razed and rebuilt from the ground up to make them equal with the high-tech schools on the north side, which until recently benefited from a higher tax base. The schools on the south side would soon all have new facilities, complete with multi-million dollar gymnasiums, computers, fully-carpeted and air conditioned classrooms and hallways, metal detectors, alarm systems–everything the students on the richer side of town enjoyed. And the unfairly rich who lived in the foothills in their split level homes with dual garages and swimming pools would get to pay for it all in yet higher property taxes.

No "thank you's" were offered for this mandatory donation. On the contrary, the article left the reader with a finally-we're-getting-even taste of revenge. Just a taste, of course ... the real meal was coming very soon.

Another free lunch feeding frenzy, Dad. Am I right? Calvin crumpled the paper into a ball and laid it in the tray. He lit a match, and watched the paper go up in flames. His smoke alarm went off. In frustration, he ripped the alarm off the ceiling, opened it, and disconnected the battery.

There. He rubbed his face, then stared at the space where his stereo had been. *They're no different, Dad. They're all thieves, aren't they?*

Oh yes ...

He stared up at the photo of Harshaw on the wall, taken at the turn of the century. At least they hadn't stolen that ... couldn't take that away. Yet.

He found his new Sony Walkman in his bedroom, opened a window, and fell into bed. When he put on the headphones and turned on the AM band, an oldies station was playing Elvis, singing "Return To Sender" again. It held a new meaning for him this time, though. Listening, he drifted away.

And dreamed of Tombstone. Wyatt was coming for him under a full moon. But that was okay now. Maybe that was his destiny.

***

They circled the six-story red brick office building twice before a parking space opened up. "What's the deal?" Vic asked. "Today is Saturday, for God's sake."

"Well, if I had to guess," Phil replied, gesturing toward the full parking garage on the corner of Congress street, "I'd say it was the Gem and Mineral show. I think this is the weekend for it. Rock hounds and dealers come from all over the world to meet at the Tucson Convention Center. It's only a couple blocks over."

"Terrific."

Vic pulled in behind a departing Lexus with California plates. It wasn't the same color, but it reminded him of Maria's car all the same.

As he suspected, all the government offices were closed, except one. They found the door one flight up a marbled stone staircase on the second floor. There was a buzzer on the door, and Vic rang it. When it opened, a Tom Cruise clone stood there in short sleeves and a 9MM automatic sticking from his shoulder holster.

"Yes?"

Vic stared for a second at the striking similarity of the man. He even had the movie star's nose; except for the graying temples and more noticeable crow's feet, he might have been a double. Here was Cruise seven years hence, after he'd made a dozen more action features and had settled down to doing remakes of old classics like *The Maltese Falcon*.

"Is Agent Delany here?" Vic asked.

"You Inspector Kazy?"

"That's right."

"Hold on."

The aging Cruise shut the door again and left them in the hallway, waiting. "He's going to see if Delany is in," Vic told Phil. "He's not sure about it, it's such a huge office."

"Yeah," Phil agreed, nodding. "Must have a thousand square feet in there. What do you think?"

After only a moment's waiting, Phil started walking away, back toward the stairs. Vic watched his odd departure in surprise.

"Where you going now?"

"Be back in a minute," Phil promised, and then began to whistle as soon as he was out of sight. The tuneless tune echoed from the stairwell, and Vic fought a strange feeling that he'd never see DeLong again—and just as he was beginning to know the man's quirks, too.

Finally, the door lettered FBI–TUCSON FIELD OFFICE opened, and this time the Cruise clone let him in and led him into a room where Delany, Manetti, and two other men stood in front of a blackboard with scribbling all over it. As he approached, Delany stopped talking and put down his stick of chalk.

"Victor," Delany acknowledged him, as a coach might to a late arrival. "Vic—this is Special Agent Scoggins and Detective Romero. You already know Detective Manetti."

"Do I?" Vic glanced at Manetti, focusing on the scar still visible on his lip. Manetti said nothing, so he turned to the agent beside him. "And you're Tom Cruise, right? And what we got here is a scene right out of *The Firm*."

"Look," Manetti complained, turning back to the group. "We don't have time for this."

"We?" Vic asked. "Don't I fit in here somewhere? Or are you forgetting that the bomber is a postal clerk who blew up a postal facility and kidnapped a *postal* inspector?"

"We're not forgetting anything, Vic," Delany said evenly.

"Then why didn't you call me back the other day? Why can't I get through to you on the phone? What's Manetti been telling you, anyway? I left three messages with Agent Cruise here, and–"

"Watson," the Cruise clone interrupted, sternly.

"What? What?"

"Agent Watson. That's my name."

"Really? Well, Agent Watson, maybe you can explain why none of your Sherlocks have called me back, although you've talked to the Postmaster General over my head and told him things I'm supposed to know. Is it some kind of conspiracy to get me fired, or what?"

No one answered. Manetti only scowled. The one called Scoggins sat down and lit up a cigarette.

"I get it," Vic said, turning to the window, as if he might jump. "You don't think of me as a cop. Even though I've got a badge; even though this investigation is technically under our jurisdiction."

"Get real," Manetti said with a grunt.

Vic looked down into the street. Up near the corner he could see Phil emerging now from a coffee shop with a cup and something else. A bag?

Yup ... A bag full of jelly donuts. No doubt about it.

Vic hung his head, and finally turned. "Okay, so I'm a new recruit. I'm green. And you're right, Maxwell is more interested in security than in capturing the bomber. Or else he wouldn't have his more experienced inspectors checking every employee who enters a postal station, and protecting him there at the Ventana Canyon resort where he's staying until this thing gets cleared up. Maybe you even think this is just a vacation for him, too. But he did assign me and Phil DeLong to this case, and he does expect results, even if we are from Phoenix. So we need to know what you have that might help us on our end. Surely you can see that."

Delany ran a hand through his hair. Manetti glared at him with open disdain, as if still blaming him for what had happened at Sominski's house. The other two were seated now, too. Bored and taking a break.

After an uncomfortable pause, Vic said, "Come on, guys. Give me a break here! Maria is my partner."

He'd said the magic words at last.

"She's a first rate field trainer, too," Delany added, half to himself. "Okay, Vic. Here it is."

The G-man moved to the blackboard, picked up his chalk again. Manetti threw up his hands and moved out of the way. Scoggins blew a smoke ring at the ceiling.

"We've been trying to trace a man given us by an engineer at Hughes Missile Systems," Delany explained.

"Gessel?"

Five heads turned to him in unison.

"You know about him?"

"Maxwell told me."

Delany seemed relieved. "Yes, of course. The engineer was given us by an ordnance supply clerk at Hughes, who was in turn given us by the officer in charge of transportation. Only two critical chemicals are missing, not much more than might be accounted for as a discrepancy in measurement during Hughes' processing. The actual amount is unknown, depending on which side of the scale you want to put your finger. In any event, you can't make plastique with just those chemicals, and not without a lot of training and knowledge."

"So this engineer first gave you somebody who turned out to be in prison?"

"That's right. He was caught with his pants down, and tried his best to weasel out of it by putting the blame on an ex-transportation officer who, he said, toured the facility on a visitor's pass and came to see him on duty, asking a lot of questions. He said the former officer acted funny. How he intercepted the chemicals at the Hughes plant and got his hands on them he had no idea."

"So the engineer, who was ultimately responsible for use and disposal of chemicals, didn't know this ex-officer was in prison."

Delany nodded. "What he knew was that this guy had since been in trouble with the law. And he knew that he'd been in the plant several times before. It would be his word against the ex-officer's; damn weak defense. But when we later told him that Andrews had been in jail for weeks on a third DUI reckless endangerment, and that he'd been searched on leaving the plant each time, he was caught in the lie. He agreed to give us the true story for nothing more than a dismissal."

"Let me guess. The engineer said Gessel was blackmailing him, had a gun to his wife's head, and told him the chemicals wouldn't be missed."

"That's about it. He also said Gessel was an ex-Special Forces member, a part-time soldier of fortune. The real truth is probably that Gessel was paying him. We've got the weasel under surveillance now."

"But you haven't found Gessel."

"Not yet. Maybe he's with Sominski. Maybe he's the one who wrote those letters."

"Maybe he's down at the Salvation Army, too," the one named Scoggins quipped, with a laugh.

"Funny," Delany said, without humor.

Vic ignored it."You know, if you run Gessel's face in the paper and on TV, you might spook Sominski out of hiding ... if they're not together, that is."

"We're considering that."

"In the meantime, can we have a photo of Gessel, along with his last known address?"

"We?" Delany smiled thinly.

"Phil DeLong and I."

"Of ... course." Delany motioned to Manetti. The Italian opened a manila envelope and withdrew a B&W photo of Gessel in uniform. The pockmarked face had a strong jaw and a Doberman's eyes. Manetti also smiled thinly, noting Vic's reaction.

A moment later the buzzer went off. Watson stamped off and returned with Phil, who wiped the last trace of white sugar from his lips as he spoke.

"Did I miss anything?" Phil asked.

27

On the way back to the post office, Vic decided to take a detour. Phil didn't catch on until they were way past Campbell and almost to Alvernon.

"Lunch?" Phil guessed wrong.

"You've already eaten," Vic informed him.

"Forget something at the hotel?"

"Nope."

"What am I playing here, then–twenty questions?"

"Call it curiosity. Following a feeling that's been bothering me for two days now. But not enough of one to mention to Delany." *Not that I would now anyway*, he realized.

He crossed Alvernon and turned south, looking for street signs. An impatient teenager in a new white Jeep Wrangler roared around them, oversize tires just missing their Chevy's front bumper. Vic leaned on the horn. The teenager beeped back, grinning. Beep, beep ... beep-beep, beep ...beeeeeeeeeep.

"Kids."

Phil ignored the confrontation. "What's with you and Maria?" he asked suddenly.

"What? What do you mean?"

"I've seen the report. Said you and her were sharing the same room."

"So what?"

"So there were plenty of vacancies that night."

"Not the night before–the night we booked. What are you asking ... if we were having an affair?"

Phil looked away. "Were you?"

Vic chuckled at the question. Obviously Phil had been meaning to ask it, looking for an opening. Maybe it was even jealousy. A man with a wife and kids who can't remember what it was like to be footloose and fancy free.

"Why do you want to know?" he asked.

Phil rolled down his window, letting out the cool air. Vic cut off the air conditioner, then continued searching for Mayfair Lane.

"Maria has a boyfriend, you know," Phil said, after almost a full minute's silence.

"*Had*," Vic corrected him. "Does that answer your question?"

Phil looked at him in disappointment that bordered on pain. "It answers mine, but what about Maxwell's?"

"He hasn't asked. Yet."

"And if he does?"

"Then I suppose I'll tell him what I'm telling you. We were tired, and Maria saw nothing wrong in taking the only room left. A room with two double beds."

"It was her decision, then?"

"I just told you. Yes, it was her suggestion."

Phil frowned. "But you have a wife."

"It's been over since the day I hit Phoenix. Maybe before. She lives in Sun City now, with a sixty-year-old trucker who's just entering puberty."

Phil folded his hands in front of him as Vic pulled onto Mayfair and began looking for number twelve-ten. "Maria is a nice lady," he announced.

"Well, thank you for telling me. I know she's special. They don't make 'em like her anymore. And furthermore, I care. Okay? That's why I'm trying to save her from this maniac bomber."

He pulled into the shared driveway of three duplexes, and stopped.

Phil unfolded his hands as a look of confusion replaced his disappointment. "What are we doing here?" he asked.

"Can't you guess? You need to grill me some more?" Vic pointed at the sectioned aluminum letter box station, marked 1210 (A–F). "Our suspect lives in apartment E. That's the west duplex, I think. The back apartment."

Phil cocked his head, like a preying mantis trying to see through a bug's disguise. "All right," he said. "What suspect?"

"His name is Calvin Beach. The one I was telling you about. Works in CFS now, but he was on the LSM, and knew Sominski. I'm building a file on him and two others, but he's the most likely."

"Your gut speaking?"

Vic nodded. "Shouldn't we check the place out? Beach is at work, and lives alone. Supposedly."

"You can't be serious."

"No, I mean we just knock on the door. Look in the windows."

"And see if Sominski confronts us with a cocked forty-five?"

"Or if there's any movement inside to give us probable cause–"

Phil wiped his forehead with one bony hand. Then smiled, considering it. "You mean like if Maria is tied up in a closet, and maybe kicks at the door when she hears a knock?"

"I admit it's a long shot."

Phil shook his head. "And you were a teacher once. Jeez. Anyway, Delany and Manetti must surely have already visited the list of acquaintances you gave them."

"Maybe they did, and maybe they didn't. I suspect there's a lot more they aren't volunteering, too. We're on our own. Stay outta their way–that's the impression I got from them. And if they need something from us, don't worry. They'll call."

After checking his gun, Vic got out. Reluctantly, Phil followed. They walked up the circular drive toward Unit E, past several large Palo Verde trees gracing the common front drive crescent. All the units looked identically old, having been constructed half of brick and half of stucco, but at least they seemed well-maintained. The individual yards were gravel and stone, with sparsely-placed prickly pear cactus growing in bunches under the front windows and beside the steps. Nearer, Vic could see the '83 Ford Econoline van Beach owned, sitting far back behind the third unit, near a fence made of dead ocotillo branches.

"I'll take the back," he said. "You ring the front."

Phil nodded, and checked his own shoulder holster as they approached. "At the count of ten," he added.

Vic barely made it around to the back window–in time to hear Phil's knocks–when he noticed that the window was open. Not just open, but missing. Tiny shattered shards of glass were still in evidence on the sill. The pulled curtain breathed.

Instinctively, he pulled out his gun.

There was no response from inside the apartment. Only the continuous rumble of an evaporative cooler motor from atop Unit B could be heard in the silence between knocks.

Vic reached in and parted the curtain, slowly. He could see through the kitchen now, into the living room. The front door banged again, loudest of all, with four even harder knocks. No one answered.

"Anyone home?" Vic called into the opening, just to be sure.

No reply.

So he crawled through the window, walked through to the front, and opened the front door. Phil was crouched to the side, his hand inside his coat, a look of shock slowly boiling into incredulity.

"Holy shit," he said. "Do you know what you've done? Nothing you find in there can be used in a court of law, now."

"Come on in," Vic replied, "and you can tell Sominski that in person." He smiled as Phil's eyes widened. "Just kidding."

***

Phil wouldn't touch anything. He kept his hands tucked under his armpits. "Really, I'm serious," he repeated. "This is way out of line. Our jobs could be on the line, too. But then what do you care–you got no kids to feed."

And he never would, he realized, unless he found Maria.

"What about all the starving kids in Chinatown, huh?" He pointed at the entertainment center which, above a stack of newspapers, was mostly filled with books. "No television," he said. "This guy reads. He's got quite a collection, too. Science and science fiction. Mystery and suspense. A set of encyclopedias up to the letter M ... probably from some grocery store chain. Some history books here too, mostly mining history. History of the Old West. And a Bible. Nothing really political, though, like Limbaugh's *See–I Told You So*."

"Don't touch any of them, for God's sake."

"Don't worry. I'm just–"

"Look at this." Phil nodded toward an old photo on the wall. "What's that?"

"Looks like an old mining town. Turn of the century, maybe before."

"In Arizona?"

"Yeah. See there? That's a saguaro in the background, isn't it?"

Phil leaned forward, straining. "You got good eyes. Wonder why he would have this on his wall? Hobby, maybe?"

"That's what he said at the interview. He's got an off-road BMW motorcycle, too. But, over here ... He didn't say anything about this."

Vic kneeled beside the coffee table set against the living room's side window. On it stood another black and white photo, this one of a woman standing in a kitchen. It was not the duplex kitchen. The refrigerator looked like the kind that had once been advertised on the *Jack Benny Show*. The metal tray in front of the photo was even more suspicious. It had a blackened bottom. Candle wax had dulled the shine on part of the table around it.

"What is it?" Phil asked, bending closer.

"That's the question, isn't it?"

Vic found a flake of soot in a crevice of the tray's scroll work. He opened the table's drawer and found a half-empty box of matches.

"You thinking what I'm thinking?" Phil asked.

"If you're thinking maybe our man here burned the fax he sent, maybe so."

"We'll never know, will we?"

"Not in time to save Maria's life." Vic searched the other rooms, careful not to disturb anything. He found nothing. No gun, no box of chemicals, nothing. "He lives a Spartan life, doesn't he? Not even a stereo here, or a clock radio. The book beside his bed is by Herman Melville. *Bartleby the Scrivener.*"

"Look here," Phil said. "A hole in the wall in the hallway. And some scrapes along the corner there."

Vic nodded. "The rear door frame in the kitchen is cracked, too. Been repaired with wood putty. What do you suppose happened here?"

"Violence, of some kind."

"I think we better go."

"I think you're right."

They locked the front door, and left by the rear after checking outside. Vic sprinted to the van, and looked quickly inside as Phil waited and tried not to appear nervous as he glanced about.

"Will you hurry up!" he called in an intense whisper.

Vic stared into the van's rear windows at the dirty, carpeted interior. A length of rope in one corner held his gaze. Had Maria been in here? he wondered. If so, why hadn't anyone seen the van at the hotel? And how could it have happened so quickly? He thought about David Sominski planting the bomb without being seen. And what the note in the park had said about his father being there ... but Sominski's father had never been there. Had Beach's?

His gut ached now, but there was no antacid for this kind of pain. Not a single substantial gram of proof. Only more questions.

Phil was checking the trash can when he returned. "Find anything?" he asked, as they walked back to the car.

"Just a rope. How about you?"

"Quite a few Hungry Man TV dinner trays; turkey and gravy, mostly."

"Fitting. TV dinners for someone without a TV."

"We telling Delany or Manetti about this?"

"How can we? We were never here. But we'll be back tonight, though, to watch him. Or rather one of us will be. 'Cause we can't watch him in CFS, and maybe he knows that. Maybe that's why he put in his bid for that job."

Phil took out a quarter, and began turning it between his long fingers. "You're pretty sure this is how we should be spending our time, aren't you?"

"You got any better suggestions?"

"How about lunch? We'll flip to see who buys."

"And whoever wins gets to watch Beach tonight?"

"Don't you mean whoever loses?"

Vic shook his head. Phil acquiesced.

"Okay. But only if you kick in money for donuts, too. One dozen, blueberry-filled. And coffee."

"Deal."

28

The distribution case Calvin chose was as far away from Ernie the Geek as possible. The night supervisor, designated a 204B because she was usually a clerk, gave them all instructions on routing the letters into the right bins in front of them. Then they were left to work with the delayed mail usually run on the LSM, along with the more typical bulky and plastic-covered junk.

The 204B made several passes by them to see if there were any questions or problems, then she sat at the only case left and began working herself.

"My paycheck will be huge next pay period," Calvin overheard one of the regulars on the next row say. "Twenty hours overtime two weeks straight."

"Yeah, but we're stuck in this joint," another said grimly. "What's the use of money if you can't spend it?" A pregnant pause. "And what kind of life is this, anyway? Nobody's here 'cause they enjoy the work. It's mind-numbing, boring as hell–and dangerous. I keep thinking those swinging doors back there are gonna open and some basket case who lost his route will come in with blazing six shooters." The others laughed. "Gotta have an imagination, for sure, or you just won't last. Nope, you'll go nutty. Can you imagine what it'll be like when they finally co-op the union, and we're working for six bucks an hour? Or when they take away our headsets? People will be dropping like flies around here, kamikaze-style."

"So look on the bright side," the second clerk responded. "If another bomb goes off in here, well, no more overtime."

Calvin smiled the smile up at the inspector's gallery, and stuck another letter into the wrong bin.

***

On the way home, he picked up the thickest T-bone he could find, a bottle of A-1 sauce, a six-pack of Tecate Mexican beer, and a pre-baked, stuffed potato.

As the steak was grilling, he sat on the front step and read the paper. The Postmaster General, it said, was giving a luncheon on Sunday for all the station managers and postmasters in Arizona who could make it to the Ventana Canyon resort's ballroom. Questions would be answered and grievances aired. Special dressing rooms would be provided for anyone who wanted to enjoy tennis, swimming, or horseback riding in the afternoon. Maxwell wanted to demonstrate to Postal Service management just how they should all work together as a team to improve employee relations.

Security, however, would remain tight.

Below the article on Maxwell, Calvin discovered, was an even better possible target for Tuesday. Easier to reach, too, since delivery to Maxwell was almost on a par with Express-mailing a package to the Pope. A judge named Mendoza had overruled a proposed 1.2% reduction in state welfare spending, on the grounds that it would prove to be a hardship to newly arriving immigrants. The same judge, the article continued, had previously been behind scrapping a Food Stamp fraud investigation on the grounds that it violated the rights of minorities.

Calvin glanced up at the Stephen King novel in his bookcase. Tucson Superior Court Judge Ramon "Peppy" Mendoza ... yes ...

He looked out at the almost-full moon.

Almost there. *Is he the one, Dad? Is he the last one? Or is it Max?*

***

After dinner, he slid his closet door open. He stared for a moment at the white shirt. Then he finished off his fourth beer and took down the old Ouija board from the top shelf. After blowing dust off the top, he opened it, and laid out the board on his bed. Then he turned off the light so only moonlight filtered in from the window.

Taking the wooden pointer in his left hand, he kneeled on the floor beside the bed.

Are you there, Dad?

Silence.

His head felt light, his belly full. As the air conditioner cycled in almost hypnotic rhythm he let his mind drift, letting all pressure off the wooden triangle.

Which one will it be, Dad? Maxwell or Mendoza?

The pointer whispered over the slick, dusty board.

When it finally stopped he looked down with only casual interest.

W

He looked back toward the moon's silver haze, and circled again, slowly. A minute passed. Then another. His head nodded down at last. He blinked twice, focusing.

A

He noted the letter and continued circling, so lightly he could barely feel his fingers. His hands moved as if directed, slowly creeping across the wood. *Who is it, Dad? Is it the Pope? I don't know his last name.*

T

Time seemed to slow almost to a standstill. The air conditioner alternately wheezed and hummed, wheezed and hummed. A car drove by outside, only half-perceived by a sweep of lights.

The pointer jerked forward, moving again. Then stopped.

E

His eyelids felt too heavy to keep open, now. His head drooped.

At last he became aware of movement–in a straight line this time, like an arrow to its target. After his hands had long stopped, he squinted down at the last letter ... at the letter which now formed a word. Then his eyes slowly widened as a realization sunk deep, parting the fog.

He got up, fighting sleep, and stumbled into the bathroom.

He splashed water into his face.

For a long time he stared at his dripping reflection in the mirror.

***

Phil was late again, and Vic wasn't happy about it. It had been hot in the office. Hotter than the intersection of Broadway and Campbell at high noon, though it had little to do with the temperature.

"Hi ya, partner. What's cooking?"

Vic looked up from McDade's desk and didn't smile this time.

"That bad, huh?"

Vic checked his watch. "You got good timing," he conceded. "You missed one lecture from Graves and Maxwell ... a bulk mailer dispute that turned into a fist fight ... the processing of a patron who threw a rock through the front window ... and an argument with Delany over how to handle the money setup tomorrow night."

Phil seemed impressed. "And it's only nine o'clock. On Sunday, too."

"Ten after nine," Vic corrected him. "And tomorrow is the Fourth."

Phil dusted his blue blazer as if for donut crumbs. "Sorry, boss. You know, you may be in charge of this investigation by default–"

"For now, you mean?"

"Right. For now. But I've been at this work one hell of a lot longer. So what I'm saying is ... you don't need to take flak from the postmaster on this, buddy. Or Maxwell, for that matter. They're not your supervisors! It's true Maxwell can get you fired, but only by recommendation."

"Oh really? Well, one of my lectures did come by telephone, too, this morning; our supervisor Simmons also asked about you."

Phil danced a crazed little jig. "It's Sunday, for God's sake! I had a long night, and I'm only half an hour late."

"Forty minutes."

"Okay, already. I'm sorry. It's times like these I wish we weren't on straight salary. We could retire on the overtime alone."

Vic nodded. "That may be sooner than you think."

"What did Simmons say, by the way."

"Just verifying my report. There's a lot of paperwork here. Most of it I haven't seen before."

"I said I'm sorry. You need help?"

Vic picked up a sheath of papers, and tapped it. "Not with this one. All I have to do here is sign on the dotted line. After that, it's all over."

"What do you mean, *over*?"

"My marriage. These are divorce papers, delivered yesterday afternoon."

"I'm ... sorry."

"You already said that." Vic tried to smile, but only managed a grimace. "Really, it's been coming for a long time. It doesn't bother me. Look." He picked up a pen and scribbled his name on the form. "See that? Done. Now let's talk about why you didn't bring in coffee and donuts. I could use some of that garbage right now."

Phil patted his improbably slim waistline. "I'm all donut-ed out, I'm afraid. Bear clawed, too."

"Long night?"

Phil nodded. "And boring. Beach grilled a steak, drank a beer, read the paper, and went to bed. You want my opinion? I don't think he's our man."

"What if I tell you he's all we've got? The other two on my list are married, with children."

"Then I'd say if he's all we got, we ain't got much. This guy is a recluse. You saw his apartment. There's nothing there."

"Except that tray. And that rope."

"Okay, I can't explain the tray."

"Or the ash."

"The trace of ash." Phil shook his head. "What else you got?"

"You mean besides a gut as tight as the rope around Maria's neck? Not much. Except there's that note from the park. The one Delany's confiscated. It said his father used to go there. Sominski's father never lived in Tucson. Beach's father did. He was a postal contract driver for a while, too. Killed himself eight years ago."

"What does that prove, though?"

"Nothing, but it does tie my gut in knots. The most I've been able to get on Ralph Beach indicates he was a loner, too. Indirectly fired by the Postal Service for alcohol abuse."

"Just like Sominski."

"You got it. Except Beach was never really a postal employee. He just worked for the trucking company that owned the rig."

Phil went to the window, looking out over the back lot—now clogged with cages and hampers of delayed bulk mail. "I take it you don't much like truck drivers, from what you've told me before."

Vic nodded. "Neither did the trucking company that let Beach's old man go, apparently. And in particular, Ralph Beach himself. Did you know Calvin's old man was a Bircher? Voted for Nixon. Used words like 'nigger' and 'spic' a lot."

Phil finally took a seat opposite him. "Like father, like son? So what do we do—wait and watch?"

"That's all we can do. Delany doesn't need us, or he would have said so this morning. And Detective Manetti thinks we're amateurs. Frankly, he may have a point."

"Speak for yourself."

"I do. I am. Don't forget, five months ago I was trying to teach high school kids there was more to life than dating and football. They weren't listening either."

"So you told Delany your suspicions about Beach?"

"Not exactly. I think they've decided to cut us out, and it riled me. They're going directly to Maxwell, too, with any news about Gessel. Trying to make Maxwell think we're incompetent, indirectly."

"But why would they do that?"

"They aren't. It's Manetti. He blames me for Maria. He's seen the report and he's jealous."

"Jealous?"

"I saw the way he looked at her. Oh, yeah. He was questioning me pretty hard about us being in that hotel room together. Even harder than you did yesterday."

"Think he told Maxwell?"

Vic shrugged. "No way of knowing. As a guess, I'd say he has.

I'm sure Maxwell has seen the report by now, so he's had the opportunity to come to the same conclusion. Maybe it didn't matter, and Manetti's insinuation was snubbed as unimportant right now. One can only hope. In the meantime I've got to take up surveillance of Beach, since it's my turn. Right? Beach's supervisor was planning on calling him into work today, to work out on the floor, but I had him cancel that idea."

"You give him a reason?"

"No, but he suspected something was up. I told him to keep his eyes peeled and his mouth shut. Or else."

"Great employee relations. Max the Ax would approve."

"Think so? Maybe I should give a lecture at his little get-together today, too. As a kind of retirement speech."

Phil looked almost serious. "It's an idea."

"Uh-huh. Right. Look ... have we got another vehicle I can use besides a white Cavalier? I was thinking maybe a Jeep. Not a postal jeep, but a Wrangler. Maria was going to get one, she said. If our suspect is on that off-road motorcycle I may need it, too. Also some binoculars, a baseball cap, and some rags. I'm going to be giving it a very long wax job across from Beach's place. Maybe an oil change and brake work, while I'm at it."

Phil grinned. "I'm sure I can find somebody here who'll donate their Jeep for a clean and lube."

"Of course you got the real dirty work, though." Vic pointed at the stack of papers on McDade's desk. "That's backlog. Have fun cleaning it up."

Phil's grin slowly faded.

***

The Wrangler was old, blue, and grungy. He parked it in the shade in front of a house that had a FOR SALE sign on it four houses up from the duplexes. He could see Beach's bike through the trees that fronted the complex from where he was. He mimicked Beach with dark sunglasses, and also wore a Tucson Toros baseball cap, a sporty jersey, shorts, and tennis shoes to complete the disguise.

Sitting there, he remembered Maria wanting a jeep, saying she'd thought about selling her Lexus to be young again, like a college student, which implied she felt old. Ironically, it made sense that if you died young enough, then maybe you could be old in your thirties. If Maria was dead already, he realized, then age twenty had been her middle age.

Rage wouldn't do any good, though. It wouldn't bring Maria back. It wouldn't generate any answers. Getting angry wouldn't lure a shark out of hiding to bite any tiny, shiny hook. Not with all the other hooks out there–not to mention Manetti's dragnet. Of course, they were mainly hunting for a smaller slippery fish. A barracuda named Gessel. Yet, what if the Great White was really right here? He would need all the adrenaline that rage could provide to reel this one in. Incredible luck, too.

Too bad this fishy quarry was disgruntled. It wasn't even biting.

After the first hour Beach came outside to sit for ten minutes on the front steps and read some magazine. *Playboy*, Vic guessed. Or was it the *National Review*? He couldn't make the title out through his binoculars. Beach was wearing shorts and a white T-shirt. No shoes.

By the second hour, the temperature had reached a hundred degrees at least, and he decided to start that wax job in order to escape the Wrangler's greenhouse effect. He put down the top, cursed the sun for taxing his shade, and then began to apply the Johnson's Cleaner/Wax in slow circular motions to the curb side of the hood–the half not in the blinding heat. His cap was tilted down on his forehead, creating an oven for his sweating scalp. His aviator sunglasses were slipping on his nose, and he had to keep pushing them back into place.

By hour three, he had finished waxing and Beach had not come outside again. What he was doing in there was a mystery. With no television or radio, he was either reading or sleeping. Or composing another letter bomb, and then maybe burning it in that little tray when he realized that the reader would never see it because he'd be plastered across two walls. It was true he could also be talking on the phone to Sominski, but a wiretap to confirm it was out of the question. He had about as much hard evidence for Beach being the bomber as they had on the Loch Ness monster. Like an old, penniless Scottish fisherman, he would just have to watch and wait. And without a pint of Guiness.

At two thirty, after the Jeep was buffed to the shine of a new corpse's eyes, the man next door finally came out for his Sunday paper. He was a bald old crony, in his late sixties, and had thick red chest hair like rusted springs, bunched at the drooping arch of his tank top.

"You the new owner?" the man called.

Vic tried to ignore the question with a little wave, but the old guy stood there waiting, barefooted on the hot walkway, a skeptical look on his unshaven face.

"Maybe," Vic said, and held up his hand again."Bad plumbing, though."

The retiree nodded once, glancing back at the motor home in his driveway, then shuffled slowly back inside while staring in suspicion.

Vic got back in the Jeep, and picked up the binoculars in frustration. Beach's front door was closed, the window curtains pulled. Nothing was happening. Nothing. Maybe he was asleep. Maybe he would go out later. In the meantime, the old man next door was probably phoning the police. It would be great if Manetti heard about that. They'd have a big laugh down at the FBI office. Maybe sketch it on their blackboard. Here's Kazy's waxed Jeep, and here's his sleeping suspect.

Screw it. It was way past lunch time, anyway. He would grab a taco somewhere, swing by the post office, come back later perhaps. Or maybe not. It was only the third of July. After work tomorrow–that would be the time to watch Beach. See if he went for the shiny, forty grand bait.

He hadn't made it back onto Broadway before the big question hit again: Did Maria have much time, or was she already dead at the hands of Sominski?

29

After a late lunch of greasy enchiladas, Vic drove up to the Ventana Canyon resort in the Catalina foothills. His motive was fear. He knew that now. If he didn't follow up with Maxwell on what they were doing, his ninety-day evaluation after the crisis would have little red check marks all the way to the right. And the essay part would recommend termination. Maria wouldn't be the one to sign it, either; it would be Simmons, at Maxwell's direction. Then, when it was over, he could go to work for Sun City as an entrance guard, at minimum wage. Of course, he'd get to see Karen and Matt come and go in Devon's shiny Park Avenue. That would be a real bonus.

The entrance guard at Ventana Canyon was Inspector Brown. Vic decided against sharing the joke that came to mind, and was then warned that he probably couldn't see Maxwell. The Postmaster General had completed his press conference and managers' meetings, and was out horseback riding with the interim mayor—who probably thought, and rightly so, that it was safer to be with the Feds than to be sitting at home waiting for a grenade or something worse to be tossed through his window.

"That your Jeep?" Brown asked.

"No, it belongs to the PEDC manager, Gary Lennox. Told Phil

DeLong we could use it for a couple days if we return it clean and with a full tank."

"Interesting." Brown cocked his head and stared at the knobby tires.

"What?"

"It's either a disguise or it makes you stick out like a sore thumb."

"Thanks a lot."

The resort was beautifully and naturally landscaped. Saguaros, many with multiple arms over fifty years old, stood at the entrance to the long, low hotel. Fronting the hotel was a waterfall with ducks swimming on the pond it created. Beside the pond was the resort's open air cafe, the Flying V, which overlooked the golf course, swimming pool, and tennis facilities. And behind it all loomed the craggy Catalinas, majestic and timeless.

After walking through the marble lobby and the massive ballroom, he ran into Inspector Weaver, who gave him the same verdict as Brown. "Come back in a couple hours," Weaver told him. "The meetings are over. Everybody's either out on the trail or getting sauced."

"What about Delany?" Vic asked.

"Been here and gone."

"Okay, thanks. I guess I won't wait. It's not important."

"How's the mail situation at the plant?" Weaver called, as Vic walked away.

"They're keeping up with the first class, but bulk and second is a mile high."

He waved to Brown on the way out. Brown lifted his hand but didn't move it. He got the edgy feeling that Brown thought he was seeing Inspector Victor Kazy for the very last time.

He drove slowly by Beach's duplex late that night. The BMW was in the same place. Ditto the van. The lights were off, but the air conditioner on. He could hear it, faintly, like a steady wheezing sound in the warm stillness.

He did not stop.

***

The Daily Star's Independence Day edition tried to give the impression that local politicians, at least, were seriously considering the bomber's words. The interim mayor was particularly vocal, and according to Phil was probably having his mail x-rayed as well. The lead piece on the editorial page was headlined **BOMBS BURSTING IN AIR–OR WHERE?**

Vic called for Delany, and got Watson instead. "I can't tell you where he is," the agent insisted.

"No?" Vic sighed. At least the man didn't sound like Tom Cruise. "Can't or won't?"

"I don't know where he is, okay?"

"He's got a beeper, doesn't he?"

"You got an emergency?"

"No, but I got questions."

This time Watson sighed. It was the kind of sigh a father gave a son who'd just knocked over a tray of woodworking chisels in the garage. A son who should be out playing with his toy truck.

"What questions? Ask me."

"No thanks. Just tell Delany I called, okay?"

He hung up and turned to Phil, who was engrossed in paperwork, half a foam cup of coffee beside him, a trace of crumbs on a napkin beside it.

"You're early," Vic noted. "I'm impressed."

Phil gave him a don't-bother-me look. "There's a lot to catch up on here."

"Save it for McDade. He'll be back tomorrow, and he deserves it. Besides, it's a holiday, remember?"

"Yeah, Sominski's favorite." Phil shook his head. "I ain't having you complain to the boss about my tardiness again."

Sominski? Not Beach? "I never complained to Maxwell or Simmons about you. They haven't called back either, have they? So maybe they've forgotten about us, anyway. It's Delany they're talking to now. Delany and Manetti."

"You reckon they've found Gessel yet?"

The look on Phil's face said it all. Mostly it said that their part in the investigation was over. *Finis.* Maybe even their careers, as suspected. Phil's look implied that if they were lucky they'd be put in an office somewhere in Glendale to do other inspectors' paperwork. The room would be like room 812, too. No windows; dry air conditioning; sickly white fluorescent lighting.

"Who knows," Vic replied, at last. *Not us, anyway.* "Maybe we should call Maxwell and get us an update?"

He could even picture it: Manetti handcuffing Sominski after repaying him with a knuckle sandwich. Delany standing beside the helicopter, counting the cash in the briefcase. Agent Tom Cruise delivering an account of Gessel's arrest to the press. The commendations ... the interviews with Tom Brokaw and Steve Croft ... the final statement by Maxwell at the airport, neglecting to mention his own inspectors–except for Brown and Weaver, of course. Meanwhile, they would still be waiting outside Beach's place in a shiny blue Jeep, watching the loner sitting on his front steps after work. Doing what? Vital stuff, like reading the evening paper and drinking a beer.

Vic picked up the *Daily Star* and turned past the editorials, searching for the funny pages. Maybe a Gary Larson clone had something to say about them today. Something sick from "The Far Side."

No, just another lame animal joke. Others were more interesting. One showed a mugger wearing a gas mask and telling a woman with mace: "Fire Away!" Another, titled "Parole 1999" showed inmates in a prison patiently dialing the combination locks on their cells. Finally, one showed a post office surrounded by a high fence topped with razor wire. Clerks were walking listlessly inside the fence, some holding onto it with expressions of fear or despair. In the background a bus had arrived with more clerks. The inspector/guards all had automatic weapons.

He was about to toss the paper aside in disgust when a piece on the facing page caught his attention:

HISPANIC TEEN IMPLICATES MOTORCYCLE KILLER

Thought to be the victim of a rival gang shooting, Carlos

> Ramirez, 17, of 2714 South 6th Ave., died yesterday at Tucson Medical Center after being in a coma for almost 72 hours. Within hours of his death, Refugio Molina, a member of the same Bloods faction, confessed that the real killer was an older man on a motorcycle who had accosted them behind the First American bank on East Broadway on Thursday night approximately between 9:00 and 9:30 PM. The shooting, which sparked another Bloods faction to retaliate by killing a black youth on Saturday, occurred at the same time and place as first reported, but not by a rival gang member. According to Molina, the mystery motorcyclist held them at bay with a gun, showed them an ID badge, lectured them, and later opened fire on them as they fled in their car. Molina denied returning fire, although a bullet hole was found in the bank's window, along with the slug of a .22 caliber bullet. Molina claimed the gunman's pistol made the hole; however, Ramirez's head wound does not coincide with the damage which might have been inflicted by a .22 at the range reported. According to Dr. Harvey Shapiro at TMC, the wound suggests a .38 caliber at least, and probably a hollow point. An internal investigation involving the Tucson Police motorcycle patrol is underway. Darrell Monroe, 15, died at 10:20 PM on Saturday at a gas station on north Thornydale in a drive-by shooting, which is being investigated separately by the TPD gang unit.

"I'll ... be ... damned."

"What is it?"

Vic folded the paper twice and laid the article face up in front of Phil. He explained nothing. He wanted to see what Phil's reaction would be. Phil read the entire piece without expression, then handed the paper back.

"Well?" Vic said.

"Well what?"

"Well, doesn't it sound suspicious? This guy on a motorcycle lectures some gang members, then shoots one, maybe with a .45. It happens on Thursday night, two hours or so after Beach gets off work, on a night we weren't watching him. The bank isn't far from Beach's home, and in fact, it's Beach's bank! Plus, the shooter shows them some kinda ID badge–did you catch that part? Wake up, Phil."

As Vic dialed the Tucson Police, Phil drained the last drop of coffee from his Styrofoam cup, crushed it, and dropped it in the waste basket, still without expression. After a long wait, Vic was put through to a Detective Bates. Bates' voice was guttural. The voice of a chain smoker who wasn't allowed to smoke in any public building in the city, and was also pissed about paying a premium tax for the privilege.

"No, I don't have much of a description," the gruff voice explained. "Who did you say you were, again?"

"Inspector Kazy. K-a-z-y. You can call the main post office operator here and ask for me, and they'll put you through."

"I'll do that."

The line went dead. Vic replaced the receiver, and stared down at it. Waiting. Always waiting.

"Your gut again?" Phil asked.

"Feels like I just swallowed sponge cake soaked in battery acid."

"I've got some Tums for that."

"Yeah, but it won't unravel the knots."

"How about a good swift kick, then, to bring you to your senses?"

"Save it for McDade tomorrow."

When the phone finally rang, Vic snatched it up. "Inspector Kazy," he said.

"Okay, here it is," Detective Bates told him over a bad connection.

"Yeah?"

"The suspect's in his forties. Stocky. Black hair."

Vic's heart skipped a beat. "Was he wearing sunglasses?"

"No, there's no mention of that. It was night, sometime after nine, you know."

"Was the bike a BMW?"

Bates paused to check. Vic felt his heart turning on him now, beating hard and slightly erratic. His gut tightened even more–like a coiled boa constricting any passage of blood. He felt almost dizzy, but giddy. BMW = Beach = *what*? Where was Maria during all this? Where was Sominski? Could the shooting be unrelated?

"It's me again," Bates suddenly announced.

Vic crossed his fingers. "And?"

"And I'm afraid we haven't got that information from the kid, yet. Apparently he didn't pay much attention to the bike. It was the gun he was looking at."

"A forty-five?"

"No, he claimed it was a twenty-two. 'Course, that was before Doctor Shapiro said it couldn't have been. Now he says he's not sure. Theory has it he's covering for another shooter, if it's not Molina himself. He won't tell us who else was in the car, and his mother can't convince him to tell, either. The kid claims he's dead if he tells, even though they did nothing wrong." Bates coughed from deep down, where the bronchitis was. "Now, you wanna tell me why you're asking me these questions?"

"I wish I could, Detective. How about I bring a photo of somebody for the kid to eyeball, see if it rings any bells?"

Bates hesitated.

"You there?" Vic asked, finally.

"I'm here," Bates said. "I was just wondering if the kid is available. He's got him a lawyer now. A public defender."

"But I would think any lawyer would–"

"You're right. They would like to see that photo. But before I ring him, you need to tell me what you got ... so I got something to say."

Vic made a fist with his free hand, and turned it, staring down at it. "What I got is a stocky forty-one-year-old with black hair who drives a Beemer off-road motorcycle."

"Criminal record?"

"No. But he's a suspect in another case."

"What case?"

"I can't say."

"That it?"

Phil waved at him. Vic held up his hand, palm out. "Yeah, that's about it."

The static grew heavier. "Tell you what, then," the gravelly voice continued in a slightly different tone, "you bring me the photo, and I'll take it to the boy. We'll go from there. I need a name, too. Otherwise no deal."

"*Vic*," Phil whispered, waving.

Vic ignored him. "You be there in an hour?"

"That I will," Bates confessed.

"Okay, then. Deal."

Bates hung up first. After a moment of figuring the dynamics of that, Vic set down the phone and turned to a sour-faced Phil—who was now waving a thick manila folder in the air.

"What's wrong?"

Phil shook his head. "No photo—that's what's wrong. Wasn't there a head shot of Beach in here from his ID badge duplicate? If so, it ain't here now."

"Terrific. Why didn't you tell me?"

"I tried to."

"So what do we do now ... go downstairs and take a Polaroid of Beach? Pretend we're taking glamour shots of the equipment?"

Phil dropped the folder heavily onto a pile. "Why don't you call the bank instead? If Beach was there after hours, he might have been there to use the ATM machine. And they keep records of that. Time records."

"Phil, you're a genius!" Vic grabbed the phone book, and starting flipping pages.

But Phil wasn't flattered. "Not a genius, really. They probably already checked that out. If he did use the ATM, they probably ran his record too, and gave him a call to see if he saw anything. That is, if they were doing their job right."

"I should have asked about that ... that what you're saying?"

"If you were doing your job right, yes."

The lady who answered the phone put him through to her boss, who put him through to *her* boss. They went through the same procedure as with Bates, and when the phone rang Vic again snatched it up. "Inspector Kazy."

"Hello? This is Roger Sinclair."

Vic explained what he could, and the bank executive offered what help he could. Both tentatively. Cautiously.

"Thank you for your offer of help, Mr. Sinclair. I didn't know I'd have to talk to the vice president of First American in order to check on this."

"Without a court order? I'm afraid you do. Normally no one would be here today. Our branches are closed, too. And I haven't promised anything yet."

"What I need to know," Vic told him, "is the same thing that was told to the police."

"You mean about the shooting?"

"I mean about the list."

A pause. "What list?"

"The list of people who used the ATM machine at the bank within an hour of nine o'clock on Thursday night."

Another and longer pause. "Why don't you ask the police about that?"

Vic sighed impatiently. "Because we're running our own investigation here, sir. It's not related to what the police are doing."

Sinclair's tone suddenly changed to curiosity. "Aren't you one of those investigating that post office bomber?"

"That's right."

Curiosity peaked into genuine interest. "What does this case have to do with that?"

"I can't say that it does," Vic replied evenly. "That's why I'm asking you for the names. Please."

The pause Sinclair now took had the feel of a grilling. The bank VP was in Manetti's usual chair for a moment, and enjoying it almost as much. A sound like the chair's rollers came faintly over the speaker, and Vic imagined Sinclair pushing the chair back from the desk and across the hard plastic carpet saver so he could put his feet up.

"You think your bomber is this guy on the motorcycle?"

Civility started to leave Vic's voice, as he detected a trace of amusement in Sinclair's question. "I don't know. And I'm afraid I couldn't say if I wanted to."

"Oh."

Vic persisted. "I would ask the police for this, except procedures dictate I get the information first hand," he lied, knowing the real reason was that he didn't want to tip his hand, because if he had the king, queen, jack, and ten, it meant zilch without the ace. Trouble was, Sinclair wanted to know what kind of ace he had himself before he turned it over, believing that maybe all he had was a deuce.

"There's no one by the name of Sominski on the short list, I can tell you that," Sinclair tried, still in the game. "Your bomber doesn't have an account with us. Maybe you should try First National. They'll take money from anybody."

Cute. "I'm not looking for Sominski right at this moment," Vic confessed.

"An accomplice, then? I don't see the connection."

And you're not paid to, either, pal. You're paid to sit comfortable as the dealer, taking little or no risk, while denying people without the right chips what they need. "Maybe there isn't any connection. That's why I'm calling. To cross off possibilities."

"Well," Sinclair announced flatly, "you can cross off any idea of this so-called motorcyclist killer being our customer, either. Police already checked that out."

"They ran the names?"

"Within the two-hour time frame, yes."

"And none of them own a motorcycle?"

"That's what I said. It puts the punk who blew a hole in our branch window in hot water, too. Kind of suspicious to me that he didn't mention this phantom biker to begin with. Luckily, we convinced the police to omit the part about the biker using our teller machine until it could be proven."

"Molina told the police the biker used your ATM machine?"

"That's right."

Vic's pulse began to slow at last. No ace; just a six of hearts. "Okay, then. I appreciate your help anyway, Mr. Sinclair."

Somewhere, a leather chair squeaked. "You want to tell me who it is you're looking for?"

"I can't say. Sorry."

"You found that lady inspector yet? The one that got kidnapped?"

Vic closed his eyes and pinched the bridge of his nose. "No, we haven't."

Sinclair hung on. "What about another bombing? Any leads on what might happen tonight, or tomorrow?"

"Security is tight," Vic informed him. "Thanks again for the help." He hung up.

Phil now sat at the window, looking out. He asked, "Did he ask you about the mess we got here, getting out the mail?"

"That was coming next, I think," Vic replied. "He said none of the people on the list of ATM users owned a motorcycle. The police checked them all out."

"Just a few welfare recipients trying their new cards, huh?"

"Either that or Social Security. Yeah. There goes another lead down the toilet. And with us running out of time." He slammed his fist down on the desk, which hurt like hell. "I was so sure of it, too, when the detective said that about the biker being stocky with black hair."

"He did? Maybe the kid was lying about the biker using the ATM machine."

"Maybe he was lying about the whole thing. Maybe he shot his own friend after an argument over tennis shoes or something. That's the more likely scenario. After that he tried to blame some rival gang member to weasel out of it."

"Why would he come up with this biker story later, then? Did he need to do that?"

"Who knows? Who cares, anymore? The kid's a stupid loser, okay? Maybe he was high on dope."

Phil stared at him, almost in surprise. Vic didn't like what he saw reflected there in Phil's eyes, either. The frustration was getting to him. It had been escalating from the first day he'd arrived in Phoenix–without Karen–fresh out of the Postal Inspector's Academy in Potomac, Maryland. He was a different person now–Phil was just trying to figure out how different.

"Did he read you the list of names?" Phil asked.

"What? Who?"

"This guy Sinclair, at the bank. How many were on the list, did he say?"

"I don't know. Why?"

Phil stood and walked behind him. Then he began to pace, just like Graves had done. Except it wasn't a worried pacing like Graves' had been. It was an excited pacing. Phil smelled a lead.

"What the hell is it? Come on, spill it, chum."

Phil's pace increased. "The names. He didn't read you the names!"

"So?"

"So Beach's bike is new, isn't it? A brand new BMW. Not even a month old, I'll bet!"

"I don't get it."

Phil stopped to pick up several file folders. Papers fell out of one, but he didn't care. It seemed to make his point. "Paperwork ... don't you understand? Beach's BMW may not be listed with the motor vehicle division yet. So his bike might not come up as being registered via a police MVD scan."

Phil kept staring, his eyes wider now. Vic saw his reflection in those eyes, sure enough. He could almost see his own face as the realization quickened the hammering at his temples. The six had become a joker.

"I'll dial for you," Phil said, and did. When he finally got through to Sinclair, he tossed Vic the receiver.

"Hello?" said Sinclair.

"This is Inspector Kazy again," Vic heard himself say, almost numbly.

"Yes?"

"I was wondering ... if you could read me the list of names we discussed. Just for the record."

"For the record?"

"It's just a paperwork thing. You know how it is."

The pause, this time, was not long at all. "Okay. You got a pen?" Sinclair sounded impatient himself now. The tables had turned.

"Go ahead," Vic said, still staring into Phil's unblinking eyes. "Please."

"Right. Well, there's only five names in those two hours. First is Isabel Donner."

"Okay."

"Robert Bantry."

"Yes."

"Alice Egglebrecht. You want me to spell that?""

"No! Please. Please, go ahead."

"The next name is Eduardo Morelos."

"And?"

"And finally ... Hold on, will you?" The squeak of a chair. The rustle of a page.

Vic gripped the phone tight. "Yes?"

"Yes. Here it is. The last name is Beach. Like at the ocean. Calvin Beach. That's the five. Okay?" A long dead silence. "Hello?"

***

Vic rechecked the chamber of his .38, and slipped it back into his shoulder holster. Safety off. "You got the cuffs?" he asked.

Phil nodded. "Right here. Think we'll need them?"

"It depends on how he reacts when we tell him we've got Gessel waiting."

Phil put on his blue sport coat. "Think he'll call the bluff?"

"We'll see. It's not a long shot anymore, though, is it?"

"You're right about that," Phil conceded.

They passed Graves' office on the way down the hall, but didn't stop. Vic pushed the button for the elevator, and then buttoned his own coat.

"You ready for this?" Phil asked.

He didn't answer. As the elevator door swung open, he thought about Maria again, since it was her they were betting for. He prayed that the hand they were about to play was a Royal Flush.

30

Calvin dropped two quarters into the breakroom's candy machine and punched A7. A chocolate brownie dropped. He retrieved it from the bin and set it beside his diet Coke. Then he sat at the table to read the ingredient label: No sugar or fat. The world's first guilt-free and fear-free brownie. And the taste wasn't bad, either. My, my.

He looked up at the TV hanging on the breakroom's wall, as he ate the thing. He burped at the KVOA news anchor who was talking about the planned fireworks display on A Mountain, which overlooked downtown and the University of Arizona. Parking would be an even bigger problem this year, since the crowd was predicted to be a record, and since construction had blocked off several streets–particularly Toole and Grenada.

To hell with the crowds, though. He could see it from behind his apartment, if he wanted to. As for working on Independence Day, he was getting double pay, so that was okay. Considering the circumstances, and because independence didn't mean much in America anymore–much less in the city of Tucson–he had no intention of simmering in the melting pot of revelers who just wanted another big show at taxpayers' expense. Fuck them. Their Fourth was a crock.

What he would do, he decided, would be to watch the news in anticipation of hearing whether Judge Ramon Mendoza would develop a taste for Stephen King. He might have lots of fun waiting for that big bang, along with all the other discrimination sniffers and animal rights pantywaists who feared they might be the next targets, and didn't realize those cute animals out there would bite into the big vein in your neck, given half a chance. *Nightmares and Dreamscapes* would be a quick read, too, for the judge. Even though there were 816 pages in hardcover, "Peppy" wouldn't be able to finish the first line, much less get to read the story titled "The End of the Whole Mess," because most of the book had been physically edited out and replaced with the real stuff of nightmares. The kind of stuff even Stephen King couldn't top. It even topped seeing the word WATER spelled out on his Ouija board. Just barely. Although he'd managed to at least partially convince himself that what he'd seen had been a coincidence, or a subconscious fabrication acted out with his hands. After all, the Ouija board had never worked before.

He thought about Sominski and the bitch, praying for dear life. Of course, they didn't know that God was on his side. They didn't realize that God was a God of War, and that the Bible was full of death and plague and judgment and sacrifice.

You tell em that, Dad. Go ahead. You make 'em see.

He polished off his diet Coke and burped.

His fifteen minutes were up.

***

"He's not here," Phil said. "Where is he?"

From the entryway, Vic scanned the room too, checking each CFS terminal and labeling case. Several spaces were unoccupied.

"Might be on break," he concluded. "It's been two hours since Beach clocked in, hasn't it?"

As Phil inspected his watch the CFS manager came out. "Can I help you?" Gilbert Allen asked.

Vic briefly showed his badge. "Where's Beach? The breakroom?"

Allen tensed, and glanced between them both as if his suspicions were verified. "It's ... likely," he confirmed. "He's not here."

Vic nodded to Phil. "Okay, we're in luck. Let's go." He turned back to the CFS manager as they walked away. "Say nothing if he returns, got it?"

Allen nodded sheepishly. No doubt he'd been watching Beach closely since his tipoff that something was up. Between answering phone calls from carriers checking on forwarding orders, Gilbert had probably been wondering why Beach always wore Army fatigues to work, staring at him, making him suspicious. Of course, Beach was probably used to people staring at his dark glasses, if he could see Allen at all from where the manager watched–at his rear desk near the entryway to the main plant floor.

If they were lucky, Beach would be alone and oblivious to their intentions. Sucking on a diet Pepsi and watching the Independence Day parade in New York. Just another disgruntled postal clerk/ bomber/ killer. That's all. Just another Vet who'd gotten preferential access to the postal exam, and thought he was still in the Army, and at war. *One sick puppy,* as Phil had tagged him.

As they walked toward the breakroom at the other end of the plant, Phil suddenly announced, without pointing, "There he is."

"Where?"

"Straight ahead. Don't react."

"Don't worry, Hoss."

Forty yards ahead, through the narrow corridor formed on one side by cages of delayed mail, a stocky figure approached, wearing dark glasses. At thirty yards there seemed to be a moment of recognition. Beach's head cocked slightly. His gait slowed.

He sees me, Vic perceived. *He knows we know.*

At twenty yards Beach ducked into the men's restroom in passing.

"Great," Phil whispered. "What if he's got a knife?"

"He's got no knife," Vic told him. "He wouldn't risk being checked."

"Right. He's a diabetic, after all. They drink and piss a lot. You ready, then?"

"Let's do it."

***

Calvin went to the urinal and stood close to it, leaving his pants zipped. If the door opened now, he realized, any piss there was might run down his leg.

The door opened.

His stomach clenched.

But he didn't look.

"Calvin Beach?" one of the men behind him asked.

"Yeah?"

"We're going to have to put you under arrest."

"You're kidding, right?"

"No, I'm afraid we're not."

He continued to pretend to piss. "What'd I do–smoke in the john?"

A pause. He heard the clicking of handcuffs, now. His heart took off like a wild stallion prematurely escaping the starting gate–leaving the thoroughbreds behind in a panic. Had they found Sominski and the girl? Had one of the punks at the bank fingered him?

"We've got Gessel upstairs," the one on the left said.

He swallowed a knot in his throat. "Gessel?"

"He described you. Now he wants to ID you."

Calvin turned his head slightly, but kept his hands at his sides, motionless. He saw them both in his peripheral vision. The one on the left had a gun out, but it was pointed down. They were waiting for him to zip up and flush.

"I have a grievance to file about Gessel," Calvin told them.

"A grievance?"

As they moved forward, he put his hands up on the wall, as if about to be frisked. "Yeah," he said, and then suddenly propelled himself backward into the man with the gun. On the way down, his hand caught the other man by the neck. They fell in a heap, the one with the gun hitting the tile wall with his head. The gun skidded. The other inspector went for his own, but Calvin scrambled like a crab on top of him and bent his long bony arm like a fulcrum until the gun pointed at the man's head.

"Pull the trigger," he ordered. "Hurry up."

The man buckled under him.

"Okay, I'll do it for you."

He jerked the man's trigger finger down. The blast sprayed blood over the first man's face, and seemed to revive him. Calvin picked up the gun on the floor, and pointed it at the live one's face. A face he recognized.

No. One shot could be interpreted as anything; two would positively be identified as a gun shot. He swung the pistol instead, striking the inspector's forehead. Then he pocketed the gun, glanced in the mirror to check himself, and left them there.

"What was that?" Mariel Grijalva asked him, walking quickly from behind the crates containing the new LSM parts.

"I dunno," Calvin replied, "Sounded like a backfire to me ... or a cage falling over."

He smiled the smile as she stopped, now, to stare after him. He walked quickly toward the dock exit.

You damn bitch.

***

The pain of the blow was intense. With a groan, Vic opened his eyes and turned his head to see Phil lying close beside him.

He recoiled, screaming.

It wasn't that Phil's eyes seemed to bulge, staring at him lifelessly. It was that blood oozed from a third eye in the middle of Phil's forehead, and ran into the donut hole of his mouth.

Oh, and buddy? This is all your fault, you know.

He turned away, gagging, and struggled to his feet. Then he bent for Phil's gun. He slid it from the holster inside Phil's coat, careful to avoid that horrid and accusatory gaze. In passing, he saw his own reflection in the mirror over the sink, and recoiled again. His face was covered in blood. He touched the welt on his upper forehead, and found it unbroken. So the blood was not his own. He wiped his face with his coat sleeve as he kicked open the restroom door.

How long had he been unconscious? Not long. The pool of blood beneath Phil's face was still widening. Still warm. Beach might still be on the property, might even be–

He pulled the fire alarm lever as he passed the pole ironically marked C4, and then regretted doing it at once. If Beach was at his bike, and about to escape, he would soon have a hundred unarmed targets. Stray bullets would find flesh.

"What is it?" the LSM manager asked as he ran past her.

He didn't answer until he'd bulled through the rear doors out onto the dock. "It's Beach!" he yelled at the dock workers who were already filing down the steps into the parking lot.

They stared at him dumbly as he blundered by them.

"Did Beach come through here?"

No one answered. They were staring at the smears of blood on his face.

He turned toward the employee parking lot, looking for the spaces designated for motorcycle parking, but the spaces were now empty. Beach's bike was gone.

"Calvin Beach?" one of the dock workers asked, suddenly.

"Yes! Calvin Beach!"

"Isn't that him, there?"

The worker pointed toward the gate. Vic whirled. Beach, without a helmet, waited on his BMW for the sliding exit gate to open. The guard at the entry side of the gate stood idly by, oblivious.

"Stop him!" Vic yelled. But it was too late. The crack had widened enough, and Beach shot through.

"Call the police!" Vic ordered as he ran for the Jeep. "Tell them Beach just shot Inspector DeLong!"

"Calvin?" old man Chambers asked in disbelief.

Vic started up the Wrangler and then roared to the gate, where he, too, had to wait.

"Come on ... come on ..."

As soon as it opened enough, he floorboarded it and cut to the right, up onto the sidewalk, taking a shortcut past the postal customer exit. The abandoned strip mall parking lot behind the Mexican restaurant on the corner came next. He dodged the few cars parked in front of the liquor store, which was the only store left open, but he scraped the last car. The old, battered Buick lost its bumper on contact, as if the thing had been attached by string. The bumper clattered after him like a string of cans behind a wedding limo.

As he jumped the curbing onto 22nd Street, he glimpsed Beach's Beemer crossing the four-lane 22nd Street Bridge, which spanned the rail yard. In the nick of time, he cut onto the bridge entry ramp by cutting off a Sun Tran bus. The bus driver leaned on his horn for a prolonged ten second blast.

"Yeah ... yeah ..."

Dodge and weave, that was the game now. Slow retired folks in the right lane, young impatient ones in the left. Disgruntled postal maniac in the lead, school teacher-turned-reckless-inspector bringing up the rear.

On the other side of the bridge a teenager in a Chevy Malibu took up the challenge by racing beside him. The punk's fragile ego was shattered, however, when Vic went right through the first red light, narrowly missing a U-Haul van crossing along Tucson Boulevard. Malibu and punk screeched to a stop in the center of the intersection, and were struck by an ancient Rambler coming the other way.

Get a life, asshole. And watch where you're going when you do.

Naturally, Beach barrelled merrily on ahead, still not turning off, and getting the next light, too. Vic swore. The lights were synchronized for the damned motorcycle. For the Jeep, the timing was off; he was seconds late, and seconds would stretch to eternity if traffic was heavy.

Green to yellow to red.

If luck were a lady, she was out of gas. Never mind that he honked in a pulsing rhythm and edged his way out with lights flashing. Drivers swerved around him, but wouldn't yield. When he finally made it across the thirty-foot span, two near-accidents had almost occurred, and others spouted four letter curses and raised middle fingers, lady or not.

Meanwhile, Beach was a mile ahead and about to make the next lucky light and disappear.

***

Calvin stared numbly into the rear view mirror. A commotion back there at the light. He decided to turn off at Alvernon and head south.

Do I go home, Dad? Does it matter now?

He cruised the streets south of 22nd in second gear, and remembered the war in 'Nam—when things went to hell quickly at the end. They'd told him he fought for nothing, then.

Nothing then, nothing now.

He would circle until the gas was gone, and try to come up with a plan. Like going to Mexico, as he'd suggested to Sominski. Like maybe selling his bike and hiding out in a sleepy Mexican town, living an existence similar to that which Americans would be forced to slave in in a few years. He might have been able to go to the bank and clean out his account, except that the banks were closed for the holiday. He could use the ATM just like the entitlement leeches planned to do, but he could only get three hundred that way. And three hundred wouldn't last long, even in Mexico. With the two hundred he had with him, that made five hundred. Figure another five hundred for the bike, which was worth eight thousand with its pink slip in the States. That meant one grand, total. One grand to set him up in a hole in Mexico, where he could then work in the fields for thirty cents an hour—if he was lucky—and live on beans and tortillas for the rest of his life. That is, if the inspectors didn't find him first, or the Federales didn't string him up.

Hey, Dad. Maybe I can help smuggle Mexicans across the border, and hasten the end?

In frustration, he roared around the corner. The houses here were now mostly stucco two-bedroom hideouts for desert rats of the Homo Sapiens variety. He went in circles around them. Hispanics, blacks, and white trash. At night, of course, these proud homeowners sat outside on their cluttered porches, drinking, because they wanted to save on electricity for cooling. In their yards were scattered children's toys, amid the scrub brush and battered prickly pear.

And there it is again, Dad—the mother of all problems.

A woman pushed a baby stroller across the street. Calvin roared at her, then swerved at the last moment as she threw up her hands in terror.

Suddenly a Jeep passed in front of him at high speed. The Jeep braked hard and pulled over to circle around, spraying up the gravel along the road's shoulder.

The blue Jeep looked familiar, too, despite the shine it now had.

It was Gary Lennox's Jeep.

Calvin geared down and peeled away, taking a wide swing onto 29th Street, around a Circle-K store. Then he popped the clutch and took off toward Harrison Road and points south, out of the city. The desert–and Mexico–lay beyond.

Within moments his tachometer topped 8100 RPM, while his speedometer inched above 90 MPH. But in his rear view mirror the blue Jeep Wrangler was gaining.

Gary, eat this, he thought crazily as he slipped into fifth gear.

31

What are you doing right now, Karen? Vic thought as he swerved around a station wagon packed to the gills with luggage. Me? I'm just chasing a killer, that's all. And you know what? If I can reach him, Karen, I'm gonna run the sucker right off the road. How about that?

He glanced down at the speedometer. He was topped out at 110 now on the straight-away, but Beach was steadily reversing the equation by putting distance between them. The maniac would reach the bridge over I-10 first, and after that there was a vast desert to get lost in.

Where were the cops? Did they get the budget ax? And just how fast could a BMW motorcycle go?

If only he had a cellular phone. A helicopter could be dispatched. Luckily, at least, he hadn't turned the Jeep's keys back to the PEDC manager yet, and it had a full tank of gas. But a Jeep couldn't go where a motorcycle might. If Beach knew a box canyon where he could escape, all it would take would be a narrow sandy wash to lose the Jeep that was racing after him. After that, he could cut directly across the desert toward Tombstone and pick up Highway 90. Then no one might ever know what happened to Maria.

"Come on ... come on!"

At the slope of the bridge the Wrangler's speed dropped to 105 MPH, then to 100. The BMW, however, did not appear to slow at all.

It disappeared over the crest, its faint wailing getting fainter in the wavy heat ahead.

Vic glimpsed no cop cars on the interstate below as he passed over. Only an intermittent line of long-haul trucks whose drivers probably had enough trouble just staying awake. Odds were against them possessing the cognitive skills needed to decipher the SOS horn honks he gave them.

Hey, good buddies, how about putting in a good word for me with your boss? I'll need a job when this is over, and I promise not to belittle your choice of music ever again.

When the road turned to dirt, he slowed to 70 MPH. But he wasn't certain if Beach did. Billowing dust obscured the view ahead. Only at a second turnoff point did he see the Beemer, two miles distant, leave the road to cut diagonally across the desert. Speeds would be much lower now, and driving much more difficult. Beach was hoping to lose him in the thicker vegetation of succulent Palo Verde. The bike bounded up and down, it seemed, and climbed over some boulders, too. Would the Jeep even be able to follow?

Did Beach have water? If only *he'd* taken a pit stop at Circle-K or 7-Eleven for one of those monster 64-ounce sodas—even an ice cube to suck on would have been worth the full price.

At the turnoff Beach had taken, Vic found what looked more like a trail than a road: full of ruts and rocks, but not too bad to drive on. He switched into four wheel drive and continued, maintaining an average speed of 30 MPH by bulling the wheel around the worst of it. He lost sight of Beach again as the terrain changed and they rode past several low hills. In the distance the irregular crests of some even bigger mountains gave a jagged edge to the horizon, and it soon seemed that the trail had begun to turn in that direction.

Ten minutes later it was a straight line southeast toward the mountains, without doubt. Not the Santa Ritas Mountains after all, but others farther east—where Beach was heading, for whatever reason. There was no way to stop him from reaching his escape route either, if that's what it was. Not without causing a turnover.

"Life's a beach," Vic muttered under his breath.

As he drove on, he forced his mind away from fear of his losing control in the hundred-ten degree heat, by considering another equation: Phil DeLong, Mayor Puerta, Manetti's cops: Randy Bates and Roger Ash, had all been murdered. Beach was the murderer. Therefore, Beach had killed them all.

The syllogism worked, somehow.

All dead.

And Beach was the one, all along.

Beach, acting alone.

One sick puppy, Phil had conceded, if his theory was true. Still, old donut-breath hadn't really believed it. Neither had Graves and Maxwell, although they could be the next targets if Beach escaped. It was just too unbelievable to conceive that a clerk could fool so many people. A clerk with a spotless record, at that. But it had to be true, nonetheless. It had to be. Because he couldn't imagine Beach going to Sominski and convincing him to blow up the city, one chunk at a time, even if Sominski did have a grievance. More likely, Sominski knew something, and Beach set him up, and later killed and dumped him personally, when the bomb he planted didn't do it. Killed him, execution style, along with Maria. Except maybe he played with her, first. Then he hunted and killed Gessel too, instead of paying him off for being his supplier.

If Beach was the sole bomber, then he was waging his own private war; a war that made him a mad zealot. Maybe it had started innocently enough, but somewhere Beach had crossed the line into obsession, and then just kept going.

Somewhere ahead, the dust finally settled. The mountains loomed. Vic pulled around yet another obstruction–this time a barrel cactus big enough to have punctured a tire. He leaned forward, straining to see any movement not blocked from view.

Nothing.

On the sandy spots of the trail he could see motorcycle tracks, but that was all. Rocks had increased in size and frequency, forcing him to slow to 10 MPH. Any faster and the PEDC manager would have to get a new suspension, if he didn't already. Not that it mattered now.

Then he saw it–Beach's BMW.

Not moving. Waiting for him.

Had Beach given up? As a diabetic, he must have been thirsty. Maybe he'd stopped to relieve himself too, certain of his ability to escape.

Closer, he could see that the bike was up on its center stand. Abandoned. He stopped fifty yards from the motorcycle, and stared at the rugged terrain ahead. The end of the line for vehicular travel, obviously. Even a motorcycle had little chance of continuing down into that deep gully of sand, where mesquite and boulders blocked the path. Beach had decided not to risk it on his heavy bike. He intended to escape on foot from here, somehow. It was the only way.

Vic cut off the ignition and was about to get out of the Jeep when a sudden thought froze him. What if it was an ambush? Beach could be belly flat behind a boulder, or waiting on the inside slope of the gully. As soon as Vic was in the open, Beach would take aim and put a bullet through his brain, then drive the Jeep back into town–or to New Mexico. No one would be looking for the Wrangler.

The thing to do would be to disable the motorcycle and then get out of there. Go find the nearest ranch and call for backup, and a helicopter. That's what Maria would do, he told himself. That's how the manual would demand handling it.

Okay, kiddo. Get a grip.

He leaned out the window, taking aim at the bike's rear tire ... and then he decided it was too distant a target. He could run it down, but that might not do the trick, either. Beach could come bounding out of his hiding place, gun blazing.

Two could play this game, though.

He stepped out on the passenger side, alert, gun raised, and ran for the nearest cover–a mound of rocky soil. No gunshots followed. He scrambled farther away from the trail, keeping low, then came around for a wide circle. If Beach was on this side, Vic would come up from behind him. If not, he would take a shot at the bike, and maybe find out where Beach was hidden. Then he would circle back, and fight if he had to. That was the plan, anyway. But when he finally got there, he couldn't see where Beach could possibly be hiding. Only one boulder was large enough to hide behind. He used it to stretch out and aim his revolver at the BMW thirty feet away. Then he squeezed the trigger, and put a hole through the lower part of the gas tank.

Bullseye.

But there was no explosion, no leaking gas. So Beach had run out. *That* was why he'd stopped. He'd had no choice. There were footprints in front of the bike, leading on, probably at a run.

He followed, first peering over the edge of the gully, down into a dry wash. Below, a battered and shattered red Ford Mustang, with its trunk open, sat at the base of an ironwood tree. Vic read the license plate in disbelief.

Sominski's car.

Wrecked and abandoned, but by whom?

By Beach, of course. Beach was the one. Which meant Sominski could be nearby, dead and buried with Maria.

Or alive and captive?

Quickly, he scanned for higher ground for a vantage point. If there was a ranch house within view, Beach could be going there to collect his hostages—or to kill them now that all bets were off. A hillock some three hundred yards distant appeared to be the highest point. Vic ran for it, ignoring the scratches he collected from ocotillo and creosote. A clump of cholla spines broke off and embedded itself in his forearm on the way uphill; when he tried to flip it away with the back of his hand, the cactus hooks embedded themselves into his hand.

Near the top, he flushed out several Gambel's quail and a jack rabbit; he took their place on the rocky summit. Panting, he wiped the sweat from his brow, and looked down the other side toward the base of the hills beyond. There was no ranch house or cabin, but over a mile away stood the crumbling adobe walls of a ghost town.

A ghost mining town, from the presence of old slag and tailings nearby.

And then he remembered what Beach had said at his interview after the explosion: he liked to explore old mining towns as a hobby. Except this was more than a hobby, now. More like a criminal returning to the scene of one of his many crimes.

Vic though about going for help–get that helicopter backup. That was the textbook thing to do. But time could be running out for Maria, if she was still alive. And it would take an hour or more for anyone to reach him, even if they knew the way. Which they wouldn't because he wouldn't know what to tell them. An unknown ghost town at the base of a mountain he couldn't name if his life depended on it? Yes, he would be a lot of help. And his life *did* depend on it. His, and maybe Maria's, too.

***

A mile run on the track at the Inspector's Academy in Potomac, Maryland, was a breeze compared to this, he soon decided. Five or even ten miles on that track would be easier than the one he now attempted in the hundred and fifteen? degree heat, with his mouth feeling like it was stuffed with cotton. For one thing, the Academy's track did not present obstacles which left broken spines embedded under your skin. It did not go up and down either, with loose sand to turn your ankles, and slate stones to suddenly slip and drop your butt onto the prickly pear. A wild desert pig known as a javelina did not become disturbed as you approached its den, and then snap its sharp teeth at you as you passed. There were not holes in the ground of all sizes, either–lairs for spiders and snakes and scorpions, waiting out the heat. It wasn't quite the same in the field, oh no. And the USPS didn't train their inspectors for anything remotely like this.

When Vic finally entered the town, or what was left of it, his throat was parched, his breathing labored. He kept to the outside of what appeared to have once been Main street, and hugged the crumbling building's walls as he inched ahead, peering into each roofless structure.

Shards of adobe brick crackled under his feet. He stopped and waited, listening. A cactus wren flittered into a window, and sat there watching him in the silence. He tried not to breathe because breathing meant lost moisture. Evaporation. After that would come heat stroke, delirium, and finally death.

The pale horseman.

Vic glanced at his watch. It was high noon, and getting hotter. The peak, he'd heard, was around one or two o'clock. And what would be the temperature then? A hundred-eighteen? A hundred twenty-two? If Maria was here, she could not be alive, not for two days, without water.

Cautiously, he stepped toward the span between the buildings–toward "Main" street. There were no tracks visible in the sand. Perhaps no one had walked there for a hundred years. Not Beach, anyway. Beach was probably miles away by then, escaping through the canyon beyond. Or maybe he'd circled back to the Jeep, and was now hot-wiring it, after drinking enough of the windshield washer fluid to allow his tongue to come unglued.

In a panic at the thought, Vic started back, slipping his gun into its holster as the idea came to him that any lost liquid would be a crime.

A sound stopped him, right in the middle of the road–if road it had been.

He turned to confront Beach. The ex-clerk stepped out from behind the low wall of the last ruin in line, where he must have been kneeling. The revolver Beach held was his own inspector's .38 special, and it was aimed right at him.

Beach smiled without humor, and then lowered the weapon. Lowered it, and finally stuck it in his belt. Now he waited, hands at his sides. Waiting, smiling, watching.

My God, Vic realized. *He wants to draw. He's waiting for me to draw.*

"This isn't the old west, Calvin," he said. But his words came out as a hoarse whisper. He wasn't sure if Beach even heard them. He tried to swallow, to clear his throat, but his mouth was as tight and dry as the bleached bull whose skull he'd seen on the wall in the clerk's duplex.

One more move and Beach would draw. Of that he was certain. There was nothing he could say to stop it. Nothing he could say at all. It all came down to this: two men and two guns. Lawman versus outlaw. No deputies. No protracted court trial. No press coverage. No appeals.

Vic looked at the squat, ugly man who stood there forty feet away, watching him through dark glasses. The unreal smile he wore seemed stitched on his face.

The postal ID badge was still on Beach's shirt pocket ... that would be Vic's target–it was right over Beach's black heart.

Vic turned and went for his gun.

But Beach was quicker.

***

For you, Dad, Calvin thought as he pulled the trigger.

The inspector dropped his weapon, clutching his chest. Then he went to his knees, just like in the movies. True to form, he even stared in shock at what had just happened to him.

Calvin smiled as he approached, watching in awe.

Did you see that, Dad? Did you see?

If he did, something was wrong this time. The script was stuck, somehow. The shot man didn't fall, he just kneeled there, the blood coming through his fingers. It wasn't like *Once Upon A Time In The West* at all. He didn't even seem to be *about* to fall forward, his eyes glazing like Henry Fonda's had as he stared up with a final realization of the irony of it.

No. He wasn't cooperating at all.

So maybe the only thing to do now was to take him to join the others, who hadn't cooperated either.

"Come on, little buddy," Calvin urged, pulling him up with one arm.

The inspector groaned.

"It's not so bad, is it? Looks like a clean shot, by the way you're holding it. Nothing vital hit, I'll bet. You can make it."

The inspector blubbered.

"I've got a canteen over there. You want a sip?"

The inspector's eyes lost any chance of a glazed look. Calvin helped him to the shade, and let him sit. Then he unscrewed his canteen and lifted it over his face. "Open wide." He poured a steady stream of water as the inspector named Kazy gulped and choked on it, greedy for more. "That's enough. Good thing I had this in my saddlebag, isn't it? Two quarts, but almost half gone already."

"My chest ..." Vic complained in a husky voice.

Calvin knelt beside him, and ripped open his shirt. The wound was deep, but misplaced. Bleeding, however, was profuse. "Glanced off a rib after probably hitting your gun. A ricochet ... no big deal. Here. Hold this fabric against it, tight. Keep it under your armpit, with steady pressure."

"Why?"

"Why?" Calvin laughed. "That's the question, isn't it? I think you know why. Don't you read the paper?"

"I mean ..."

"What? ... You mean, why didn't I just finish you?"

Kazy nodded once.

"Hey, I'm a man of honor. Besides, I got something to show you. You're gonna love it, too."

He went back for the inspector's gun, pocketed it, then returned. He slipped the canteen around his neck, and then pushed the inspector forward. The semblance of road soon disappeared into tall dried grasses and mesquite.

"Maria ... is she alive?" Kazy asked as they walked.

"Well, let me tell you, Victor. You mind if I call you Victor?" No response. "Anyway, Victor, the answer is ... I don't know."

Vic digested that for a moment, then asked, "What about Sominski?"

"You mean Davy boy? Same thing. Flip a coin."

Kazy slowed even more, and Calvin had to push him again.

"Don't worry, though. They're not in one of those ruins, out in the sun. Although some people in Tucson don't expect to live in houses much better, 'cause they got no ambition, no guts." He glanced back in derision at Tucson, expanding like a cancer on the horizon beyond Total Wreck. "You'd never make it on the frontier, you know. Your kind will probably run pipes out here, start building tract houses for all the poor families who can't even afford to feed the kids they got now."

"Where are they?" Kazy asked him, not listening.

Calvin smiled the smile. "Be patient, big boy. You'll see."

They reached the fence. Kazy saw the sign, and the confusion on his face was evanescent–there and gone.

"An old missile base," he concluded at last.

"Hey, you're good," Calvin admitted. "But did you know that the Air Force forgot to dismantle one of the missiles?"

"What?"

"A Titan missile. I got one. It's all ready to launch, right at downtown Tucson. We're gonna start all over, see. Start from scratch. Make it a true melting pot, and really level the playing field. No more radical liberals on the city council. No more radical judges named Mendoza. Of course, I already sent him a little surprise. Hope he likes to read scary stories."

"I don't like them either," Kazy said.

Calvin laughed. "You think I'm lying?"

The inspector stumbled foreward on a rock and then squinted at him. "You'd need fuel, electricity. You got neither out here."

"Oh, but that's where you're wrong. The base is self-sufficient. It's got a generator. Storage tanks. And–"

"Stop it."

"What? You don't believe me? You never saw the movie *Twilight's Last Gleaming*?"

"Give it up, Beach. It's over."

Calvin frowned. "Maybe you're right there, Victor. Maybe it is over–but for you, not me, and not my plan."

He shoved Kazy through a hole in the fence. Then he dragged the ladder to the center of the clearing, and began rolling it out to its full length so he could drop it in the hole.

Victor stood watching, while holding the wound below his armpit. "What you're doing isn't helping anyone," Victor told him, and then grimaced in pain.

"I can't get to the King and Queen," Calvin replied. "I can only try to wake up the pawns. As it is, the pawns are enemies too, you know. Just like the Bishops."

"This is not a game, though. Not one you can win."

"I know that now. But at least I tried, didn't I?"

"By hurting a lot of people."

"Casualties of war. Pawns."

"Just like you."

"Yup. Just like me. And you, too."

Calvin lowered the ladder. It clanged at the bottom.

"You'll like it," he said. "It's cool down there."

He gripped the inspector's other shoulder, and led him to the opening. They descended, Kazy first. Victor stood at the base of the ladder, looking up at him coming down, no doubt wondering if he had the strength to dislodge him and cause a fall. Blood soaked his entire side, though, from chest to knee. He nodded weakly, instead.

Calvin smiled. "I'll need those keys so I can get us some groceries."

Kazy fumbled in his pants pocket. "We can't stay here forever," he rasped.

"You can," Calvin corrected him. "Me, I'll be heading south, shortly. So I'll need your debit card too, to make a withdrawal. My five hundred plus your three will make eight. Any cash you got would be appreciated, too."

"You leaving me here, without water?"

"What can I say? At least you'll have company."

Calvin went to the chain fastening the steel door, and placed the padlock in a bent outward position. Then he got under it, aimed upward at the padlock's body, and fired.

He jerked the lock, but it still wouldn't open.

"I don't have the key with me today," he explained, and fired again.

This time the lock severed and he managed to twist it off. He slipped the chain out of the grommets and then pulled open the heavy door.

The dark opening widened.

"I did remember to bring a flashlight, though," he said, and then dug in his pocket for his new pen light. "Ladies first."

32

Vic felt weak, but with a gun to his back he was forced over the threshold of the base's blast door. As he suspected, there was no light switch. No sound of a generator, either. Only exposed wiring remained where instruments had once been. Beyond the metal bridge stretched a round floor supported by springs. He paused at the mouth of the inky blackness.

"You lied," he said. "No one's here."

"Keep walking," Beach told him, "and we'll see."

He stumbled forward, over some debris. Some kind of matting. A soda can. Then he smelled a stench. The stench of urine, of feces, and something else. Something worse.

Beach turned on the penlight behind him as they got farther in. The beam was a wide pale sword of light stretching–dimly–to the other side of the room. As they got closer, Vic squinted at what he saw.

It was Maria and Sominski, chained together.

Dead.

"You *bastard*," he muttered, his dry throat twisting the words into a gargle.

Beach stepped closer and shined his penlight past a shattered toilet onto the grisly scene.

Sominski's head was cocked back. His white, clouded eyes stared sightlessly up. His lips, cracked and clotted, formed a perfect O, just as Phil's had. His hair was a tangle of dried blood–black and hard. His bandaged arm stretched toward Maria, whose head hung down, motionless, her hair hiding her face. The handcuffs attached to the chain on Maria's wrist bit into her purpled flesh as it arched toward one of the giant springs behind her.

"You did this," Vic heard his own voice say in a strange and unfamiliar timbre. "You want to talk about responsibility? You want to tell me about freedom? Go look in a mirror and you'll see what the real problem is."

He kicked over an empty jug between them for emphasis.

"Shut up," Beach said, almost defensively.

Vic pointed at a bag on the floor behind Beach. "What's that?"

Beach turned the light. The beam funneled down, and lit up a bag of groceries, just out of reach.

"You're sick," Vic said, half to himself. *One sick puppy, oh yes.* "This is not about Tucson, or America. This is about insanity. And you're the one to blame. The only one, for this."

Beach tried to laugh, but it was hollow. Unreal.

A sudden moan drew Beach's light back–first to Sominski, then to Maria. Maria's head moved, slightly. Vic dropped to his knees beside her, and lifted her head, pushing her hair back.

She opened one eye. A dilated pupil stared at him.

"Maria!"

Her other eye was shut, clotted. Her lips were broken and crusted.

"Maria!"

She moaned again, from deep in her chest, but she was too weak to keep her head up. Vic tilted her head gently in his hands. Then he felt something touch the back of his fingers.

Something crawled onto his right hand.

He pulled his hand from behind her head, and saw it, perched there.

A giant spider.

He jerked and tossed the thing away, into the air, with a whiplash motion. The spider landed on Beach's neck, and ambled quickly up his face into his hair.

Beach dropped both gun and flashlight, thrashing wildly at his own head. The flashlight struck with a pop and extinguished. Vic heard another popping sound amid Beach's curses as Beach's glasses fell and broke.

Vic dropped to the floor, and scrambled on all fours for the gun–hoping in the darkness not to find the spider instead. It had been a big spider, too fast and agile to be a tarantula. As he groped the dark floor with his hands, he remembered seeing such a spider on a PBS show called *Nature.* It was a sun spider, said to have the largest jaws in relation to body size of any creature on earth.

A sun spider, which had been crawling on the back of Maria's head in the pitch darkness as she lay chained to a dead man by a madman.

He found Beach's foot instead. Beach kicked him, and Vic yelled out in pain. A few inches higher and Beach's heel would have found his wound.

Now Beach was on the floor beside him. A hand closed on his neck. Powered by an adrenaline rush, Vic threw up his elbow and caught the clerk's chin.

A sharp click of teeth.

He rolled away, skimming the floor with his left hand. He brushed over what felt like a ball of yarn. The ball opened and wriggled.

Then Beach's bulk eclipsed the dim light coming from the opening across the room. The bulk bent over him just as his knee struck something, which skittered two feet at the impact. Something hard and compact.

The gun.

He stretched, pinwheeling his arm in that direction.

"I got you," Beach said as a hand gripped Vic's leg.

Vic's fingers closed on a blunt fragment of porcelain first–from the shattered toilet. Then on the barrel of the revolver.

"Come to papa."

Beach jerked his leg now, twisting it.

Vic fired at the silhouette above him. Twice. Beach dropped Vic's leg and stumbled back, out of the dim light. Vic fired again in the direction Beach had moved. The blast was loud, and echoed with a dual ricochet.

Then silence.

No groaning. No body falling. Nothing.

He looked at the dim opening across the room. *No. He'll kill Maria*, a voice inside told him. He rose painfully to his knees instead, then got to his feet. His head filled with noise, like static. Like white sound. He nearly passed out, then recovered a bit, and bunched part of his soaked shirt back under his armpit.

He stepped slowly toward Maria, gun raised. Listening intently, past the static and the wind in his head.

Was Beach already there? Where was he? Was he dead? Was he wounded? Was he standing just feet away, listening, too?

He held the gun close to his side in case Beach grabbed his arm.

He stepped toward the wall, where Maria was chained.

Suddenly, there was a terminating clang. The trace of dim light behind him was snuffed out, like a vacuum. The blackness deepened into infinity.

He whirled, and now saw ... nothing. No frame of light at the end of a short tunnel. No trace of light anywhere. Beach had locked them in, and it was as black as the inside lid of a coffin buried six feet deep.

The silence was heavy too. He stood frozen, listening to it.

This is what hell is like, he realized. Outer darkness ... wasn't that how the Bible described it?

In hell you would be alone forever, in the dark, tortured by your own thoughts and memories. Forever and ever, amen.

Suddenly he heard a sound. After it faded, his heart began to beat again, its tempo increasing rapidly, hammering at his temples. Had he imagined it? No. The sound was the ping of a can ... as if it had been struck, accidentally, by a foot. It had been distinct and was magnified by the acoustics of the reinforced crew quarters. And it meant only one thing.

"That's right," Beach said out of the darkness, as if reading his thoughts. "I'm coming to get ya, little buddy."

Vic lifted his pistol and fired. The ricochet lent a triple beat to the blast.

"Missed again," Beach announced. "How many ya got left, now? Me, I got six."

He moved out of the way just in time as a spurt of flame shot from the end of Beach's gun. The bullet whizzed by Vic's ear. He fell to the floor and opened the chamber of his .38, emptying the shell casings into his hand. He felt for heavy slugs, and found just one. The rest were empty casings. He slid the good slug into the chamber nearest the barrel, and carefully closed it. It made a clicking sound.

"How many did you find?" Beach said. "The way I calculate it, you fired that gun four times, and I fired it once. That means you got one left. Right? So you better not miss again, Wyatt."

Footsteps, coming closer, across the matting, from the bridge of the steel door.

Vic hugged the floor, aiming up with one arm. He kept the other arm tucked. Then he remembered the spider.

"See if I can calculate where your lover is," Beach said. "Is she *there*?"

Another shot and spurt of flame. Another quick ricochet and reverberation.

"No? Well, I still got four shots left, don't I?"

Closer, Vic thought. *Come on, bastard.*

Suddenly, the footsteps stopped.

Silence. Beach was listening for movement. Gauging his target. His voice, when he spoke, echoed hollowly. It was impossible to tell exactly where it came from.

"You know, you were wrong about me. You may not think there's a missile in the silo here, but there is. I'm the missile. A regular instrument of destruction. But just a tool, really. A tool that's not responsible how it's used."

Like hell, Vic thought.

"I'm not responsible for anything I do–isn't that the way it goes? It's not me. It's society. It's society's fault. And when I'm caught maybe they'll give me six lashes with a wet noodle, and then Hollywood will offer me millions for the TV rights. It's not my fault for anything. In fact, I'll probably be applauded for making your boring world a little more interesting."

Maybe you should shave your head, too. Become a neo-Nazi skinhead.

"You can't teach me morals, either. It's against the law. You hear that? The NEA would pitch a fit."

Tell me about it. Been there, shithead.

"They won't teach junior his ABCs, but they can sure teach him how the founding fathers who built this country were racist, sexist SOBs."

As Beach talked, Vic crawled closer. Sliding carefully, on his side. Vic stopped crawling only when Beach stopped talking. Something crawled over Vic's leg; he didn't move. Beach was closer now. He could hear him breathing. Panting, almost. Had he lied about not being hit? One of the bullets must have struck, at that range. How could he have missed?

"I remember Tucson twenty-five years ago, before it turned into a concrete jungle. My dad was alive then. So was my mother. But Total Wreck was already a ghost town for over seventy years. How about that? They used to mine silver around here, too, and my great-grandfather even found a silver vein in this very spot. But it must not have panned out ... and here we are. Aren't we? By the way, you getting thirsty again, little buddy?"

Yeah. Hold on and I'll be right there.

"It's running out, you know. All the water. They can't ship in enough by canal because California wants it, too. Except they're already bankrupt out there, just like we're gonna be. Right? All it takes is just doing nothing. Sitting on your ass. Making sure everybody is given an equal shot at all the handouts, even if it ain't fair on the people who were born here."

Vic felt the edge of the matting. He touched something wrapped in a ball. He squeezed it hard, clenching his teeth. It was a rag.

I'll give you a fair shot, all right, he thought.

He crawled even closer, lifting his pistol. A dribble of warm water struck the matting in front of him, and a drop splattered on his hand.

Beach emptying the canteen?

No. Beach pissing.

Vic pulled the trigger.

The blast arched up from the floor at the voice directly above him. Immediately, he rolled away, just in case.

He heard a groan. A deep ragged groan like the kind that Maria might have given had her bone-dry throat been able to fully utter it. He smiled in the darkness, and waited for the fall.

A belly shot ... yes ... how do you like it? Is it painful enough for you?

A staggering sound. Another long groan.

No judge or jury, just like you wanted. Right?

Walking now. The sound of Beach walking unsteadily away, but not toward Maria or toward the base's steel door. Disoriented in turning, perhaps, he was walking in a new direction. A bullet in his gut, he was lost in the dark and walking away–with the canteen of water dangling and sloshing from his neck.

Vic struggled to his feet, and felt instantly light-headed. An intense high-pitched rushing sound began in his left ear and spread through his brain, causing phantom flashes of light across his inner eyelids. When the pulsing finally slowed, he clutched the clotted bundle of fabric under his armpit, and walked in the direction of the moaning he heard. Whether Beach still had his gun or not, he had no idea.

***

The pain in Calvin's stomach was the worst he'd ever imagined feeling, even in Vietnam. It eclipsed the pain in his right shoulder, where the inspector's first bullet had struck. Now that his gut was filling with blood it wouldn't be long before he passed out. If only he could make the door, push it open somehow. The moon might be high enough to see, one last time. Then he could say goodbye. Or was it hello? He would see.

He reached the metal bridge spanning the space between the room's floor and the round wall. He crossed over into the threshold as his pain began to fade into numbness. He stumbled forward, stretching his hands out to push the door.

But the door wasn't there.

Where was it?

He took three more steps. Then two more, balancing like a blindfolded acrobat on a high wire. His legs about to give, he took a final step ...

... into the void.

He seemed to fall forever. Then he struck the pile of plaster and bricks he knew would be there. The snap in his back was distinct and loud. He tried to move, but couldn't, anymore.

Sorry, Dad, but I did the best I could. Didn't I?

No answer. Not quite yet, anyway.

Can I go back now? Can I be born again, back then? I want to see Total Wreck, Dad. I want to visit Helvetia, Harshaw, and Tombstone back when Tucson was a little horse-and-buggy town. There's a life there waiting for me, isn't there? Maybe even a wife like mom? Break a wishbone, make a wish ... So what I wish is that you were there too, waiting for me, Dad. You and mom, and the friends I never had here. Okay?

He opened his eyes in the dark. A tunnel of light suddenly appeared as if by magic, and careened down toward him from above. The tunnel opened to swallow him. The colors were beautiful. Gold, and purple.

Yes, Dad, I'm coming. Take me! Yes!

But then the tunnel slowed its onward rush. It finally stopped to turn the other way. Now it began to retreat, and slip away.

Wait!

As quickly as it had opened, the tunnel began to withdraw and close down. Soon he was slipping out of it, as there was nothing to hold on to. Then it slipped exponentially faster.

No!

The tunnel narrowed toward infinity, toward extinction. The blackness around it engulfed it, like the event horizon of a black hole. He watched in horror and shocked disbelief as it left him in a darkness that was darker than any he had ever known.

So was I wrong, Dad? Why didn't you tell me?

Then even the darkness winked out.

33

Vic found Beach at last, after a search of what must have been close to an hour. Beach lay across a pile of what felt like building materials in the control room below and beside the gutted crew quarters. He put a hand to Beach's face, just to be sure. But there was no breathing. The killer was dead.

He slipped the canteen's strap off Beach's head, and pulled it away.

Less than half-full.

Maybe only a pint and a half.

He unscrewed the cap, and tilted the canteen to his chapped lips.

Forgive me, Maria.

He took a sip of the precious fluid. Just a sip, although he could have emptied it in seconds ... could have drained it, along with half a gallon more. Then he searched for the other gun, but couldn't find it.

When he found the staircase again, by feeling along a wall of exposed pipes and conduits, he had to force himself up every step. On the upper level, he fought his encroaching fatigue to edge his way back along the tunnel, past the hole in the floor where he'd heard Beach fall. Next came the second metal bridge leading over the crack along the round wall, past the giant springs which supported the metal floor where Maria lay.

"I'm coming," he said.

He walked right into her in the dark, or so he thought. He kneeled and groped with his free hand, finding Sominski's encrusted head instead.

"Maria?"

He followed the chain to her. He cupped her head, loosely, and put his face next to hers to hear her shallow breathing. She was alive, barely. Somehow she had held on through the nightmare.

He opened her mouth with his fingers so none of the water would be wasted. Then he placed the canteen to her lips, and tilted her head up to let a little water run down her throat. There was no effect. He poured more in. Still nothing.

Then she coughed. A dry, hollow, rasping cough.

He fed her more.

Soon, she began to drink.

***

He found the gun where Beach had dropped it after forcing open the three-foot-thick door to let in the dim, late afternoon sunlight. He cursed himself for forgetting to look for the key to the handcuffs in Beach's pockets, but then remembered what Beach had said outside, about forgetting the keys to the padlock. He used the gun on the cuff's chain, freeing Maria at last.

"Victor," she said, after the reverberation died.

He put an arm around her, and pulled her close.

"Yes ... I'm here."

She began to cry, but whether at the horror of her memories or at the joy of being rescued he couldn't tell; it was probably both.

"I'll go for help now," he said. "I'll help you to the door, and you can wait there."

"No," she whispered, almost in terror. "I'm coming, too."

"Can you walk?"

"Don't ... know. I know I can't see yet."

"You want to try?"

There was no hesitation in her voice, only gravel. "There's no choice."

"Okay. But I don't think I can carry you. I've been shot ... lost some blood. The wound isn't too deep, and the bleeding's stopped, but I have to keep pressure on it. Broken rib hurts like all hell."

Maria squeezed his hand. "Barbecued ribs?"

***

The light and heat were too much for her, so they waited until almost dusk. By the time they reached the ghost town, the sun was only a glow on the horizon. The full moon now rode high over the crumbling adobe buildings like a sentinel witnessing a prison break. Supporting each other, they walked without speaking to conserve moisture. Then, at the edge of the town, Vic heard a noise behind them. He glanced back, half-expecting to see Beach standing there in the silver moonlight with that vacant Sphinx smile on his face, and those same dark glasses. Glasses through which he'd seen a darker world.

A coyote howled suddenly, as if on cue.

Is that you, Calvin? he thought. *It would be frontier justice if it was. A wild dog is what you are. A lone wolf preying on the weak. Except Maria wasn't weak, was she? And neither am I, anymore.*

"How much farther?" Maria asked.

"We can make it," Vic replied, looking back at the Tucson valley in the distance ahead. He pulled her even closer.

On the horizon was the silhouette of the jeep, lit up by a tracer of red flame which suddenly arched up from the horizon and burst into a flower of blue and white sequins. It was the first of many, although they were too far away to hear the explosions. Vic thought about freedom and independence, and wondered if there was anyone watching the display who appreciated those concepts that very moment more than they did.

***

From his room adjoining Maria's at the Tucson Medical Center, Vic made several phone calls. The first was to Vincent Manetti, through the TPD's paging system. When he was finally put through, the detective sounded tired.

"Hello. This is Vince Manetti."

"And this is Victor Kazy," Vic told him.

"Kazy?" Manetti's tone instantly changed. His voice rose an octave, and he sounded as if he'd just finished a pot of strong coffee. "Where are you?"

"I'm at the TMC, with Maria. We both just got out of emergency, and into our rooms."

"Holy ... shit."

"There's nothing holy about it. Listen. You need to contact a Judge Ramon Mendoza. He's got a package coming, I think. Priority mail."

"A bomb? From Sominski?"

"It's a bomb, all right. But it's not from Sominski. Sominski is dead."

"He's *what?*"

"You heard me. The bomber is dead, too. I know, because I killed him."

"You ..?"

"Right–me. You can get the other details from Delany later; tend to Mendoza for now."

Vic hung up, waited for a dial tone, and then called Delany.

"FBI," Special Agent Watson's voice answered.

"Victor Kazy for Agent Delany," Vic announced.

The pause wasn't long.

"Vic!" Delany almost shouted. "That you?"

"The same. Working late, are we, Frank?" No response. "Just wanted to let you know ... the case is solved." *No thanks to you.*

"Was it Beach?" Delany asked, hesitantly. "That's who killed your partner, right?"

"I think you should get that information from the Postmaster General," Vic replied.

"He knows?"

"He will shortly."

Delany ignored it. "What happened?"

"I just told you what happened. I solved the case. What happened with your money drop for Sominski?"

"We've just picked up Gessel, and that takes priority."

"So he hasn't talked yet?"

"Only enough to rule out Sominski by description. We've got two men watching the pickup site just in case, though. And a photo of Beach is in transit now. So you want to tell me why the cat and mouse?"

"It's a game I'm learning." Vic started to hang up, then added: "By the way, Frank, you can pull your men from the drop site. Sominski and the real bomber are both out at an old Titan missile base in the desert southeast of town. Dead."

He hung up and next dialed Maxwell. But the receptionist at the Ventana Canyon resort told him the Postmaster General was not to be disturbed.

"You don't understand," Vic said. "I'm the inspector on the bomber case, and I want to report ... a final bomb."

"One moment, please."

He was put through to the Canyon Cafe, where Maxwell was dining with Postmaster Graves and Inspector Brown. A phone was brought to Maxwell's table.

"Yes?"

"This is Victor Kazy, sir."

Silence, then: "Victor?"

"I'm the rookie inspector on the bomber case, sir."

"Yes, yes, I know! Where are you, Victor?"

"At the hospital, sir. Gunshot wound and broken rib. I just got off the phone with Agent Delany and Detective Manetti. I told them what they needed to know, but I thought I should tell you everything else first."

"Good thinking, son. Now come on ... tell me. Like Ross Perot, I'm all ears."

***

They released him the next day, but kept Maria for observation. Estimates were a week to ten days, with particular attention paid to Maria's eye and hand. Her prognosis was good.

Under orders from Maxwell, Vic rested in a suite at the Ventana Canyon hotel, where he was guarded from a bevy of reporters by both

Brown and Weaver. He *did* allow Steve Croft through briefly, however, for a follow-up interview before the *60 Minutes* reporter flew back to Washington with the Postmaster General. Then he gave in again and did an interview with Leslie Stahl. Inspector McDade, back from vacation, tried to get his autograph. As did Rick Matuska. But no one, he was told, had even asked to talk to either Delany or Manetti. Sympathies ran high for Phil DeLong's family.

"What's the news like?" Vic asked Brown, around noon.

"You mean besides being about you? Well, let's see. Some little old lady in Indianapolis drove by a prison yard and opened fire with an automatic weapon she found in the alley behind her house. An emergency session of Congress is considering the latest migration of Third World refugees, and how to pay for it. And there's been an explosion on Tucson's south side, I understand."

Vic sat up in bed, ignoring his soreness. "An explosion?"

"An Air Force A-ten training jet crashed into a house near the airport. Pilot ejected just in time. No one home at the house. Kids at camp, parents at work."

Vic sighed and laid back. "Just as it should be ..."

"What's that?"

"Nothing."

A knock at the suite's door. Weaver opened it. "Got a message here from Karen Kazy," he announced, pushing in a food cart from the porter in the hallway. He handed the note to Vic. "That your sister?"

Vic studied the signature and shook his head. "Nope. Probably just another celebrity chaser. Thinks Hollywood will be calling me next. It's a good try at an introduction, though, wouldn't you say?"

He wadded the note into a ball, and pitched it for two points.

Brown laughed, then lifted the silver lid on the cart. The aroma of barbecued beef ribs filled the room. "You think you can get over all this by the end of next week, when you and Maria get assigned to cover security at some postal exam back in Phoenix?"

"That's a long time from now," Vic replied with a smile. "In the meantime, let's eat."